STEPHA

2-99

THE PRINCE'S CHOSEN

THE FOUNT BOOK 1

Syafant Press

Syafant Press

New York, New York

Stephanie Fazio

Visit www.StephanieFazio.com

Printed in the United States of America
First Printing: March 2020

Library of Congress Control Number: 2019914458

ISBN 978-1-7335929-9-4

*To my amazing husband…for always having my back
and for a life full of love*

had moved to a corn farm in the middle-of-nowhere upstate New York soon after. Her only memories were of corn fields in the summer and snow in the winter. Their town was called Nowell, and had a population of 15,000. When she said the name, she pronounced it so it sounded like *Nowhere*, New York.

She shooed Cluckers Numbers 1-5 into their henhouse. All she got in return for saving them from the fox that had been prowling around lately was a mouthful of feathers and a shrill protest from Cluckers Number 4.

Addy washed her hands and face in the mudroom sink. She kicked off her muddy boots and shed her windbreaker. Even though it was June, it had been an unseasonably cool week. It had her dad in a tizzy over the corn.

"Everything alright with the corn?" her mom called out. She was peering into the oven, appraising the pot roast inside.

"Yes, everything's fine," Addy replied. "Not a stalk out of place."

There never was. Everything was always fine…because *nothing* ever happened. It made her want to set something on fire or blow something up, just to see people's reactions. But she didn't think her parents would accept *impending death by boredom* as a valid excuse for vandalism.

Addy's mom poked a fork into an apple pie on the counter. The smell of cinnamon wafted across the kitchen.

"Addy!"

Lucy, the youngest of Addy's four sisters, came skidding across the linoleum floor of the kitchen in her fuzzy socks. Even though Addy had only been gone for a few hours, Lucy acted like they hadn't seen each other in weeks. Grinning down at her baby sister, Addy picked her up and spun her around in a circle.

"Wheeeee!" Lucy squealed as she waved her short legs in the air.

"Be careful with Baby Lucy," Addy's mom said as she put a casserole dish full of cheesy potatoes into the oven.

At three years of age, Lucy wasn't a baby anymore, but everyone still called her *Baby Lucy* anyway. Lucy didn't seem to mind.

Addy put her sister down. When her mom turned back to the oven, Addy reached across the counter and broke off a flaky piece of pie crust.

"Adelyne Deerborn!" her mom scolded when she saw the evidence of Addy's theft.

"Wha'?" Addy gave her mom an innocent look as the cinnamon and sugar melted on her tongue.

When her mom turned back to the oven, Aunt Meredith, who was visiting from Texas, gave Addy an *ahem*. Addy stole another piece of pie crust and tossed it to Aunt Meredith. Her aunt caught it and stuffed it in her mouth just before Addy's mom turned back around. Her mom frowned at Aunt Meredith.

"You're as bad as the girls," her mom tsked.

"I'll take that as a compliment." Aunt Meredith winked at Addy.

Aunt Meredith's face was tan and a bit leathery from so much time spent outside. Even when she wasn't on the farm, she wore her cowboy boots and cowboy hat and said ya'll.

Before she had become a cattle rancher, Aunt Meredith had been a volunteer in the Peace Corps. Addy loved hearing about all the places she'd gone and the people she'd met. Aside from being born in Texas, which didn't count since she didn't remember it, Addy had never traveled farther than a few towns over. When she laid in bed at night, she tried to imagine what it would be like to travel the world like Aunt Meredith had before she retired to the ranch.

Addy wanted to see everything, go everywhere. It was some twist of irony that she'd been born into a family whose big yearly outing was to the mall an hour-and-a-half away.

The rest of Addy's sisters came through the swinging door to the kitchen in a tornado of laughter and good-natured arguing that was the constant background noise in the farmhouse.

Stacy came in first, complaining about how Rosie had stolen her nail polish...*again*. Rosie was flatly denying it even as she kept her hands noticeably hidden behind her back. Livy, Addy's very non-identical twin, followed the other two, picking up the toys and books they left discarded on the floor. Addy grinned at her twin across the room. In spite of the mayhem, Livy sensed Addy's gaze and returned her smile.

Literature class, and he'll move into the farmhouse here. Our kids can grow up together." She beamed at Addy.

"You've really thought all this out, haven't you?" Addy asked, feeling her throat start to constrict.

"What's a Chaucer?" Rosie asked.

"His last name will be something wonderfully British, like Hampton." Livy continued, lost in her fantasy. She smiled. "Olivia Hampton," she murmured.

Add scoffed. "That sounds too pretentious. How about Livy Shufflebottom?"

Completely ignoring the epic last name suggestion, Livy asked, "How about you? Will you change your name to Addy Brown when you marry Fred?"

"Please don't ever say "marry" and "Fred" in the same sentence again," Addy said, forcing a lightness she didn't feel.

Stacy twisted Addy's head back into position. "If only you weren't so freakishly pale," she complained, rubbing foundation over Addy's skin. "You look mostly dead."

Addy couldn't argue with that observation. Like her height, red hair, and light green eyes, Addy had apparently gotten her pale skin from her great-great-Grandma Ellen. She cursed the woman regularly for making her nothing like her soft and petite sisters. Livy was doll-like, with perfect hourglass curves, soft brown curls, and rosy cheeks. If Stacy and Rosie had been older, they would have looked like Livy's twin rather than Addy.

"And yet," Livy said, coming to Addy's defense, "Addy looks like a walking, talking magazine cover. And she never gets sunburned like the rest of us."

It was true, at least the *not getting sunburned* part. Even in the hot July and August months when they were outside the whole day, Addy never tanned or burned, not even when she "forgot" the bottle of sunscreen their mom made them take with them.

"Don't get me wrong, you're gorgeous. Just pale and flat as a board." Stacy surveyed Addy with a critical eye. "A padded bra would help, although there isn't much to be done about your flat butt."

"I'll file that assessment in the appropriate place," Addy said dryly.

"How about a butt pad?" Rosie suggested.

"That would be a diaper," Addy told her.

Rosie dipped her finger into the cream blush, and Stacy slapped at her hand. Pouting, Rosie went to sit next to Livy.

"I just don't see why we can't play cowboys and Indians like we used to," Rosie told Stacy.

At ten and thirteen, arguing was a constant state of being for Rosie and Stacy.

Stacy heaved a dramatic sigh. "Because it's culturally *insensitive*. Duh." She gave Addy's face an appraising stare. "I need purple eyeliner." She hopped off the bed, Rosie and Baby Lucy scrambling to follow her. "Purple looks good with green eyes," she was telling the younger ones as the three of them made their way to the bedroom down the hall that they shared.

Rosie shut the door behind her, leaving Livy and Addy alone. The silence their younger sisters left behind was deafening.

"You okay?" Livy asked in a soft voice. Her pretty brown eyes were bright with concern.

"Just tired," Addy replied, offering her twin a weak smile.

"You had the dream again last night," Livy said.

Addy cringed. She remembered her chest burning like water was filling her lungs. She remembered the panic of trying to breathe.

She'd been having the dream for as long as she could remember, and it was always the same. She was standing on the sandy beach of a lake that was ringed by bright green trees. The lake was so still it was like glass. It was peaceful.

And then the water began to suck at her feet. She fought it, but she could never escape as the water dragged her in. Deeper and deeper she went, until she couldn't stand anymore. The water pulled her under its surface, except it wasn't like real water. This water was thick. It was more like mucus than lake water. It filled her lungs and swelled her veins. She could see the sun overhead, but no matter how much she waved her hands and kicked her legs, the water kept her under.

"How's your dad been doing?" Addy asked quietly.

Fred shrugged. "He's lost a lot of his fine motor skills, but that's part of the deal with MS. It's been gettin' harder for him, though, now that he can't do much aroun' the farm."

Fred's mom had died ten years ago, and since then, it had just been Fred and his dad. Addy knew how much it was killing Fred to see his father slowly wasting away. The banner over their garage got it right—Fred really could fix anything. Except he couldn't fix his father's health. Addy didn't know what to say, so she just gave his hand a squeeze.

Fred squeezed hers back. He rolled his shoulders like he was shrugging off the sadness.

"Wanna go for a drive?" Addy asked.

It was the only thing that could always make them feel better, no matter how bad their moods. Addy could almost feel the truck's tires pummeling the dirt into dust and the night air whipping her hair as they raced down the empty road.

"Nah," Fred said. "I wanna talk to you about somethin'."

"Oh?" Addy raised her eyebrows. "What do you want to talk about?"

"Us."

The way he said the word, *us*, seemed weighted with a meaning Addy didn't want to understand. Fred stood up from his chair and began to pace back and forth across the dining room. A feeling of dread crawled up Addy's spine.

Fred came around the table and kneeled in front of her, his red bow tie askew.

"What are you doing?" Addy demanded, snatching her hand out of Fred's sweaty palm.

"I'm so proud of you, Ads," he began.

"Jeez, Fred. I thought you were proposing to me or something." Addy clutched her heart. "Don't ever scare me like that again."

Fred's face didn't lose any of its seriousness. "I'm not proposin', exactly."

Addy's relieved grin froze on her face. "What do you mean, *exactly*?"

"Listen, I got a plan." Fred tried to take Addy's hand again, but she was gripping the sides of her chair. "You're only gonna be an hour away at Cornell. I can come visit on the weekends."

"Um…."

"We can go to that dairy farm just off campus that's famous for their milkshakes, or have a picnic on the quad, or we could hang out with your new friends."

He looked so eager Addy didn't have the heart to suggest she might not want Fred visiting every weekend.

"Or we could get off campus if you want," Fred continued, spurred on by her silence. "There's a lake—"

"No," Addy said, cutting him off. "No lake."

She had been to a lake exactly once in her life. Her parents had rented a cabin about an hour away. Addy had gotten out of the car, seen the sun glistening off the lake, and had a panic attack. She hadn't stopped crying and shaking until her parents packed the whole family back in the van and drove far enough that she couldn't see any hint of the water.

It wasn't one of her favorite memories.

She'd had a similar reaction the next summer when her mother enrolled her and Livy in swim lessons at the YMCA. Addy hadn't been able to even get near the pool, and with the Y being a fifty-minute drive away, her mom hadn't pushed the issue.

Addy's paranoia about water had only gotten worse with age. It had gotten to the point that she hadn't taken a bath in two years, and God forbid the shower drain clogged and the water started to rise around her ankles….

Only her family knew about her paralyzing and completely irrational fear of water, and about the dream. Fred knew almost everything about her, but not this.

"Okay," Fred said, his grin faltering. "No lake."

Addy gave him a stiff nod.

"But here's where we get to the exactly part." Fred cleared his throat, and Addy had that vague sense that Fred was about to say something

CHAPTER 7

TOL

Purgatory. The Fount lived in Purgatory.

That's all Tol could think about as he left his fourth farm. Back in the rental car, he crossed off the name on the list with so much force the paper tore. Tol had started at Cornell University, and when that proved fruitless, he'd worked his way outward to all of the surrounding corn farms.

He had used precious time and even more precious Source questioning every person on every farm within two hours of Ithaca, New York. He had looked into their eyes and asked them. He hadn't known exactly the questions to ask, but he had known that none of the simple, hardworking American women he'd met were the one he was searching for.

It had been three days since he left England. Three days without any sense of whether his vision would lead him to anything besides another dead end. He would soon find out. There was only one place left on his tattered list: Deerborn Family Farm.

He turned the rental around in the muddy, unpaved lot and coaxed it onto the main road. He got a blast from a truck horn for his trouble. Tol cursed. As if it wasn't bad enough that the future queen of the Chosen came from Hicksville, America, he kept forgetting that Americans drove on the wrong side of the road. Despite his gran's confidence that the "Cornell University" T-shirt meant the Fount was a student there, he didn't have high hopes for her intelligence if her family lived in a place like this.

Tol slapped at his cheeks, forcing the exhaustion away. Three days he'd been searching for her. Three days he'd come up with exactly nothing. Deerborn Family Farm was his last hope.

If she wasn't there, Tol had no idea what he'd do. The thought of going back to England, of seeing the rest of his family battered and bruised from their fight with the Forsaken, and having nothing to show for his own search, was intolerable. Even a continent away, he could see Erikir's smirk and that expression he always wore that said his cousin would have made a better prince—a better king.

Tol was desperate to find the Fount. At the same time, he wished he wouldn't find her. Erikir's comment about being bound to someone with a hairy mole for eternity was still bothering him. Not because of the mole...maybe she had a nice personality...it was the eternity part that made him feel ill.

He couldn't imagine spending that long with anyone, least of all someone he didn't want to be with, and who wouldn't want to be with him. His gran had been married to his grandfather for five-hundred years, and that seemed like a number too great to fathom. Eternity was just...impossible. And yet, if he succeeded in the task that had consumed his life up to this point, that's what he would get.

Tol wondered if this mortal girl had any inkling of who she was. He wondered if the Celestial had given her any awareness of Vitaquias and its two races that had been expelled to the mortal world.

What if she had no idea about any of it?

There certainly weren't any other mortals who were aware of them. Since there wasn't enough Source to control six billion people, it was essential the mortals stayed ignorant.

"When my people destroyed our world, the gods deserted us," he imagined explaining to the wide-eyed, hairy-moled girl. "And the only way for us to survive and get back to the Old World is if you bind yourself to me...for eternity. Oh, and by the way, you'll have to rule an alien race of people alongside me. Cheers."

CHAPTER 8

ADDY

"Mom! Dad! Livy!"

Addy ran through the living room, where the coffee table was upended. Shattered glass crunched under her sneakers. Addy screamed the names of her family as she ran through the house.

Terror pulsed through her veins.

Blood streaked the floor and led to the swinging door of the kitchen, like an enormous brush had painted a pathway for her to follow.

Not a brush, she realized. *A body.*

Addy threw open the swinging door, heedless of whatever—or whoever—might be hiding behind it.

Unlike the living room, the kitchen was intact. All the chairs had been pushed into the table. All the placemats were set, with the knives and forks already laid out in preparation for breakfast (Rosie's chore). The only difference was the bodies strewn across the floor.

A choked, tortured sound escaped Addy's throat as she fell to her knees.

"Mom?" she managed, crawling on her hands and knees to the nearest body.

Blood soaked through her jeans, but she hardly noticed. She turned her mother's body so her face was pointed up.

Addy's chest started to heave. Her mother's face was covered in blood, and something metal protruded from her neck. Her skin was still warm. There was even a trickle of blood still leaking from the wound. Her mother's eyes were open, glassy and unseeing. Addy let go of her mother and reached for her father.

She checked for a pulse, cried his name, tried to wake him. But his body was cold and had already started to stiffen.

She vomited into a pool of blood and…innards….

Her need to breathe warred with her gasping, gut-wrenching sobs that tore at her lungs. She found Stacy and Rosie next. The only blood on their bodies was from what had flowed across the floor from their parents' and soaked their hair and clothes. When Addy gathered each of their limp bodies into her arms, begging them to wake up, their heads rolled back on broken necks.

Baby Lucy, her youngest sister, was lying in a pool of blood behind her other sisters, as though they had tried to shield her. Her throat had been sliced open.

Addy crawled from one to the next, sobbing their names in a voice she didn't recognize.

"What happened, Daddy?" the voice was begging the corpse. "Wake up, Rosie! Please. *Please.*"

She surveyed her family through eyes too blurry to make out anything more than the lifeless bodies curled on the linoleum.

Livy.

Addy's breath caught. She blinked furiously, trying to rid herself of the tears that clouded her vision. *Where was Livy?*

She wasn't in the kitchen. Addy got to her feet, slipping on the blood-slicked floor. She tore through every room of the downstairs. She yelled her twin's name, throwing aside furniture and checking inside cabinets.

Livy must have hidden and been too scared to come out. She had to be here…Addy just had to find her. She ran up the stairs, calling her twin's name as she went. This was all just some nightmare that would disappear as soon as she found Livy. Just like when she had the dream and Livy woke her and drew her out of its watery depths, she'd be safe from this one too, as soon as she could find her sister.

But Livy wasn't in the house.

Addy shut the hatch to the attic, her breaths coming in ragged little gasps. The shed, maybe? Or maybe she had run away from the murderers. Maybe she had been running to the Browns' house—to Addy—and Addy hadn't even seen her because she was so wrapped up in her stupid anger.

Was all of this because of the thief she'd killed? Had his friends come back for revenge on his killer, like she'd originally thought?

Oh God.

Her parents had wanted to leave the farmhouse. They'd wanted to hide, but Addy had talked them out of it. *Paranoid.* That's what she'd said to her parents three days ago. And now...and now....

Addy's stomach heaved. If there was anything left in it, it would have been on the floor. She moved to the stairs, telling herself she just had to keep going...just had to find Livy...when she heard the front door creak open.

Addy fell back into Stacy, Rosie, and Lucy's bedroom, her heart hammering. She kept her body against the doorframe and peeked over the railing, where she had a view of the three massive men and one woman stalking through the front door.

She knew at once these brutes had nothing to do with the skinny thief who had broken a window and tried to steal their cash with a knife. These men and women wore army camouflage and stomped into the house with military precision. They didn't carry guns. Instead, they each held a different weapon. Two carried swords, and one held a baton. The fourth had what looked like throwing stars, which Addy recognized from a Kung Fu movie she and Fred had watched together. All of the weapons were surrounded by a faint blue glow. The man with the baton raised a fist, and Addy saw that his hand was stained with blood.

Hatred churned inside her. These monsters had done this. They were the reason her family's blood was cooling on the floor downstairs.

She would kill them. She'd kill every one of them if it was the last thing she did.

They were speaking to each other. She couldn't make out the words, but the sound of their voices was as hard and cold as the rest of them. They moved farther into the house, and Addy lost sight of them.

She melted deeper into her sisters' room. What should she do? She knew from one glance at those people that whatever strength had come over her in her fight with the thief wouldn't pose even the smallest challenge to these brutes.

Addy moved to the window and looked out. She could try escaping, but there was nothing to use to climb down and only a stone patio at the bottom to break her fall. Even if she didn't break a leg, instinct told her they would hear her and get her before she could lose them in the cornfields.

She could try to hide, but if they were looking for her, they'd find her sooner or later.

She moved to Stacy's desk and picked up the tarnished silver hand mirror their grandma had given Stacy before she died. It was heavy, and if the glass broke, maybe the shards would embed themselves in her assailants.

A mirror against swords. Addy almost laughed at herself. But then she remembered her family downstairs.

These people murdered her family.

The rage she had felt when she held the garden shears over the thief came back to her. She let the feeling wash over her. She let it fill every space inside her, until there wasn't room for anything else. She saw the glow of golden light seeping out of her skin and filling the room.

Addy gripped the mirror in blood-slicked hands. She eased the bedroom door closed, slid against the wall, and waited.

At the first sound of boots on the stairs, her heart flew into her throat. They stopped on the landing, said something to each other, and then continued up. Addy counted the steps and knew when they'd reached the top.

She held her breath. Her heart was pounding such a furious rhythm, she was sure it would give her away. If the sound of her heart didn't, the golden light spilling out of her would. When there were no more footsteps or sounds, she peeked through the crack of the door.

A single, gray eye was staring back at her.

"Ahh," the man said, his voice deep and accented. "We've been looking for you."

Addy screamed.

CHAPTER 9

TOL

Tol was in some kind of laundry room, with dozens of muddy shoes thrown onto metal shoe racks. Nothing useful here.

He went into the next room, and caught his breath. He knew this room. It was the place where the Fount had been when he felt her. The television, the couch, the dirty windowpane with the view to the cornfields outside—it was all here, just as he'd seen it. Tol stood for a moment, marveling at how the Celestial's magic had enabled him to see through another person's eyes from a continent away.

A scream came from upstairs. He ran toward it.

Tol took the stairs two at a time.

Forsaken. He knew it from the sight of their towering figures as they kicked open a door and strode inside.

"Get away from me!"

Tol heard the girl's voice, and his blood went cold. The Fount was inside that room, and the Forsaken had come for her.

Move, you bloody idiot.

Tol raced for the nearest Forsaken. His enemy was so focused on the girl, the man didn't notice Tol until he'd wrapped his hand around the man's bare wrist.

The Forsaken man's muscles went slack as Tol's Influence took hold.

"Kill the other Forsaken," Tol ordered the man, gesturing at the sword in his hands. "Then, kill yourself."

Tol didn't wait to see the Forsaken's eyes glaze over, or for the man's slack arm to tighten around his sword hilt. The others were already on the Fount.

Tol grabbed for one of the others, but the man backhanded him without even looking up. Tol fell backward into a solid desk, feeling all the air leave his lungs. As he wrestled for breath, he saw the Forsaken man under his control knock down one of his comrades and engage another. They were locked in combat, which meant there was still one who was free to go after the Fount.

The girl was bloody and leaning back over a small bed, but she wasn't cowering. She wielded a hand mirror like it was a sword, lashing out at the Forsaken's arms as he tried to grab her.

The man finally managed to wrench the mirror out of the girl's hands. He threw it across the room. Still, she didn't curl into a ball and give up like anyone else would have. She stood her ground, fists raised.

Any doubts Tol might have had about this girl being the Fount vanished in an instant. There was no mortal who could stand up to the Forsaken.

Still, Fount or not, Tol felt an enormous respect for this girl who defended herself against the most ruthless warriors in two worlds with nothing but a hand mirror and her fists.

The man grabbed the Fount by her shoulder. Tol's mind went white with fury. He lunged.

Tol shoved the man. He had been leaning over the girl, so Tol was able to knock him off balance.

The girl took advantage of the space that had opened between her and the Forsaken. She launched herself at him like a cat. She punched him in the throat, and to Tol's complete amazement, the Forsaken faltered. He put his hand to his thick neck, like he couldn't breathe.

Tol knew they only had a millisecond before the Forsaken attacked again.

"Look at me," he commanded.

Without thinking, the Forsaken turned to him. As soon as their eyes met, it was over for the Forsaken.

"Don't look away," Tol commanded.

The man's tense shoulders relaxed. The sword in his hand slid to the ground.

"Good." Tol walked up to him, keeping his gaze fixed on the Forsaken. "Now, give your other weapons to the girl."

The Forsaken's glazed eyes never left Tol's as he removed knives from hidden pockets inside his jacket and dropped them onto the floor by the girl's feet.

The Fount jumped at the sound of the knives thudding to the ground before her. Her wide-eyed stare moved from the daggers, to the Forsaken man, to Tol.

"W-What?" she stammered.

Tol ignored her, keeping his eyes locked on the Forsaken's.

"Good," Tol told him, like the man was a dog that had just come when called. Tol turned his head just enough to look at the girl, while keeping the Forsaken in his sight. "Do you want to kill him, or do you want me to do it?" he asked.

"No, don't."

The girl's voice trembled.

Great, Tol thought. The Fount was a pacifist.

He didn't have time for this. "Listen," Tol told her. "If we let him go, he's going to come after you again. And the next time, there won't be four of them, but fifty. We won't stand a chance."

The girl came to stand in front of the Forsaken, and to Tol's surprise, she didn't quake or look away like any normal person would have. Even most Chosen would cower before these warriors, and they'd be right to do so. This girl didn't seem afraid, though. She seemed angry.

"He has my sister," the Fount told Tol. "Or at least," she swallowed, her face twisting in anguish, "he might know where she was taken."

Tol turned his full attention on the Forsaken. "What did you do with her sister, barbarian?"

The man hesitated for a second, his gray eyes going wide with emotion Tol wasn't allowing him to express. Tol flared his Source, and the man sunk to his knees.

"The others took her."

"Who took her?" the girl asked. "Where? Is she still alive?"

The Forsaken didn't say anything.

"Answer her," Tol commanded. The sooner this interrogation ended, the sooner he could get the Fount and himself out of here. There were bound to be more Forsaken nearby. It wasn't safe here.

"My comrades took her. I don't know where. The mission is top secret. Only the officers know anything."

"So, she's still alive?"

There was so much hope in the girl's voice it tugged at Tol's heart. He knew the Forsaken didn't take captives unless they needed something from them. If they had the Fount's sister, it was because they intended to use her against the Fount.

"Yes," came the mechanical answer.

"How do I find her?" the girl was yelling now.

"I don't know," came the robotic reply.

Enough of this, Tol thought. This man didn't know anything about where her sister had been taken.

"What were you planning to do with *this* girl?" Tol demanded, tightening his mental hold on the Forsaken.

The man winced, like Tol was exerting physical pressure on him, rather than just a mental one. "We were to bring her back unharmed."

Tol opened his mouth, but before he could say even a single word, the girl picked up a knife from the ground and slashed it across the Forsaken's throat.

Blood sprayed through the air. Tol stepped back to avoid it, but the girl didn't even flinch as her already-bloodstained clothes were splattered anew. When the man's body hit the floor with a thud, she didn't even blink.

Okay, so definitely not a pacifist.

There was a *pop*, and then the Forsaken's body disappeared in a puff of blue smoke. That got the girl's attention.

"What the—?" Her mouth hung open.

"You've never seen one of them die before?" Tol asked. He should have said one of *us*, but he couldn't bear to lump himself and the rest of the Chosen in with the barbarians.

"One of *who*?"

"Never mind."

Tol went to the four piles of clothes, which were all that remained of the rest of the Forsaken, and started to search for their necklaces.

"Where—" the girl swallowed. "Where did those people go?"

"Their essence returned to Vitaquias," Tol said, knowing full-well the explanation would mean nothing to this girl.

He found the necklaces. He opened their vials—similar to Tol's, only much smaller—and added the few drops of Source from their vials into his own. He let the empty vessels fall onto the wood floor. If they had been made of regular glass, they would have shattered on impact. But these containers were from the Old World; any other material would have caused the Source to be leached out as soon as they entered the mortal world.

It was why they had such a finite amount. When Vitaquias started to burn, the survivors could only bring as much Source as their vials would hold. It was all they had to sustain themselves in the mortal world, and it was fast-draining.

"Ohmygod...those people just...disappeared." The girl was pacing back and forth between the piles of clothes. "They just disappeared!"

"Yeah, like I said—" Tol's words trailed off as he really looked at the girl for the first time. He started.

In the commotion before, he hadn't noticed her Haze. There was no vial of Source around her neck, and yet golden light surrounded her, shimmering in a way that set her red hair aflame. Her Haze was strong. Even as he watched, it seemed to recede back inside her until it was no longer visible at all.

Tol had never seen Haze work that way before. His was always present; it just got brighter when he ingested Source. Tol supposed he shouldn't be surprised the girl's Haze worked differently. She was a mortal with the Celestial's powers. None of the regular rules applied.

The Chosen scholars had devoted the last eighteen years to trying to guess what the Fount would be like, and what it would do to a mortal body to possess other-worldly magic. But all their charts and diagrams were just fancy guesses.

Everyone from Vitaquias had some amount of Haze, which indicated their natural inclination to the Source, the power that fueled their immortality and abilities. Once Source was ingested and got into the bloodstream, it infused the body with added strength. It basically supercharged their natural abilities. For the Chosen, it was their mind-controlling Influence. For the Forsaken, it was their strength and weapons.

One drop of Source was enough to create the magical reaction, which made their golden Haze flare brighter.

Since the girl wasn't wearing one of the Vitaquias-forged necklaces, which were made from the only material that could contain the Source, it meant her power came from somewhere else. It meant the Source was somehow a part of her very being. It meant that Tol was looking at the woman his people had been trying to find for eighteen years.

He was looking at the Fount.

The Fount had pale green eyes that reminded him of spring. They looked nice with her coppery-red hair. She was someone most people would consider very attractive, although, at the moment, she was covered in blood.

Tol noticed the girl was looking at him, too. Not him, he realized, so much as his prosthetic arm. The way she was staring at him made him feel like she was undressing him with her eyes, and not in a good way.

Tol shifted his body so his good arm was facing the girl, even as a dark dread crept over him. If he told this Fount-supermodel who he was and what he needed from her, she'd laugh in his face.

How tall was she, anyway? Tol wondered. He was tall, but she looked about his height. Tol knew from his experience in mortal school with Gerth, who was slight like most of the Chosen, that mortal girls hated being taller than their male counterparts.

"They have my sister," the Fount said in a hoarse voice. "I have to find her."

The words seemed to jolt her out of some kind of trance. She hurried out of the room.

Tol followed her into another bedroom. The girl took a duffel bag out from under a bed and started stuffing clothes into it.

"What exactly is your plan?" Tol asked.

She paused. "I—" She looked at the bed on the other side of the room, and her body seemed to shrink in on itself. "I don't know. I just have to find her."

Tol understood her feeling of helplessness.

"I'm sorry," Tol said, "but if they have your sister, you're not going to be able to get her back."

Instead of the resignation he expected to appear on her face, her eyes brightened and her despair fell away. "You know these people? Do you know where they might have taken her? Can you tell me where to find them?"

Tol put up his hand, trying to slow her down.

Instead of answering any of her questions, he asked one of his own. "What's your name?"

She blinked at him.

"My family calls me Addy." And then, "Called me Addy."

She yanked off her bloody shirt. Embarrassed, Tol turned around to give her some privacy while she changed into a clean T-shirt. Not that she seemed to notice, or care, that he was there. She pushed past him, now more or less free of blood, and headed for the stairs. Tol had to hurry to keep up with her.

"What should I call you?" he asked.

"My name is Adelyne Deerborn," she replied, without turning around.

"Adelyne," Tol repeated.

Part of him expected the ground to tremble and the sky to open as a flock of doves flew down to perch on both their shoulders. But of course, nothing happened. It was just a name…a mortal name.

It didn't matter. He'd found the Fount.

Tol looked at the girl who he'd have to convince to spend eternity with him. She took the stairs slowly, as though she didn't want to reach the bottom.

"Look," Tol began, "we should get out of here. It's not safe, and—"

"I don't know what you expect from me, but I'm not going anywhere with you."

She didn't even bother to turn around to look at him when she said the words.

Tol faltered. He didn't expect her to want to stay here, not when there were sure to be more Forsaken on their way.

"Those people who attacked you," he said, trying a different tack. "There are more of them. A lot more. When these blokes don't report back, more will come."

They reached the bottom of the stairs. Adelyne turned back to look at him. He felt uncomfortable under the scrutiny of her gaze, but he forced himself to hold her stare.

There was something startling about her. *Definitely no hairy moles.*

The thought brought him little comfort. He remembered the way her gaze had gone straight to his prosthetic arm, and it made the flame of his hatred for this mortal burn a little hotter.

"Where are you going?" Tol demanded, following the girl away from the front door. "We have to leave."

"If more of those people are coming, then one of them will be able to tell me where to find my sister," came her curt reply.

Tol's mouth fell open. "You can't be serious."

"Just do that thing you did before," Adelyne said. She narrowed her eyes and made some ridiculous motion with her hands like she was imitating a TV magician.

Anger pulsed through Tol. He knew it was unfair—there was no way for this mortal girl to understand Source and what it meant to spend even a single drop—but it didn't stop him from spitting back, "I'm not just going to *do that thing I did before.*"

"Fine. Then get the hell out."

Tol wanted to shout at her. Instead, he followed her into the kitchen. He sucked in a breath.

"Oh, gods," he whispered.

Adelyne stood, seeming as paralyzed as he was, as she looked down at a small child. The little girl couldn't have been older than three, and there was a red slash across her neck. Bile rose in Tol's throat.

Tol counted the bodies in the room. There were five of them.

"I'm so sorry," Adelyne was telling the dead little girl. "I should have been here."

Tol's heart constricted. This was what the Forsaken did. They killed, they took, and then they disappeared without remorse.

"This isn't your fault." Tol's voice came out rough.

Adelyne looked up at him, her tears pouring down her cheeks. "Yes, it is," she whispered. "My parents knew—they knew—" she hunched over the child's body, sobbing.

Tol felt helpless. Should he put a hand on her shoulder? Too forward. He wanted to say something to comfort her, but he had no idea what words could help her right now.

"Um," Tol cleared his throat. "I know you want to stay here, and I don't blame you, but we really do need to go before more of them come."

She looked at him, her eyes dull. "Why didn't they kill me, too?" she asked in a whisper.

Tol blew out a breath. "It's kind of a long story. I can explain it to you in the car."

"I said I wasn't going anywhere," she snapped.

"And I said I couldn't protect you if—*when*—more of them show up," he shot back, and then immediately felt guilty.

Don't be a prat, he told himself.

"They'll take me to the same place they took Livy, won't they? I'll be able to find her—"

"Trust me, you won't." Tol felt sorry for this girl, but the urgency of their situation was trying his patience. "There won't be some happy reunion or whatever you're imagining. They'll use her against you. And then, once you've given them what they want, they'll kill her."

"What do you know about these people?" Adelyne asked. The hope in her voice made it clear she hadn't heard a word Tol just said.

"Nothing you're going to want to hear," he said.

He was taken aback when she grabbed his shirt with her bloody hands.

"Can you help me find her?" her voice was full of desperation.

"I'm sorry," Tol said, and he meant it. "The Forsaken—I mean, those people—are very good at hiding."

His gran had been pushing the scholars and guards to discover the Forsaken general's hideout since they'd been in the mortal world. Jariath had gotten close, and they all knew how that story had ended.

"But it might be possible," Adelyne pressed.

"Loads of things are possible," Tol replied, his gaze flicking to the window. Had he seen something move?

"Please." She was still holding onto his shirt. "Help me find her."

"I can't—"

"I'll do anything," she said, practically dragging him to her by the force of her grip. "I'll do anything. Just help me find her."

Tol paused. Before he did or said anything else, he had to be sure this girl was who he thought she was. If he got back to the manor and it turned out she wasn't the Fount....

He was being paranoid. Or maybe just hopeful.

There wasn't a regular mortal on earth who could have stood up to the Forsaken the way Adelyne had. Still, his tutors' reminders to check and double-check all evidence before confirming anything had stuck. He wasn't taking any chances, especially not with something as important as this.

"There's something I need to be sure of before we go any further," Tol said, looking at Adelyne. "How old are you?" he asked.

"Eighteen," she replied. "Last week."

That was about right. He scrutinized Adelyne, who stared back at him.

"Is there anything about me that seems, um, strange to you?" he asked.

Her eyes immediately went to his prosthesis. Tol rolled his eyes. "Besides my arm, I mean."

Adelyne looked up at him. "You have a gold halo all around you." She swallowed. "Like mine, and those people who attacked me. But yours is brighter."

That was it, then. Regular mortals couldn't see their Haze. And they certainly didn't have one of their own.

This girl was the Fount.

"Okay, then," Tol said, feeling the weight of his responsibilities, finally coming to fruition, bear down on him. "Will you agree," he paused, his mind fitting the pieces together as he spoke, "to come with me and, um, perform a ritual my people need—"

"Yes." Her answer came without hesitation. "If you'll agree to bring an army of your cultish magician friends to rescue my sister first."

"Cultish magician friends?" Tol raised a brow.

Adelyne looked down at the bloodstained floor, which immediately sobered him.

"Look," Tol said. "If I told my people we were going to find your sister instead of returning for…the ritual…they'd come here and drag us back. They wouldn't help you, and they certainly wouldn't spare any of their Influence for a mortal who…they don't care about." Tol almost said *doesn't matter*, but stopped himself. "I'm all you've got."

Her gaze flicked to his prosthesis, and it was like he could read her thoughts. *How could you, with only one real arm, be of any use to me?*

He hardened himself against the resentment that was building inside him.

"None of my people would waste the time to help you." He winced at the way his words came out, even if they were true. "But I will," he said, trying to soften the blow.

"Whatever, fine," she said. "I'll do this ritual. But you have to find my sister *first*." She glared at him, making it clear she wouldn't budge on this point.

Tol looked at Adelyne. There was a stubbornness to her features that told him there was nothing he could say to change her mind.

What should he do?

He knew what his parents would say. They'd tell him to get her back to the manor first, and then leave the business of gaining her consent to the poets and mortal psychology experts.

One of the Celestial's contingencies of the blood marriage was that it was entered into by both the prince and the Fount of their own free will. This stipulation was intended to temper the Chosens' belief in their own superiority and to make them realize the limitations of their powers. In all their planning, the king and queen had insisted Tol bring the Fount back to the manor, and let the scholars do the convincing on his behalf.

Now that Tol was here, he had no intentions of starting out his eternity with this girl by forcing her to do anything.

He also felt certain, just from the few minutes he'd known her, that this girl wouldn't fall for any of the scholars' sweet words. All she cared about was finding her sister, and she wouldn't agree to anything until she'd gotten what she wanted.

But if he helped her, it would be that much longer before the blood marriage. That would mean more Chosen would die when their Source ran out. And it wasn't just that. Every moment that went by without the ceremony being completed was one more day they were vulnerable to the Forsakens' attacks. It wasn't just his and her lives they'd be risking. If the blood marriage wasn't complete by Adelyne's nineteenth birthday, Tol's entire race would be doomed.

This blood marriage was their only hope of survival. So, why was Tol considering risking everything to search for a girl in the custody of his enemy, who would probably be dead before they found her?

"Okay," he said. The word sounded like a death sentence for his people. "I'll help you find your sister, if you'll promise to come with me after and complete the ritual."

"After," Adelyne clarified.

"After," he agreed.

"Done."

He knew she didn't have the slightest clue what she was promising. On the other hand, he'd technically just gained her consent. If she knew what she was agreeing to, if he had used the words *blood marriage* and explained their meaning, Tol felt sure it would be a price she wouldn't be willing to pay no matter how desperate she was. And so, he did what any of the Chosen would do in his position. It made him feel sick with self-disgust to be so deceitful, but he forged on.

"If you're serious about this, I need you to give me your word," Tol heard himself say. He hated what he was doing. He hated that he had no choice. "I'll help you get your sister back, and then you'll come with me to perform the ritual."

She cocked her head at him. "You're in some kind of cult, aren't you?"

"Not exactly," Tol replied, biting his lip to keep his temper in check.

"Whatever." Adelyne shook her head. "I'll do it."

Guilt and self-loathing swept through Tol, but he forced them down. "Swear it, on your life."

Her gaze was unblinking. "I swear on my life."

It wasn't enough. This oath was too important to leave any room for ambiguity.

He kept his eyes fixed on hers as he said, "I, Tolumus Magnantius, prince of the Chosen and son of King Rolomens and Queen Starser, swear on the Celestial of Vitaquias that I will do everything in my power to help you find your sister."

Tol's oath rippled through him, tightening around his chest like invisible cords.

Adelyne scoffed a little, but there was an uncertain look on her face, like she wasn't sure whether he was the crazy one, or she was. Her eyes were fixed on his Haze, which had flared brighter with the power of his words.

"Now you," he said, when the force of his oath had lessened enough for him to speak. "Do it the way I did, using your full name and swearing on the highest authority you obey."

Her green eyes gleamed as she said, "I, Adelyne Deerborn, daughter of Sue and Gary Deerborn," her voice broke on their names, but Tol saw her steel herself. She continued, "Swear on my sister Olivia Deerborn that I will perform this ritual after we have rescued her."

She sucked in a breath as she was bound in the same invisible chains as he. Tol felt the power of her oath fill the blood-soaked room.

CHAPTER 10

ADDY

Addy instantly regretted telling the boy to call her Adelyne. The only time anyone ever used that name was when she was in trouble, and her parents were saying something like "Adelyne Deerborn, did you forget to shut the chicken coop and make your younger sisters chase them all over the farm?" And then Livy would cover for Addy, and her parents' disappointment would be smoothed over.

Addy's eyes stung. She shook her head at the terrible sweetness of the memory…sweetness she would have scorned only a few days ago, and which she now longed for with every ounce of her being.

Her nickname had just seemed too familiar to give a stranger. She didn't have much experience with strangers; the only new people she ever met were the farmhands her family and the Browns hired to help during their busy season.

But even with her limited experience with new people, she wasn't a complete idiot. She knew there was nothing normal about this strange boy, surrounded by a gold shimmer, who appeared out of nowhere and saved her life.

She still thought he was a lunatic, the saving her life part aside. He'd called himself a prince and looked like he believed it. Maybe he was one of those fanatic alien-loving conspiracy theorists. She knew the type. She and Fred had watched a documentary about Jonestown a while back.

But he didn't have the look of a fanatic, and he'd killed her attackers without laying a hand on them. The only blood on him was from when she'd grabbed his shirt with her own bloodstained hands. It also hadn't escaped her that the boy was surrounded by a more intense version of the gold halo she had first seen around herself when she killed the thief. Unlike hers, though, his never disappeared. Instead, it seemed to go from bright to super bright depending on how long it had been since he drank from that vial around his neck.

None of that mattered, though. All that mattered was that Livy was alive, and this boy was going to help her find her sister.

This boy. She didn't know his name, because she hadn't cared enough to ask. He had called himself something when he made that oath, but she hadn't been paying attention to anything except his promise to help rescue Livy.

Under normal circumstances, Addy would have had a lot more questions about what this ritual entailed before agreeing to participate. But these were not normal circumstances. Those people had her sister, and Addy would agree to anything if it meant finding Livy.

At least this boy didn't give off the creepy religious zealot vibe, and he had saved her life. For now, that was enough for her to agree to anything if it meant rescuing her sister.

The thought of sweet, kind Livy in the hands of those monsters was all that kept her from curling into a ball on her bloody kitchen floor and sobbing. It was all that kept her from thinking about how, if she hadn't talked her parents out of leaving, they might all still be alive.

This was what her parents had been afraid of. It was why they'd kept exchanging those scared looks. At the time, she had just thought they had PTSD from the thief's attack.

Addy felt a surge of anger toward her parents. *Why hadn't they told her?* If she'd known what they knew, she might have been packing her sisters' bags and chasing them out of the house herself.

As soon as the anger flared, it spent itself up. Whatever secrets her parents had, whatever reasons they'd had for not telling their daughters, didn't matter now. While she was sitting at Fred's table eating chocolate pie and talking about the Daytona 500, her family was getting slaughtered. The thought of it made Addy want to throw up.

She wanted to undo whatever had made those people upstairs turn into blue smoke so she could kill them again.

"I guess I need to call the police," she said, heading for the phone.

"No." The boy put out his arm as if to stop her, and then snatched it back before their hands met. "The police can't help you find your sister, and if they find out the rest of your family is dead, they're going to take you into custody."

He was right.

"We can't just leave them," she choked.

A look of sympathy flashed across the boy's face before it hardened again. When he looked at her, Addy got the sense the boy couldn't stand the sight of her.

The back door slammed. They both went rigid.

"Get back," he said.

Addy watched as he uncorked the little glass vial hanging around his neck. He tipped it over. A perfect bead of clear liquid glistened on the tip of his finger for a moment before he put it in his mouth. The golden glow around the boy flared so bright Addy had to look away.

"Get behind me," he told her.

Addy grabbed two knives from the block on the counter. She tried to give one to the boy, but he just shook his head. She would have insisted, but he seemed to do just fine without a weapon before. Maybe that metal arm had poison darts that shot out of the fingers, or something. Addy thought she'd read a book like that once.

"Ads?"

Fred. Elation, followed by horror, filled her at the thought of Fred being here...seeing *this.*

The door to the kitchen swung open, and Fred came in. He halted, and stared. He didn't even blink when the door swung back and hit him.

"Addy," he breathed.

She ran to him. The wildflowers bunched in his hands fell to the ground as his strong, familiar arms came around her. She had thought all her tears were spent, but they poured out of her eyes anew. She was crying so hard she barely heard the question Fred kept repeating.

"What happened? What happened? What happened?"

"Who are you?"

Addy and Fred broke apart at the sound of the other boy's voice. There was a furious look in his eyes, and he had already moved toward Fred like he was going to do…something…to him.

Fred grabbed Addy and tried to shove her behind him. "Who are *you*?" Fred demanded, his hands curling into fists.

The boy didn't say anything, but his gold halo flared. It was more frightening than any reply he could have spoken. Fred didn't seem to notice, though.

"Addy," Fred said. "Run. I'll take care of him."

The boy raised an eyebrow at Addy, looking amused rather than angry for the first time since he'd shown up.

"It's okay, Fred," she said, disentangling herself from him. "He isn't the one who did this. He saved me from the ones who—" She swallowed, unable to finish.

"Uh-huh," Fred said, not looking in the least bit convinced. "And what did you say your name was?"

"I didn't," the boy replied, his voice low and dangerous.

The two of them were still facing off, and Addy knew if she didn't do something, it would come to blows.

"Fred, there's no time," she told him. "Those people took Livy, and he's," she gestured at the boy, "going to help me find her."

"Is that righ'?" Fred asked, his voice and face twisted in sarcasm.

"I'm sorry," the boy said, not sounding at all sorry, "but we don't have time for this."

He stepped forward, and Addy thought he was going to punch Fred. He didn't.

"Look at me," the boy said.

Fred did. Neither of them blinked, like they were in some kind of trance.

"Adelyne," the boy said without taking his eyes off Fred. "Who is this person to you?"

"He's my best friend," she choked out. "Don't hurt him."

"You're lucky," he told Fred in a quiet voice that should have sent shivers of dread down Fred's spine. Instead, Fred gave the boy a stupid smile Addy had never seen on his face before. His eyes were glazed over, too, like he was trying to see the hidden image in those magic eye illusions in the Sunday paper.

"Here's what you're going to do," the boy said. "You'll bury these bodies where no one will find them. You'll clean up this house and all evidence of bloodshed. And then, you'll go home and never speak of this to anyone. Do you understand?"

Fred nodded his head, that stupid grin still on his face.

"What are you doing to him?" Addy gasped, even though it was obvious. He was mind-controlling her best friend.

She wouldn't have believed it was possible if she wasn't witnessing it with her own eyes.

The boy broke eye contact, and Fred immediately went to her mother's body. He picked her up like she was as light as a ragdoll and started to carry her out of the room. Addy cried out and went to follow him.

The boy put out a hand to stop her, and she flinched away. She thought she saw him wince, but she might have just imagined it.

"Undo whatever you just did to him," she demanded.

"I told you those people wouldn't rest until they found us," he replied through gritted teeth, like he was the one who had a right to be furious. "I understand you want to bury your family, but there just isn't time. That bloke is going to do it for us."

Simultaneous rage and helplessness filled Addy.

"But we can't just—"

"Do you want to find your sister or not?" he demanded.

Those were the magic words—the words against which she would brook no argument.

"What if more of those people come back while Fred's still here?" she asked. "I won't let—"

"They don't want him," the boy growled. "They're after us."

With one final look at Fred, who was lumbering back to the farmhouse like he didn't notice his shirt was soaked with her mother's blood, she nodded.

"And Fred," the boy said his name like an insult. Fred stopped mid-stride to look at him. "Don't forget to dispose of your bloody clothes before you go home."

Fred nodded, and then continued on with the business of destroying the evidence of her family's existence.

"It's Tolumus, by the way. Tolumus Magnantius."

"What?" Addy looked at looked him.

"My name," he said.

"What kind of name is Tolumenuous?" she asked, stumbling over the unfamiliar syllables.

The boy was looking at her like she was some kind of disgusting beetle.

"Some people call me Tol," he said, turning his back on her, "if that's easier for you."

There was derision in the way he said it...*if that's easier for you*. Like she was stupid or something. Not that she cared what he thought about her.

"Okay." She shrugged. "Tol."

He was watching Fred clean up her family's bodies. He didn't really seem to be watching Fred, though. His mind seemed far away in some dark place. She stared at the strange boy with the weird name so she wouldn't have to watch her best friend carrying away all that remained of her family.

He was about her height, which was to say he was tall. *Tol was tall*, she thought, a bitter humor to her thoughts. He was thin, especially compared to Fred, but not lanky. There was something almost regal in the way he stood there staring at Fred, like he was used to people doing whatever he told them, and the novelty of being obeyed had long since worn off.

Tol wore jeans and a button-down. Both looked tailored and expensive, the opposite of Addy's ratty jeans and faded T-shirt. He had that kind of layered shoulder-length black hair all the skater boys had in the movies she and Fred watched on Netflix. The skater boys' hair always seemed greasy and stringy, though. Tol's hair was thick and shiny, and unlike the goth kids who hung out by the 7-Eleven in town, his didn't seem dyed. She wondered for one ridiculous moment if it felt as soft as it looked.

His accent was English, but he didn't look British. His skin was a deep olive, almost bronze. His eyes had a slight almond shape and were such a dark brown they seemed to match his black hair. All of it together gave him an other-worldly appearance.

Addy noticed Tol kept his body slightly angled whenever he spoke to her, like he was trying to hide his metal arm from view. It seemed like an unconscious gesture, and she doubted he even realized he was doing it. The metal arm aside, Addy could imagine seeing his grainy picture taped to the ceiling over Stacy's bed.

The breath went out of her lungs as grief struck her anew. Her sisters. Her parents.

How could they be gone?

"I have a car," Tol said. "I can bring it around."

Addy didn't respond. It was only the sound of the closing door and Fred's truck driving away that made her react. She moved mechanically, throwing a few more things into her duffel bag. She went into the living room and grabbed the cloth bag filled with cash that the thief had tried to steal. For the first time, she was glad her parents hadn't listened to her about taking it to the bank rather than keeping it in the farmhouse. There was more than $2,000, and she figured it would come in handy at some point. She stuffed half the wad in her duffel and put the rest in the front pocket of her jeans.

As an afterthought, she grabbed the garden shears resting on top of the coffee table, the ones she had used to kill the thief and which her mother had cleaned afterward. They fit nicely in the palm of her hand, and she liked the feel of their weight. She tucked them into the back pocket of her jeans.

She looked at the phone on the table next to the couch.

Aunt Meredith. The thought sent simultaneous feelings of relief and dread through her. She still had her aunt. She wasn't alone. On the other hand, she was the one who'd have to tell her aunt what had happened to their family. A cold panic went through her at the thought that maybe, whoever was after her family had killed Aunt Meredith, too.

Addy went over to the phone and picked up the receiver. With trembling fingers, she dialed the number she knew by heart. Her aunt picked up on the first ring.

Addy sagged with relief to hear her aunt's voice.

"Aunt Meredith."

"Addy? Oh, thank God. I've been calling and calling, and I haven't heard from your mom in two days…." She broke off, like she could hear Addy's panic through the phone. "Addy, what's wrong? Has something happened?"

Addy didn't know how she found the words to tell her aunt what had happened, but somehow, she managed it between bursts of sobs and hiccups. She could hear her aunt's own choked sobs on the other end of the receiver.

"Your parents told me, but I never believed them." Aunt Meredith's voice was a hoarse whisper.

"What did they tell you?" Addy asked, her heart pounding.

Paranoid. She had called her parents paranoid when they wanted to run.

How could Addy have been so stupid? Why hadn't she bothered to dig deeper, to understand why her parents were afraid? They had never been the type of people to act crazy for no reason.

"Where are you, at the farmhouse?" Aunt Meredith asked, ignoring Addy's question.

"Yes, I—"

"Then you need to leave, right away. And you can't come to my house, either. It isn't safe. Go to Fred's and stay there until I come for you."

"I can't. Aunt Meredith…they took Livy."

Her aunt let loose a string of curses she never would have said in front of Addy's mother. But her mother was dead now. Addy had to keep reminding herself, because it felt too impossible, too horrible, to be real. It felt more like her drowning nightmare, except Livy wasn't here to wake her up from this one.

"Stay at Fred's house until I get there," her aunt was saying. "We'll figure it out together."

"But Aunt Meredith, what did my parents tell you? What do you know about all of this?"

There was a long pause on the other end of the receiver.

"Honestly, I thought it was all some trick of their minds after your mother's miscarriages. They were so desperate for a child, and I assumed something just kind of snapped in them. I didn't really take any of what they said seriously, but it was so important to them that you girls never find out—"

"Find out what? Aunt Meredith? Hello?"

"Are you out of your mortal mind?"

Tol, holding up the dangling cord, had a furious look on his face.

"How dare you," Addy spit, but Tol cut her off.

"The Forsaken are undoubtedly tapping your phones. They'll be watching and listening to anyone you might contact, and they'll use them as a way to get to us."

He threw the cord onto the ground, making a sound of disgust. "The car's around back. Let's go."

Addy wanted to punch him in the face. She wanted to grab his stupid glass necklace and smash it against the wall.

What had Aunt Meredith been about to tell her?

Addy grabbed her duffel bag and ran past Tol. She slammed the door behind her. She didn't get into the sedan, which was too clean and too quiet to exist naturally on Deerborn Family Farm. She ran over to the pickup truck that was bouncing back over the dirt-and-gravel path. Fred leaned out the window and smiled at her. There was a smear of blood on his cheek.

Fred stopped the truck, and she leaned into the open window.

"Fred, you have to look after the farm for me while I'm gone." She shoved a wad of bills into his hand. "Hire people if you have to, just…." She swallowed. "Please, just don't let it go under."

Her family loved this farm, and when Livy came back, she'd be devastated if she found it in ruins. And the Cluckers…Rosie would want them taken care of even if there was no one on the farm. The corn would be ready soon, and her dad—

Addy slipped the bracelet off her wrist, the one Fred had given her last night when her biggest concern was his sort-of proposal. She hadn't noticed the metal cutting into her flesh, but there was a faint scratch on her forearm, and blood was crusted on the inside of the metal. Addy couldn't stand the sight of one more drop of blood. She gave Fred the bracelet.

"And hold onto this for me. Please."

"'Course, Ads," Fred said. "I'd do anything for you."

But he wasn't looking at Addy when he said those words and took the bracelet from her. He was looking at Tol, who had come down the back steps and now stood next to his car.

Tol gave Fred a curt nod. A grin spread over Fred's face.

"What the hell did you do to him?" Addy demanded.

"It's called Influence," Tol said, "And it'll wear off as soon as he's finished the job I gave him."

"So, you can just force people to do whatever you want, just by asking them?"

"It's a little more complicated than that," came Tol's dry response.

Addy stared at her best friend, who was unloading cleaning supplies from the truck bed. "What if someone doesn't want to do what you tell them?"

Tol shrugged. "That would never happen. Their only will is to do what they've been compelled to do."

"So, he'll be totally back to normal as soon as he's finished…." *Finished cleaning up the remains of my dead family.*

"Yes," said Tol. "Now get in the car."

"Fine." Addy threw her duffel into the backseat. "But I'm driving."

CHAPTER 11

TOL

Tol should have told her about the blood marriage before he made her swear that oath. He had used the word *ritual* instead, knowing it would invite far fewer questions.

According to the Celestial's stipulations, he hadn't broken any rules, and he had gained Adelyne's consent. Technically speaking, Tol could compel her based on their agreement, so long as he held up his end of the bargain, without ever having to utter the words *blood marriage*.

Adelyne was so desperate to find her sister it was possible she might have agreed to the blood marriage even if he explained it to her. It was easier to keep things vague, though. For now, at least.

From the short time they'd had together, Tol sensed Adelyne wasn't someone to put much store in faith. Even if he had tried to explain it all to her, she either wouldn't have believed him, or she wouldn't have understood what it really meant. When it came to eternity, there was a big difference between theory and reality.

But if Tol was being honest with himself, none of those reasons had been the one why he'd kept his explanation of *the ritual* vague. He'd seen the way she assessed him, making him feel stripped bare. He had seen right through that look she gave him when he said he could help her. Her eyes had gone straight to his prosthesis.

Tol could only imagine Adelyne's horror if he told her he expected her to bring herself to the brink of death, revive herself with his Source-infused blood, and then do the same for him. He knew the way her mouth would twist with disgust if he told her about the blood marriage and that it would link them, in mind and body, for eternity...that they would be inextricably bound in a way that wouldn't permit one to survive without the other.

Tol could imagine her response: *bound to the cripple for eternity? Pass.*

Tol's thoughts went to the ruddy, stocky bloke who looked like a caricature of a farmer. Or a wrestler.

Adelyne had called him her best friend. What did that mean? It was obvious Fred thought of them as more than friends. Tol thought about Nira and winced. He called Nira a friend, but that didn't mean he spent his nights with her the same way he spent nights with Gerth.

"What kind of a name is Tolumus Magnantius, anyway?" Adelyne asked, pulling Tol out of his thoughts.

Despite her earlier butchering of his name, she had no trouble pronouncing it now.

"Family name," Tol replied.

He knew he should give her more than that. For what felt like the hundredth time, he reminded himself that none of this was her fault. She didn't want any of this any more than he did.

It was the reminder of those dead little girls on her kitchen floor that softened him. Even though he was too young to have witnessed the death and destruction at the Crossing for himself, he'd spent his entire life seeing the after-effects of so much heartbreak. He knew what losing someone's entire family did to a person, and his heart ached for her.

Adelyne had been drawn into his world through no fault of her own. The least he could do was give her an explanation.

Adelyne stopped the car at the end of the driveway.

"Syracuse International Airport," Tol said, assuming she was waiting for directions. When the car still didn't move, he turned to look at her.

Her gaze was fixed on that hand-painted "Deerborn Family Farm" sign Tol had seen on his way in.

"Livy and I painted that sign when we were kids." She said it so quietly, Tol wasn't sure if she knew she had spoken aloud.

Tol recognized that look on her face. It was one he had seen on too many of his people. It was that sinking helplessness and hopelessness he felt when another of their elders died, or there was another attack by the Forsaken.

"We're going to get her back," he said, hoping it was a promise he could deliver.

Tol felt a growing anger, but this time it wasn't toward the Fount. It was on her behalf. He hated that his people were the reason Adelyne's family was dead.

He was angry at his own people for overdrawing the Source and causing the downfall of Vitaquias. He was angry at the Forsaken...for his enemy's abilities that were so much stronger here, and their unquenchable thirst for revenge for the loss of their world. And most of all, he was angry at the Celestial for giving him and this mortal girl the responsibility of saving his entire race through a binding that would force their two separate souls into one.

Adelyne wiped her eyes, and then, before Tol could say anything else, she hit the gas.

"It's a long drive to the airport," Adelyne said, all hints of emotion gone from her voice. "You'd better tell me what all this is about."

Tol raked a hand through his hair, trying to decide how to explain Vitaquias and the centuries-long conflict with the Forsaken to a girl who probably had never traveled outside of New York. "Do you know what you are?"

"What I am?" Adelyne used one hand to steer around some obstacle in the road Tol couldn't see.

He'd been only too happy to give her control of the car. Night was just starting to turn to dawn, but it was still too dark to make out the potholes Adelyne navigated around with ease.

"Oh." Adelyne's face cleared in understanding. "It's more of that cult stuff, isn't it?"

"What? No." Tol huffed out an exasperated breath. "It's not a cult. It's...who we are."

"I'm an atheist." She waved a hand, dismissing his people and his world. "But by all means, go ahead and tell me what you think I am. We've got time to kill."

Tol gritted his teeth and bit back the first, decidedly unproductive comment that came to mind.

"I'm not from this world, Adelyne, and neither are those people who attacked you and took your sister." It took an enormous effort to keep his voice from displaying his irritation. "Eighteen years ago, our world was ruined." Tol took in a breath, trying to figure out how to say the next part in a way that wouldn't make her laugh in his face. "The Celestial—she was basically the intermediary between the immortals and the gods—wanted to protect my people. When our world started to fall apart, she opened a portal between Vitaquias, where we come from, and the mortal world for us to escape.

"Since she was too connected to the Source of our power to come with us, the Celestial extracted her power and sent it through the portal. She told my parents, the king and queen, that her power would find a mortal vessel, where it would stay dormant until," he swallowed, "the ritual."

"I see." Adelyne still had her eyes on the road, but she had a smirk on her face that made fury well inside Tol.

She didn't believe a word he was saying.

"And you think her power is inside me." She cleared her throat, and Tol thought she was suppressing a laugh. He clenched his right hand into a fist.

"I know it is," Tol said. "I…felt you."

"Excuse me?"

"Four days ago, I was asleep, and I heard you scream." This admission seemed strangely personal, and Tol felt heat creep up his neck. "I woke up, but I wasn't in my room. It was like I was seeing the world through your eyes. I saw your living room, with the view of the cornfields outside, and that 'Cornell University' shirt someone was wearing. That's how I knew where to find you."

Tol couldn't help feeling the slightest bit of satisfaction at the way Adelyne's mouth was hanging open.

She cleared her throat again. "And you think I'm this vessel, the one who has all of your Celestial's powers?"

"I know you are," Tol replied, feeling those words settle like a weight between them. "I would never have seen into your thoughts like that otherwise."

Adelyne didn't say anything for a minute.

"My people call you the Fount," Tol said.

"The Fount?" Adelyne's words were full of derision. "What am I, a water fountain?"

Tol smirked. "No. You're called the Fount because you're the wellspring of my people's salvation. The power and knowledge inside you are the answer to saving my people."

It was an over-generalization, but Adelyne didn't seem to be taking any of this too seriously, anyway. Tol supposed there was only so much a person could absorb at once, especially when she was fleeing the people who had just murdered her family.

"And this ritual?" Adelyne asked. "What is that all about?"

Tol's blood ran cold. This was the question he'd been dreading.

"You have information inside you that belongs to the Celestial." He was convinced Adelyne would be able to see everything he was holding back if he looked at her, so he kept his gaze fixed on the corn passing by outside his window.

"That's what the ritual is all about," he continued. "You have the Celestial's knowledge of how to undo the damage that was done to the Old World, but you can't access it on your own."

"Do those murderers want me for the same reason, to use me to get back to their world?"

Tol sighed. "They want you because your blood is the only way to re-open the portal between the worlds. But all they can do with you is return to our world. They wouldn't be able to use you to access the Celestial's knowledge."

"Why not?"

"Because they'd need me," he said curtly. "But I'm not sure they know that. They interrogated one of my people, and I don't know how much he told them. My guess is they're using your sister to lure you to them. The Forsaken can't control people like we do, so they use more violent methods."

Tol wanted to smack himself across the face. He realized, belatedly, that he should have found a more delicate way of conveying his theory to Adelyne. When he looked at her, though, her expression just seemed thoughtful.

Tol took that as a sign he should keep talking. "The Forsaken are named that because the Celestial chose my race as her people."

"The Forsaken are murderers," Adelyne said, her voice low and full of terrible emotion.

"Yes," he said. "The Celestial loved my race, the Chosen, and ignored the Forsaken, who were the gods' afterthought. The Source was stronger for us than it was for them on Vitaquias, and we had more power over them. It turned the Forsaken into hardened warriors. They became barbarians, refusing to obey the gods who made them and then abandoned them."

The gods had forsaken them. The Celestial had forsaken them. They were, and ever would be, less than the Chosen.

He continued, "On Vitaquias, my people were stronger. But in the mortal world, the Forsaken have the advantage. Their race is younger, and thus needs less of the Source to sustain themselves. They've also honed their ability to fight and kill even without Source, whereas our Influence only works when there is Source inside us." Tol took a breath. "The Forsaken have been picking us off one by one. If we don't complete the ritual and return to Vitaquias, the war brewing between our people won't just mean our end. It could threaten the mortal world, too."

That familiar, furious helplessness washed over Tol, making him feel sick. He should be bringing the Fount back to his people. Instead, he was postponing the blood marriage to go on some wild—and most likely fruitless—chase for her mortal sister, who could in no way contribute to the survival of his people. He was being stupid and irresponsible. He was gambling his people's lives, and for what? For a mortal girl who would hate him either way when she found out what she'd agreed to.

Adelyne jolted him out of his thoughts with another question. "So, if I'm the supposed savior of your entire race, then how come you look at me like my existence is some kind of death sentence for you, rather than salvation?"

Tol started. "I didn't—"

"You hated me from the second you saw me," Adelyne interrupted. "Don't try to deny it."

Tol was dumbfounded. He couldn't believe this girl, whom he'd just met, had so easily seen through the emotions he had hidden from people he'd known all his life…emotions he was sure no one except for Gerth had even had an inkling about.

"I really couldn't care less what you think about me," Adelyne continued with a shrug. "As long as I get Livy back, you can hate me as much as you want."

"I don't hate you," Tol mumbled when he got his voice back. "It's just…complicated."

"What the hell?"

Tol looked at Adelyne, but her gazed was fixed on something on the road ahead. Tol blinked. Two sets of headlights were bumping along the road toward them. The headlights were high above their sedan. Trucks, maybe? Whatever they were, they were coming down the road too fast.

"Get on your side of the road," Adelyne complained.

The vehicles continued to barrel down the center of the road. Adelyne hit the brake.

"No," Tol said, "Keep driving."

"They're going to run us off the road—"

"Then drive off the bloody road!" Tol was already reaching for the vial around his neck.

She hesitated for only a moment before cutting the wheel. Tol clung to the door as the car bounced and rattled over uneven ground. Stalks of corn scraped against the doors on either side of them.

"Sorry," Adelyne said.

Tol wasn't sure if she was talking to him, the car, or the corn.

Tol saw the flash of headlights in his side mirror as the Forsaken followed them.

"Are those Army trucks?!" Adelyne asked, looking in her rearview mirror.

"Yeah." Tol gritted his teeth as they caught air off a bump in the path. "They've got people in every major country's military."

"Why didn't your people think of that?"

Tol ignored the jibe. The Forsaken were gaining on them, fast. It didn't take a mechanical engineer to know their car would lose this fight when the military jeeps caught up.

"Stop the car," Tol said.

She did. The rental creaked and groaned as it settled on the uneven ground. When Adelyne killed the engine, they heard the audible roar of the army jeeps as they barreled closer.

Tol unstopped the cork of his vial and let a drop fall onto his finger. He was loath to use any more of the precious liquid than he already had, but he had no choice now. Gods only knew how many Forsaken would pour out of those jeeps once they caught up.

He put the drop in his mouth, feeling his Haze flare. He turned to Adelyne to offer her the vial, but her own Haze already surrounded her even though she'd taken no Source. Whatever power was inside her was lending her strength.

They looked at each other. As though reaching an unspoken agreement, they got out of the car.

"This way," Adelyne said.

Tol followed her deeper into the cornfield. They crouched down, just as the sound of metal crashing into metal cut through the silent night. The rental car went flying through the air before crumpling like a tin can some way away.

Adelyne winced. "Sorry about your car."

"Trust me," Tol replied. "That's the least of our problems."

Flashlights swept over where they were crouched. Voices called to each other.

"Come on!" Tol grabbed Adelyne's hand and pulled her to her feet.

He took a step, but Adelyne stayed put.

"We have to go—"

All the air went out of Tol as Adelyne tackled him. He hit the ground with her on top of him.

"Are you bloody—"

Adelyne's raised hand held something in the air where he'd been standing moments before. She rolled off him and showed him the glowing blue hatchet she was holding. She gave him a mischievous grin, and then she threw the weapon back with a flick of her wrist. There was a scream. Tol looked up in time to see one of the Forsaken vanish in a puff of blue smoke.

Tol didn't have a chance to marvel over the fact that he wasn't lying on the ground with a hatchet buried in his chest, or that this mortal girl had used the Forsaken's own weapon against him—something that shouldn't be possible. She was already running, like some kind of mad warrior, straight for them. Tol cursed, and then he hurried after her.

Adelyne had ripped a jewel-encrusted sword away from one of the Forsaken and sliced it across two of their throats by the time Tol caught up to her. Tol stood, frozen in place. He watched this mortal girl, who had never heard of Forsaken or Vitaquias before tonight, decimate the most skilled warriors in two worlds.

Tol saw the Forsaken were reluctant to attack her. Instead, they seemed to be trying to surround her. All they were managing to do was get within her reach. She showed no hesitation as she approached one after another, leaving nothing but blue smoke in her wake.

"The cripple Chosen prince is here," one of the Forsaken called.

"Kill him!" another voice shouted.

Tol stopped gaping at Adelyne and moved. He raced into the fray, catching the eye of the first warrior in his path.

"Look at me," he commanded.

The man did, and it was only a matter of seconds before Tol's Influence had the Forsaken running into the fight, his dagger aimed at his own people.

Tol cursed as the man under his Influence fell, cut down by a different Forsaken who hadn't hesitated when he saw the dazed expression in his comrade's eye. There was a *pop*, and then all that remained of the man disappeared in a cloud of blue smoke.

"Look at me," Tol said to the nearest Forsaken.

The woman's gaze slid to him, and it was enough for Tol to Influence her.

"Give me your necklace," Tol demanded.

She did. Tol saw the vial was almost empty, with only a few drops clinging to the bottom.

The Forsaken woman didn't immediately disappear in a puff of blue smoke, though. She aged and shrunk before Tol's eyes. Her brown hair turned gray, her back curved, and her eyes went milky with age. She hobbled up to Tol, but she wasn't strong enough to raise her axe against him.

This happened when someone lost their Source but was of an age sustainable in the mortal world. The Forsaken woman was probably eighty or so years old, and would continue to age at a mortal rate without her Source.

The last thing Tol wanted to do was kill an old lady, but he knew from a lifetime of experience that if he didn't, she'd get more Source and end up killing a dozen of Tol's people. Hating himself a little, he walked over to the woman and put a hand on her bare cheek.

"Kill yourself," he said.

He turned away before he could see his order carried out.

Tol moved from one Forsaken to the next. The vials clanked together around Tol's neck as he gathered his enemy's Source before their essence turned to smoke.

He looked up in time to see Adelyne backflip. She hooked her foot around a Forsaken's leg. The man thudded to the ground.

Tol stared, mesmerized by her deadly grace. The scholars' history texts described the power of the Celestial as being a similar type to his own, with an ability to manipulate the thoughts of others. But Adelyne wasn't bothering with Influence. She whirled and kicked and jabbed, her hair streaming behind her like a red-gold flag. She pulled something out of her back pocket that looked like a pair of scissors and hurled it at one of the Forsaken. The sharp point embedded itself in the man's eye. He fell to his knees with a scream.

Tol couldn't take his eyes off Adelyne. Before this moment, he hadn't truly accepted who she was, even though all the evidence made her identity irrefutable. There was nothing mortal about the way she moved, the way she fought. She moved like her blood contained the strength of the gods, which, he supposed, it did.

Adelyne walked up to the man who was clawing at the scissors in his eye. There was a grim smile on her face as she took the soldier's head in both her hands and gave it a vicious twist.

Tol shuddered as Adelyne let the body fall and immediately turned for another opponent.

She killed with such ease. On the other hand, he reminded himself, these people were responsible for murdering her entire family. Tol understood that kind of hatred well.

Something behind Adelyne made Tol turn all of his attention on the movement.

"Adelyne!"

It was too late. The Forsaken launched to his feet and wrapped his arms around her. She struggled and kicked, but the man was at least a foot taller and built like the Hulk. He was dragging her back to the nearest jeep.

Tol raced after them. Another Forsaken jumped out at him, but Tol caught his eye before the Forsaken could so much as lay a finger on him. Tol sent the barbarian chasing down the one who was wrestling Adelyne into the jeep.

Tol caught up with them just as Adelyne's captor was forced to let go of her to address his comrade, who had grabbed him from behind and was trying to choke him.

Tol took advantage of the distraction as the two Forsaken wrestled with each other. He managed to grab the wrist of the Forsaken man not yet under his control. His Influence was starting to ebb, and the exhaustion that always came after was beginning to build. Tol ignored the feeling as he commanded the warrior to lay down his weapons and kneel on the ground. He made the other Forsaken use his own sword against himself.

"Where is she?" Adelyne was screaming at the Forsaken kneeling in a pool of his comrade's blood. "Where's my sister?"

The man looked away. Tol used the last of his Influence on the Forsaken, making the man fall forward on his hands and knees. Tol spared Adelyne a glance. "Look him in the eye, and ask him again."

Adelyne knelt before the Forsaken, gripping his chin to force his gaze to meet her own.

"Where is my sister?"

To Tol's surprise, there was defiance in the man's eyes. Tol's own Influence was spent, but Adelyne's stare was unblinking, *and* she was touching his bare skin. Her Haze was still intact, which meant she was accessing the Celestial's power within herself. The golden glow warmed the strands of gold in her copper hair. So, why wasn't her Influence working?

"Here." Tol took Adelyne's hand, measured out a drop of Source from his vial onto her finger, and nodded for her to take it.

She did, but nothing happened. Her Haze was already bright. Tol realized she must not need Source to access her power. She could clearly access some of the Celestial's knowledge, but he figured they would need to wait for the blood marriage for her to gain the rest.

The Forsaken was still kneeling on the ground, but he was growing restless as Tol's Influence wore off. Tol measured out another drop of Source. He felt actual physical pain at the thought of how much of the precious liquid he was wasting on this encounter.

His energy was drained, and so it took almost a full minute for his Haze to flare. When it finally did, Tol crouched beside Adelyne and looked into the Forsaken's gray eyes.

"Where is her sister?" Tol asked, his voice thick with exhaustion.

"I don't know," came the immediate reply.

"You'll have to give me more than that," Tol pressed, gripping the Forsaken's mind with his own.

The man held his head like he was trying to rip Tol's Influence away. "We weren't told."

Adelyne let out a frustrated scream.

Tol bent and looked the man in the eye. "That isn't helpful."

With that, he ripped the vial of Source from the Forsaken's neck.

CHAPTER 12

ADDY

Addy watched as Tol pulled the vial from the man's throat. She sucked in a breath as the man started to change before her eyes. He had been a young, rock-solid man in his twenties when he wrapped his arms around her and dragged her back to the jeep. He wasn't young anymore.

She watched as streaks of gray appeared in the man's thick, white-blonde hair. His smooth skin creased into lines and began to wrinkle. His muscles seemed to melt away. He was looking more like an inhumanly tall skeleton than the strongest foe she'd ever encountered.

The ageing continued. The man's hair thinned until his wrinkly scalp was visible. He continued to shrink and shrivel and stoop. And then, with a pop, he disappeared in a puff of blue smoke.

Addy blinked, thinking maybe the light of dawn was playing tricks on her eyes. But when she looked again, the man was still gone.

When she had seen those people turn into blue smoke back in the farmhouse, she had been sure she was hallucinating. But now….

Addy turned to Tol. She felt her mouth hanging open, and it was an effort to force it closed.

"What did you do to him?" she asked.

"I took his Source. For the people of my world who are too old to survive naturally, the necklace's chain lets trace amounts of the Source seep into their skin to keep them young. If they lose their Source," Tol gestured at the pile of army fatigues, which were all that remained of the people who had worn them, "they die."

Tol was looking at her with the same kind of wonder she felt at watching him take down those men without spilling a drop of blood. She didn't know what to say. She didn't know how to feel…whether to be disgusted, amazed, or both.

"You were brilliant," Tol said.

A flood of warmth went through her at the compliment.

"You weren't bad yourself," she replied. Her blood was still singing from the power of that golden light that seemed to surround her whenever she needed to defend herself. It made her feel like she had an endless reservoir of energy to draw from. She had never felt more powerful in her entire life, and she wanted more of it.

But as the adrenaline and golden light wore off, she remembered the way her garden shears had looked, embedded in that man's eye. She remembered the way she'd broken his neck with her bare hands…and enjoyed it.

She had been so overcome by that fury deep inside her that she hadn't been able to see anything else—hadn't been able to think about anything else. She had let it rule her mind and body without question.

Addy shivered. It was the same inner turmoil she'd felt after she killed the thief. It was violent and horrible and wrong, and yet, it had felt so right.

Addy shook her head. These people had taken Livy from her. They'd tried to kill her. She wouldn't lose any sleep over killing them, even if she'd enjoyed it more than she knew any normal person should.

"Maybe we should take more of that," she gestured at the multiple mostly-empty vials now hanging around Tol's neck—necklaces that now seemed anything but stupid. "In case those men come back."

"I've already used too much," Tol said quietly, like he was talking to himself. He looked at Addy, and then said, "Right now, we just need to get out of here."

Tol gestured to one of the jeeps, which was still running. "The next ones who come will be higher-ranked than these blokes, and they'll be even more powerful."

The golden glow around Addy had faded, leaving her with an emptiness that made her ache. She wanted to sink down onto the cold ground and wrap her arms around herself.

"That gold light is a drug," she said, realizing that somehow, after only feeling it a few times, she was going through withdrawal.

Tol shook his head. "There's nothing addictive about the Source itself. What you're feeling is an addiction to the strength it lent you. That strength has greater limitations than you'd think, though." He was silent for a moment. "The reason my people are in your world in the first place is because we tried to push the boundaries of what the Source could do."

Addy massaged her head. She couldn't wrap her mind around everything that had happened. There was all this crazy talk about a different world and different races, and the thing Tol had said about her being the Fount who possessed the secret to returning their world to its former glory. It made no sense. And yet, Addy couldn't come up with a single logical explanation for everything that had happened in the past few hours.

Addy didn't know what to think anymore. She was bone tired, confused, and heartsick. She wanted her parents and her baby sisters. She wanted Livy.

Tol went to the tangled remains of the rental car. He grabbed their bags and headed for the driver's side of the army jeep.

"I'm driving," Addy announced, cutting ahead and climbing in before he could protest.

"Sorry again about your car," she said, exploring the gears and buttons on the dash.

Tol looked out the window. "I'll just distract everyone by telling them I've found you but we aren't coming back yet. That ought to get their minds off the car."

Guilt, followed by irritation, flashed through her. Whoever— whatever—this boy thought she was, she didn't owe him anything beyond the confines of their agreement. He had promised to help her get her sister back. Until then, his worries weren't her problem.

"So, where are we going?" Those people hadn't given them even the slightest clue about where Livy might be. That thought was enough to make her want to resurrect the people so she could kill them all over again. "Once we get to the airport, I mean."

Addy hit the gas, and the jeep lurched forward. In a different time and place, she would have been thrilled out of her mind to be behind the wheel of this jeep. Now, she barely thought about it beyond the mechanics of getting where she needed to go.

"Washington, D.C.," Tol replied. "There's someone there who might be able to help us."

Might be able to help us wasn't the answer she wanted to hear, but it was all she had. So, she clung to it as the jeep ate up the road between them and the airport.

They drove in silence for some time while she tried to organize her thoughts.

"The way I fought," she began. "Is that because of this power you say I have?"

Tol looked at her. "Don't tell me you still think this is just some cult."

"No." Her voice was quiet as she struggled with how much to say. "That night the thief broke into our house," she glanced at Tol, "the night you...saw me...I knew how to fight him, even though I'd never been in a fight in my life."

Addy didn't know why she was telling Tol any of this. Maybe she was just desperate for some explanation...some way to convince herself that the thing now coiled and asleep inside her wasn't insanity or an uncontrollable murderous rage, but something real and sensical.

Tol nodded. "You have knowledge inside you that belongs to the Celestial."

"But I didn't know I knew how to fight until I just kind of did it."

Tol looked out at the lightening sky and shifted in his seat, like he was uncomfortable. He said, "That's what the ritual is all about. You have the Celestial's knowledge of how to undo the damage that was done to the Old World, but you can't access it on your own."

From the way Tol kept his gaze fixed out the window, Addy could tell he was keeping something from her. *Lots of somethings, most likely.*

Addy kept her eyes on the road as a new realization crept up her spine. "You said before my blood is the only way to re-open the portal between the worlds." She paused, and then just said it. "You're going to kill me, aren't you?"

Tol jerked his attention away from the corn and back to her. "What? No! Of course not."

She looked at him. He seemed genuinely horrified at the thought, but she wasn't an idiot. A ritual…her blood….

She gripped the steering wheel. "I'll do anything for my sister," Addy said. "Whatever price you want me to pay, I'll do it, so long as we get her back."

Tol's face paled. "Adelyne, I swear." He put up his right hand, like he was taking an oath. "No one will harm you." And then, after a pause, "At least, as long as the barbarians don't get to you. But I won't let that happen. My people have been searching for you for eighteen years, and any one of us would die to keep you safe."

She didn't feel any gratitude for his pledge, but she believed he didn't want to hurt her. After all, if all he needed was her blood, he could have just let those warriors kill her back at the farmhouse.

TOL

Adelyne was insatiable with her questions. Now that she believed Tol wasn't just some crazy person in a cult, she wanted to know everything.

"I just don't understand why you don't drink that water stuff all the time," she was saying now. "If it makes you stronger, smarter, and better, then why not just keep it flowing?"

Tol bit back his reply, knowing there was no way she could possibly understand what his people had been through. He squeezed his eyes shut, reining in his temper. He waited until he could trust his voice before he started to speak.

"Back in the Old World, Vitaquias, we all had access to the Source. It's what gives us vitality and strength."

Adelyne glanced over as he tapped his necklace.

"This is what gives my people, the Chosen people, an ability to Influence anyone except for our own. For the Forsaken, it gives them extraordinary fighting abilities and enhances the strength of their weapons.

"But something happened." He swallowed, feeling like saying too much would be a betrayal of his family. "The Source was drained, and our world became a wasteland. Our only option was to flee to the mortal world."

Adelyne kept her inscrutable gaze fixed on the road ahead. "You keep calling us *the mortals*. Does that mean you're immortal?"

"We were," Tol said, his voice sounding weak to his own ears. "The Source gives us our immortality, and we don't have much of it left." He thought of Gran, with her curved spine and white hair. "My people are dying."

This admission cost him. He felt a great weariness take hold of him.

"You don't look like you're dying," Adelyne said.

"That's because I'm only eighteen. But some of our people are hundreds of years old, and we don't have enough Source to sustain them for much longer."

"So, when the Source runs out…?"

Tol nodded in response to her unfinished question. "They'll die."

"Is that why those people died when you took away their necklaces?" she asked.

Tol nodded again. "The vial and chain are from the Old World. They work together, extracting trace amounts of Source from the vial and feeding it into the wearer's skin. The greater the person's years, the more Source they need just to survive in the mortal world. Those of us who are of mortal ages don't need the life-sustaining qualities of the Source, we just need it to use our abilities."

"You know that golden light you have around you that gets brighter when you drink the stuff?" Adelyne asked.

"Source," Tol corrected, before feeling like a prat. "The golden light is called Haze," he said in a gentler tone.

"Whatever." Adelyne waved a dismissive hand. "How come my golden light just comes and goes, especially since I never drink any of the *Source*?" she imitated his accent on the last word.

He couldn't decide if he wanted to laugh or knock his head against a blunt object.

"There's never been another like you, so no one knows for sure how your abilities work," Tol said. "But I believe your Haze appears when you're drawing on the Celestial's powers inside of you, which are tied to the Source. I'd guess that until…the ritual…you'll only be able to access them when you're in a threatening situation."

Tol was sure that, after the blood marriage, Adelyne would be able to Influence and do a thousand other things. He wasn't about to tell her that yet, though.

Adelyne looked thoughtful. "If I have the same powers as you, then how come I can't," she took her hands off the wheel to make a strange flailing motion and bugged her eyes.

"Beg pardon?" Tol asked dryly.

"You know, force people to do whatever you want."

Tol gave her an irritated look. "I don't," he imitated Adelyne's gesture. She just rolled her eyes.

Tol sighed. "My best guess is that for now, you can only access the basest of the Celestial's abilities, and that would be the Forsakens' ability to fight."

Tol had been startled to see the Fount fight more like the Forsaken than the Chosen. It shouldn't have been surprising, though. The Forsaken were the children of the gods and goddesses, even if they had been abandoned. It only made sense for the Celestial to share their fighting talents, and thus, for the Fount to possess those abilities, too. And like he told Adelyne, physical fighting required far less finesse than Influence. She likely wouldn't be able to access anything more powerful until after the blood marriage.

Adelyne sniffed. "I'd hardly call what I did back there *base*."

"No, that's not what I meant—" Tol clenched his jaw until it ached.

How could this girl manage to irritate him so much? When he looked over at her, he saw there was the hint of a grin on her face.

Bloody hells. She knew she was getting under his skin, and she relished it. He wasn't sure if the realization made him angry or feel a grudging respect for this mortal who wasn't intimidated by either the Forsaken warriors or the Chosen prince.

Adelyne asked, "So, you can make anyone do anything you want just by looking them in the eye or touching their skin?"

"It's not quite that simple," he replied. Tol had never had to explain any of this before, and he didn't think he was doing a very good job. "Different amounts of Influence are needed, depending on the request. It's harder to compel Forsaken than mortals, and it takes more Influence for a request that takes more than a few seconds to complete. Influence only lasts until the drop of Source runs out or the Influencer releases the one they're manipulating. If enough Influence isn't used, the person just gets confused and starts wandering around because they know they were supposed to do something but can't remember what it was."

A troubled look crossed Adelyne's face.

"Don't worry," he said, following the line of her thinking. "That won't happen to Farmer Fred."

"Farmer Fred?" she scoffed, but she looked relieved.

Tol wanted to ask her about Fred and how she felt about him, but he didn't want to come off as creepy. Not that *everything* about the blood marriage wasn't creepy, but he didn't have to make a bad situation worse.

Adelyne's face pinched with another thought.

"Could you Influence me?"

The question threw him off guard. "I—" he stuttered.

He realized he didn't know the answer to her question. She was a mortal, which meant he should be able to Influence her. But she was also the Fount, so maybe he couldn't. He guessed the Celestial's powers inside her would protect her from Influence.

"My guess is no, but I'd never try," he said honestly.

"You did it to those men. You did it to Fred."

"Yes, but the Forsaken are barbarians, and Fred is—"

113

Unimportant, he was about to say, but then thought better of it.

Tol clenched and unclenched his fist, frustrated at his inability to give a decent explanation. Technically, it was illegal to use Influence against a mortal, but it was one of those laws the king and queen generally turned a blind eye to, so long as the Influence was used for a reasonable purpose.

"Influencing someone takes away their free will," he said finally. "It's an invasion of the person's privacy, and it's not something I would ever do to someone I wanted to trust me."

"You want me to trust you?" Adelyne asked.

Tol couldn't read the tone of her question, and it flustered him.

He scowled. "Well, if we're going to be stuck together for," he stopped, horrified by what he'd almost just revealed. "Er, I mean, if we're going to be stuck traveling together for a while, I just think it would be better if we didn't see each other as enemies."

"I guess I can agree to that," she said. There was a thoughtful expression on her face. "You did save my life again, so thanks for that, I guess."

"Thanks for saving mine."

They exchanged a look. For a moment, Tol felt like he and Adelyne were co-conspirators instead of living shackles that would forever deprive each other of their free will.

CHAPTER 13

ADDY

Addy still wasn't sure if she believed everything Tol was saying, but she liked listening to him. He was a natural storyteller, and she almost didn't care if it was all real or not.

His voice might be the most striking part about him. It was like black velvet, if black velvet had a sound. It rippled and flowed in her head as he spoke. Its tenor held the promise of something magical and dangerous. That, combined with the golden Haze surrounding him, gave him the air of a man capable of burning down the world.

She had thought he was all bluster when he called himself *Prince Tolumus*, but she'd heard those murderers call him *the prince* too. She had no idea what he was the prince of, but she couldn't deny there was something prince-like about him, starting with the black velvet of his voice.

She turned at the sound of a muffled *crack*. Addy turned to see that Tol had just broken his very expensive-looking cell phone.

"What are you doing?!" she demanded as he threw the pieces out the open window.

"Making sure neither my people nor theirs can track us," Tol replied. "Now give me your phone."

"I don't have one," she replied.

"You don't?"

Addy didn't have to look at him to know he didn't believe her.

Instead of arguing the point, she turned to him and arched an eyebrow. "Would you like to search me, *Your Highness?*"

Tol's face reddened. "That won't be necessary," he mumbled.

Addy smirked.

They got to the airport just as others were arriving for the first flights of the day. She'd been here before with her mom to pick up or drop off Aunt Meredith, but she'd never actually gone into the airport itself.

Tol told her just to leave the jeep idling outside the airport. Addy thought it was a shame she couldn't somehow take the jeep with them. It had the smoothest engine of anything she'd ever driven, especially compared to the Benz and her parents' truck. Fred would have loved to take it for a drive.

The thought of her best friend filled her with an intense homesickness she'd never had cause to feel before. It took her breath away.

"Come on," Tol said, tossing her duffel at her.

He said a few words to the cop standing outside the airport, who got into the driver's seat of the jeep with a glazed expression on his face. It fascinated Addy to see the way Tol could just make people obey him. It scared her a little, too.

"Wow." Addy stopped just inside the sliding glass doors.

"What?" Tol asked, his hand going to his necklace.

"It looks just like it does in the movies." She gestured at the men and women in uniforms standing behind the desks, taking luggage and passing tickets over the counter.

Tol raised an eyebrow. "You've never been inside an airport before?"

Addy shook her head. "I've never been outside of upstate New York, except for my aunt's farm where I was born, but I don't remember that."

Tol gave a short laugh, like he couldn't believe anyone could possibly live such a sheltered life. It made her defensive.

"I'm sure I'll figure it out just fine." She pushed past him and walked up to the board displaying the departing flights. "Which flight to D.C. do we want?"

"We're not going on any of those," Tol said.

"But you said D.C.," she argued. If he thought he could pull one over on her....

Tol rolled his eyes, like he knew exactly what she was thinking. "We're going to D.C., but we're not taking any of those planes."

"Which plane are we taking, then?" Addy asked, her limited patience unraveling.

"My family's private plane. Now come on."

* * *

Addy had promised herself she wouldn't let Tol see how impressed she was, no matter how awesome it was when the airport personnel smiled and led them to the front of the security line. Addy didn't let a single emotion show on her face as they got onto one of those airport carts and were driven right onto the tarmac. She didn't even blink when the stairs of the not-so-small plane lowered, and a flight attendant dressed in a tailored navy suit bowed to them. But every promise she'd made to herself evaporated the moment she saw the plane's interior.

"Holy shit."

A grin warmed Tol's face. "Make yourself at home."

She knew her mouth was hanging open, but really, this plane was nicer than Air Force One, which she knew about from the movie *Air Force One*.

Everything was polished wood and cream leather. There were two long couches and eight overlarge armchairs on either side of the plane. There were crystal decanters filled with amber liquid and neatly stacked magazines in mesh compartments.

"Madam, may I offer you a beverage?" one of the *three* flight attendants who were on board just for them asked in a heavy British accent.

"I'm good, thanks," Addy said, her gaze still roving over the plane.

She sat next to Tol in one of the large chairs. It was quite possibly the most comfortable chair she'd ever sat in. It was even better than Mr. Brown's La-Z-Boy.

The captain came out of the cockpit and actually bowed to Tol. He called him Prince Tolumus, and then wished them both a pleasant flight.

Tol, for his part, was adjusting the recliner of his seat like he'd done this a thousand times before…like it was no big deal.

He noticed her staring, and narrowed his eyes at her. "Are you really telling me you've never been out of New York?" he asked.

"That's right," she replied. "Us poor plebeians were too busy harvesting the corn to feed your lordship to dally about." She said the words in what she thought was an admirable impression of a British accent.

Tol looked like he didn't know if he wanted to laugh or scowl, and that suited Addy just fine.

"That's not what I meant," he said, looking a little chastened. "I just thought, I mean—" his voice trailed off.

"What?" she demanded. "You want to criticize my parents some more? Maybe take a shot at the way I was raised?"

"No." He looked genuinely distressed. "I was just wondering if your parents knew about you and were trying to keep you hidden." He rubbed his eyes. "If they were, they did an ace job of it."

Tol looked exhausted, which made Addy feel a little bad for giving him such a hard time. His words also made her think. Was it possible her parents had known something about what she was? Could that have been the reason they were so terrified after the thief, and why they had been so desperate to get away?

Addy felt sick.

"My parents were just so…regular." She said the words quietly.

Tol gave her a sympathetic look. "I'm sorry for what happened to your family," he said.

She cleared her throat and looked out the window as the plane started to move.

"Tell me more about these people who came after me." She gripped the armrest of her seat, digging her nails into the soft leather. "I want to know everything."

"They're barbarians," Tol replied. From the way he said that word, Addy could tell she was far from the only one to lose loved ones to those monsters.

As the plane took off, Tol told her about the Forsaken, who had been his people's enemy for hundreds of years in their own world before they came into the mortal one. He told her how his people, the Chosen, had possessed more power in their world because of the liquid he called Source. Here in her world, though, the murderers were advantaged. He told her how the Forsaken were hunting his people. Like animals. With each word, her hatred grew for the people who had taken Livy and killed the rest of her family.

She would get Livy back. Then, those monsters would pay.

Tol told her that if he didn't get his people back to their own world, the mortals would be in danger of getting caught up in the war the Forsaken were waging against the Chosen. If they lost all hope of ever returning to their own world, the Forsaken would try to take over Earth.

Addy could barely breathe. It wasn't enough that these people had taken her family away from her. They were threatening every person in her world. The Forsaken were parasites...deadly ones. And, if she believed what Tol was saying, she was the only one who could save Earth.

A few days ago, she'd been feeling trapped because her world was too small. Now, it had expanded in a way that terrified her even more.

As the plane climbed into the air, Addy looked down at the cars below. They looked like ants, with headlights, zooming along in their anthill. When she glanced up and saw the rising sun spilled across the sky ahead of them, she gasped.

"It's so beautiful."

She turned to Tol, who was looking at her with a thoughtful expression on his face.

"What?" she demanded.

"Nothing." He shook his head. "You're just...not what I expected."

"Oh?" she raised a brow.

Tol didn't elaborate, so she asked, "Does this mean you don't hate me anymore?"

Instead of the snarky reply she expected, a sad look came over his face. "It was never you I hated. It was my...lack of choices in the matter."

"Which matter?" she pressed. Addy didn't like beating around the bush.

Tol seemed to be wrestling with how much to say.

"If we're going to be stuck traveling together, you may as well just be honest with me," she said.

Tol gave her a sharp look. After a moment, he said, "My whole life has been one giant search for the Fount who would save our people."

"Me."

"You," Tol agreed.

He raked his hand through his hair. "It just frustrated me that everything had been decided, and I was powerless to change anything. I've been watching my people age and die for the last eighteen years, and all I could do was try to find you. It was a life I didn't choose and had no ability to control."

Addy almost laughed. "I know exactly what you mean."

Tol looked surprised. "You do?"

She nodded. And then, she surprised herself by telling Tol about how she had never wanted what her family wanted. She was wracked with guilt over it now that they were gone, but it still didn't make her want to return to the farmhouse. It still didn't make her want to accept Fred's...proposal.

"My parents had this grand plan that I would marry Fred, and Livy and her husband would stay on our farm, and we could just keep the cycle going. Livy loved the idea." Addy smiled at the thought of her sister. *Sweet Livy.* "I was the only one who felt like I was going nuts."

Tol's posture had stiffened when she mentioned Fred. She assumed it was one of those macho things. She didn't pretend to understand it.

"So, you don't want that life?" he asked, like he was choosing his words carefully.

"No," she replied. "And that makes me a terrible person, because all they wanted was for me to be happy. They just didn't realize how weird and messed up I am."

Tol's lip quirked. "I'd hardly call wanting to live the life you choose, rather than the one that is chosen for you, weird *or* messed up."

She bit her lip. If Tol knew that the first time she'd felt truly alive in her entire life was when she was murdering someone, he'd take back what he said. Instead of going there, she asked the question that had been burning a hole through her insides.

"The other night, when you…saw me," she began, needing to say the words, but terrified of his answer. "There was a thief who tried to steal from us. I killed him, and I was just wondering—"

She couldn't finish.

"If he was alone, he wasn't a Forsaken," Tol said. He gave her a sympathetic look, like he understood how guilt was tearing her apart. "I felt you that day because you must have accessed some of the Celestial's power inside you, which is what connected you to me. I think the Forsaken showing up a few days later was just coincidence."

He said the words that should exonerate her, but he looked troubled. She understood why. It was too big of a coincidence to be unconnected. Her parents had been afraid and wanted to leave. They knew something was going to happen. She had just been too dumb to listen.

Addy tipped her head back and closed her eyes, trying to banish the thought of all the ways she had failed her family.

"There are blankets and pillows in the couch," Tol said. "You should get some sleep while you can."

Addy didn't think she'd be able to sleep ever again, but she wasn't going to tell Tol that. She went over to the couch and unloaded a soft pillow and fluffy blanket from the opening beneath the seat. She felt weird about lying down on this strange boy's plane, but his eyes were closed, and it looked like he might already be asleep. She stretched out on the couch and pulled the blanket over her. It had the same faintly spicy smell as Tol. She wondered how often he was traveling if the blanket on his plane smelled like him.

It was her last thought as her eyes drifted closed.

CHAPTER 14

TOL

The Fount wasn't what Tol had expected. He never thought they'd share the same fear of being trapped…the same desire to escape a future that had been determined without their input.

Tol could hear the undercurrent of frustration in her voice when she talked about what her family had wanted for her. And now, he was going to do the same thing to her that they had. Except, instead of a lifetime of something she didn't choose, he was going to give her an eternity of it.

The thought made him feel ill.

As soon as Adelyne was asleep, he used the phone at the front of the plane and made the call he'd been dreading.

Gerth picked up on the first ring.

"Where in the two hells have you been?" his friend demanded.

"Keep your voice down," Tol replied.

"Do you have any idea how pissed your parents are?" Gerth demanded, talking louder to spite Tol. "Your gran is beside herself because no one has heard from you and—"

"I found her."

Gerth went quiet.

"Did you hear me?" Tol asked. "I found the Fount. She's on the plane with me."

There was a strange sound on the other end of the line.

"Are you crying?" Tol asked.

"You did it, you stupid arse," Gerth sniffled. "We can go back. Our elders…."

In typical Gerth fashion, he was about a hundred steps ahead, calculating moves and counter-moves…actions and reactions.

"There's just one thing," Tol said, interrupting Gerth's monologue about the house he planned to build himself on Vitaquias.

He told Gerth about his bargain with Adelyne, and then held the receiver away from his ear as Gerth shouted at him.

"Are you out of your gods-damned mind?" he was demanding. "We've kept you safe from the Forsaken for your whole life, and now you're going *right to them* with the Fount in tow?!"

Tol had expected this reaction, but it still filled him with fresh guilt. "Gerth, listen—"

"No, you listen. It's been nice knowing you, mate."

Tol hadn't expected the bitterness in his best friend's voice. Gerth was never bitter.

"I need you to cover for me," Tol said. "A week or two at the most."

Gerth's harsh laugh came across the line. "You know what, Prince Tolumus?" he said it like Erikir, in that scathing you-don't-deserve-your-title way. Gerth had never spoken this way before, and it cut Tol like a knife. "Any of us would lay down our lives for you in a second, so for you to be so frivolous with yours—and ours—is intolerable."

Tol sucked in a breath.

"It was the only way she'd agree to come back with me," Tol said, his voice pleading. He'd thought Gerth of all people would understand.

"It was your duty to bring her back to us," Gerth hissed. "We could have sent others out to get her sister. It didn't have to be you."

Tol pressed his forehead against the cool side of the plane. How could he explain he felt like it was his duty…his penance…to give this girl something before he took away everything from her? Maybe if he helped her rescue her sister, it would in some small measure make up for the fact that he was going to take her future in exchange.

"Listen to me," Gerth said. "There's been talk of an uprising. There are some who say the Magnantius family isn't fit to rule."

Anger and guilt filled Tol in equal measures.

"Nothing is going to happen in the next few weeks," Tol said when he trusted himself enough to speak. "Once everyone sees the Fount and the blood marriage is done, any whisperings of a rebellion will fade."

Gerth didn't say anything. Tol could feel his friend's skepticism radiating over the phone.

"Give me two weeks," Tol said. "I promise—"

"What? That you won't die?" Gerth said. "You can't make that promise, mate, and we both know it."

"I'll see you in two weeks," Tol said. "Just make up whatever excuses you need to for me until then."

Tol gently returned the phone, like Gerth could somehow feel his apology through that gesture. He sunk back in his seat and covered his face with his hand. His left shoulder was aching, and there was a tight knot in his stomach.

He shook his head, like the motion would be enough to clear it. He'd help the Fount rescue her sister, and then he'd save his people. Whatever else happened, and whatever Adelyne thought of him when he told her the whole truth of what she had agreed to, he'd just have to find a way to live with it.

He sat up as a bloodcurdling scream ripped through the airplane.

✷ ✷ ✷

ADDY

Addy didn't dream of her dead family like she had feared she would. Instead, she fell into *the dream*.

It was the same every time. In the dream, she was standing on the shore of a lake. It was surrounded by trees, but they weren't like any trees she'd seen before. Their leaves were a too-bright shade of green, and they were

124

too tall and narrow to exist in any place she knew. The lake was too still. There wasn't so much as a ripple.

She was barefoot, and the sand beneath her feet felt more like powder than the grainy sand they used to melt ice on the driveway during winter.

It was peaceful, serene.

And then the water started to rise. It lapped at her ankles. As the water touched her skin, it started to draw her into the lake.

The water was thick and dense, and even though she tried to fight it, it wrapped around her like watery vines and drew her in. She kicked at the water and flailed her arms, but it only made the water drag her in faster.

When it closed over her head, she wasn't in water, but in some kind of clear oil. It got in her eyes and burned her lungs, and still, it dragged her deeper. She saw the glare of the sun just above her, beckoning her. Taunting her.

She screamed, but that only made her lungs fill faster. The oily water flooded her stomach and swam through her blood. It filled her until there wasn't room for anything else. She was choking and crying. And still, the water filled her.

"Adelyne."

There were hands in the water, pulling her out.

"Adelyne, wake up!"

She was coughing and gasping, trying to expel the horrible oily water. Her lungs burned and her nose smarted. She opened her eyes and saw Tol, kneeling on the floor of the plane next to her. His face was drained of color.

She looked down at his hands, which were clutching her shoulders. He followed the direction of her gaze and snatched his hands back.

"I'm sorry," he said. "But you were screaming."

Addy winced as she came fully awake and the remnants of the dream slipped away, like oily water sliding back into a lake.

"You woke me up."

"I'm sorry," Tol said again, looking puzzled. "I thought about letting you sleep through it, but you seemed so scared...."

He didn't understand. Livy had been the only one whose voice could draw her out of the watery depths of the dream. Her parents and other sisters had tried, but it was only Livy who could ever wake her.

Whenever Livy woke up from one of her seizures, it was Addy kneeling beside her and holding her hand, and whenever she woke from the dream, it was Livy beside her. This was the first time in her life someone else's voice had brought her out of the nightmare, and it belonged to a near-stranger.

Addy sat up, clutching the blanket to her like she was naked underneath and it was the only thing she had to cover herself. She was fully clothed, but she felt exposed. Until today, her family had been the only ones to know about the dream. Not even Fred knew.

Tol handed her a box of tissues, and she was mortified to realize there were tears streaming down her face.

"Thanks," she mumbled, taking a handful of tissues and wiping her eyes. "Just a nightmare."

"You," Tol swallowed. "You said they were drowning you."

"Yeah." Addy shrugged, clutching her ball of tissues so Tol wouldn't see the way her hands shook. "I have this recurring nightmare of drowning." She let out a shuddering laugh. "It's so stupid. The closest I've ever come to drowning was when we bathed Fred's dog in the kiddie pool."

Tol's face was still pale.

"You can stop looking at me like that now," she snapped.

Her embarrassment at being seen like this—especially by Tol, who probably wasn't afraid of anything—transformed to irritation.

"Your breathing," Tol began, and then shook his head. "It sounded like there was actually water in your lungs."

She knew this already. Livy had told her more or less the same thing.

"What can I say," she said, with a forced lightness. "I'm a head case."

She'd had this dream for as long as she could remember. It never changed, and it never got easier to bear. She was ashamed of herself, but it didn't stop the dream from terrorizing her. It didn't stop her from wanting to curl into a ball and sob.

Tol still looked worried. "Can I get you anything?" he asked.

"It was just a dream," she said. "Do you freak out every time you have a bad dream?"

The scowl she was becoming familiar with returned to Tol's face. She felt relieved to see it, rather than concern and pity.

The captain's voice came on, announcing they were arriving in D.C. It gave Addy an excuse to turn away from Tol and stare out the window at the city below.

CHAPTER 15

TOL

Tol felt on edge from the conversation he'd had with Gerth and Adelyne's nightmare. But as he watched the sheer wonder on Adelyne's face as the city came into focus, Tol's unease evaporated. Tol had been to D.C. before on a number of occasions to track down leads on the Fount, and so he pointed out the buildings to her as they descended.

He laughed as she came away from the window and there was a smudge from where her nose had been pressed against it. He couldn't fathom what it would be like to only know such a tiny corner of the world. He felt a small, undeserved sense of pride at being able to show her something new.

But then he reminded himself of why they were here, and all he was risking for a girl who would come to truly loathe him, and he sobered.

Tol's gloom subsided once again as they descended into the metro. Adelyne looked around like she was a kid in a candy store, pointing at the trains rushing past on either side of the platform. She practically leaped onto the train car when it arrived.

When she wrinkled her nose at the city smell, Tol couldn't hold back a laugh.

He led Adelyne to two open seats, where they sat squashed together between a heavyset businessman and a woman whose knitting was practically spilling onto his lap. There were two older women sitting across from them, and they were staring at the prosthesis peeking out from Tol's sleeve. He shifted his body to try and hide it from view.

Adelyne felt his movement. She looked at him, and then at the women across the way. Tol saw her understanding dawn. He felt his face heat with embarrassment.

"What are you looking at?" Adelyne snapped at the women.

Tol looked at her, shocked, but she was glaring at the women. They both stared down at the floor, their cheeks turning pink.

"That's what I thought," Adelyne grumbled.

Tenderness swelled inside Tol. Adelyne rushing to his defense was the last thing he had expected from her. There wasn't a hint of pity on her face, either. She gave the women another glare for good measure and then settled back against the seat.

Tol felt an enormous rush of gratitude. He was used to people staring, and he'd endured more than his share of teasing about it all through mortal school. Tol learned early on that primary school children were the cruelest of all mortals.

Gerth had always defended him. As the prince, Tol wasn't allowed to get involved in fist fights or use his Influence on mortals. So, Gerth had gotten into all the fights Tol couldn't. He'd used his own Source when he really wanted to teach a bully a lesson, even though Tol had always begged him not to. Gerth had even made a game out of coming up with more and more outlandish explanations for Tol's missing arm.

His own people knew the reason why he'd lost his arm, of course. But still, there were comments here and there that made it less a badge of honor and more something to hide under a long-sleeved shirt.

There was one time when Nira, tangled in his sheets with her face still flushed from exertion, said, "Imagine what that would have been like if you had two hands."

He'd laughed it off, made some joke about how she could barely keep up with him as it was, but her words had stung.

Tol had certainly never expected Adelyne to be different. He tried to smile his thanks, but her attention was on the subway map overhead.

They got off and walked to the Senate Office Building. They had to stand outside for a few extra minutes for Adelyne to stare up at the building and gawk at how big it was, but Tol didn't mind.

"You know a senator?" Adelyne asked, her voice full of wonder and disbelief. "That's so cool."

Tol snorted. "I guess. Our people have made a point of getting involved in every major political organization in the mortal world."

"That's smart," Adelyne said, still looking up at the building.

"Not as smart as controlling every country's military," he replied darkly, thinking about the Forsaken.

After the security officer checked Tol's ID against a list on his desk, he ushered them into a nearby elevator and directed them to the right floor. When the elevator opened, a highly caffeinated woman not much older than they were took down their names and informed them in a bubbly voice that Senator Michaels was out of town.

A noise of protest came from Adelyne.

"Where is he?" Tol asked.

"London." The secretary gave them a bright smile. "But he'll be back first thing tomorrow. Shall I take down a message?"

"Yes. Tell him Tolumus will be back to see him at 8:00 sharp."

The secretary's smile faltered. "I'm afraid he's all booked up for tomorrow." She let out a breathy laugh. "Busy, busy."

"Just give him the message," Tol said. "Please."

Tol watched as she wrote down the message, and then muttered his thanks as he and Adelyne went back to the elevator.

Adelyne was cursing—and not quietly, either.

"What now?" she demanded once they were back on the street.

"We get a hotel for the night and then come back tomorrow," he replied.

"But the lady said he was busy," Adelyne argued. "What if he won't see us?"

"He'll see us," Tol promised.

ADDY

They had tried two other hotels nearby, but they were all full for the July Fourth festivities taking place that weekend. If she wasn't in such a bad mood from the senator being out of his office, she would have liked to walk around and look at everyone dressed in red, white, and blue. There were more people than she'd ever seen in her life.

She lost interest as soon as she thought about how much her sisters would have loved to be here. The last thing she deserved was to be wandering around a new, beautiful city while Fred was back at the farmhouse disposing of their bodies.

She shoved the thought of them out of her mind, like she'd been doing every other minute since she got in Tol's rental car and left Deerborn Family Farm behind.

When they stepped into the third hotel's lobby, she gasped. Everything was marble, except for the chandeliers, which were crystal. A bellboy took one look at her torn jeans and actually sniffed. She couldn't blame him. She probably should have taken Tol up on his offer and used the shower *on the plane*, but she hadn't felt comfortable showering in the air. What if the plane tilted? Would she spill out into the aisle?

Tol strode up to the counter and rested his right elbow on the marble like he did this kind of thing all the time. For all Addy knew, he did. She assumed his title of 'Prince' didn't actually mean royalty, but there was a quiet surety about him, like things just *happened* for him, Source or no. It must be a rich person thing, she decided.

"Two rooms, please," Tol told the hotel clerk.

"Yes, sir." The portly man behind the counter, dressed in a black suit, started typing on his computer.

Tol pulled out his wallet, and then seemed to realize something.

"Um." He turned his back to the clerk and gave Addy an apologetic look. "Would you mind paying?"

"Spend all your money on the plane?" Addy nodded like it made perfect sense.

"No." Tol look flustered, and Addy had to admit she kind of liked being the cause of his discomfort. "I only have a credit card, and if I use it, my family will know where I am."

"So?" Addy tapped a sneaker on the marble, liking the tap-tap-tap sound it made.

"So, in the time it takes to get from London to here, there will be a swarm of angry, Source-wielding people who will drag us back to England."

With all his words implied, she stepped up to the counter. "I've got this," she announced, pulling out her wad of bills.

"My apologies," the clerk said, giving Tol puppy dog eyes, "but I'm afraid we only have one room left in the whole hotel." He glared at the computer, like it was the machine's fault he couldn't offer better news. "July Fourth has all the hotels in the city at capacity, I'm afraid. But this room is spacious and is one of the newly remodeled ones. I do think you'll enjoy it?" He said it like a question.

Addy looked at Tol, who muttered, "Whatever you want to do is fine."

When the clerk told her the price of the room per night, she had a heart attack, and then decided that one room was more than enough. She wasn't made of money. At least it would only be for one night.

"You're paying me back for this," Addy informed Tol, who gave her a formal nod.

She wasn't too worried about the sharing a room part. After what had happened on the plane, she had no intention of sleeping.

There was a flurry of activity as bellboys came to scoop up their bags. Tol nodded politely as the clerk walked them to the elevator and jabbered on about the renovations. He seemed desperate to impress Tol even though he had no way of knowing who Tol was…whatever he was. Addy had no idea what Tol was. He had told her so many fantastic, impossible things over the last day-and-a-half. She also couldn't believe it had only been that long. It felt like an eternity had passed since she came home from Fred's and found her family….

As soon as they were alone in the elevator, Addy gave Tol a look.

"Should I start bowing and stuttering around you, too?" Addy asked. "I'm afraid I've been too informal, *Your Majesty*." She bowed, flourishing her hands as she did so.

Tol made a sound of disgust, and then, seeing that Addy wasn't serious, laughed.

A satisfied feeling passed through her. Something told her he didn't laugh often, and she liked the sound of it. Tol opened the door to their room and stopped just inside. He swore.

"What?"

Did their enemies somehow know they were here? Impossible.

Addy pushed past him, fists raised.

"Oh."

In spite of the hotel clerk's assurances to the contrary, the room was small, and it was dominated by a single, king-sized bed.

Tol's bronze cheeks darkened, and he was actually stuttering…something about the gods-damned Americans and their July Fourth.

His hair was ruffled from the way he'd been raking his hand through it. In the short time she'd known him, Tol had always seemed so together and sure of himself. It was more than a little gratifying to see how uncomfortable he was now. Seeing Tol's embarrassment put Addy strangely at ease. It was obvious he didn't want any more to do with her than she wanted to do with him.

"It's fine," she said, tossing her duffel onto the small, polished desk. "I'll sleep in the chair."

"No, you bloody will not," Tol said, his embarrassment turning to offense. "Do you know what my gran would say if she heard I let you do that?"

"That chair is tiny," Addy pointed out. "And you're taller."

Tol scoffed. "By a centimeter. Maybe."

"You're also royalty," she said. "Isn't there some kind of law about heads rolling if the royal family is inconvenienced?"

"Only in France," Tol replied, swiping a finger across his throat. "But like I said...Gran. She'd make the French seem downright civilized if she found out I shirked my gentlemanly duties."

"She sounds like a tough lady," Addy said in sympathy.

"The toughest seven-hundred-year-old bird you'll ever meet," Tol agreed.

"You're kidding," Addy said.

"About her age, or her being a bird?" Tol replied.

In response, Addy threw a pillow at his head.

CHAPTER 16

ADDY

They must have argued for close to an hour about who would get the bed, but Tol had refused to budge on the issue, using his "Gran" as the excuse for being unnecessarily chivalrous. In the end, it hadn't really mattered.

Addy didn't think either of them had gotten much sleep. Her fear of falling back into the dream in front of Tol kept her wide awake for most of the night. Tol had seemed consumed by worries of his own. He kept rubbing at his left shoulder like his prosthetic arm was hurting him. She almost asked him about it, but she had a strong suspicion he liked talking about his arm as much as she liked talking about the dream.

In the last hour before dawn, Tol nodded off, squished into the straight-backed chair.

As soon as it was light out, she went out for provisions. She had no idea what Tol liked to eat, but she got him a tea, since she wasn't completely ignorant about the British. When she got back to the hotel, Tol was running out of the lobby. He skidded to a stop when he saw her.

"Where in the two hells were you?" he demanded. His face was drawn, like he'd been really worried.

Addy held up the bag of donuts and tea and gave him a *duh?* look. Tol seemed to sag in relief.

"I didn't realize I needed your permission to go out and get breakfast," she said.

"You don't," Tol muttered as he sunk into one of the overstuffed chairs in the lobby. He buried his face in his hand.

"Did you think those men were going to find me?" she asked, all teasing gone from her voice. He looked physically ill.

"Maybe," he said, raising his head to look at her. "You're just…important." And then, as though afraid she might misinterpret his words, he said, "The ritual is important. If you disappeared, we'd be lost."

"I'm not going anywhere," Addy said, sliding the tea into his hand. "We made a deal, right?"

Tol nodded, his hand curling around the foam cup.

"And you're welcome for the tea," Addy said. "I'm putting it on your tab, along with our hotel room."

Tol gave her a small smile. "Fair enough."

* * *

They were back on the metro so they could get to the senator's office early. Tol was confident the senator would be waiting in his office for them whenever they showed up, but Addy wasn't taking any chances. She wanted to be there, outside his office, when he arrived in the morning.

The metro was crowded, full of men and women dressed for work and shuffling briefcases and children. Tol and Addy stood, pressed against a lady with spit-up on her dress and a little girl on her hip. There was a boy, probably about Rosie's age, standing next to her. He was rummaging around in his mother's purse. Finding what he wanted, the kid pulled out a leftover dish filled with Cheerios. Addy watched as he wrestled with the cap. He finally managed to wedge his small fingers under the tab. There was an explosion of Cheerios.

"Jack!" the mother yelled, trying to gather up the dish and scattered Cheerios.

"Damnit," she said.

She turned to Addy, frazzled. "Would you mind holding my daughter for a sec?" She didn't wait for Addy to reply. She just plopped a fussing toddler in Addy's arms and went back to collecting Cheerios and soothing a now-crying Jack.

The little girl looked at Addy. She had a purple bow clipped into her fine brown hair. She looked, and felt, about the same age as Lucy. All the breath went out of Addy's lungs. She saw her youngest sister, lying in a pool of blood on their kitchen floor, surrounded by the bodies of the rest of her family. Addy's knees started to buckle.

"We're getting off."

Addy heard the voice like it was coming from far away. Then, the little girl was taken out of her arms.

"Almost done," the woman was saying, but Tol took her arm with his prosthetic one. It looked gentle enough, but the feel of metal on her skin must have thrown her off, because the woman gave a little "Oh!" and took the child that Tol held out to her. Addy saw all this without really processing any of it. The feel of the toddler in her arms had reminded her of too many memories to count…memories she hadn't appreciated when she was living through them.

Every emotion she'd been fighting to keep at bay was boiling to the surface. She couldn't think. She couldn't breathe.

She slipped on some brown liquid on the floor of the train, and she could have sworn it was her family's blood beneath her feet. Addy's legs turned to rubber as acid churned in her stomach. Tol caught her arm and steered her through the crowd of commuters.

She made it to the trash can before she started to vomit.

Images of blood and broken necks and her family on the kitchen floor swam through her mind. Addy clung to the garbage can as she sobbed and threw up, and tried to catch her breath in between.

A few passers-by were staring. She was aware of Tol using his body to block her from view as she continued to retch long after her stomach was empty. He was holding her hair so it didn't hang into the garbage. He said something in her ear. She couldn't make out the words through the screaming of her own mind, but she understood the tenor of his voice. It was low, and it was saying something comforting. She opened her mind to the sound, letting its velvet sweep in and clear out her own thoughts.

"My baby sister," she gasped when she could breathe enough to talk. "She—"

"I know," Tol said, sinking onto the ground beside her. "I know."

CHAPTER 17

TOL

Tol had been at every elder's death in the mortal world since he was old enough to comprehend what was happening. When the oldest Chosens' allotment of Source was no longer enough to sustain them, there was no choice but to let them expire. As the future king, Tol saw it as one of his duties to be there with his parents when they sat with the elders through their last moments.

After thousands of years of immortality on Vitaquias, none of the Chosen elders could fathom the meaning of death. Every time he saw them remove their empty necklaces and take their last, shuddering breaths, Tol felt a crushing powerlessness. He had tried to give them his own Source when he was younger, but of course, they never accepted. The value they placed on his life, the hope they had that Tol would make things better for the younger generations, only made him feel worse.

As he got older, Tol's sense that he was failing his people only grew. No matter how many days and nights he traveled in search of the Fount, she was still missing, and his people were still dying.

Tol felt that same helplessness as he watched Adelyne take that child on the train and see her dead sister. He saw that look in her eyes, and it gutted him. It was worse that the only comfort he could give was some meaningless platitudes and to keep her hair out of the rubbish bin.

He'd promised her they'd find her sister, and he was determined to keep that promise. Not just because it was the only way to get what he needed, but because he knew the truth was that her family had gotten mixed up in something that never should have touched them. Her family would still be alive if it wasn't for his. The crushing unfairness of it all made him want to fall to his knees and beg for her forgiveness.

"I should have been there," Adelyne said. "Maybe if I'd been there—"

"No," Tol wanted to grab her and shake the preposterous idea out of her. "This is not your fault."

"If I'd been home, they would have taken me instead of Livy."

"And your sister would be dead, rather than captured," Tol replied.

She looked at him with so much pain and guilt in her green eyes he couldn't take it.

"If you want to blame someone," he said, "blame me."

"You?"

And so, Tol explained. He told her about his people's unquenchable thirst for knowledge and desire to expand their powers. He told her how their greed and ambition had led to the Source being drained beyond the point at which it could regenerate.

"The balance of Vitaquias was disrupted," he said. "Our world couldn't sustain itself."

Tol repeated his people's grim history, which he'd learned from written records in his parents' library. He knew the more emotional parts of the story from elders who remembered the Crossing.

"When you say your world was damaged," Adelyne began.

"Imagine the worst forest fire in existence, and what that place looked like after the fire."

"Oh." Adelyne's face was pinched in sympathy.

"Yeah."

Tol took a breath.

"My people caused our world's destruction because we pushed the limits of what Source could do. It's why the Celestial chose to give her powers to a mortal instead of one of us. She didn't trust us after what we'd done."

He wanted to stop there, but he forced himself to keep going. He felt like he owed it to Adelyne to explain, at least as much as he could for now.

"You absorbed the Celestial's knowledge and power, and that's why my people need you. If my people hadn't drained the Source, we never would have been expelled from our world, and your family would have been left in peace."

Tol went quiet, waiting for Adelyne to rail at him, maybe even try to call off their bargain. She did neither.

"I don't blame you for what your people did before you were born," she said after a while. "The only ones who set out to harm me and my family are those barbarians. I'm going to save my hate for them."

Tol thought that was more than he or his people deserved, but he nodded anyway.

"I'm good now," Adelyne said, rising to her feet. "Let's go."

She looked like the exact opposite of good. Her pale skin had turned a little gray, and her eyes were bloodshot from vomiting. But Tol didn't argue. If their places were reversed and the Forsaken had Gerth or Gran, he knew he wouldn't rest until he had them back.

By the time they reached the Senate Office Building, Adelyne had stopped shaking. She ducked into a restroom, and when she came out, her color was back and the tears had been scrubbed from her face.

Tol gave her a *you okay?* look, and she nodded.

"I'm sorry," she said with a wan smile. "I'm not usually like this."

He felt stricken. "If you think I'm judging you for grieving for your family," he didn't finish the thought. "To go through something like that and still want to fight the Forsaken, knowing what they can do," Tol shook his head. "I think you're one of the bravest people I've ever met."

Adelyne let out a small laugh. "I don't think brave people have nightmares about drowning."

"Everyone's afraid of something," he replied.

* * *

ADDY

The bubbly secretary from yesterday was at her desk, and Addy had the vague sense she'd never left.

"Ah," the woman leapt to her feet. "Senator Michaels is expecting you. Wait here, please." She scurried down the hall like a mouse in high heels and rapped on a door at the other end.

Addy found it hard to believe that this alien race of immortals was so much a part of her world…governments, militaries…and she'd never known. And yet, no matter how hard the logical part of her tried to dismiss everything Tol had said, she didn't think there was any other way to explain the insanity of the last couple of days.

"You might want to stay out here," Tol told her. "This man is a bit…odd."

Addy just gave him a withering look. "I'm coming with you."

Tol looked like he wanted to argue, but then thought better of it. "Fine," he said, "but let me do the talking."

The secretary was back, a little out of breath. "Senator Michaels will see you straight away." She led them over to the senator's office, rapped once on the glass, and ushered them into the room. She gave them a bright but quizzical smile on her way out of the office, as if to say *you don't look very important*, and then shut the door behind her.

"Prince Tolumus." The senator came around his desk and bowed. He held the pose for several seconds before rising.

"Migelian," Tol said, holding out his hand.

The senator shook it, keeping his head bowed over their hands like Tol's visit was the highest honor he'd ever received.

Addy just stared. It was one thing for Tol to tell her he was some kind of royalty, but it was quite another to see a senator bowing to him.

The senator had olive skin and dark hair and eyes like Tol. Unlike Tol, his hair was trimmed in a short, neat cut. He was a slight man, and Addy felt like a giant next to him. He looked to be in his mid-forties, but from what Tol had told her about his people's longevity, she knew appearances could be deceiving.

Tol motioned to her. "Adelyne has a question she thinks only the Forsaken officers can answer," Tol said.

"Majesty?" The old senator put a hand on his heart. "If there is any issue with the Forsaken in my territory, I assure you—"

"We just want to have a chat with them." Tol put his hand on the senator's arm in a friendly, kingly sort of way. He leaned in, like he was sharing a secret. "And I'd appreciate my parents not finding out."

"But, Your Highness." The senator looked troubled, and Addy felt a little sorry for him.

"I need you to tell me where to find one of their officers," Tol said, steering the senator around his desk. "Just give me a home address. Somewhere we can talk in private without anyone getting hurt."

The senator's eyes bugged out. "Prince Tolumus, you can't possibly be thinking about going *yourself?*"

"Just a quick chat," Tol said again. "In and out. No one will be in any danger."

The senator took the paper and pen Tol offered him. He didn't write anything, though.

The senator looked up and caught Addy's eye. Something seemed to register in the senator's gaze, and he straightened.

"Prince Tolumus," he said, his hand wavering slightly. "Who did you say this young lady of yours was?"

Addy saw Tol's posture stiffen.

"I didn't."

"Ah, of course." The senator put his pen to the paper, but he still didn't write anything down.

"Better yet," Addy said, "Why don't you just tell us how to find their leaders?"

Tol gave her a look, but she continued. "Why bother with officers, if we can go straight to the top?"

The senator laughed. "Dear mortal girl, no one knows where the Forsaken general's hideout is located. If we did," he gave Tol a knowing look, "we would have destroyed it long ago."

"My gran is the only one of us alive who has ever seen the Forsaken general," Tol explained. "I'd guess most of their own people couldn't tell us where to find the general even if they were under Influence."

"A suspicious, paranoid lot," the senator put in. "Although," he gave Tol a rueful grin, "I suppose that's why their people are surviving in the mortal world better than ours."

Addy saw a muscle flex in Tol's jaw. The senator had struck some kind of nerve without realizing it, but his attention was no longer on Tol. He was staring at Addy.

"I heard a rumor," he smiled at them both, "and mind you, you know how rumors abound in Washington."

Tol just waited, but Addy could see the tension in him.

"The Forsaken were looking for a mortal girl, and I can't help but wonder…."

"The address, Migelian," Tol said firmly.

"Right, of course." He picked up the phone, dialed a number, and waited several beats. He hung up when the person on the other end didn't answer. "My secretary has my address book out at her desk," the senator explained. "I'll go get it." He started to rise from his chair, but then a thought seemed to occur to him.

"You do understand I am compelled to tell the king and queen of all that passes in my district?" He gave Tol an apologetic smile, but it didn't seem genuine to Addy. "Once you're gone, I'll have to tell them about your visit." He shrugged, like he wished it wasn't the case, but what could they expect from him, really? "They are my sovereigns until you come of age."

The senator's eyes slid to Addy again. A cold feeling slithered up her spine. This man was more than odd. He was creepy. Addy just wanted to get the address and get out of there.

"Funny," Tol said, his light tone not fooling her. "But I don't think you ever mentioned to my parents that you were involved in trading Source in exchange for the Forsakens' weapons."

The senator gasped. "Your Majesty, I was only—"

"Afraid for your life and wishing to protect yourself." Tol nodded. "I understand why you did what you did, and why you kept it a secret from my parents. I, too, would like to keep my visit here a secret. I'm sure you understand."

The senator's face had taken on an ashy hue. "I understand perfectly." He sunk into his chair, looking exhausted. "If you'll be so kind as to give me a moment, I'll go get that address."

"Don't trouble yourself," Tol said. "I'll get it."

He gave Addy a look as he left the office. The message was clear: *watch him.* Tol left the door open behind him as he strode back down the hall. As soon as Tol was gone, the senator took out the necklace hidden under the collar of his shirt. He uncorked the vial, measured out a single, glistening drop on his finger, and put it in his mouth.

Addy narrowed her eyes on the senator. *I wouldn't try anything if I were you, buddy.* Addy reached around to her back pocket where her garden shears were nestled in her jeans. She kept her eyes on the senator, whose pallid skin had transformed into a dull gold.

"Adelyne, is it?"

Addy looked at the senator, and the moment she met his gaze, everything else slipped away.

"Don't look away from my eyes," the senator said.

Addy found that she had no desire to do anything except look at the senator. It was her only purpose in the world, and every other thought fled from her mind.

"Who are you, really?" the senator asked. "What business do you have with the Forsaken?"

Addy wanted nothing more than to tell him, and so she did.

"You're a very beautiful young woman," he told her when she'd finished explaining.

Addy was pleased that he was pleased.

"Come here," the senator said.

She did, because she couldn't fathom doing anything else. The senator patted his legs, and she came around the desk to sit in his lap. The senator picked up his phone and spoke into it, telling the person on the other end to "Keep him busy."

Addy heard the words, but they were unimportant. All that mattered was to stay on the senator's lap, to let him sweep back her hair and murmur into her ear about how he only needed a little, tiny bit of her blood, and she wouldn't mind, would she?

Of course, she wouldn't mind. She watched with a kind of dull fascination as the senator took a small knife from a drawer in his desk.

It was like padding had gone up inside her mind, and everything except for the senator's voice was of no significance. She was still aware of what was going on around her, she just didn't care about any of it. All that mattered was staying very still so the senator could cut her skin and collect as much of her blood as he desired.

She heard footsteps and shouting, and then Tol was pulling her to her feet. She didn't want to leave the senator's lap, and she fought him. Tol took her face in his hands, forcing her head to face him, but her eyes swiveled around to stay locked on the senator's. She heard Tol gasp, but it didn't concern her.

"Release her," Tol said in a voice that wasn't velvet, but steel.

"Your Majesty, I—"

"Release her!"

"I release you from my Influence."

The Senator's words tore away the padding in Addy's mind. She gasped as sensation and clarity rushed back. She would have collapsed, but Tol caught her. Horror swept through her at the memory of what she had told the senator. And why in the world had she sat on his lap?

"Are you alright?" Tol lowered her in a chair and knelt in front of her.

She nodded, even though she wasn't sure it was really true. She felt…violated. Like her mind had been emptied out onto the senator's desk, and he'd been picking through the contents while she stood by. *While she sat on his lap*, she reminded herself with a shudder.

Tol rounded on the senator. He didn't say anything. He just held out his hand.

The senator was apologizing, begging for forgiveness, saying he was an ignorant old fool. Tol just stood there with his hand outstretched, not saying a word. The senator began to weep.

Addy felt shame and confusion, but she could see there was nothing but cold fury in Tol as the senator took the glass vial from his collar, unhooked it from the chain still around his neck, and handed it to Tol with shaking hands.

Tol wrenched the vial from the other man's grip. It took Tol several seconds to uncork the vial. His prosthesis seemed too clunky to do much about the small cork, and his right hand was shaking. Except unlike the senator, Tol wasn't scared. He was furious. His eyes had gone dark with the emotion.

When Tol managed to uncork the vial, he all but drained it into an empty one from his pocket, and handed it back to the senator.

"I've left you enough to get your affairs in order," Tol said, his voice all the more brutal for its quiet calm. "If even a single word about our meeting—about whatever Adelyne told you—gets out, I'll make sure this," he held up the vial, "never reaches your daughter."

Tol moved in front of the senator's chair. He put a hand on each armrest and leaned over until he was in the senator's face. "Have I made myself clear?"

A shiver went through Addy at the way Tol spoke to the senator. His voice was low and deadly. But whatever fear she felt was nothing compared to the senator's terror.

"Y-yes, Your M-Majesty."

Tol glared at the senator for another moment before pocketing the vial. To Addy, he said, "Let's go."

"Did you get the address?" she asked.

Tol nodded, giving her the paper with the address written out in what she assumed was the secretary's flowing script.

Neither of them looked back as they left the office.

CHAPTER 18

TOL

Tol could barely see through the fury that pulsed through his veins. He'd left Adelyne alone with Migelian, his own subject, and the man had Influenced her. Tol wanted to retch every time he remembered Adelyne sitting on Migelian's lap with her eyes glazed over.

He'd known the old man had been buying Forsaken weapons, but that wasn't so unusual among the elders whose Source was running low, and who needed a means of protecting themselves without always turning to Source.

But Tol had never guessed the man would try to Influence Adelyne.

"I'm so sorry," he said for what felt like the thousandth time.

Tol had convinced himself that Adelyne, like all of the Chosen, couldn't be Influenced. She had the Celestial's blood after all, and the Celestial certainly hadn't been subject to Influence. But Adelyne was also mortal. Too late, Tol realized she likely wouldn't be able to resist Influence until after the blood marriage.

"I just feel dirty," Adelyne said, brushing at her clothes as if to rid herself of the filth of what Migelian had done to her.

"It's a violation of your mind," Tol said. "Your free will was stolen away."

The only mortal Tol had ever Influenced was Adelyne's friend, Fred, and he hadn't been there to see the effects wear off. He had seen the way the mortals who tormented him in primary school had wandered around for hours after Gerth Influenced them, looking dazed and a little lost.

Adelyne had been in a bit of a fog on the metro, but she seemed to be recovering quickly.

"When you told him to release me," she said, swallowing, "was that the only way for me to get my mind back?"

"We could have waited until that drop of Source expended itself," Tol said. "But to return your free will before then, only the person who cast the Influence could take it back."

"Teach me how to protect my mind," Adelyne demanded.

"I can't. It's impossible." Tol shook his head. "The strongest minds can be more difficult to hold, but Influence is impossible to resist. Only the Chosen are immune."

Adelyne looked ill, and he didn't blame her. For his people, Influence was their only weapon against the Forsaken warriors, but mortals had no defense against either.

"I didn't think you could be Influenced, but now that we know, I'll never let that happen to you again." Tol meant it with every ounce of his being.

He'd taken Migelian's Source for it. He'd left the man only a couple of drops, which wouldn't keep him alive for more than a week. And Migelian wouldn't dare return to the manor to beg for more from his parents' reserves.

Tol should have felt more distress at condemning one of his own subjects. He should have sent the man back to England for his parents to judge and punish, but the logistics of that course of action aside, it hadn't even occurred to him. He'd been so angry when he realized what the senator had done, he had wanted nothing more than to kill the man right there in his office.

"Are you sure you're up for this?" Tol asked when they got off the metro.

"Never better," Adelyne replied, her eyes on the paper they'd both memorized.

Tol let the matter drop. They found the quiet street lined with brownstones, and located the right one. Tol watched Adelyne's Haze flare around her. No matter how many times he saw it happen, he didn't think he'd ever get used to seeing her Haze just appear whenever she had need of the Celestial's powers. For his part, Tol took a drop of Source and waited for its warmth to envelop him.

"Ready?" he asked.

"More than ready," Adelyne replied.

Tol knocked on the door and moved away from the peep hole. After a few seconds, the door cracked open.

Adelyne shoved the door. There was a yelp of surprise on the other side as she barged in. Tol hurried in behind her. He scanned the room quickly, confirming from the military decorations on the Forsakens' uniforms that they'd found the ones they were looking for.

"The Chosen prince is here!" the Forsaken who had opened the door shouted.

Screams of rage echoed through the house.

Adelyne cracked the first man's jaw with her fist, leaving him doubled over as she went deeper into the house.

Tol Influenced the man clutching his face. He barely managed to keep up with Adelyne as he took control of the bloodied and battered Forsaken she left in her wake. Her limbs flew. The only weapon she wielded was that pair of shears he'd seen her use against the Forsaken in the cornfield.

Tol had no idea the damage a pair of scissors could exact, but in her power-infused state, Adelyne was unstoppable. Daggers, crossbows, and swords did nothing to hamper her progress as she tore through the Forsaken.

Tol watched in awe as Adelyne drew forth the Fount's powers and wielded them against her foes. Tol didn't think five of his own people would have been as effective in this fight as Adelyne with her shears.

Still, the Forsaken weren't giving up easily. After blows that would have left any of the Chosen unconscious or worse, these warriors got back up for more. An already-dazed mind was easier to take hold of than a lucid one, but even with the blows Adelyne was dealing them, these Forsaken kept their heads. It made Tol's job more difficult.

Tol had encountered Forsaken on many of his earlier searches for the Fount, but he'd never had to Influence so many at once. He knew he could control three of their minds at the same time, but he'd never had cause to push himself beyond that. He didn't know the limits of his strength, but he had no choice now but to trail behind Adelyne and keep Influencing their enemies until his hold on their minds began to splinter.

Most Chosen could only exert Influence over a single mind at a time. More gifted Chosen could manipulate two. Tol now had seven in the grip of his mental hold.

If he hadn't been so preoccupied, he would have been more surprised by the power radiating from his own mind. It was greater than he'd ever felt before, and more than he thought any Chosen could be capable of.

There was no one else here who could appreciate what he was doing. Tol knew if Gerth was with him, he'd talk about nothing else for days afterward.

Gerth had often theorized about how powerful Tol must be if the gods had tried to keep him on Vitaquias even as an infant. Because of the risk involved any time Forsaken were around, and the laws against Influencing mortals, Tol's true strength had never been tested.

Tol and Adelyne were many times outnumbered. All that saved them was that the Forsaken hadn't had time to take Source, and so their ability to resist Tol's hold over their minds was dampened.

Tol knew if the playing field were more even, he would be dead and Adelyne would be in chains. Since the two of them were the only ones with Source in their veins, they were stronger than all nine of the Forsaken combined.

But both of their energy was spent, and Source or not, they were still only two against nine. Adelyne knocked weapons across the room, which flared blue and flew back into their owners' hands. She sunk to her knees after slamming the last Forsaken into a wall. Tol saw the strain of the last few days on her face.

For the moment, everyone in the house was either unconscious or under his control, but Tol was exhausted. He could tell his Haze was less bright than usual. He felt the effort of holding so many minds at once like a leaden weight on his skull.

"Where's Olivia?" Adelyne screamed at them. "Where's my sister?"

Tol pulled at their minds, forcing out whatever information they had. Of the nine men and women sprawled out in the austere living room, Tol could tell from the insignia on their lapels that eight of them were lieutenants. The ninth was a captain. Tol focused as much Influence on the man as he could spare.

"Answer her." Tol gave the man's mind a vicious tug.

The captain winced. "The girl's location is top secret," he reported.

These Forsaken were strong, both in mind and body, and it was taking all of Tol's strength to Influence them. He knew he didn't have much time before his control over them started to slip.

Sweat was rolling down the captain's face. "Only the Forsaken general's top officers know where she was taken."

Tol ground his teeth. "And where do we find these officers?"

"The Forsaken hideout is on one of the islands outside Baltra. I don't know which one."

Baltra. Tol searched his mind for the maps he'd been forced to memorize in mortal school.

"The Galapagos?" Tol groaned.

That would add at least a week to this insane journey, maybe more. If the Forsaken didn't manage to kill him at some point during their trip, Gerth and his parents would do it for them.

"I don't believe the girl was brought there," the captain continued. "Rumor was the general left the hideout to bring the mortal girl somewhere else."

"Where?" Tol asked. "Where else might they have taken her?"

The man managed a jerky shrug. "She could be anywhere. Only our people in the Galapagos will know where."

"Is there anything useful you can tell us about my sister?" Adelyne demanded.

"Adelyne." Tol gritted his teeth against the strain of keeping so many minds in his control. The ones who had been stunned from Adelyne's beating were coming back to themselves, and Tol felt his hold on them fading.

Adelyne wasn't ready to give up, even though it was obvious these Forsaken had nothing more to offer. A bead of sweat slid down Tol's face. Spots were dancing at the edges of his vision. He knew if he didn't let go of these minds soon, he was going to lose consciousness, and then the Forsaken would be free of his Influence. Out of the corner of his eye, he saw Adelyne was leaning against the wall. She looked as weak as he felt.

"We need to get out of here," he managed. "Now." To the Forsaken, he said, "Forget everything we asked. You don't remember why we're here."

With the amount of Influence needed for that request, Tol's Haze shuddered. His control fell away.

"Run!" he yelled.

She did, knocking the captain out of the way as she reached for the door. Tol took one step and fell to his knees.

Adelyne reached the door and turned back.

"Go," he demanded.

The other eight Forsaken were on their feet. They were confused and bloody, but they were Forsaken.

"Go!" he shouted.

Adelyne ignored him. She ran back, hauling Tol up and winding his right arm over her shoulders. She half-supported, half-dragged him out of the house. They stumbled down the front steps and onto the street, the Forsaken on their heels.

Adelyne struck out behind them one-handed with the shears. Tol heard a scream and then cursing. Somehow, they made it onto the street.

"Wait," Tol gasped. He managed to unstop the vial of Source and swallow a drop. His Haze flared, but his wasn't the only one.

A glowing blue throwing star *shinged* past his ear. It stopped in mid-air, and then flew back toward him like the thing was heat-censored. He barely managed to dodge it. The Forsaken were amassing in the doorway of the brownstone, their golden Haze spilling out around them. One of them had a bow and arrows, and Adelyne was using her shears to deflect the shafts hurtling at them.

"Come on," Tol said, forcing himself to carry his own weight. They needed to get off this street and lose themselves in traffic. Adelyne pushed him in front of her as she defended them from behind with nothing but her shears. If he'd had more energy, he would have been humiliated to need her protection. Instead, he was grateful.

A car was idling on the other side of the street. Tol made for it.

He could hear the Forsakens' boots as they pounded the pavement behind him. He opened the car's passenger door, which actually turned out to be the driver's side door. Tol took hold of the surprised mortal's mind and ordered him to shove over.

"Get in!" he yelled to Adelyne, who was holding the Forsaken off.

Tol got in the driver's seat with the placid mortal sitting next to him. Adelyne opened the back door with one hand, using the other to deflect another arrow, and swung herself in. Someone shrieked in pain. Tol couldn't tell if it was Adelyne or the Forsaken she was wrestling. He turned back to her.

"Drive!" she screamed.

Tol hit the gas.

CHAPTER 19

ADDY

I t took two cars, three metro lines, and a bus to lose the Forsaken trailing them. It hadn't helped that Addy and Tol had barely been strong enough to walk, let alone fight. Even the extra Source Tol took hadn't helped much. Apparently, the stuff had its limitations, which Addy thought was inconvenient to say the least.

They stumbled into their hotel, bloody, filthy, and tired in a way Addy had never been in her life. She thought hauling hay into the Browns' loft in July, in 100-degree weather without even the hint of a breeze, was exhausting. But that didn't even compare to how she felt now.

The doorman gave them a dubious look, but Tol must have Influenced him, because he didn't say a word as they passed. Addy's vision was blurry. She stumbled over her own feet. Tol caught her arm, steadying her. Somehow, they made it up to their room in one piece. Addy just collapsed on the floor, not wanting to get her grime all over the pristine white bed. Tol sunk into the chair and closed his eyes.

"Just a quick nap," Addy murmured. "Then we'll figure out how we're getting to the Galapagos."

She knew the Galapagos were made up of islands, which meant they were surrounded by water. But she wouldn't let herself think about that now. It was their only lead on Livy. Even if she had to swim there, she would.

"We're not going anywhere until tomorrow," Tol replied without opening his eyes.

"But—"

Tol sat up with an effort and looked at her. "People die from using Source when their physical bodies are too weak to handle it."

"So, what are we supposed to do?"

If Addy hadn't been too damn tired, she would have stomped her foot on the ground.

"Shower, food, sleep. In that order," Tol murmured, his eyes falling closed again. "Tomorrow, we'll go to the Galapagos."

Addy wanted to argue, but she didn't have the energy. "Fine," she said. "Then I get first shower."

"Not a chance," Tol replied, rising to his feet.

Addy was quicker. She grabbed her duffel and shut the bathroom door against his weak protests.

It was the best shower of her life. She turned the temperature up as hot as she could stand and let the dirt and blood wash off her. She used the hotel's soap to wash herself twice, and then she used the coconut-scented shampoo and conditioner she'd brought from home for good measure. Addy stood under the hot water until guilt at hogging the bathroom finally drove her out.

Addy threw away her clothes, which she decided were unsalvageable. She changed into a fresh pair of jeans and T-shirt and dried her hair using the hotel's blow dryer. When she emerged, she felt like a new woman.

"Oh good," Tol said. "I assumed you died in there."

"Do you think this look happens by accident?" she replied, gesturing to her wrinkled clothes.

She expected Tol to come back with some snarky comment, but when he just looked at her in a way that made her cheeks warm, she faltered.

"Shower's all yours," she said, trying to mask her awkwardness. She wrinkled her nose in his direction. "And the sooner the better."

Tol rolled his eyes at her as he stood up. He had turned on the TV, and when he moved, Addy could see the breaking news banner on the bottom of the screen.

Senator Michaels unexpectedly retires, was scrawling across the TV in an unending loop. There was a reporter standing next to the Senate Office Building where they had been earlier in the day, and he was talking about the senator's "sudden and unexpected departure." The feed cut to a clip of the senator, flanked by bodyguards, outside what must be his home.

"He looks like he's aged a decade since this morning," Addy said.

Tol gave her a short nod. "Our immortality comes from the Source, which is what keeps us young in mind and body. The more years someone had in the Old World, the more Source is needed to keep their youth in the mortal one." Tol inclined his head in the direction of the TV. "Migelian was almost two-hundred years old, so without his Source...." Tol didn't need to finish that thought.

"If someone took your Source, you would get old, too?"

The thought held no humor. Instead, it chilled her to the bone.

"No," Tol said. "I'm eighteen years old, so I'm ageing the same way as you."

"Weird that we're that same age," Addy mused.

A strange look passed over Tol's face, but he didn't say anything more.

"So, who gets to decide how old or young your people look?" Addy was thinking of Migelian, whom she had guessed was in his forties, not in his two-hundreds. She gritted her teeth against the involuntary shudder that came with even thinking the senator's name.

"At the age of nineteen, the vial and chain we wear take on a life of their own and start to deposit trace amounts of Source into the wearer's skin."

Addy tried to picture that. She squinted at the chain around Tol's neck, but it just seemed like an ordinary metal chain. She didn't see any gold sparks or a glowing light that would indicate it was magic.

"Okay," Addy said, "so how does that effect how old someone looks?"

Tol was staring longingly in the direction of the shower, but she couldn't help herself. Now that she accepted Tol's story, she wanted to know everything. It was mostly because she thought any detail, no matter how small, might be important in helping her to rescue Livy. But she was also just plain curious.

Addy had thought her world was small before, and now she was learning about a whole other planet. It blew her mind. It was also awesome in a way she couldn't begin to wrap her head around.

"It's an imprecise magic," Tol said. "Not even the scholars really understand it. All we know is that everyone's body reacts to the Source differently, and so the ageing process varies for all of us depending on how our own chemistry is affected by the Source. At some point, we stop ageing…assuming we have access to Source. It's why some of us look young and others old, and it's impossible to tell our real age just by looking at us."

Addy shook her head, trying to make sense of it all.

"Once someone loses their connection to the Source, they revert back to their true age," Tol said.

They both turned back to the TV. Reporters were shouting questions at Senator Michaels, most of them asking for updates on his health. The senator didn't comment as his bodyguards escorted him inside the house.

Addy knew she should feel bad. She knew Tol did what he did to that man because of what had been done to her. All things considered, what the senator did to her wasn't *that* bad. Still, just the memory of it made her cringe. She'd had no control over herself or her thoughts. She would have done anything the senator told her without a second thought, and that was terrifying.

"I'll get dinner," Addy said as Tol moved to the bathroom.

He stopped and turned to her. "You can bet the Forsaken are scouring the city for us. You're not leaving this room without me."

"Well, the minibar leaves something to be desired," she said. "So, unless you want to split a fun-sized bag of M&M's for dinner, I'm going out."

Tol opened his mouth to argue.

"I have a hoodie," she said. "And I'll find somewhere nearby. No one's going to see me."

Tol seemed like he was going to argue, but with a distasteful look in the M&Ms' direction, he relented. "Don't talk to anyone, don't linger, and for gods' sake don't try to make any calls."

"Yesssir." Addy saluted, and then, just because she knew it would annoy him, said, "I mean, yes, your Royal Highness." She dropped into what she thought was an excellent imitation of a curtsy.

The look he gave her was totally worth it.

"You know, you could have just made them forget they had seen us," Addy complained.

"I would have," Tol retorted, "but they kept throwing pointy things at me, and I guess I lost my focus."

Addy had another reply on the tip of her tongue, but Tol slammed the bathroom door before she could get it out. Chuckling to herself, she tucked her hair into her hoodie and left the room.

As it turned out, she really didn't have to go far for food. There was a pizza delivery guy in the lobby with a stack of pizza boxes. He was arguing with the woman at the concierge desk, and Addy came to understand that there had been some kind of mix-up. A guest had ordered ten pizzas and then claimed to have only ordered two. The concierge woman was shrugging and apologizing, and saying there was nothing she could do.

Addy went up to the delivery guy and tapped him on the shoulder. "I'll buy a couple of those pizzas off you," she said.

The delivery guy sniffed. "I have eight I need to get rid of."

"Well, I can't help you with that," Addy replied, "but I can take two." She narrowed her eyes. "Depending on the toppings, of course."

It was a short negotiation.

When they parted ways, Addy had three pizza boxes. The delivery guy had given her the third pizza half off, and her mother's mantra of *never buy something without a discount* had her shelling out the cash, even though she had no idea what she and Tol would do with three large pizzas.

Addy had taken it as some kind of good omen that the delivery guy had two pepperoni-and-mushroom pizzas—her favorite. She got both of those, and one that was just plain cheese, because she didn't know what kind of pizza British people ate.

She brought the boxes back up to the room and let herself in.

Tol was leaning over his bag in nothing but a towel. Addy froze as he whipped around and gave her a deer-in-the-headlights look.

The first thing Addy noticed was how…good he looked. Droplets of water glistened on his chest, which was bare except for the glass vial that always hung from his neck. He didn't have cut abs like the guys in Stacy's magazines, but his stomach would still have earned him a spot on her sister's ceiling.

The second thing Addy noticed was that Tol wasn't wearing his metal arm. Tol seemed to realize it at the same moment she did. He shifted his body, but not before she saw that everything below his left shoulder was gone. His prosthetic arm lay on the bed like a little corpse, with its straps and buckles hanging loose like splayed limbs. Addy saw the arm wasn't metal like she had thought. Instead, it was some kind of hard plastic.

As he snatched up the arm along with a bundle of clothes, their eyes met. Addy saw shame on Tol's face.

"I thought you'd be out longer," he muttered as he moved to the bathroom. He kept his body turned so his missing left arm was hidden.

She wanted to tell him there was nothing to be embarrassed about, but he shut the bathroom door before she could get out a word. Flustered, Addy started setting out the pizza boxes on the desk just for something to do. She switched off the TV, having had enough of the looping news footage of the senator's unexpected retirement.

Tol came out of the bathroom and sat on the edge of the bed. He was wearing dark jeans and a gray polo that clung to him in all the right places. He smelled amazing.

"Pizza?" he asked.

Addy opened up the boxes. "Pepperoni-and-mushroom, and cheese. Take your pick."

Addy thought it indicated something positive about Tol's character that he had good taste in pizza. They both went straight for the pepperoni-and-mushroom.

They sat cross-legged on the bed, a slice of pizza in hand. Addy folded her slice in half and took a huge bite, surprised to find she was ravenous.

There was one can of coke in the mini fridge, which they shared, even though it would probably cost ten dollars. They were on their third slices when Addy got up the nerve to ask about Tol's arm.

"So." She cleared her throat. "Have you always had—" She broke off, realizing it was probably insensitive to ask how someone lost their limb.

Tol followed the direction of her gaze to his arm, which was mostly covered by his long-sleeved shirt and angled away from her.

"I've had a prosthesis for most of my life," Tol said.

He didn't say anything more, so Addy didn't press him. She was still curious, though. She'd never met anyone with a prosthetic limb. She thought it was kind of badass.

"Do you always wear it, except for when you're in the shower?"

She felt her cheeks warm at the memory of Tol's bare torso.

"Usually not when I sleep," he replied. He got up to get another slice of pizza. He kept his face turned on the boxes like he couldn't decide which one he wanted.

"Usually?" Addy pressed.

"Well, when I sleep by myself."

"Oh." Now it was her turn to be embarrassed.

Tol came back to the bed. "What about you?" he asked.

"What about me?"

"Have you made love?"

She had just taken a sip of coke, and she started to cough. It took all of her concentration to keep the soda from coming back out through her nose. Tol waited, an amused look on his face, while she gasped and thumped her chest.

The sound of those two words, coming from his lips, replayed in her head. A fire raced up her neck.

"That's none of your business," she huffed.

"I'm sorry." Tol shrugged, an infuriating smile tugging at the corner of his mouth. "I thought we were asking each other personal questions."

"Not *that* personal."

"It's nothing to be embarrassed about," Tol said.

"Neither is your arm." She hadn't meant to say the words, but she was inexplicably flustered, and they just sort of came out.

Tol gave her a surprised look.

Addy stood up. "Time to sleep?"

Tol nodded. She was gratified to see his smirk had disappeared.

She took the mass of pillows piled at the head of the bed and lined up all but two of them down the center of the bed.

"What are you doing?" Tol asked, eyebrows raised.

"I'm not watching you sleep squished in that chair for a second night," she said without looking up from her arrangement of the pillows. "You stay on your side, and I'll stay on mine." She gave him a glare, making it clear what would happen if he crossed the pillows.

"You're not doing this out of pity, are you?" he asked, a suspicious look in his dark eyes.

"Pity? Pity for what?"

Tol gave her a casual shrug that didn't fool her. "Because I'm crippled."

Addy scoffed. "I'm doing it because I don't want you to bruise your royal backside and be useless tomorrow."

Tol gave her a penetrating look that she had to force herself to hold.

"You sure?" he asked, his serious gaze boring into hers.

"Just respect the pillows," she said, climbing under the covers still fully dressed.

Addy didn't believe in an afterlife, but if there was such a thing as ghosts, her mom would be blowing gusts of cold air on her right now.

A strange boy in your bed, Adelyne? she would have asked, that disappointed look on her face. *Not until you're married, thank you very much.*

Addy knew she should feel more discomfort about being so close to a boy she'd known for mere days. On the other hand, if Tol had wanted to harm her, he'd already had plenty of opportunities to do so. She'd lost track of how many times they'd each saved each other's lives since they met. Addy figured there had to be some kind of *saving each other's lives* clause in the sleeping proximity rule.

It wasn't just them saving each other's lives, either, Addy realized. She trusted Tol.

"Don't worry," Tol said, getting under the covers on the other side of the bed. "I won't touch you until you want me to." He gave her a cocky grin.

"*Until?*"

162

"I'm a prince with an English accent. You won't be able to hold out forever."

His words were full of arrogance, but Addy thought she saw a sadness in his dark eyes that kept her sarcastic reply at bay.

"What exactly are you the prince *of*?" Addy asked.

"Vitaquias, the world where my people are from."

"So, that makes your parents…."

"The king and queen."

Addy grinned. "Do you live in a castle, Your Highness?"

Tol raised an eyebrow. "We had a castle on Vitaquias. I'm told it was rather nice. But in the mortal world a castle would be too conspicuous, so we have a manor where the most important scholars and my family live."

Addy didn't have a comeback for that, so she stayed quiet as she tried to picture a castle in another world.

Tol lay down on his back and sighed. "Do you always sleep sitting up?" he asked when Addy made no move to lie down.

"Not usually," she replied. She certainly wasn't going to tell him that, as exhausted as she was, she was afraid she'd have the dream as soon as she fell asleep.

Addy searched for a change in subject before she'd have to admit what she was thinking.

"Is it uncomfortable to wear that arm?" she asked.

"Yeah." After a pause, Tol said, "My shoulder always hurts, especially when I'm tired or stressed."

This admission seemed to cost him. His cheeks were dark with embarrassment.

"So, why not take it off, at least while you're sleeping?"

Tol turned to face her. "Because, it would be like standing naked in front of you while you were fully clothed."

Addy hadn't expected that response. Words died on her tongue.

Tol gave a soft laugh at her speechlessness.

"Well, you should stop being an idiot and take it off if it hurts," she said when she finally managed to get the word *naked* in relation to Tol out of her mind. "I'll shut off the light if it makes you feel better."

Tol propped himself up on his elbow. "I'll make you a deal. I'll take it off, if you tell me about that nightmare you had on the plane."

Addy was dumbstruck. She considered lying, trying to brush it off again. But he had been honest about his arm. So, she told him the truth.

"I've had it since I was a little kid," she admitted. "I feel like I'm drowning and can't breathe. No matter how much I kick or try to swim, I can't reach the surface. The water just keeps coming and coming. It fills up my lungs and veins and even my eyes. It's…terrifying." And then, more quietly, "Livy was always there to wake me up."

Even she heard the longing in her voice at the mention of her sister.

"We'll get her back," Tol said.

Addy knew he was just trying to make her feel better, but the words still infused her with a warm glow.

Tol sat up. She expected him to go turn off the light, but instead, he pulled off his shirt.

Addy's breath stuck in her throat. His beautiful chest was crisscrossed with straps. With his right hand, he unbuckled the clasp at his sternum. One by one, the straps fell away.

There was something strangely intimate about watching him, which had nothing to do with the fact that he was now shirtless. *Well, maybe it had a little to do with him being shirtless.*

Tol pulled the prosthetic arm away from his body and let it drop to the floor. It hit the carpet with a dull *thunk*. Then, he got up and turned off the light. They both lay quietly in the dark for a while. Addy didn't know what was keeping Tol from sleep, but her heart was racing.

The only boy she'd ever shared a bed with was Fred, and Fred didn't count. Their parents had insisted on separate bedrooms for propriety's sake when they reached their teenage years, but that didn't stop them from falling asleep on the couch, tangled in Mrs. Brown's old afghans, at the end of one of their movie binge sessions.

Being in a bed with Tol felt nothing like that. Even on opposite ends of a huge bed and separated by a line of pillows, she was intensely aware of him. He was very quiet, and yet she felt his smallest of movements. His masculine, spicy smell just barely reached her, and she had to stop herself from scooting closer.

"Tol?" she asked.

"Yeah?"

"You said earlier everyone is afraid of something." She paused. "What are you afraid of?"

Tol was quiet for so long Addy thought he was either asleep or ignoring her. But then, he started to speak.

"My parents are the reason why our world was ruined."

Addy sucked in a breath.

Tol continued, "But that isn't the secret. Everyone knows the king and queen let the Chosen draw too much Source, which damaged our world beyond repair. Because of what happened on Vitaquias, the Magnantius line is being threatened by other Chosen who want to usurp the monarchy. I'm my people's only hope, and I'm the reason why my parents haven't already been overthrown. Everyone thinks I'll be the king to return our world to its former glory."

"So, what's the secret part?" Addy asked.

There was another long silence. Addy could tell Tol was trying to decide whether or not to tell her. She realized she wanted him to…more than she'd ever admit out loud.

"I've wanted to be king my whole life," Tol said. "It's all I've ever wanted. But I'm afraid."

"You don't want that much responsibility?" Addy guessed.

"I do want it, more than anything, and that's the problem."

The bed shifted as they both turned to face each other. Tol's eyes were just pinpricks in the dark. Addy couldn't see the expression on his face, but the black velvet of his voice deepened to something rougher.

"I'm afraid I'll fail my people. I'm afraid I won't be able to stop them from pushing limitations that aren't meant to be pushed. My parents are brilliant people, and they aren't prone to impulses. It was their ambition, their desire for true greatness for all our people, that made them drain the Source.

"I'm afraid if we ever make it back there, I won't be able to stop my people from doing the same thing again."

Addy opened her mouth and then closed it. It wasn't at all what she'd expected Tol to say, and she found she didn't know how to respond.

Tol continued, "Most of my people feel the same drive to be more than they should be. I'm afraid, when it comes down to it, my people will fall to ruin while all I can do is stand by and watch." Tol gave a soft laugh. "I've never admitted that out loud before."

Addy felt strangely honored.

"You seem like someone people listen to, even without your Influence," she said. "Maybe you'll be a better ruler than your parents."

Tol didn't say anything for a few minutes, and they just lay in silence. "What about you?" he asked. "Anything besides drowning keep you up at night?"

"Besides not being the daughter and sister my family wanted me to be, and hating the idea of a future I couldn't control?" she let out a short laugh, which died on her tongue.

And taking all of them for granted…and being too stupid to see my parents were afraid for all our lives…and for not being there when my family needed me….

"I get angry sometimes," she whispered.

Addy didn't know where the words came from. She hadn't even been aware the thought was in her head until the words had already spilled out.

"Everyone gets angry," Tol said. "There's nothing bad about that."

"It's more than that." Now that she had started, Addy wanted to try to understand the feeling that had been growing inside her since the night she killed the thief. "I never got in a fight until a few days ago, but it felt…good. And when I killed that man, I didn't feel bad about it."

"You were protecting your family," Tol said. "You shouldn't feel bad for protecting the ones you love."

Addy remembered the fear in the thief's eyes, and his promise to leave her family alone if only she let him live. She remembered driving the garden shears into his chest over and over again.

Killing him had been about more than protecting her family.

Her parents had always referred to the twins as Sweet Livy and Firecracker Addy. She had never given much thought to her temper before that night. Now, she thought about it a lot.

"Tol?"

"Yeah."

Addy bit her lip. She hadn't asked this question because she had feared the answer, but she had to know. "That thief I killed," she began. "Do you think if I hadn't killed him, the rest of those people wouldn't have come after my family?"

"From what you said, that thief sounds like he was just a mortal," Tol replied.

"But doesn't it seem like too much of a coincidence? I mean, our house had never gotten broken into before, and then three days after, the Forsaken came."

Tol didn't answer right away. "I don't know exactly how it works, but my guess is that when the thief threatened your life, you accessed the Celestial's powers. That's what connected you to me." He paused. "Maybe the Forsaken had some way of sensing you, too, although I doubt it."

Addy thought there might be more to it than what Tol was telling her, but she was just relieved not to have any more blame added onto the load her conscience was already carrying.

"Get some rest, Adelyne," Tol said, his voice deepening with sleepiness.

"Addy," she said.

"What?"

"Call me Addy."

"Addy." He said it like he was savoring her name.

She liked the way it sounded in his black velvet voice.

"Night, Tol."

"Sweet dreams, Addy."

✳ ✳ ✳

Addy woke up at some point in the night. She couldn't see the clock on the bedside table, but she guessed it was two or three o'clock in the morning. She had been in the midst of a blissfully dreamless sleep.

She blinked the darkness from her eyes and saw that her left hand was resting on top of the row of pillows. She had fallen asleep on the edge of her side of the bed, but while she slept, she had shifted so her body was flush with the pillow barrier. She saw the dark outline of Tol, in a symmetrical position to her. His right hand was on the pillows, his curled fingers a hair's breadth from hers. Their bodies were facing each other, separated only by the pillows. They were close enough that Addy could feel his warmth through the barrier.

Addy had no desire to move over and put more space between them. She liked being close to him. She didn't close the millimeters-wide gap between their fingers, but she liked knowing that she could. With that thought, she fell back into her dreamless sleep.

CHAPTER 20

TOL

Tol woke to find Adelyne—Addy—asleep next to him, her hair splayed across her pillow like a sunrise.

Addy.

It seemed impossible those two little syllables, so small and insignificant on their own, combined in a way that evoked a flood of feelings in him. He couldn't imagine how, only a few days ago, he'd thought she was just another pretty girl. She wasn't just pretty...she was beautiful. She also smelled like a piña colada, but that was beside the point.

She was as full of complexity as only the Celestial's Fount could be.

Tol's feeling of protectiveness over Addy didn't surprise him. She was, after all, one half of his people's salvation. His feelings of tenderness toward her, of trust, did surprise him.

None of these emotions meant he was any more interested in the blood marriage than he had been before he knew her. He was as reluctant as ever to lose his freedom in exchange for her voice eternally in his head. Perversely, knowing he was starting to care for Addy made him even more loath to go through the blood marriage. Now, not only would he be dooming himself to an eternity of being bound in body and spirit, he would be condemning someone he actually cared for to the same fate. She would hate him, and whatever might have grown between them under different circumstances would turn cold with resentment.

Tol thought Addy might be the fiercest person he'd ever met. She loved her family deeply, and she hated their killers with the same passion. It was why he'd known the moment he stepped back into Migelian's office that her empty expression could only mean she was under Influence.

He still felt a stab of guilt every time he remembered her sitting on the senator's lap, staying perfectly still while Migelian raised his knife to her skin. The memory made Tol's insides roil. He should have guessed that since the Fount wasn't yet able to Influence, she could in turn be Influenced. But there was no precedent for a mortal with her powers, and the scholars hadn't had any prior cases on which to base their theories.

Tol didn't feel any pity for what he'd done to Migelian. Killing one of his own subjects for the crime of defiling the Fount's mind was only natural. His parents or any member of the royal court would have done the same in his position. But his actions in the Forsakens' house…telling Addy to leave without him…that was unforgiveable.

He had told Addy to go. He hadn't given a thought to how, if he died, the rest of his people were doomed. All he had thought about was how he couldn't stand for the Forsaken to take her away the same way they had her sister.

He didn't know he could care so much about someone he'd known for less than a week, but impossibly, he did. If his parents, or Gran, or any of the Chosen knew what he'd risked, all for the sake of gaining intelligence on a mortal of no importance to anyone except Addy….

And they'd be right to react that way. How stupid was he, to risk everything for the sake of rescuing one mortal?

But Addy hadn't listened to him. She'd come back. She'd fought her way through eight Forsaken to drag him out of that place.

Tol could sense Addy's feelings toward him shifting from resentment to something like his own. He could lie to her, convince her they needed to go back to the manor for supplies, and then try to renegotiate with her.

Even as the possibility entered his mind, Tol knew he would never do it. He found that the more he saw her as Addy, a fearless mortal who had saved his life more times than he cared to remember, and not just *the Fount*, the more he wanted to help her. He knew now that she shared his desperation to escape a life that had been pre-determined. He also had a good idea of what it would do to her when she found out what she'd agreed to out of desperation to save her sister. If there was anything he could do to soften that blow, no matter the risk to himself, he wanted to do it.

Tol got out of bed and found his arm where it had fallen to the floor. He couldn't believe he'd taken it off in front of her, like some kind of deformed stripper.

When he asked Addy to tell him about her dream, he'd seen the stubborn expression on her face and had assumed she wouldn't take his bait. When she surprised him, he figured he'd make a spectacle of himself and prove this girl was exactly what he had first suspected her to be: the same as every mortal girl he'd ever known.

And yet, as he'd watched her face for the disgust he expected at the sight of his missing arm, he'd seen only curiosity.

His arm hadn't been all he'd revealed to Addy last night. He wasn't sure if it was the exhaustion, the dark, or something about lying in the same bed that made them both share their secrets. Tol had never spoken out loud about his fear that he wouldn't be a strong enough king to temper his people's ambition. He hadn't told anyone that he was afraid he would witness another cycle of destruction, this one under his own reign.

Addy had shared things, too. For someone as strong as she was, admitting to having an irrational fear couldn't have been easy. In a way, it made Tol feel closer to her than many people he'd known his entire life.

Tol wanted to let Addy sleep longer, but he knew she'd want to get going. Besides, it was only a matter of time before the Forsaken tracked them to this hotel. He had no intentions of still being here when they showed up.

After a breakfast of cold pizza, they packed their bags and quietly exited the hotel. They got in a cab, since Tol was willing to bet there were Forsaken at every metro stop in the city, and headed straight for the airport.

Luckily, Washington Dulles Airport was in the throes of morning flights, and they lost themselves in the crowd of passengers. Tol broke his own people's laws for the second time that week when he Influenced the American Airlines woman behind the counter into giving them two first class tickets for free. Addy didn't have enough cash left to cover even the economy seats, and Tol figured if he was going to break his people's law, they may as well be comfortable on the multiple flights that would eventually bring them to the island of Baltra.

"Why couldn't they have just taken your sister to Florida?" Tol muttered as the placid woman handed over their tickets.

"Why can't we take your plane?" grumbled Addy.

"Baltra is too far for a small plane," Tol began, but Addy wasn't listening to him. Someone in the mass of people had caught her attention.

"Forsaken?" he asked, turning to look.

Addy didn't answer. She started to run away from the ticket counter.

"Addy? Addy!" Tol followed her, weaving through people when he could avoid them, knocking into them when he couldn't. When he finally caught up to her, it wasn't to find her locked in battle with one of the barbarians. Tol groaned.

Farmer Fred, as he had taken to calling the bloke, was there, in the airport. And his arms were wrapped around Addy.

A lightning bolt of irritation went through Tol. He had to force himself to stand still to keep from *making* the farmer remove his hands. But Addy was holding him, too. It drove an unpleasant, unfamiliar feeling through Tol that couldn't be jealousy. Tol wasn't the jealous type.

"What are you doing here?" Addy asked Fred.

Farmer Fred still had his pudgy hands on her waist, and Tol had to clench his fist to keep from doing or saying anything inappropriate.

"Lookin' for you, obviously." He gripped Addy's hands in his meaty ones as he looked up at her.

It was petty, but it gratified Tol to see how he had to reach up on his toes to look Addy in the eye.

"How did you know we were here?" Addy asked.

Tol saw the farmer reach into the pocket of his overalls and clutch something. When he removed his hand, though, it was empty.

"I ain't just an ignorant hick," he said. "And I haven't just been sittin' around since you disappeared, neither."

"I never thought—"

"Are you okay? What are you doin' with *him*?"

Tol gave Farmer Fred a cool look. It was the look he'd seen Nira give Erikir, like he simply wasn't worth the effort it would take to frown. It had the desired effect.

Farmer Fred's face turned scarlet. Spit actually flew from his mouth when he said to Addy, "Who is this guy?!" he looked at Tol. "Have we met?" the expression on the farmer's face was uncertain, like he recognized Tol but couldn't remember where they'd met before.

"I—" Addy looked at Tol, who shook his head.

Don't tell him a damn thing, he told her with his eyes.

"I met him at a Cornell event," Addy told Fred.

"Don't lie to me." He turned on Tol. "Who are you? And what the hell are you doin' with my best friend?"

Tol didn't spare him another glance. "Addy, we'd better get going. We don't want to miss our flight."

"You ain't goin' nowhere with him!" Fred spluttered.

Tol was honestly worried for Addy's sake. She was right in the line of fire for Fred's spit.

"Fred, listen," Addy tried, but the poor lad was beside himself.

"I may not be goin' to college, but I ain't an idiot. Tell me what's goin' on with you."

Tol made an exaggerated show of looking at his watch. "Should I just Influence him and be done with it?" he asked Addy.

"I'll kill you if you come near either of us," Farmer Fred growled.

Tol gave him a pleasant smile. "You're welcome to try."

"No." Addy gave Tol a pleading look. "Promise you'll never do that to Fred again." She shuddered, and Tol knew she was thinking about her own experience under Influence. It transformed his anger into guilt.

"I need to tell Fred what's going on," she said.

"Absolutely not." Tol was horrified. "He's a mortal. It's against every law we have."

"I already know, you big idiot," Farmer Fred said.

Tol stepped forward, feeling his golden Haze flare before he even thought about what he was doing.

"Tol, don't."

Her touch on his arm made him go still, but it did nothing to cool his anger.

"What do you know?" Tol demanded. "And how exactly did you find us here?"

Farmer Fred's hand went to his pocket again. When he spoke, it was only to Addy. "Your Aunt Meredith stayed with Dad and me for a few days. She said—"

Something behind Addy drew Tol's attention. He sucked in a breath. There was the white-blonde hair, gray eyes, and height that outmatched all of the surrounding mortals and made it impossible for the Forsaken to hide.

"Addy."

She followed the direction of his gaze and, seeing what he saw, swore.

"We have to go. Now." Tol took her hand and pulled her toward the security line.

Fred followed.

"I'm comin' with you," he was saying to Addy.

Tol kept his attention on the Forsaken, who were stepping through the sliding glass doors, their eyes scanning the crowd. Tol hunched his shoulders, indicating for Addy to do the same.

"Fred, I'm so sorry," Addy was saying. "I swear, I'll tell you everything as soon as I can."

"Wait, Ads—"

Tol saw the exact moment the Forsaken spotted them.

"Run!"

They bolted through the crowd.

They had a lead on the Forsaken, but their enemy had the benefit of police uniforms and weapons. He and Addy were just civilians. Tol turned to Addy, whose Haze had flared up alongside his own.

"No," Addy gasped as Tol pulled her through the people already on line at security, who were shouting protests at them. "Fred. He'll—"

"Be fine as soon as we're gone," Tol replied. "It's us they're after."

"Where are you going?" Fred shouted at them.

Tol caught the TSA officer's gaze, and the man waved them right through.

"To get Livy," Addy called back. "I'll tell you everything...."

The Forsaken were pushing their way through the crowd. They were waving batons and shouting. They were gaining on Tol and Addy fast.

Fred disappeared in the crowd as the two of them sprinted through the terminal.

"Did we lose them?" Tol managed, looking around.

"Tol!" Addy grabbed his hand and yanked him in the opposite direction. He looked back in time to see three Forsaken separate to flank them. They ran.

One of the Forsaken tackled Tol from behind. They collapsed on the carpeted floor in a tangle of limbs. There wasn't a centimeter of the huge woman's skin that wasn't covered by her uniform, and she kept her eyes squeezed shut as she pinned him.

As quickly as her weight had settled on his chest, it was gone.

Addy, bear-hugging the Forsaken from behind, had lifted her all the way off the ground and thrown her into a crowd of onlookers.

"Come on!" she shouted.

They clasped hands and continued their mad dash for the plane.

When they got to the gate, their flight had just started to board. Tol shoved Addy onto the gangway ahead of him. He didn't even bother with tickets. He put his hand on the startled attendant's cheek and said, "Close the doors behind us and don't let anyone else on the plane."

He didn't wait for her assent before running after Addy.

The doors shut just behind him. He hadn't taken two steps when he heard angry voices and pounding on the other side of the door. He looked back once to see the Forsaken beating the door with their fists. Tol was too relieved to feel victorious.

He used the last of his Influence to tell the pilot to ignore air traffic control, take off, and re-route them from Panama City to San Salvador. There would be some confused passengers, but at least the Forsaken wouldn't be able to force their plane to land or be waiting for them in the city where they were expected to arrive. With that done, Tol collapsed into his seat.

CHAPTER 21

ADDY

The plane was relatively empty, courtesy of Tol shutting the doors to the jet bridge behind them. She felt bad for all those people who had missed their flight, in addition to the ones on the plane who didn't yet realize they were now bound for a different city. She felt even worse for leaving Fred behind. But as the plane lifted off the runway, the only emotion she really felt was an overwhelming sense of relief.

The Forsaken hadn't been able to stop them. They were now one step closer to Livy.

As she watched the city fall away below them, Addy felt like she could breathe again. But as soon as she started to relax, her conversation with Fred made her sit back up. He said he knew something. Aunt Meredith had come to New York, and she had told him…what? What did she know about all of this madness?

And how had Fred managed to find her in Dulles Airport? Addy was desperate to know, and now, she wouldn't.

She had no idea how those murderers had tracked them to the airport, but she wouldn't risk trying to call Fred or Aunt Meredith once she landed. She didn't want those barbarians to think either of them had anything to do with her.

The golden glow that seemed to conveniently appear around her whenever she needed extra strength had worn off, and that empty feeling she was growing accustomed to had returned. Her dark thoughts spiraled as exhaustion warred with her anxiety and sense of loss.

It was an hour into the flight before the maelstrom of thoughts in her head quieted enough for her to take in her surroundings. It certainly wasn't as nice as Tol's plane, but it was still awesome. To sit in a cushy chair and *fly* through the air was a novelty Addy didn't think she'd ever get used to.

She looked at Tol, who was passed out next to her. His golden glow had dimmed, and now he just looked drawn. She was fighting exhaustion herself, but she'd only had to yank that woman off Tol. He'd had to Influence about a dozen people to get them off the ground without a host of Forsaken on the plane with them.

She marveled at how easily these words—Source, Forsaken, Influence— had become a part of her vocabulary…a part of her life. A week ago, her conversations had been about corn, Cornell, and purple eyeliner.

Tol was slumped against the window. His prosthetic arm lay across the armrest between them. His shirt sleeve had come up enough to expose the wrist joint. Curious, she reached out to feel it. The material was cool to the touch. It didn't seem like metal or plastic, but something both hard and light.

"It's carbon-fiber."

Addy snatched her hand away from Tol's prosthesis, only to realize he'd been watching her.

"I'm sorry," she began, but he waved away her apology.

"It doesn't freak you out?"

She shook her head. Feeling a little shy, but too curious to stop, she brushed her fingers over the smooth surface of the prosthesis.

"Can you feel this?" she asked.

He shook his head. "There are electrodes that let my brain think it's controlling a real arm." He wiggled the prosthetic fingers. "But I can't feel anything with it."

He looked a little wistful as he watched her hand, which was still exploring the plating at his wrist joint.

"Were you born like this?" she asked. "Without your arm, I mean," she added quickly.

"No." He was watching her hand, which was still resting on his prosthetic one. She had no desire to move it, and he didn't seem to want her to, either.

Tol said, "I was a baby when our world started to burn. My parents were carrying me into the portal, but the gods didn't want to let me go." A frustrated look passed over his face, like he didn't quite know how to explain. "All of my people have a certain amount of innate connection to the Source. The stronger our connection, the stronger our abilities are when we take Source.

"When my parents took me out of Vitaquias, my arm got ripped away as the gods fought to keep me."

Addy shuddered at the thought.

"Do you remember?" she asked.

"All I remember is a pain in my shoulder that felt like fire."

"So," Addy bit her lip, "do all of your people have something…missing?"

"Just me." Tol gave her a rueful smile.

"Why?" Addy wrinkled her brow. That didn't seem fair.

"Because I'm the most powerful of my people, and the gods didn't want to let me go."

If he'd said it differently she would have scoffed, but there wasn't a hint of pride or arrogance in his words. He'd said them like it was just fact.

"I guess it's hard for you to believe," he said.

"Not so hard," Addy replied. She was thinking about the way he could just look at someone and make them do anything he said. She wrapped her arms around herself, remembering what it had been like to be so powerless under someone else's gaze.

"It is a little ironic," Tol said.

"What is?"

"To talk about my strength when I have only one arm, and you've done all the real fighting."

Addy brightened. "I have done all the real fighting, haven't I?"

Tol squinted at her. "I believe the correct response is some kind of compliment to sooth my fragile male ego."

Addy laughed. "You're right." She put on her most serious face and cleared her throat. "Prince Tolumus, you are the strongest, smartest, bravest, sexiest man in the whole world."

"Just in this world?" Tol nudged her with his shoulder.

"I can't speak for other worlds," she said with a shrug. "I'm sure there's someone better *somewhere* out there."

"Well." Tol acted affronted. "I'll just have to bring you to the other worlds and prove there isn't."

Addy tried to ignore the little thrill that went through her at the thought of exploring other worlds with Tol. She lifted his hand to examine the intricate plating of the fingers.

"Gerth, my best mate, is always trying to convince me to install darts and tasers in the fingers," Tol said.

"It's a good idea," Addy replied. "The most high-tech thing my family owns is a computer that looks like it's from the early 2000s. It takes about six weeks to boot up, and then we all fight about who gets to use it, and so our parents—"

Addy was talking like she'd go home and her family would play out the very scenario she was describing. But they wouldn't, because her family was decomposing in an unmarked grave.

The realization that she'd never bicker with her sisters again hit her with a force that took her breath away.

Tol, who had been watching her, saw the change come over her face. He covered her hand with his right one. The warmth of his skin said more than any words.

"We're going to find Olivia, okay?" he said, squeezing her hand.

She nodded, managing a small smile. "Okay."

CHAPTER 22

TOL

Tol had told Addy he was the most powerful of his people. It was true. Even though the full extent of his abilities had never been tested, there was no debating Tol's Haze. His people's connection to the Source, and thus their abilities, was dampened in the mortal world. He could only guess at what he might be able to do with Influence on Vitaquias. Now, for the first time, it seemed there was a chance he would find out.

When he told Addy, he'd expected her to take one look at his arm and say *powerful?* in the derisive way she had spoken to him when they first met.

For his own part, Tol had never felt anything but power*less*. Even the woman he would be bound to for eternity had been chosen for him by someone else. It was that feeling of powerlessness that woke him in the middle of the night, his own version of Addy's drowning nightmare.

During the three flights and two days of travel it took to get to the Galapagos, Tol planned. He knew there had been a military base on Baltra during World War II. It was just the kind of remote location the Forsaken would use for a hideout. The captain had said one of the islands near Baltra, though, which meant they'd have to search them one by one. Tol had used their most recent layover to learn as much as he could about the Galapagos islands. It turned out there were a lot of them.

With every drop of Source Tol expended, his anxiety rose. The reserves his parents kept under constant guard were running low, and every bit needed to be conserved to fight Forsaken who attacked them and keep their elders alive. And here he was, using more Source in one week than he had in months. He knew what Gerth and his parents would say if they knew what Tol was doing now.

And yet, in spite of all of the counter-arguments he knew could be made, Tol didn't regret his choices.

He tried not to think about anything beyond the next few days. Tol had no idea what they would find when they got to Baltra. Maybe they'd get lucky enough to find a lone high-ranking official they could interrogate about where the Forsaken were hiding Addy's sister.

Right. And mortal pigs could fly.

Gerth was going to kill him if the Forsaken didn't get to him first. At this rate, he'd never be able to keep his promise to be back in two weeks. Even if everything went according to his plans, which, so far, it hadn't, it would be closer to a month before they returned to the manor.

Addy, who had been asleep for most of their last flight, stretched and opened her eyes.

"Are we there yet?" she complained.

As if on cue, the plane jolted as it hit the runway.

"Oh my God," she gasped.

Tol looked at her, but her attention was focused on the view outside the window. Her pale face had gone white as a ghost. Addy was staring at the ocean just past the runway.

"You do know Baltra is an island, right?" Tol asked.

"Yes."

Tol had thought Addy's fear of drowning had been confined to her nightmares, or maybe if she was actually swimming...not something she would dread by the light of day. He realized now how wrong he'd been.

The other passengers had started to de-plane, but Addy stayed rigid in her seat.

"Everything all right, you two?" the flight attendant asked when they were the only ones still on the plane.

"Just give us a minute," Tol told her.

He turned to Addy, trying to think of what he could say to make her feel better. "You won't have to set foot in the water. We're just going to get out, interrogate some Forsaken, and hop back on the plane."

Addy swallowed. "Just like that?"

He offered her his hand. "Just like that."

* * *

When they were inside the airport, away from the view of the water, Addy calmed down. She was still holding his hand, and her fingers were ice cold even though the air was balmy. Tol rubbed the pad of his thumb over her hand, trying to warm it.

"They're not here," Addy said, looking around like she would simply be able to spot the Forsaken if they were.

"They could be," Tol said.

"I don't think so. I can't feel them."

Tol turned to look at her. "What do you mean, you can't feel them?"

Addy lifted a shoulder. "I don't know how to explain it, but I sensed their presence before we went into that townhouse, and then I felt them again at Dulles Airport. I don't feel them here."

"Well, I prefer to do things based on fact rather than feelings," Tol said. "So, let's find out for sure."

"They're not here," Addy repeated, stubborn.

After searching the airport, Tol was willing to concede Addy had made a lucky guess.

"I told you," she said.

"They could still be somewhere else on the island," Tol said, frustrated by Addy's insistence the Forsaken weren't on Baltra.

There was just no way she could know that. In spite of what the Forsaken captain had told them, Tol wasn't going to leave the island half-searched.

They got on a bus full of tourists that was headed for the old U.S. Air Force base. The road ran parallel to the coast, and Addy actually shuddered when she looked out at the ocean. Tol took the seat next to the window. It didn't seem to help much. Addy sat with her fists clenched and her face drained of color.

"Close your eyes," he said in her ear. "Pretend we're somewhere else."

She did, and Tol was gratified to see her relax just a bit.

The tour bus ground to a halt.

"Bus departs in half an hour," the heavyset woman at the front called out when they arrived.

"Stay here," Tol told Addy as he got up with the other camera-wielding tourists. "I'll check it out and come back for you either way."

Addy looked like she wanted to argue, but after glancing out the window at the sea shimmering around them, she nodded and squeezed her eyes shut again.

Tol was in the midst of scouting around some old ruins when a security guard came up to him.

"You can't be back here, sir," the man told Tol.

Tol looked at the man. He wasn't Forsaken, but he was military. Tol took a drop of Source and caught the man's eye.

* * *

"Well?" Addy asked when Tol got back on the bus.

"They're not here," he said.

"Told you—"

"But," Tol put up a finger. "They were."

"They were?" Addy stood up so fast she hit her head on the bus's ceiling. She didn't even seem to notice.

"They left the island by boat." Tol pulled her back down into her seat. "Two days ago."

"Where did they go? And who exactly are *they*?"

There was so much hope and fear in her eyes. It killed Tol that he couldn't tell her anything more than "must be one of the other islands around here, and some high-ranking Forsaken."

"What do we do now?" Addy asked.

This possibility had already occurred to Tol, and he had an answer ready. "We're going to have to search the islands one by one. I chartered a yacht—"

"A yacht?"

"That won't be a problem, will it?" Tol asked.

"Why can't we fly?" Her eyes were wide as she stole another glance at the ocean.

"There aren't airports," Tol said, trying to be patient.

It had been no small feat to charter a private yacht and crew that would serve their unique needs. He'd done what he could from the airport in San Salvador, but there was the matter of payment and other logistics he'd have to use Influence to solve when they got down to the docks.

He only now realized his irritation was because he had expected Addy to be impressed. He'd wanted to impress her. Tol tried not to dwell on what it meant that he cared so much what she thought.

"But like I said," Tol continued. "We'll have our own boat and crew. They'll take us right from one island to the next. We'll start nearest to this island and work our way out. They'll bring us to each island, we'll have a quick look around, and then we'll go on to the next one until we find someone who can tell us where your sister is."

Addy was breathing faster. Tol was concerned she was going to hyperventilate.

"Look, do you want to find Olivia or not?"

Those were the magic words. She swallowed, getting her fear under control with an enormous effort, and nodded.

"It's going to be fine," Tol said, as much to convince himself as Addy. He had no idea if they were going on a wild goose chase. All he could think about was the two weeks he'd promised Gerth slipping away. He'd called home and left a message with one of the servants, saying he was safe but would still be gone for another couple of weeks. Tol knew it wouldn't be enough to keep his family from being worried sick about him.

By the time they reached the docks, Addy was visibly shaking. She had taken on the most fearsome warriors without batting an eye. But now, standing on the dock with water on all sides, she seemed to be falling into a black hole of terror.

Tol pointed out their boat. It was a sleek, beautiful yacht that most mortals would kill to be on. Addy just shuddered. Tol was getting worried about her.

"Look," he began. "We don't have to—"

"There's no other choice," Addy said.

"I can take you back to England, and then my people can go search for her. You don't have to do this."

Tol saw the effort it took her to calm her breathing.

"It'll be fine," she said. "Let's go."

CHAPTER 23

TOL

The friendly captain, a man with a white beard and deep laugh lines around his eyes, was waiting to welcome them on board. The moment they set foot on the ship, they were surrounded by a staff of five. They were offered cool, lavender-scented washcloths and island punch in crystal glasses.

Addy's gaze took in the water surrounding them on all sides, and she collapsed.

Tol caught her, lowering her to the leather seat on the edge of the boat. The crew swarmed around them. They were crouching in front of Addy, asking her what was wrong, and patting her on the back.

"I can't breathe," she gasped. Her eyes were huge with fear.

Tol didn't know what to do.

"Give her some space," he snapped at a woman who was trying to dab at Addy's face with a washcloth.

Carefully, like she might break in her fragile state, he wrapped his arms around her.

Tol expected Addy to pull away or say something sarcastic, but she just shivered against him.

"Tol, they're drowning me."

Addy's panicked voice tore at him. He needed to do something.

"It's okay," he told her, rubbing her back with his good hand while he continued to hold her with his prosthetic arm. "I've got you."

Addy took a shallow breath, and he though he heard that rattle in her lungs again. She coughed, and it really did sound like her lungs were trying to expel water.

Was the mind powerful enough to do that? The Chosen neuroscientists would have known the answer, but Tol didn't. Maybe they were both going crazy.

"Here you are, darling. Right into the bucket."

Tol looked down to see one of the crew had put a bucket next to Addy, like she was going to throw up.

"She's not sea sick," Tol said. "She just…doesn't like the water."

He saw the woman's expression out of the corner of his eye, a *then what are you doing bringing her on a boat* look, which he chose to ignore.

"What can we do to help?" asked a woman in a skimpy uniform who was crouching beside them in her stilettos.

"Get her a blanket," Tol ordered.

One was brought on deck almost immediately. Tol took it from the overly-helpful woman. He wrapped it around Addy's shoulders and held her against him. She buried her face against his chest, and he could feel the wetness of her tears through his shirt.

Flustered by their proximity, which under other circumstances would have taken on a very different meaning, he asked the crew, "Are there any rooms without windows on this boat?"

Through a lot of frantic hand gestures and more questions about Addy's well-being, all of which he ignored, Tol came to understand that the ship was all windows. There were curtains, though.

"Draw them all," he told the crew. "I don't want her to feel like she's on a boat."

Tol looked at Addy. Her eyes were open, but she didn't seem aware of what was happening around her. She was still gasping for air. Tears were streaming down her cheeks. Tol brushed them away without thinking about what he was doing.

"Sir?" the captain, his face pinched with worry, kept his distance and spoke gently. "Do you want to push off?"

Tol released Addy enough to look at her. "What do you want to do?" he asked.

"I'll be fine." Her lips were bloodless, and her voice was hoarse.

"Addy—"

"Get going," she told the captain. Her voice wavered, but she glared like she was challenging any of them to defy her.

The captain gave Tol a questioning look, and Tol just nodded.

The boat's engines revved. Addy's shaking got worse.

"Let's get you inside," Tol said.

Addy couldn't stand without her legs giving out, so Tol scooped her up and carried her down the polished wood staircase below deck.

Tol was aware of the opulent lounge, with its overstuffed chairs, a bottle of champagne chilling next to the couch, and even a grand piano in one corner, but none of it made an impression. He put Addy down on the couch and adjusted the curtains to hide even a sliver of the view outside.

As the boat picked up speed, the staff on board reconvened around them. Tol tried politely telling them not to trouble themselves. When that didn't work, he ordered them to leave using an imperious voice he only ever resorted to with Erikir.

Tol watched through a slit in the curtain as they sped away from the island, checking to make sure they were headed in the right direction and that no one was following them. Then, he turned all his attention back to Addy.

He adjusted the blanket so it was wrapped around her. She was shaking. He could see her pulse fluttering at her throat and hear her teeth chattering. She looked so fragile, he almost didn't recognize her.

Tol realized he'd gotten used to thinking of her as fearless.

"What can I do?" he asked Addy, and he could hear the desperation in his own voice.

Addy seemed beyond words. She just continued to tremble under the blanket. Wanting nothing more than to offer her comfort, he sat on the edge of the couch next to her and gently shifted her head so it was propped against his leg. Carefully, he brushed her hair away from her tear-stained face.

Tol might have been imagining it, but it seemed like whenever he touched her, Addy seemed a little less frightened. He liked touching her. He liked the way her piña colada-scented hair felt between his fingers.

Gods, she was beautiful.

The moment the thought crossed his mind, he recoiled from it. Addy was half-dead with fear, and he was thinking about…that? What in the two hells was wrong with him?

"Do you want me to talk or just sit here?" he asked. When she didn't say anything, he added, "Or, I could leave you alone."

He hoped she didn't pick that last option, but he felt compelled to give it.

"Talk," she said, her voice so small he almost didn't hear her.

So, he did. He told her about Gerth, and warned Addy that she should never accept Gerth's challenge to play any game unless she fancied losing spectacularly. He told her about Gran and his parents, and even about the sour looks his cousin gave him whenever they were together.

He told her everything he knew about Vitaquias, which turned out to be quite a lot. By the time he felt her breathing even out in sleep, his voice had gone raspy from so much talking.

CHAPTER 24

ADDY

When Addy woke up, her head was in Tol's lap. She had a vague recollection of his voice in her ears and his spicy, masculine scent surrounding her, but the rest was vague. She should sit up, but she couldn't bring herself to move. Tol must be getting sick of playing the knight in shining armor to her damsel in distress routine.

Addy couldn't even imagine what he must think of her now. Probably something like *Mortal girl with irrational terror of water…avoid at all costs*. Or maybe just *Batshit crazy*.

"How are you feeling?" Tol asked.

"Better." Her voice sounded pathetically weak to her own ears. She cleared her throat. "Thanks."

"Approaching Isla Floreana," the captain's voice announced over the speaker.

"I can go on shore and check it out," Tol offered, but Addy was already on her feet.

The room spun. Tol put a hand on her waist to keep her from falling back down. Objectively, the water was calm and the boat was hardly moving, but her legs insisted on turning to gelatin the moment she tried to use them.

"I'll be fine once we get on land," Addy said, hoping with all her might it was true.

She hated anyone seeing her like this, especially Tol.

They got off the boat, and she felt only slightly better than she had on the ocean. She was still surrounded by water, and as much as she tried to tell herself her fear was completely unfounded, her brain wouldn't listen. She squinted so her field of vision was narrowed and she could pretend like the beach in front of her went on forever…without any ocean. It helped a little.

"You okay to walk?" Tol asked.

Addy looked at him. "They were here."

Tol's brow wrinkled. "How do you know—"

"I just do," she said, but her attention was on the ground. There were blobby footprints in the sand, which she followed. She picked up a broken twig from the ground and studied it.

"What are you, some kind of tracker?" Tol asked.

She shook her head. She had no experience with following enemies on foreign islands. Her family didn't even hunt. And yet, she knew what she was looking for.

"Come on."

There wasn't much—a drop of blood on a rock, a tiny piece of cloth stuck to a branch—but she noticed it all, and she understood it. It was like the clues were rearranging themselves in her mind, and all she had to do was watch the pictures unfold. She didn't even need to interpret them; they did it for her.

If she'd had any room for an emotion other than fear, she would have been amazed by this new ability. She saw the golden light radiating around her, telling her she was somehow tapping into the hidden powers inside her. But she was too focused on the ocean and Livy to give much thought to anything else.

"They were here a day ago," Addy said, after she had found and examined all the evidence.

"Okay," Tol said, still looking puzzled. "Any idea where they went?"

She shook her head. "I think they were only here for an hour or two at the most. There are too many people who live on this island, and they wouldn't have wanted to stay here for long." The clues rearranged in her mind once again. "I think they're on one of the uninhabited islands."

Addy knew what she was saying sounded crazy. She also had absolutely no idea how she knew any of what she was saying, except she knew it was all true. It was kind of like how she'd sensed the Forsaken's presence the first time she encountered her family's assassins. Later, she had gotten the same feeling when she stood outside the brownstone in D.C. and had known they were inside.

Tol looked at her for another minute, considering, and then he said, "It must be an ability the Celestial gave you. Maybe you're sensing their Source."

It was the only explanation that made sense. The only alternative was that she was insane, and she preferred not to dwell on that very real possibility.

"I guess that means on to the next island?" Tol asked.

The thought of getting back on the boat made Addy want to throw up. *Livy*, she reminded herself for the millionth time. *Do it for Livy.*

If it hadn't been for those words, which had been running through her mind on repeat since the plane touched down on Baltra, she would have given in to her terror a long time ago.

At least Tol didn't seem to pity her. She had been grateful when he told the boat's crew to leave her alone, and even more grateful he'd stayed with her while she convulsed and wept. As much as she didn't want him to see her in that state, the thought of being alone with all that water was unbearable.

Tol didn't try to talk her out of going to the next island or offer her some meaningless words of comfort. Instead, he just slipped his hand into hers, like it was something they did all the time. The island was small, so it took only a few minutes for them to know it wasn't the Forsaken hideout. As they walked back to the boat, Tol even coaxed a laugh out of her by telling her about the birds that roosted on the island, which he swore were called "boobies."

They got back to the yacht as the sun was setting. If she hadn't been overcome with terror, she would have felt guilty for being on a boat like this without appreciating it. Stacy would have committed actual murder for a chance to be here, with the marble columns and full staff just for the two of them. There was even a hot tub on the top of the yacht, which she wouldn't go near if her life depended on it, but which her sisters would have loved.

As they went down to the second level of the boat, Addy saw the dining room table. It was nestled in an alcove and had been set for dinner. The sunset was streaming in through the surrounding windows. Candles burned on the table, and there were rose petals strewn across the white tablecloth.

"Er, I didn't specify the reason for our travel," Tol said, dropping her hand and looking uncomfortable as he went over to close the curtains. "I guess they just assumed...."

Under any other circumstances, this ridiculous situation would be funny. Instead, she felt the boat's engines roar to life beneath them, and she wanted to die.

"We'll check out Isla Española as soon as it's light out," Tol said. "In the meantime, do you want food? Sleep?"

Addy felt the thick, oily water pooling in her lungs. As the boat rumbled beneath her, she felt her mouth and throat fill with water. She couldn't speak. She couldn't breathe. The water was everywhere....

"Addy. *Addy.*"

Her vision had cleared enough for her to see Tol kneeling over her. She was lying on the floor. *How had she gotten here?*

"Can you stand?" Tol asked.

He didn't wait to hear the lie on her lips. He bent down and lifted her, his right arm warm against her back and his prosthetic one cool beneath her legs. Her head was too heavy for her to hold, and she slumped against his chest.

He carried her into a bedroom and laid her on the bed. If she'd had any ability to think about anything besides the endless ocean stretching out all around and beneath her, she would have appreciated the sheer luxury of this bedroom. The mattress was soft. Everything was dark wood and warm light. Tol made sure all the curtains were drawn, which helped, but she still knew where she was. She was a miniscule speck floating on top of a bottomless sea that could suck her down at any moment.

"Lights on or off?" Tol asked, pulling a blanket over her.

She tried to answer, but she started coughing up the phantom water in her lungs.

She really must be going crazy. She was self-aware enough to recognize it, she just couldn't do anything about it.

In the end, Tol made the decision to turn off all the lamps except for the one on the bedside table.

He looked at her, uncertainty in his gaze, and moved for the door.

"Tol?" She sounded so weak. So useless.

"Yeah."

She hated to ask…she knew how he must feel about having to babysit a sniveling coward. But her terror at spending the night on this flimsy, floating hunk of wood and plastic banished any pride she had left.

"Stay with me?"

CHAPTER 25

TOL

Something was tickling Tol's nose. He opened his eyes, only to see a curtain of red clouding his vision. It was the smell of piña coladas that reminded him where he was. He remembered Addy asking him to stay. He remembered sitting down on the bed next to her.

He didn't remember precisely how they'd ended up with their bodies curled together on the bed.

Addy's back was pressed to his chest, and his right arm was wound around her. He was acutely aware of the fact that if he shifted his arm just a few centimeters higher, it would graze her breasts. That thought was enough to make him extricate himself from Addy before he woke her up in a way that embarrassed them both.

Tol slipped out of the room and went up the stairs, needing the fresh sea air to clear his mind. They were in sight of the next island on their route, and the sky was just beginning to lighten.

A table was on the upper deck with two places set. A sideboard with fruit and pastries was laid out. The crew were waiting patiently beside it, so that whenever Tol and Addy decided to make use of the yacht's amenities, they'd be ready to assist.

Tol was used to being waited on, but he didn't relish the effort these people were going through for their sakes.

"This isn't necessary," Tol said, even as one of the crew pulled out a chair and ushered him into it. "This is really more of a...business trip for us. Please don't trouble yourselves on our account."

"We're here for you," one of the two scantily-clad crew members said. They both sauntered over to Tol. They approached the table from opposite sides, like they intended to corner him.

"Thank you," he said, "but Addy likes her privacy, and so do I." He let a note of possession come into his voice when he said Addy's name, letting the women know he wasn't interested in whatever entertainment they were offering. "Please don't trouble yourselves," he said again. "I'm afraid your efforts will be wasted."

He felt a little bad at the crestfallen looks on their faces. He knew this crew was probably used to wild parties on the deck, with champagne flowing and music blaring, while guests moved from the hot tub to the wet bar.

"Morning."

Tol stood up from his chair so fast it would have fallen over if one of the crew hadn't caught and righted it. "Addy."

She looked so pale. Even her lips were drained of color.

He motioned to the glass partitions surrounding the table. "Can we get these covered?" he asked the crew.

As they scurried around, hanging tarps to block out the view of the ocean, Tol turned all of his attention on Addy.

How are you feeling?" he asked.

Tol heard the eagerness in his own voice, and mentally punched himself.

"A little better. I slept well."

It might have been Tol's imagination, but he thought she gave him a smile that was a little secret and a little shy. It made him think last night had meant something to her, too.

"Can I get you anything?" he asked.

Her eyes went to the ridiculous display of watermelons carved into roses. "Maybe some orange juice?"

Before she had even finished her sentence, the staff ushered her into the chair across from Tol with a glass of fresh-squeezed orange juice. The cook came on deck and was trying to entice Addy with all manner of delicacies.

"I don't know that she's really in the mood for caviar," Tol broke in after Addy had declined and apologized for the third time.

Addy looked away, hiding her smile from the cook.

"How about some tea and toast?" Tol suggested, and then winced.
Gods, he sounded like Gran.

In the end, the cook set all manner of hot and cold food out for them. Addy made Tol eat a little of everything so the cook wouldn't feel bad. She nibbled on a piece of dry toast while the cook stood over her and shook his head in disgust.

Tol felt more relief than he should have as she took a small bite of bread and a sip of juice. She hadn't eaten since they got off the airplane, and her face had taken on a hollow look that worried him more than he cared to admit.

Addy kept her chair turned inward so she was looking at Tol rather than over the now-covered partition at the ocean, which suited him just fine. The crew hovered around them, seeming almost as relieved as Tol to see Addy alert.

Once the cook descended back into the ship, muttering to himself, Addy convinced the rest of the crew to help them out with the food as they sailed for the next island. They resisted at first, but as Tol was coming to find, there was something about Addy that brooked no argument. After a few minutes, the crew had pulled up chairs to the small table with plates balanced on their laps. It wasn't long before they were all talking and joking as they ate. When Tol said something that made Addy laugh, it felt like the sun coming out after weeks of the dreary English winter.

Addy looked at the island in front of them. "I'll need to get on shore to be certain, but I don't feel them here."

Tol nodded. He had no idea how it worked, but some Fount ability made Addy able to sense the Forsaken. She could probably put the infamous Forsaken trackers to shame.

He'd been skeptical when they were on the previous island. He'd followed as she led him on a winding trail through the sand, and he'd been amazed when she bent to pick up an arrow shaft that had clearly belonged to a Forsaken.

It seemed like the Celestial's powers appeared when Addy needed them without her doing anything conscious to bring them out. Tol couldn't imagine what kinds of abilities she'd have after the blood marriage when she could access all of the Celestial's knowledge.

On shore, Addy kneeled in the sand and closed her eyes, like she was listening for something. After a few silent minutes had passed, she stood. "They weren't on this island," she said, her voice hollow.

"We're going to find them." Even Tol was getting sick of hearing the same refrain in his voice, but he had nothing else to offer. "Even if we have to search every single island."

Getting back on the boat seemed to be the worst time for Addy, but she did it without complaint. She pressed her lips tight together and grasped the railing so hard her knuckles turned white. While Tol couldn't begin to understand her terror, he admired her for leaving the dock each time even when it seemed to be sucking the life out of her.

Tol understood determination and desperation, but what Addy felt for her sister was stronger than both. It made her courageous even as she huddled under a blanket shivering. He had no right to feel anything like pride for her bravery, since he could lay no claim to it or her, but he felt it anyway.

Whatever had made her feel better in the early hours of the morning had worn off. Addy was back on the couch, shaking under the blanket Tol had wrapped around her.

"Sir?" The captain, a hesitant smile on his face, stood in the doorway to the lounge. "We're approaching the next island."

Tol nodded and turned to Addy. "You ready?"

"There's just one thing." The captain held up a finger. "This island is small and uninhabited. There's no dock, and the shoreline is rocky."

As soon as Tol heard that, a suspicion took root inside him. It sounded like the perfect place for a Forsaken hideout.

"You said the shore was rocky?" Tol asked.

The captain nodded. "I'll get you close, but you'll have to swim the last little bit."

"Swim?" Addy, who had been staring at the floor, jerked her head up like an animal that had just scented a predator.

"It's barely six feet deep, and it gets shallow quickly," the captain said. "You can probably walk to the island." His voice was kind, grandfatherly, but it did nothing to quell Addy's growing panic.

Tol was starting to understand the signs, and he knew she was about thirty seconds away from passing out.

"Addy."

Her eyes started to roll back, so Tol grabbed her face and forced her to look at him. His touch wasn't gentle, and it got her attention.

"I'll be with you the whole time—"

"I can't swim," she gasped, like she was already drowning. "I've never done it. I can't."

"I'll carry you," he said. "I'm a good swimmer. You'll be fine."

"You have a metal arm," she said, hysterical. "It'll sink like an anchor, and then we'll sink. And then we'll die!"

"It isn't metal," Tol said, his patience deserting him. "And neither of us is going to sink."

"Darling girl, with your height, you'll be able to stand," the captain said, a puzzled look on his face.

Tol gave him a *don't help* look. The captain backed away, his hands raised like he was trying to show this snarling girl he wasn't a threat.

"Look, why don't I just go?" Tol suggested. Addy had refused every other time he'd offered to go ashore without her, but maybe this time....

"No. I'm the only one who can sense the Forsaken. You won't know what you're looking for."

"It's a small island," Tol said. "I'll figure it out."

"If they're there, you'll need me," Addy argued, even as her body shook. "You won't be able to fight them alone."

She had a point.

"It's up to you," Tol said.

Addy rose to her feet and made her way to the staircase.

On deck, Addy's teeth were chattering with so much force Tol was afraid she was going to break a tooth. The crew hurried around, putting supplies into a dry bag and offering hushed assurances to Addy. A ladder was lowered into the water at the other end of the boat.

Addy gripped the railing, staring down at the floor as she tried to catch her breath. Tol went over to stand beside her.

"Do you trust me?"

The better part of Tol expected Addy to say *no, you idiot. You've been nothing but trouble for me since the moment you stepped into my life.* She didn't, though. She gave him a short nod.

"Okay then." Tol put an arm around her waist to keep her from falling and cracking her head on the furniture. Slowly, he led her to the back of the yacht.

"I'm going to get into the water first, so as soon as you climb down, I'll be there to catch you. Okay?"

Addy clung to the railing. She didn't say anything. Her terror seemed beyond words.

The yacht staff hovered just behind them, looking as helpless as Tol felt. He gave them a look, which they understood. They moved in to stay with Addy while Tol pulled off his shoes. His shirt was long-sleeved, as were all of his shirts, but he left it on. Even though Addy had seen him once without his arm, it didn't mean he was comfortable with it now, especially with a boat full of people staring at him.

He put his sneakers in the dry bag one of the crew had given him, along with the first aid kit he'd requested. Since they were kids, Gerth had drummed into his brain the need to be prepared for all possible outcomes. When Forsaken were involved, the need for a first aid kit was more than a possibility.

Addy's hands shook as she handed over her garden shears for Tol to put into the dry bag along with everything else.

The crew members were kneeling in front of Addy. They unlaced her sneakers as she stood there, completely frozen. Tol doubted she heard a single one of their comforting words, but he appreciated their efforts, anyway.

Tol lowered himself into the water. It was cool and calm, and it made him feel a lightness that was more than just buoyancy. There was a freedom of movement in water that wasn't possible on land. It eased the weight of responsibility.

Tol imagined it was the exact opposite for Addy. He felt a pang of regret that she couldn't feel the water's freedom, too.

One of the yacht's crew tossed Tol the dry bag. He caught it and slung it across his back. He looked up, waiting to see Addy come down the ladder.

But she didn't climb down. She jumped.

There was a splash, and then Addy was in the water. Tol struck out for her, but before he could reach her, she was...swimming.

Like a sea nymph or a mermaid, she cut through the water like she'd never known any other way to move. Her strokes were even and perfect. There wasn't a hint of uncertainty in her movements. She *glided* through the water more than swam.

Addy had reached the island by the time he came out of his stupor enough to follow her...far less gracefully, in spite of his years of swim lessons.

"I thought you said you didn't know how to swim," Tol said when he reached the craggy shore.

"I don't. I mean, I didn't." Addy's face was still pale, but there was a spark of life in her eyes that hadn't been there on the boat.

She even laughed a little, and the sound was music to Tol's ears. "You didn't tell me the Celestial was an Olympic swimmer."

"I...didn't know." Tol was grinning, too. He sloshed through the shallows to her.

Addy looked like a goddess, with her red-gold hair on fire in the light of the setting sun. She was dripping wet and gorgeous, and he didn't hesitate before wrapping his arms around her. He felt her hands come around his waist.

"Adelyne Deerborn," he murmured, "you astonish me."

She raised her eyes to his, and the look in them stole Tol's breath away. She reached up and brushed a strand of wet hair from his face. Even that small touch sent a ripple of feeling through him. He was aware of her smallest movements...the dart of her eyes to his lips, the slight intake of breath.

He wanted to kiss her. Badly.

He thought she wanted it, too, but he didn't trust himself to read the expression in her green eyes.

Tol stayed perfectly still, letting Addy decide what would happen next. She closed her eyes and leaned in.

Their lips met. There was more magic in it than in all the Source on Vitaquias. They melted together, like their bodies already knew each other. The kiss should have brought him relief, but it only made Tol's longing for Addy fiercer.

He had only a few precious seconds to sense what it might be like to really kiss Addy... to feel the perfect fit of their lips and bodies...and then Addy was pulling back.

"They're here," she said, her eyes wide and full of a mix of emotions.

He was just as full of feeling, and it took him longer than it should to process what she was saying.

"What?"

"The Forsaken. I can feel them here."

"Right." Tol forced himself to let go of Addy so he could take the Source from around his neck.

"There are a lot of them." Addy's forehead was creased.

The last thing Tol was prepared for right now was an army of Forsaken. His mind just wanted to replay those few blissful seconds.

Snap out of it, he ordered himself. If he ever wanted to kiss her again, he'd have to live long enough to do it.

Tol swallowed his drop of Source and used the flare of his Haze to ground his thoughts.

Addy was already running, and he could barely keep her in his sight. She was so damn fast. She flew over the sand like it was as stable as flat ground. He stumbled after her.

"Duck!"

Tol had barely made sense of the word when he saw something hurtling through the air at them. He swerved. The glowing blue knife that was on course for his heart grazed the side of his chest instead. Tol felt heat flare across the spot, but he didn't give it a second thought as Forsaken wearing camo appeared out of nowhere.

There were at least ten of them, maybe more. Tol knew immediately these were the Forsaken they'd been looking for. They were huge. They looked like humans, but had the height and girth of grizzly bears. The barbarians' white-blonde hair was almost luminescent in the darkening sky, and they moved with a swiftness that came from centuries of Source-infused training.

Even as strong as they were, these Forsaken still didn't stand a chance against Addy's ferocity. She punched a man in the face with so much force he flew backward and hit a rock with an audible thud. She used her own momentum to flip in the air and plunge her shears into another Forsaken's side. She somersaulted away from the dagger he threw, coming out of her roll to sweep the legs out from another warrior. Getting a running start, she slid through the sand and pulled a Forsaken's own weapon from his hands.

Before Addy, Tol had never seen a Forsaken lose his weapon, let alone be killed by it. Addy was ruthless, slicing the blade so fast it blurred. Screams and blood filled the air as she wielded the stolen blade in one hand and her garden shears in the other.

Tol managed to grab one warrior's ankles in a far less graceful way than Addy's most recent move. He Influenced the Forsaken and turned the woman on her own comrades.

The rest of the Forsaken became confused and suspicious. They knew some of them were not under their own control, but they couldn't decipher which of their own people they could trust. That, coupled with Addy's unrelenting attack, made the disadvantage of having five Forsaken to one of them all but irrelevant.

Tol wrested control of another Forsaken's mind. He used his Influence to sow terror among their ranks as they attacked their own people.

Addy leapt out of the way of a saber that came hurtling toward her. She grabbed it out of the air and threw it back.

The Source-infused weapon tracked the movement of the Forsaken who had thrown it. Tol winced as the saber cleaved the Forsaken's skull. The man thudded to the ground, sending up a spray of sand.

Only one Forsaken remained alive who wasn't under Tol's Influence. The man dropped his sword and raised his hands.

"On your knees!" Addy yelled in a voice that was like and unlike her own. There was authority in that voice, as well as brutality.

Tol caught the man's eye, adding his consciousness to the others under his control.

Tol's hold on their minds felt…slippery. The edges of his mind had gone fuzzy, like the mist that hung over the English Channel. He clung tighter.

"Where is her sister?"

The Forsaken smiled and bared his yellow teeth. "You'll never get her."

Tol felt the man sliding out of his mental grasp. He couldn't understand it; his mind was stronger than all of these Forsaken. And yet, holding the warrior's mind was like trying to grasp a live eel. A live, red eel. He didn't know why, but everything in his view was tinged with red.

Maybe he needed more Source. When Tol tried to grasp the vial, he found his arms were too heavy to lift.

Strange.

He gripped the man's mind with all of his concentration.

"Where is she?"

"Elmendorf Air Force Base, but you'll never get her. The general and a hundred Forsaken warriors are there. They'll kill you before you even get a look at her."

"Where is that?"

Tol heard Addy's question, but he couldn't see her.

"'laska," Tol slurred.

And then he blacked out.

CHAPTER 26

ADDY

The moment Tol hit the ground, his hold on the Forsaken shattered. Addy hadn't realized how many of their minds he was controlling until he wasn't, and now, they were after her.

She needed to get to Tol, who was lying motionless in the sand. But half a dozen of the murderers separated them. Addy screamed Tol's name, but he didn't move. A horrible feeling came over her. She put every ounce of her strength into killing the Forsaken as fast as she could.

The golden light surrounded her as fury washed over her...fury at these monsters who had killed her family...who had taken Livy...who had hurt Tol. There was no end to the misery she wished she could cause them. The thing inside her sprang to life, devouring every emotion until all she felt was a rage that wouldn't be satisfied until every one of her enemies lay dead.

She barely noticed the geysers of blood and clouds of blue smoke as she used her trusty garden shears to slice through flesh and end lives. She ducked and twisted and stole weapons from pockets she hadn't even know were there until she reached for them.

Addy didn't have time to feel satisfaction when the last of her enemies fell. She raced back to Tol. When she reached him, she fell to her knees beside him. He wasn't moving.

"Tol. Tol!"

An icy fear slid through her veins, replacing the anger that was now coiled back up inside her.

She leaned over Tol to lift him into a sitting position. That was when she felt the blood. There was a long slice in his shirt. His side was sticky from congealed blood, and slick from where it was still oozing from a gash in his chest.

For a moment, she couldn't move. She couldn't think. All she could see was her family, the people she loved most, lying in pools of their own blood. And there was Tol, lying next to them.

Tol was here because of her. He was dying because of her.

The thought was enough to jolt her out of her stupor.

She pressed her fingers against his neck. He had a pulse, but it was faint. His skin was clammy and a sheen of sweat coated his brow.

Addy looked around, like there was someone who could help her. Too late, she realized she should have left one of the Forsaken alive to…do what? Carry him somewhere? Stitch him up?

She needed to think. She needed some of the Celestial's survival knowledge right now. The moment the thought came to her, her golden light flared as though she'd drunk from the vial around Tol's neck. Her panic faded. Some voice in her head forced her numb limbs into motion.

Get him somewhere safe. Assess the damage. Fix him.

The first aid kit in Tol's dry bag called to her. She wanted to dump out the medical supplies and do what she could to stop the bleeding here and now, but some instinct she knew better than to ignore told her there were plenty more Forsaken on this island. She had to get him somewhere safe, first.

She pulled Tol up as gently as she could. He was heavier than he looked; his prosthetic arm weighed him down, but whatever power was inside her gave her the strength to lift him.

With Tol dangling awkwardly in her arms, Addy stumbled to her feet. She paused as she tried to figure out what to do next. The thought of going back into the water with Tol passed out was enough to make her want to curl up in the sand and sob. Addy didn't know if their swim to the island had been some kind of fluke. She didn't want to get back into the water, only to find her body no longer knew what to do. She also didn't know if there were sharks around here that would be attracted to the blood leaking out of Tol.

It was getting dark. The only option was to find somewhere to hide on the island until Tol woke up.

And he would wake up. She kept promising herself that he would. The thought was all that kept her going.

She let the golden light radiating from her guide her steps, since she had no idea where to go. She let the same tracking instinct that had helped her feel the Forsaken guide her now. It didn't let her down.

Her path ended at an outcropping of rocks. There was a small cave, which would protect them from the elements and prying eyes. It wasn't perfect, but it would have to be enough to get them through the night.

Addy laid Tol down gently inside the cave. She gathered kindling for a fire. The magic inside her told her how to start a fire without a lighter, and she rubbed sticks together until she'd coaxed a small flame to life.

The fire was weak, but it was enough for Addy to work by as she tore away the bloody remains of Tol's shirt. She sucked in a breath.

There was a long slice down his side. It was impossible to tell how deep it was with all the blood. She ran her hand across his skin, and her fingers were instantly wet with fresh blood. Tol didn't even react to her touch.

Addy's hands started to shake. The worst injury she'd ever seen was when Fred fell out of the hay loft and broke his ankle, but all she'd had to do then was ride in the truck and hold his hand as Mr. Brown raced to the hospital. She'd never stitched a wound before.

Pull it together, she commanded herself. There was no hospital here. She'd just have to save Tol herself.

She took Tol's vial from around his neck, measured out a drop the way she'd seen him do, and put it between his lips. She didn't know if the magical fluid would speed his healing, but she figured it couldn't hurt. Addy wouldn't admit the real reason she gave it to him was that she couldn't stand his silence and stillness.

She saw his golden light flare bright enough to illuminate the whole cave, but Tol still didn't move.

"Come on," she begged him. "I need you."

"Don't look so worried." Tol's eyes cracked open.

A sob of relief escaped from Addy.

"I won't die before we get your sister."

Addy faltered. "No, that wasn't what I meant."

And it wasn't. Livy had filled her thoughts every minute since Addy left the farmhouse. Or, at least, that had been the case before they'd come to this island. Addy realized she hadn't thought about Livy once since she saw Tol's body hit the sand.

"Why do you care what happens to me if not to help get your sister back?"

Tol was trying to watch her, but his eyes kept fluttering closed.

Because I love you.

She said the words in her head. The thought came immediately, and it was preposterous. She had known Tol for three weeks. Addy was certainly no expert on love, but she knew it took longer than three weeks...didn't it?

Addy tried to reel the thought back, but the words rang with a truth she couldn't deny. She schooled her features and tried to think of a response that wouldn't give her away, but when she looked back at Tol, his eyes were closed.

Addy opened the first aid kit and started taking out packets of sterile gauze, distilled water, and alcohol wipes.

"Sorry," she said as she cleaned away the blood.

Tol flinched when she got near the open wound, but he didn't say anything.

The wound was long, but blood was only coming from the center of it along Tol's chest. Addy didn't need to be a doctor to know it needed stitches.

"Okay, I can do this," Addy muttered as she opened the vinyl case labeled "the stitch kit" and assessed the various tools inside.

"Not inspiring much confidence," Tol said with a weak smile.

"I've never done this before," she admitted as she looped the suture thread through the needle. "You might have a scar at the end of all of this."

Tol shrugged and then winced. "Maybe it'll take some attention away from my missing arm."

"I like your arm the way it is." Addy didn't look at Tol as she readied the needle.

She moved the needle in and out of his skin with a confidence she knew didn't come from her. It was so bizarre to have so much knowledge in her head that she had no idea was even there until she needed it. It was convenient, just weird.

Her whole life, Addy had felt like she didn't quite belong. She hadn't understood why. It was just a feeling she always had in the back of her mind. She didn't look like the rest of her family, and she had wanted different things than they wanted, but she'd never realized how far those differences went.

Addy longed to talk to her parents, to find out what they knew about her, to understand why they never told her. It made her angry to think they had kept such a secret from her, and the last thing she wanted was to feel anger toward her dead parents.

Tol watched Addy work without saying anything. He didn't move or make a sound, even though Addy was sure each stitch must be agonizing.

"You know, if you were really good at this, you'd be trying to distract me from the pain," Tol said as she worked the needle through the layers of skin on his chest.

"Sorry," she winced, even though he didn't move.

Tol was right. It was no less than he'd done for her for days on the boat. There were more than a few times when his stories about Gerth or his grandmother talking to dead people had kept her from the brink of insanity.

"Why do the Forsaken use strange weapons like hatchets and throwing stars?" Addy asked.

Tol raised an eyebrow. "Is there something that would be less weird?"

"Well, yeah. Like guns," Addy said. "Why don't they ever have guns?"

"Because then I'd be dead right now," Tol replied.

He laughed at the horror on her face, which she cut off by poking the needle back into his flesh.

"In all seriousness," he said, "Source doesn't enhance mortal weapons. The Forsakens' were forged on Vitaquias and are more powerful for it. The blue halo you always see around their weapons means they're infused with

Source. That's why their weapons are impossible to destroy, can track their enemy's movements, and return to their owner's hand once they've done their job. The barbarians don't use any other weapons except for their own if they can help it."

Addy thought she could understand that. She'd grown very fond of her trusty garden shears and would prefer to wield them over seemingly more lethal weapons.

"For the Forsaken, their weapons are their pride," Tol continued. "They would see it as beneath them to fight with guns or anything else from the mortal world, just as my people would never use any weapon besides our own minds."

"That Senator was buying Forsaken weapons," Addy pointed out, remembering how Tol had used that knowledge to keep the senator from telling his parents about their meeting.

"Migelian has no integrity," Tol said, anger making his voice stronger.

Addy still wasn't convinced.

"You have to remember," Tol said. "Many of our people are hundreds of years old, and we've only been in the mortal world for eighteen years. It isn't easy for them to let go of the way they've lived for centuries."

Centuries. Tol had said they were immortal, but the concept was too big for Addy to fathom. Dying was part of life. Eternity was…too big for comprehension.

Addy tied off the suture and then rummaged through the first aid kit until she found sterile bandages.

"Not bad," Tol said, examining the stitches.

"Hold still," Addy commanded as Tol pushed himself into a seated position and leaned against the rock.

She examined the wound. There was no new blood flow, and the stitches did look pretty neat. She put on the bandage, and then used medical tape to keep the bandage in place. It was only as she pressed the last piece of tape on top of the bandage that it occurred to her that she was touching Tol's bare chest. For the first time, her attention moved to something besides his gaping wound.

She was finished with the bandage and didn't need to be touching him anymore, but she liked the feel of his skin beneath her fingers now that she wasn't jabbing it with a needle. As light as a feather, she let her fingers move farther from the bandage as she traced the flat plane of his chest.

Addy lifted her eyes to Tol's. He was watching her fingers on his skin. He seemed to be holding his breath.

Tol's gaze met hers. Whatever expression he saw on her face made him smile. Before she could react, he wrapped his arms around her and shifted her onto his lap so she was straddling him.

"Tol!" she gasped. "You'll pull out your stitches."

"It'd be worth it," he murmured as he leaned forward.

The first time they had kissed, it had been a tease. She'd gotten just a hint of what it would be like to really kiss him. At least, she thought she'd had a hint. Now, as their lips met, she realized she hadn't had a clue.

She'd thought the farmhand she had kissed was good. He hadn't even compared to this.

Tol's mouth was warm and soft, and moved over hers in a way that made her whole body turn liquid in his arms. If Tol hadn't been holding her against him, she'd be a puddle in the sand.

Addy raised her hands to his face, tracing the sharp lines of his cheekbones and jaw, feeling the rough stubble on his chin. Tol deepened the kiss. It awoke a thousand sensations inside her.

The taste of him was like a drug. The more she got, the more she wanted. It was only when he pulled her even tighter against him that a small, unwelcome voice in her head made her break away from him.

"Your wound," she managed in a breathless voice that didn't sound like her. "I don't want it to open—"

"I don't care." Tol's voice was different, too. His was deeper, rougher. It made her crazy for him.

"I like your blood better inside you than all over the sand," she said, gently pushing back so there was space between his bandages and her body.

"But I have such a good surgeon." Tol traced her bottom lip with the tip of his tongue. Shivers of pleasure traveled from her lips to the rest of her.

To keep either of them from doing something that would hurt Tol, Addy moved off his lap and snuggled against his uninjured side. Tol's prosthetic arm came around her. He used his right hand to trace the lines of her face like she'd done to him moments before.

Addy shifted so she could see his expression. She expected to see the same kind of wonder and longing that she felt, but instead, Tol looked…conflicted.

"What's wrong?" she asked.

Tol continued to brush his fingers across her face and neck, which would have made her close her eyes and give in to the feeling of bliss, but Tol's expression kept her alert.

He said, "I've spent my life searching for you, of thinking about the Fount. And in all that time, I never expected…to feel like this."

"Feel like what?" Addy breathed.

Those three words she'd thought before hadn't gone away. In fact, their clamor had grown louder inside the confines of her own mind. She didn't want to say them out loud for fear that Tol, who obviously had far more experience in this area than she did, was on a completely different page.

"Addy, I have to tell you something."

She could tell by the expression on his face that whatever he had to tell her wasn't anything remotely like what she was hoping he'd say.

"When you promised to do that ritual, I didn't tell you all that it entailed." He let out a breath, and then dropped his hand to his side. "You're going to hate me."

"Don't tell me tonight," she said. "Whatever it is, it can wait until tomorrow."

All Addy wanted was for the space that had gathered between them to disappear. She wanted Tol to gather her into his arms again, when now she felt like he was pushing her away.

"Hating you will be a good distraction for the boat ride back," she continued.

Addy saw the moment Tol's self-control broke. She knew he didn't want to stay away from her any more than she wanted to be separated from him.

When she kissed him, she felt Tol sigh against her lips. His body, which had gone rigid with whatever bad news he was going to share, melted against her like he couldn't resist her touch.

I love you.

Addy's heart beat in time with Tol's as those words looped through her mind.

She decided when two people had saved each other's lives so many times they lost count, it sped up the clock on how they were allowed to feel about each other. She knew what she felt, and she felt its realness in her bones. Her feelings for Tol were as intense as the anger that had driven her slaughter of the Forsaken. Except this emotion didn't scare her.

She didn't say the words out loud, but she felt them in the way she kissed Tol. And she thought his lips answered hers as they came together.

CHAPTER 27

TOL

Addy had to help him back to the yacht. He'd lost a lot of blood, and his chest felt like someone had dragged a hot iron across his skin. When the salt water seeped under the bandage, Tol bit down on the inside of his cheek until he tasted blood to keep from screaming.

Although he could tell she hated getting back in the ocean, Addy swam as gracefully as she had the day before. It never ceased to amaze him the way she continued to draw from a reserve of knowledge she didn't know she had to save them both.

Tol knew that if it hadn't been for her ability to close his wound, he'd probably be dead. The thought didn't concern him the way he knew it should. Instead, it made Addy even more precious to him.

When the crew helped them back onto the boat and saw the dried blood and Tol's bandaged chest, they swarmed him. While the cook—who apparently had the most first aid experience of them all—replaced Tol's bandages, he praised Addy's skill with the sutures. Tol was only half-listening. His mind was back in the island cave, with the dim firelight and Addy warm and alive in his arms.

He shouldn't have kissed her like that. Tol knew he had no right...not when he hadn't yet told her about the blood marriage. But he'd been mad for her and hadn't been able to stop himself.

Tol wished for ten more wounds if it would prevent even one ounce of the pain he knew he was going to cause Addy.

This beautiful, powerful woman, whose only fears were water and being forced into a future she didn't choose, was going to hate him. Tol thought he had been prepared for the blood marriage and how the Fount would blame him for the union the same way he had always blamed her. But in all that time, there was one possibility he hadn't accounted for. In eighteen years, it had never occurred to him that he would fall head over heels for her.

Somehow, it made everything so much worse.

"So, we're going to that Air Force base now?"

Addy, her face bloodless, was standing in the doorway to his room—the room he hadn't slept in because he'd spent every night with Addy. She came and sat on the edge of the bed. She had showered, and that piña colada smell that was just so Addy filled the room. His desire to reach for her, to let his mind empty of every other thought except for the thought of her, was overwhelming. He clenched his fist to keep from pulling her to him.

"Elmendorf Air Force Base is in Anchorage, Alaska," Tol said. "It isn't one of the Forsaken refuges on our radar, but it makes sense. There are plenty of mortals to lend support, and the infrastructure is already there to keep a prisoner under guard."

He'd been so wrapped up in Addy the night before that he hadn't thought much about their next steps. Now, he mulled over the Forsaken man's words from the day before.

"With the general there," he continued, "we'll never make it on our own."

Tol saw worry tighten Addy's features, so he said quickly, "We're going to need more help, and more Source."

"But you said—"

"I know what I said," Tol put out his hand, "but we won't be able to get Olivia without my people's help."

"So, we have to go to England, and then to Alaska?" Addy demanded. "That will take forever. Livy might not have that long."

"It won't take more than a couple of extra days," Tol said, trying to keep his voice calm to ease her growing panic. "But going up against the general and her best warriors would be suicide without having a force of our own."

Addy slitted her eyes. "What makes you so sure your people will help us? You said before they wouldn't be willing to put themselves at risk for my sister."

They wouldn't be happy about it, that was for sure. Tol hadn't told them where he was going or asked for their help before because he knew exactly what they'd have to say about the deal he made with Addy. That was also before he knew the Forsaken general had gotten involved with Olivia's kidnapping.

Everything was different now, and not just because of the higher stakes of the rescue. He would do anything, sacrifice anything, for Addy. Even if it meant putting himself and his people at greater risk.

"They'll help us because I won't give them any choice," Tol said.

Addy pressed her palms into her eyes. Tol longed to gather her in his arms and comfort her, but her next words made him go still as a statue.

"I need that distraction now," she said.

Tol looked around, like there might be some escape from this conversation. Of course, being stuck on a boat meant there was nowhere to go. The only upside to waiting until now to tell her, Tol thought darkly, was that at least he didn't need to worry about Addy running away from him as soon as she knew the truth.

Tol looked at Addy, trying to memorize her beautiful green eyes before they clouded over with hate. And then he started to speak.

ADDY

Tol was nervous. It was obvious from the way he was picking at the bandage through his shirt, and she had to swat his hand away before he peeled it off.

"Just get it over with," Addy told him as he continued to look around the room like he was a wild animal stuck in a trap.

Tol let out a breath, and Addy could see the frantic flutter of his pulse in his neck. His nervousness was contagious, and she found herself distracted by the feeling of water sucking at her ankles as her own anxiety rose.

"Do you remember the promise you made in exchange for getting your sister back?"

As always, Tol's black velvet voice brought her away from the edge of her despair.

"The ritual," she said. "I remember."

"We made an oath that was bound by Source. If either of us doesn't hold up our end of the bargain, we'll die."

"Okay...."

"I've never lied to you," Tol continued, "but I haven't been wholly honest, either."

"Just spit it out," she demanded. "What is the ritual all about?"

Addy knew it must be something unpleasant. Tol had always been evasive about it, but she hadn't cared enough to push. After all, she would have sold her soul and her life for the chance to get Livy back. No price was too high to pay to rescue her sister.

"When our world became uninhabitable, the Celestial couldn't come with us because her powers were too connected to the Source and Vitaquias. She knew she'd be split apart if she tried to make the Crossing."

"Like what happened to your arm," Addy said, wishing Tol would just get to the point.

Tol nodded. "She wanted to protect my people, especially since she knew we'd be at the Forsakens' mercy once our Source ran low." He swallowed. "But she didn't give the gift of her power for free. She was angry at my people for pushing the Source past its natural limitations, so instead of transferring her power to one of us, she sent it through the portal to bind to a mortal woman."

"Me," Addy said.

Tol nodded again. "The Celestial decreed that the mortal who possessed her powers would become the Fount, whose mind and blood would hold the answer to returning to Vitaquias and repairing the damage that had been wrought. But the only way for the Fount to access her power would be through a blood marriage to the Chosen prince."

"Blood marriage." Addy had no idea what that meant, but it sounded evil. She wanted nothing to do with it.

"Yes." Tol looked like he was in physical pain. Addy wondered if it was his wound, or the pain of what he was about to tell her.

"Few couples in our world have chosen to undergo the blood marriage because of what it entails."

"What does it entail, Tol?" Addy was losing patience.

"An exchange of our blood and Source, which binds us in body and spirit for eternity."

Tol was staring wide-eyed at her, like these words were supposed to mean something to her. They didn't.

"The connection will be in our heads. I'll know every thought that crosses your mind, and you'll know every thought that crosses mine. Whatever emotion one of us feels, the other will feel. We'll be so connected that if one of us is wounded, the other will feel it like it was their own blood being spilled. If one of us dies, so will the other."

Addy's throat was starting to close, and for once, it had nothing to do with the ocean surrounding them.

Was he saying....

Tol pushed on. "We'll never be able to be with another person. Any kind of disloyalty, whether physical or otherwise, would cause us an unbearable amount of pain. The only way we can ever part is in death."

Addy tried to speak, but she couldn't get a word out.

Blood marriage...eternal...can't live without each other.... Tol couldn't be serious. It wasn't possible. And yet, one look at his face told her he was serious, and it was possible.

"How dare you." Addy was shaking, but this time, it was from fury rather than fear. "You trick me into a bargain, and then you expect me to do this insane marriage thing with you?!"

She was shouting, but she didn't care if every member of the crew heard her.

"My entire race is dying," Tol said, pleadingly. "Our Source is running out, and unless we do the blood marriage before your nineteenth birthday, my people will die."

"I don't give a rat's ass about your people," Addy yelled.

Even as she said the words, she knew she didn't mean them, but she was too angry to care.

"Do you think I wanted this, either?" Tol's voice was rising to match her own.

"You didn't tell me because you know how insane this is." Addy felt her mouth twist into a sneer. "You acted like you…cared…when all along you were just getting ready to own me!"

She was crying, and she hated herself for it.

"I had no choice." Tol's anger disappeared as quickly as it came. "But things are different now."

Addy was too furious to speak. He had lied to her. He meant to use her.

A niggling voice in the back of her mind whispered that she wasn't being fair. She was using him, too. But her anger won out.

"I won't make you do it."

Addy was so wrapped up in her own mind that she didn't process Tol's words at first.

He raised his dark eyes to hers, and she saw his heartbreak as clear as day.

"I'll release you from our oath, Addy. I'm still going to ask you to marry me, but if you say no, I won't force you. I'll help you get your sister back, and then I'll disappear from your life."

All of the air left Addy at once, and with it, her fury.

"If I refuse," she said, "your people will die."

Tol didn't say anything. He didn't have to. The horror and sorrow in his gaze spoke for him.

"Why?" Addy's voice cracked with her own pent-up emotions. "Why let me out of the bargain?"

"Because. I…love you." The words sounded like they were ripped from Tol's throat. "I'm in love with you."

Those words from Tol's lips was the most beautiful sound she'd ever heard, and yet, it seemed to torture him to say them. His shoulders had collapsed, and there was a pain in his dark eyes that tore at her heart.

Addy had thought—hoped—he felt the same way she did. She had been desperate to hear those words…desperate to know she wasn't on this island of unfamiliar emotions alone. And now, she did. But it felt nothing like the way she'd thought it would.

Addy cleared her throat. "I would think that'd make things easier for you."

Tol shook his head. "I couldn't bear it." His voice was raw. "My whole life, I was prepared to be eternally bound to a mortal who I didn't love, and who didn't love me. I expected that. But you." He shook his head again. "I couldn't stand to spend an eternity seeing you unhappy, and knowing I was the reason for it. I can't do that to you."

It was a few moments before Addy got her breath back enough to speak.

"So, you would have held any other mortal girl to her word? You would have made her bind herself to you for eternity?"

"Yes. Maybe." Tol raked a hand through his hair. "I don't know." He rose to his feet. "But I do know it would destroy me to spend eternity with the woman I love who only tolerates me because she has no other choice."

He was as powerless in all of this as she was, Addy realized.

He walked to the door.

"Tol, wait."

Her thoughts were a tumult in her head, but one truth emerged.

"I do care about what happens to your people. I'll marry you, and do all the blood stuff that goes with it."

Addy had been holding her breath. She let it out, but it didn't stop her heart from trying to pound out of her chest. She expected Tol's torn expression to transform into relief. She expected him to rush back to her, take her in his arms, and kiss her senseless.

He didn't do any of that. He just gave her a small nod before turning and leaving her alone.

CHAPTER 28

TOL

Tol went to the bow of the boat and sank down behind the rigging. He'd told Addy she didn't have to go through with the blood marriage. The words had come out of his mouth before he'd thought them through. A part of him was glad he'd said them. Offering Addy a way out was the only way Tol would ever be able to keep his sanity intact.

The other part of him, the greater part, was being crushed beneath a mountain of guilt. He still couldn't believe he had even suggested letting his people die, and letting their dream of returning to Vitaquias die with them, for the sake of one girl.

And yet, the thought of forcing Addy to marry him seemed equally impossible.

Tol buried his face in his hands.

He didn't deserve to be king of a people whose lives he was willing to sacrifice, no matter his reasons. He was the worst person imaginable to be responsible for the fate of so many.

Tol had given Addy a way out of their bargain, but she hadn't taken it. He knew she didn't understand—*couldn't* understand—what the blood marriage really entailed. He had spent his whole life trying to comprehend the magnitude of it. He knew she had only agreed to it out of guilt for his people's lives.

Tol didn't know how he was supposed to survive being bound to Addy. She would know how deep his feelings were for her, and he'd be constantly reminded that she had agreed to the blood marriage out of guilt.

He saw the irony of his situation. When he thought he'd hate the Fount, he didn't care about making her as miserable as he would be. But now that he was in love with her, he couldn't stand the thought of forcing the union.

He was in love with Addy.

Tol didn't know how true it was until he'd said the words out loud. They had unleashed a torrent of feelings that were stronger than anything he'd ever felt in his life.

He had no idea he was capable of feeling so much for one person. He and Nira had been...whatever they had been...for more than a year. He cared about her and knew she cared about him, but Tol rarely thought about her when they weren't together. They had both known it would end as soon as the Fount was found. For as intimate as they'd been, Tol had never shared his secret fears with her. They hadn't talked much at all, in fact, unless it was about what they were doing or had just done.

Gerth and Gran were the only ones who really knew him. But Gran was family, and Gerth was more like a brother than his mate.

Whenever Tol thought about the Fount, all he saw were the mental shackles and resentment he knew would come from their binding. He'd read about love and seen it in the way his parents interacted, he just knew it wasn't for him. Until he met *her*.

Footsteps on the wooden boards of the deck made Tol raise his head.

Addy stood over him. She had a determined look in her eyes that was one of about a thousand things he admired about her.

"Tell me more about this blood marriage," she said.

Addy sat down next to him, close enough for him to feel the warmth radiating from her skin. She was wearing a tank top, and it looked fantastic on her.

"There is a ritual of sorts," Tol gave her a half-smile. "We bring each other to the brink of death, and then use each other's Source-infused blood to revive each other. It creates a bond that is forever."

"So, if the bond is forever, does that mean I'd become immortal?"

Tol nodded. "We would both live forever, so long as the other one was alive. But you could never be with anyone else. You would be stuck in my head, and with me in yours…eternally. That means forever."

"I know what eternity means," Addy said, but Tol could see from the glazed expression on her face that she didn't really understand the magnitude of it all.

How could she? He was from that world, and he barely understood the concept of forever.

Tol was hyperaware of how close they were. If he moved his arm only a little, it would brush hers. He didn't move.

"Look," Tol said, "I understand what I'm asking of you. I have to imagine the only thing worse than being locked into a future you didn't choose is being locked into a future you didn't choose…for eternity."

Tol hadn't forgotten what Addy said about not wanting the life her family wanted. Their shared disdain for being stuck, of not wanting the life that had already been decided for them, had bonded them. And now, Tol was the one forcing that life on Addy.

"It wasn't your choice," Addy said. "It's not like you wanted this."

Tol wasn't sure that was true anymore. At least, if Addy felt differently, it might not have been true anymore. Now, though, it was worse.

"I accepted this burden a long time ago," Tol said. "It's my duty as the future king of the Chosen. But you," he shook his head. "This shouldn't be your problem. You shouldn't have to pay for my people's mistakes."

"It's no more your fault than mine," Addy said.

They didn't speak for several minutes.

"Could you have Influenced me to forget about Livy?" Addy asked.

Tol started. "What?"

"Could you have made me forget about her so you wouldn't have had to do this," she swept her hand around at the boat, "and we could just have done the blood marriage right away?"

"I never would have done that," Tol replied.

The idea had occurred to him, especially at first. It was what any of his people would have done in his position. It's what Gerth had told him to do when he'd called his friend to tell him where he was.

225

"But you could have," Addy said.

Tol didn't say anything, and Addy nodded.

"Why didn't you?" she asked.

"Because I didn't want to start off our eternity together with a lie," Tol said. "And then, after Migelian…." Tol broke off. He still couldn't bring himself to think about the old man rooting around in Addy's mind. It made him sick. "I promised you I'd never let anyone Influence you again, and that included me."

Addy shifted slightly, so the fingers of her left hand and his right just touched. Tol wasn't sure if she had done it intentionally, and he had to restrain himself from his instinct to thread his fingers through hers.

"Blood marriage just sounds so morbid," Addy said.

Tol looked at her, but he couldn't read the emotion on her face.

"Does it hurt?" she asked.

This time, Tol didn't stop himself from taking her hand. She didn't pull away, and even curled her fingers around his.

"Very few couples choose to be blood married, and the ritual has only happened once since I've been alive."

Tol was ten years old when he'd witnessed his first and only blood marriage, and all he'd been able to think about was how that would someday be him.

"There is a lot of blood being lost and gained," he gave her a wry look, "obviously. But the two I saw go through it seemed too busy looking at each other to even notice the pain."

At the time, Tol had been disgusted by what Gerth had referred to as their gaga faces. He'd decided then and there that he would never look at any girl like that, even though he knew he'd do the rest of it with the Fount, whoever she turned out to be.

Addy nodded, like she didn't think all of this was too insane for comprehension.

"If we have to go back to your world," Addy swallowed. "Can Livy come with us?"

A flash of guilt went through Tol. It had never occurred to him what would happen *after* the blood marriage, but of course, the whole point was for them to return to Vitaquias.

"I'm not sure," Tol admitted. "A mortal has never been involved with our people before, so there's no real precedent for any of this. I don't know how a regular mortal would fare in the Crossing."

Addy's features tightened.

"We'll figure it out," Tol said. "Either she'll go with us, or we'll come back to the mortal world to visit. Either way, you'll be able to see your sister."

Tol hoped he would be able to give Addy this. He really didn't know what would be possible after the blood marriage. The scholars didn't know if the portal would remain open, or if it would seal itself off as soon as they were through like it had the last time. And he had no idea if Olivia, a mortal without any connection to their world, could even survive on Vitaquias.

"Why does all of this have to happen by my nineteenth birthday?" Addy asked. "Last question, I swear," she added when Tol shook his head and smiled a little.

"Nineteen is the age on Vitaquias when our people begin their immortal lives. It's the age when the vial and chain start depositing Source into our very beings."

Tol paused. "That's why nineteen is a symbolic age. We're considered adults under the laws of my people." He didn't look at Addy when he said the next part. "My parents have said they'll pass the crown to me on my nineteenth birthday."

He heard Addy's intake of breath as she worked out what that meant...what that would make her.

The yacht picked up speed, and a spray of mist came over the bow. Tol turned to Addy. She had gone stock still.

"I think I need to go below deck," she said, her voice quavering slightly.

"I can come with you—"

"No." Addy got up, clutching the railing to support herself. "I just need to be alone for a little while."

Tol nodded, trying to ignore the crushing disappointment of those words. What did he expect from her, anyway? He just unloaded this bombshell on her, and she was taking it as well as he could have hoped.

He didn't expect anything more, but it didn't stop him from wanting more. Tol turned his attention to the sea and listened to Addy's steps grow fainter until he couldn't hear her at all.

Despite the crew's entreaties, Tol couldn't bring himself to eat anything and shut himself in his room before the sky had gone fully dark. He lay on his bed, fully clothed, and stared out the window without seeing anything.

He hadn't slept in this room yet. After that first morning when he'd woken up curled around Addy, they'd spent every night together in the same way.

Until their night in the cave, Tol had thought it was only Addy's fear of water that drove her to nestle against him each night. But she hadn't been afraid in the cave, and she'd still wound her limbs with his before falling asleep with her head on his chest.

The room was too quiet, his bed too empty.

He felt raw and exposed. He shouldn't have told her he was in love with her. He could only imagine what she was thinking, because they were the same thoughts going through his mind. *It's been three weeks. You couldn't possibly love her after so little time. You're a sentimental fool.*

Tol struck his head back on the pillow, like it might be enough to knock his humiliation loose and free him from more emotions than he'd felt in his entire life up until now.

Tol had asked the sweet old stewardess to check on Addy and make sure she was alright, since he was determined to give her the space she needed. Still, it was pride alone that kept him from going to sit outside her door in case she needed him.

What if she had the dream? Would he hear her screams from in here?

Tol was about to get out of bed—his pride be damned—when his door creaked open. The lights were on in the lounge, framing Addy's silhouette in the doorway. She was wearing a tank top and shorts, which showed off her perfect everything.

"Are you awake?" she whispered.

"Yeah."

Addy came over to the bed. Tol pushed himself over, making room for her. She climbed on and scooted closer to him. Her piña colada smell filled the air, making him feel a little drunk.

He didn't know what she wanted from him, so he waited, even though it was agonizing to be so close to her without touching her.

Addy took his arm and pulled it across her stomach. The tank top clung to her unlike the T-shirts she usually favored, and he could imagine the feel of her skin just beneath the material.

He stayed still as her breathing evened out and she relaxed against him in sleep. Tol gently extricated his arm and swept her sunrise hair over her shoulder so it wasn't tickling his face. He leaned forward and kissed the triangle of bare skin at her neck.

Addy sighed and pressed closer to him. Tol wrapped his arm back around her and fell asleep.

CHAPTER 29

ADDY

There was a strange shyness between them that hadn't been there before. So much had been said, and so much had been left unsaid. Addy knew there were things she needed to tell him…things she was now sure he wanted to hear, but she was still trying to grasp what it all meant.

She'd spent their flight from Baltra to Quito and from Quito to Bogotá lost mostly in her own thoughts. Tol had seemed preoccupied with worries of his own, and they'd barely spoken as they each tried to make sense of what was going to happen after they got Livy back.

Tol had convinced Addy to spend a day at his family's manor in England. He'd said they needed more of his people to help them rescue Livy and enough Source to defeat the murderers holding her sister captive.

With the rage boiling inside Addy, she was sure she could defeat the Forsaken one-handed without any help, but Tol hadn't been persuaded.

Before, she hadn't given much thought to what Tol was risking by helping her. It didn't matter that he had agreed to help her for his own reasons. Now that she knew he was putting himself and his entire race at risk just for her, it humbled Addy.

By the time they finally made it to London Heathrow airport, things had more or less gone back to normal between them…if there was such a thing as normal for Addy and Tol. They kept their conversations to the logistics of getting Livy out of a Forsaken stronghold and the lighthearted sniping that had characterized their relationship up until it hadn't. There was still so much unsaid, but Addy didn't have the right words. Every time she thought she had worked up the nerve to say what she was feeling, she'd turn to find Tol asleep, or there would be a flight attendant asking them if they'd like something to drink.

Addy's relief at being off the water had been overwhelming, but there was a part of her that missed the yacht. Mostly, she missed the excuse she'd had to curl up next to Tol every night. Her fear of the water hadn't left her, but after she made that swim to and from the Forsaken island, she had conquered her terror enough that she could have slept alone. Tol didn't need to know that, though.

She spent more time than was probably reasonable remembering the way they had kissed in the cave. Addy badly wanted to repeat the experience, but there hadn't been the opportunity, and she had gotten the feeling that Tol was trying to give her space. Either that, or he was trying to put distance between them for some other reason. They needed to get off this plane and just have some time alone together.

But as they carried their duffels down to the Arrivals of Heathrow, any hope she'd had of being alone with Tol went out the window. There was a group of men waiting for them. They were all wearing suits. Five of them had on dark sunglasses and those cords behind their ears that told everyone they were bodyguards. Addy didn't think any of the men reached above five feet in height, but she also knew their power wasn't in their size. She was sure if it came down to it, they'd use their Influence to dispatch any threat with as much brutal effectiveness as Addy with her shears.

The last man was dressed impeccably in a suit and had a cap that made him look like the stereotypical British limo driver. He took Addy's bag and tipped his hat at her before bowing to Tol. The bodyguards all greeted Tol with slight bows of their heads. The driver chatted with Tol as the other men escorted them outside to three black cars.

The driver held open Addy's door while one of the bodyguards got into the front and the others separated into the remaining cars.

"Sorry about all this," Tol said as the convoy sped away from the airport. "This is my parents' way of saying I'm in trouble." He grinned and shrugged.

Addy had been with Tol when he called his family from the airport in Bogotá to tell them they'd be back the next day. She didn't know who he was talking to, but when Tol pulled the phone away from his ear, she'd heard yelling on the other end.

"Sorry I've caused so much trouble," Addy told him.

Tol shook his head and smiled. "It's good for my parents. Keeps them on their toes."

"We've all been worried about you, Prince Tolumus," the driver said.

Addy noticed the driver kept glancing in his rearview mirror at her, a curious expression on his face.

"You know me," Tol replied. "I always come back."

"Yes, sir," the driver said, returning his gaze to the road.

Tol told the driver to make a detour through London proper so she could glimpse the sites of the city. When she saw her first double-decker bus, Addy actually squealed. Tol laughed and took her hand in his, pointing out the buildings as they drove through Westminster.

Addy saw the driver's glance stray to their joined hands, but he didn't ask about it, and Tol didn't offer an explanation. As they passed Big Ben, Addy practically broke her neck leaning out the window to gaze at it. Tol told the driver to pull over so she could have a better look.

The driver had muttered something about the king and queen wanting to see him straight away, but one look from Tol had the car screeching to a halt so Addy could gaze her fill.

"After we get Olivia back and everything else is settled," Tol whispered in her ear, "I'll take you around the city and show you everything."

"I'd like that," she said, scooting closer to him on the seat and resting her head on his shoulder.

Tol put his arm around her and kissed her forehead.

With the warmth from Tol's body against her, Addy fell asleep sometime after they left the city.

"We're here," Tol said, smoothing her hair back from her face in a way that sent chills through her entire body.

"Holy…."

Addy didn't finish the thought. The driver had opened her door and was waiting for her to get out.

"You really do live in a castle."

Tol laughed. "It's a manor, but I guess you could call it that."

They were at the end of a long, tree-lined driveway. In front of them towered the stone mansion. Part of it was covered in green ivy, while the rest was a weathered stone that looked like it was out of a fairytale. The lawn, which was bordered by trees, was lush and green. It had been mowed in a diagonal striping pattern that her dad would have gone nuts over.

There were people in uniforms waiting for them, who immediately relieved Addy of her duffel and bowed to Tol. They were absorbed into a grand marble foyer, which made Addy feel a little bit like she'd stepped into one of those Jane Austen novels that Livy loved so much. She wished her family was here to see all of this.

Addy was pretty sure her jaw had been hanging on the ground since they arrived at the manor. Tol, for his part, seemed only interested in Addy's reaction to their surroundings. He accepted the servants' well-wishes and bows courteously, but Addy noticed his attention never strayed from her.

It gave her a warm feeling that Tol cared so much what she thought of his home.

"Tol didn't tell me he was bringing home a supermodel."

A boy about a foot shorter than Addy, with long black hair tied back in a messy ponytail, reached out a hand to her.

"This is Gerth," Tol said, grinning at his friend.

Addy shook his hand, returning Gerth's easy smile. Unlike the servants who were standing around them, there was nothing stiff or formal about Tol's best friend. Addy liked him immediately.

Gerth and Tol gave each other one of those back-slapping hugs and exchanged a knowing look.

"Nice of you both to bother dropping by," Gerth said. He leaned closer to Addy, and she bent down so he could fake-whisper in her ear, "The king and queen have been talking about putting Tol in the stockades."

Gerth laughed at the expression on Addy's face, and she glared at him.

"Gerth fancies himself quite the comedian," Tol said with a roll of his eyes. "He thinks it makes him popular with the ladies."

A strange look came over Gerth's face before he laughed. "Well, what do you think, Adelyne?"

Addy pretended to give it some thought. "You might want to work on adding a bit more sarcasm." She mimicked his fake-whisper. "It might make you sound smarter."

Gerth's smile widened until it stretched across his whole face. "Oh, I like her, Tol."

He raised himself on his tiptoes and studied Addy. "And no hairy moles, either. Erikir is going to be devastated."

Addy cocked her head at Tol, who laughed and gave her an *I'll explain later* gesture.

"You don't happen to play chess, do you?" Gerth asked, an eager look in his eyes.

"Sorry," Addy shrugged. "Checkers was more my speed."

Gerth brightened. "I can play checkers."

"I don't advise playing any game with Gerth," Tol told her, "unless you enjoy losing."

"Is that coming from personal experience?" Addy teased Tol.

"It's not my fault Gerth's a freak of nature," Tol complained. "He's always a dozen moves ahead of his opponent."

"He weeps like a little girl every time I win," Gerth confided in Addy. "It's really rather sad."

Tol opened up his mouth to retort.

"Tolumus."

They all turned as a small woman swept into the room. She had the same bronze skin and dark hair that all of Tol's people seemed to have in some variation. She was dressed in a neat skirt and blazer with pearl buttons. Her black hair was twisted in an elegant coif. She was tiny compared to Tol, but she had the same slant to her eyes and same sharp cheekbones.

Everyone in the room except for Tol and Addy sunk into bows and curtseys.

"Hi, Mum." Tol didn't let go of Addy's hand until his mother pulled him into a hug.

He had to almost fold himself in half to be on her level, but there was something imposing about the queen that made Addy feel like she was the short one.

The queen gave Tol a once-over, and Addy got the impression the woman had X-ray vision. The queen's gaze even lingered on Tol's chest where his wound was, even though his shirt covered all evidence of the bandage beneath.

"Well." She turned her attention on Addy, and Addy panicked. "I'm Queen Starser. It's a pleasure to make your acquaintance."

"I—I'm Adelyne Deerborn."

Addy looked at Tol. *Do I curtsey? What do I say?*

Tol just smiled at her, so she stayed put.

"Come," the queen commanded.

Tol took Addy's hand in his, giving it a reassuring squeeze as his mother, who Addy decided was the most terrifying woman she'd ever laid eyes on, led them down the hall.

Addy gave Tol an accusing glare. *Why hadn't he warned her about his mom?* Tol just snickered, which earned him a look from his mother that made Addy want to hide behind one of the enormous potted ferns.

No one said anything as Queen Starser led them through a set of double doors and then closed them as soon as they'd all stepped inside. The room was small and cozy, which put Addy more at ease.

There was a fireplace in the corner that, even though it wasn't lit, seemed to give the room added warmth. All the furniture was plush, from the overstuffed armchairs to the leather couch. There were artfully-arranged pillows everywhere. The walls were painted a deep red, and the tall bookshelves were lined with books. Heavy drapes had been pulled back to reveal a stone patio just beyond the glass doors bordered by flowers and shrubs, which had been pruned with careful precision.

The queen appraised her in a way that made Addy want to put on more clothes, even though she was wearing a sweatshirt and jeans.

"So, you're the Fount, then?"

Addy looked at the queen. "That's what Tol told me," she managed.

Queen Starser's face was inscrutable as she turned her attention back on her son. "And I suppose you have an excellent reason for being away so long and practically giving your father and me a heart attack?"

"Yes," Tol said.

He didn't say anything more, and Addy could see the queen's irritation mounting. Addy thought it was very brave, or very stupid, of Tol to challenge this woman.

"I told Gerth to tell you not to worry," Tol added.

If he was as uncomfortable as Addy, he didn't show it.

"Yes, I know." The queen's face twisted in annoyance. "We'll discuss that later. For now, there is a far more pressing matter. The blood marriage."

She looked from one of them to the other. "I've set it for tomorrow at sundown."

Addy's throat started to constrict, but before she could even form a thought, Tol said, "That isn't going to work. The Forsaken are holding Addy's sister at Elmendorf Air Force Base. That's why we came back. We need help getting her out."

If it had been her parents in the room, and she had dropped a bombshell on them equivalent to the one Tol had just dropped on his mother, shouting would have ensued. Her sisters would have come into the room to see what the fuss was about, and then they would have joined in the yelling. It wouldn't have been angry yelling, just the kind of raised voices that came naturally when there were a lot of people with loud voices in one place. Tol's mother didn't raise her voice.

She raised one perfectly manicured eyebrow. "Then it seems you and I have some matters to discuss. In the meantime, as far as we're all concerned, Adelyne is just a guest in our home. If any of our subjects discover the Fount is here and we are waiting on the blood marriage, we'll have anarchy on our hands."

"I agree," Tol said.

He and his mother looked at Addy.

"Of course," she managed. *Your Majesty? Your Highness?*

Why hadn't Tol gone over protocol with her on the plane? Addy made yet another mental reminder to kill him as soon as they were alone.

The queen went to the doors and opened them a crack.

"Henroix," she said.

Addy heard the sound of shoes clicking across the marble, and then an older man in a black suit was bowing at the queen through the doorway.

"Please see Ms. Deerborn to the guest cottage. Have Viola and Marise help her settle in."

"Very good, Your Majesty."

Tol walked with Addy to the door. "Don't worry," he whispered in her ear and gave her hand another squeeze. "I'll see you in a little bit."

Addy nodded, and then followed Henroix out of the room.

CHAPTER 30

TOL

Gran and Tol's father came in next, and then the whole conversation he'd just had with his mother had to be repeated. His father gave him the same speech his mother had, nearly word-for-word, about his responsibility to his people and the risk he'd put them all at by disappearing for so long. He took their quiet chastisement, knowing they weren't wrong. He drank the three cups of tea Gran practically forced into his hands.

"The blood marriage must happen first," his mother said. "On that, we are all agreed."

Gran and his father nodded.

"No, we aren't," Tol said.

"Tolumus, I know you may have needed to give the Fount certain assurances to get her here, but now is not the time—"

"I made her an oath bound by Source," Tol interrupted his father. "We get her sister back first, and then she'll go through with the blood marriage."

Everyone else in the room sucked in a collective breath.

"You'll just have to get her to agree to new terms," his mother said. "It isn't possible to wait for the blood marriage."

"That's not for you to decide." Tol kept his voice even. "Addy and I are the ones going through the ritual, so we'll decide when it happens. And I'm telling you it isn't happening until we get her sister back safely."

"Tolumus, be reasonable—"

"You can help us, and the whole process will go faster and smoother, or you can stay here and we'll go alone. Either way, we're going."

"She's just a mortal girl," his father tried to reason with him. "She isn't one of us until she is bound to you."

Tol clenched his jaw to keep from saying something he'd regret. When he trusted himself enough to speak, he said, "She is not *just a mortal girl*. She is my future wife and queen of the Chosen, and we will do this one thing for her before she gives up her freedom for our people."

Tol stared his parents down, daring them to argue with him. They didn't.

His parents exchanged a look.

"We'll organize a small party," his father said at last. "We'll leave tomorrow morning and be back in a few days. The blood marriage will take place upon our return."

Tol nodded.

"Good, now that that's settled," Gran said, "let's get down to the important matters."

Gran settled herself on the couch and took a long sip from her teacup. "Tell me about the Fount."

The Fount. It had been a long time since Tol had thought about Addy that way. It seemed like such a cold, removed title that wasn't deserving of the woman he'd come to love.

Tol swallowed. "She's incredible," he said.

He decided not to mention how she'd saved his life...multiple times. The less his parents knew about how close he'd come to dying, the better.

"Is she pretty?" Gran persisted.

Gorgeous.

"Yes," Tol managed.

Gran's smile widened. "You like her, don't you?"

"Even if there was no Celestial and I could choose any woman, I'd choose her."

His parents exchanged a skeptical look, but his gran clapped her hands together and laughed with glee.

"You're in love with her." His seven-hundred-year-old grandmother bounced up and down on the couch.

"Yes," he said. *So much.*

"Then my prayers to the gods have been answered," Gran said. "I am so very happy for you, my boy."

His gran gave him a squeeze that would be impressive for someone his own age. She looked into the corner of the room that was empty except for the fireplace and said, "You hear that, Walidir? Our grandson is in love!"

Tol's parents just shook their heads. They had all long-ago given up on trying to convince Gran that her husband was dead.

"And I'm sure she's just as smitten with you. Lucky girl," Gran said, oblivious to the way her son and daughter-in-law were looking at her.

Tol managed a weak smile that he hoped concealed all the uncertainty and depth of emotions that lay beneath. He and Addy hadn't talked about anything serious beyond rescuing Olivia since they'd gotten off the yacht. He had wanted to give her the space she needed to figure out how she felt about everything he'd unloaded onto her. Tol had watched complex emotions unfold on her face when she hadn't realized he was watching her.

Tol was desperate to know what she was thinking…how she was feeling…but he forced himself to be patient and wait until she was ready.

Gran stood up, waving away his offer to help her. "We have so much to celebrate tonight."

The king shook his head. "We don't want anyone to suspect who the girl is. We'll keep her in the cottage tonight so no one will ask questions."

"Oh for gods' sake, Rolomens." Gran peered at her son over the rims of her spectacles. "Don't be such a sour puss. This girl is the savior of our race and the love of my grandson's life, and you want to sequester her in the cottage?"

Tol's father pursed his lips.

"Getyl, we need to be practical," Tol's mother began, but Gran cut her off.

"Oh poo," Gran said. "Starser, I depend on you to make sure my son doesn't stiffen into a statue."

"I don't think preserving our reign, especially at this tenuous time, is a joking matter," Tol's father replied.

"I'm telling Henroix to arrange dinner on the cliff garden to celebrate my grandson's return." Gran hobbled to the doorway, leaning on her cane. She turned back. "Drink some tea, Rolomens. It might help wash away some of your cynicism."

To Tol, she said, "I can't wait to meet your Adelyne." She gave him a warm smile, glared at Tol's father, and then left the room.

His Adelyne.

He wanted her to be, but that was for her to decide.

CHAPTER 31

ADDY

The guest cottage was as big as her family's farmhouse. Everything was cream and lace, and Addy was afraid to touch anything until she'd showered and put on her last clean outfit. After she changed, she wandered around the bedroom, which had enough opulence and charm to delight both Stacy and Livy, respectively.

A large four-poster bed sat on one side of the enormous bedroom. The long wooden dresser was topped with expensive-looking glass bottles and silver jewelry holders. There was a lamp with crystals hanging from the shade that made a pleasant clinking sound when Addy ran her finger along them.

Across from the bed was a sitting room with floor-to-ceiling windows that looked out over a private, tree-bordered courtyard. There were two couches and a coffee table with a silver tea set perched on top. Pillows covered the couches, and they had been fluffed so they all had a dimple right in their center. The walls were covered with pastoral landscapes, all of which were hung in gilded frames.

No sooner had Addy settled herself on the fluffy white comforter of her bed, she heard a knock at the door.

"Come in?" she said, scooting to the edge of the bed.

Two women bustled into the room, looking flustered. The first was very old and chubby. The second looked just like the first, except less old. They both had smaller versions of Tol's necklace, and Addy noticed that the liquid in them was nearly empty.

"Hello, darling," the older woman said, unloading the boxes she had been balancing in her arms onto the dresser. The younger woman gave Addy a nod as she dumped what looked like dress bags onto Addy's bed.

"Viola," the younger woman pointed to herself, "Marise," she pointed to the older one.

"Nice to meet you," Addy said, deciding it would be impolite to ask these women what they were doing here.

"My lady." Marise sunk into a low curtsey. "The pleasure is all ours." She took a handkerchief out of her pocket and started to dab at her eyes, which Addy realized were leaking tears.

"I'm sorry," Addy began, not knowing what she should be apologizing for.

"Rubbish!" Viola planted her hands on her hips. "We're just grateful is all."

"Grateful?" Addy asked.

"This curse," Marise said. She gave Viola a furtive look and then lowered her voice. "We're just so grateful to you."

"To me?"

Viola nodded. "You're going to save us."

"We don't have more than a month between us," Marise said. "And we're better off than some."

"Jeniala only has a few days left," Viola said. "We're lucky the prince found you when he did."

Addy stared at Viola and Marise in horror. These women were dying, and they were grateful to her because they thought she was going to rescue them.

"Don't worry," Viola said, misreading Addy's distress. "The servants all know who you are, and your secret is safe with us."

Addy forced a smile. "Thanks."

"The royal family has done all they could to keep us safe," Marise was saying. "They barely take enough Source for themselves. The only reason our dear Tolumus has so much is because he needed it to search for you."

Both women beamed at Addy. She had no idea how to respond.

Marise started dumping eyeliner pencils, foundation, and makeup brushes onto the dresser. Stacy would have been in heaven, but Addy was overwhelmed.

"Um, what are you—" Addy began.

"We're getting you ready for dinner." The older woman gave her a warm smile before going back to arranging the makeup on the dresser.

Addy thought about dinners at home. The only requirement for sitting at her parents' table was clean hands. Even that rule was hard to enforce, though, especially for Rosie and Baby Lucy.

Viola was pulling beautiful dresses out of bags and holding them up to Addy with a critical look at both the dress and its potential wearer.

Both women took breaks every so often to sit on the couch and fan themselves. They pressed the chains around their necks into their skin. Addy remembered Tol telling her about how the vial and chain worked together to implant the life-giving elements of Source into people older than the mortal world would allow. The women's Hazes were dull, and Addy could swear Viola had gotten a few more gray hairs since she'd come into the cottage.

"Blood marriages really can be a beautiful event," Marise was saying. "My cousin…."

Addy wasn't listening to her. She was thinking about Jeniala, who only had a few more days, and the rest of Tol's people who might die before she and Tol could save them.

She had known, at least in theory, what Tol was sacrificing to help her get Livy back. But seeing these women, with their near-empty vials of Source and the way they wheezed and limped around the room, made her heart ache.

Marise perched Addy on one of the couches, adjusting the curtains to let in more sunlight.

"How do you usually do your makeup?" Marise asked as she sifted through the bottles and pencils on the dresser.

"I don't," Addy admitted. "My sister used to do my makeup…."

Addy couldn't catch her breath. For a moment, she just sat on the couch and waited for the crushing pain to ease.

She wanted Tol.

"I just need some air," she managed.

"Oh no, you don't." Marise pulled Addy back down onto the couch. "We don't have much time, and I promised Queen Starser you'd be ready in time for dinner."

She looked at Addy and pursed her lips. "Viola, go get this darling girl a petit four. The sugar will do her good."

That's how Addy ended up eating tiny desserts while trying to hold still long enough for Marise to do her makeup and Viola to take her measurements. The younger woman disappeared with one of the dress bags, a tape measure wound around her neck like a snake. Addy was grateful that Marise kept up a stream of chatter the whole time, which saved Addy from having to talk about herself.

She learned that Marise was Viola's niece, which confused Addy since Marise looked older. It overwhelmed Addy to consider how much about these people she still didn't understand, and how much she'd need to learn if she would be worthy of becoming…their queen. That's what Tol had said she'd be. It still didn't seem possible on this planet or any other.

Marise blew Addy's hair out, curled the ends, and then worked the lengthy coils into place with bobby pins. Marise didn't let her look in the mirror, saying she "loved the big reveal at the end."

Addy resigned herself to looking like some overdone caricature and just let the woman work her over in any way she saw fit. Maybe she'd be able to wipe some of the makeup off and change her hair on the sly after Marise left.

Viola returned, the doily pinned in her hair askew, with one shoebox and one dress bag. The shoebox contained a pair of lavender shoes that looked like ballet slippers. As Viola slipped them onto Addy's feet, she complained about how it was next to impossible to find shoes that wouldn't make Addy any more giant than she already was.

"You don't want to tower over the prince," Marise said in sympathy.

Addy just smiled as the women continued to fuss over her.

The dress Viola slipped over Addy's head was lavender silk to match the shoes, and it clung to her like a second skin. The two women exchanged a look of pride. Marise led Addy over to the floor-length mirror on the other side of the room.

Addy steeled herself, and then took in her reflection.

"Wow," she breathed.

With all the work Marise had done on her, she'd expected to look more clown than human. She didn't.

Her makeup was understated, making her look like a less pale, prettier version of her normal self. Lavender eyeliner brought out the green of her eyes and matched the dress perfectly. Her hair was elegant, but not fancy or overdone. It was twisted and swept in a graceful knot on the side of her head. A strand of hair had been artfully pinned over the top to make it look like a sash.

The dress was the most impressive part of the whole ensemble. There were thin straps at her shoulders, and then the dress plunged in a V-shape in the front in a way that made it look like she had far more cleavage than she did. It had a similar cut in the back, except it was even more revealing. Everything from her shoulders to her lower back was bare.

The dress molded to her hips, giving her shape where she'd never had it before, and then flared out all the way to the floor.

"Stacy would love this," Addy managed.

She missed her sisters with a ferocity she hadn't been prepared for. She sat on the bed before her legs failed her.

"Ad-dy!"

There was a knock at the door, and then it burst open before any of the women could say anything. Addy leapt to her feet.

Gerth strolled into the bedroom, dressed in a tux.

"You wait until the lady says 'come in'," Viola huffed.

Gerth shrugged. "I figured there was at least a ninety-eight percent chance you were all dressed." He turned to Viola and Marise. "I'll be escorting Addy to dinner. You can go."

"Thank you!" Addy called as the two women gathered up the makeup and clothes bags and bustled out of the room.

When they'd gone, Gerth looked Addy up and down. He grinned.

"Tol is going to lose his gods-damned mind when he sees you."

Addy felt her cheeks warm. Gerth offered her his arm, and she took it.

"Where is Tol?" Addy asked.

"Just finishing up getting dressed. His parents gave him quite the verbal lashing, and you know Tol, he gave it right back."

Addy smiled, picturing it.

"You've been Tol's friend since you were kids?" she asked as they crossed the lawn between the cottage and the manor.

"Best mate, protector, subject, brother," Gerth said. "I've been all of it."

"Protector?" Addy lifted an eyebrow as she looked down at Gerth.

He gave her a mock-offended look. "Not everything is about height, Ms. Supermodel."

Addy laughed. "Fair enough."

Gerth sobered. "When the elders had the bright idea of making us fit into the mortal world by acting like actual mortals, they didn't account for how merciless primary school kids can be. Combine that with my best mate having a missing arm, and us not being able to tell any of them it was because he's so damn powerful our gods tried to yank him back into their world, and you've got yourself hell on a stick."

Addy thought about how, even now, Tol angled his body so his prosthetic arm was out of view of whoever he was talking to. She thought about how he still slept with his prosthesis most nights, even though she told him to take it off. She wanted to go back in time and kick those kids' asses.

Gerth continued, "I'm not embarrassed to say I used up more of my Source than I should have getting revenge on those prats."

Addy felt a ridiculous gratitude toward Gerth for defending Tol back then.

"Ah, good." Gerth pointed to an old woman hobbling up the path toward them. "You can meet Tol's gran."

Nerves shot through Addy. Tol had told her about his grandmother, and she knew that next to Gerth, his gran was the most important person in

Tol's life. Addy wished suddenly for a sweater or something to cover up the more revealing parts of her dress.

"Stop fussing," Gerth told her, batting her hands away from where she'd folded them across her chest. "Getyl isn't one of those prudish grannies."

The old woman stopped a few paces ahead of them. Addy's smile faltered at the expression on her face. Tol's grandmother let out a piercing scream.

She dropped her cane on the grass and started to run toward them.

Addy and Gerth exchanged a puzzled look.

"Lezha Bloodsong!" she shrieked.

Tol's grandmother raised her vial to her lips, foregoing the single drop Tol always used and taking a glug straight from the vial. Her golden light flared around her.

"Murderer!"

The old woman lunged…at Addy.

CHAPTER 32

ADDY

Addy was too stunned to even move. Gerth stepped between them and caught the old lady as she came barreling at Addy.

"Getyl, what's the matter with you?" Gerth grunted as he wrestled Tol's grandmother back.

"Murderer!" she shrieked at Addy. "You killed my boy!"

All Addy could do was shake her head.

"Getyl, this is Adelyne," Gerth said as he continued to wrestle her. For an old lady, Getyl was holding her own.

Addy winced as a streak of blood appeared across Gerth's cheek. Tol's grandmother was literally clawing him in her attempt to get to Addy.

"Lezha Bloodsong," Getyl continued to yell. "You will pay for the death of my son!"

"Getyl, you're attacking the Fount," Gerth said, finally managing to pin her arms by her sides. "This is Tol's Adelyne. She isn't the Forsaken general."

Addy started. *Tol's grandmother thought she was the Forsaken general?*

"Oh." Getyl seemed to shrink into herself. "Adelyne, of course." She let out a crazed little chuckle. "You hear that Walidir? It isn't our son's murderer." She looked at Addy. "Forgive me, dearest. I thought you were...someone else."

Addy was shaken, but she managed to give the old woman a small smile.

Gerth motioned to a servant standing just off the path. He passed off Getyl to the servant, telling the man to "Please see Lady Magnantius to the clifftop garden."

"I really am very sorry," Getyl told Addy, looking both puzzled and contrite. "You'll have to forgive an old woman's eyesight." She accepted the cane the servant held out to her and hobbled away.

"What was that all about?" Addy asked.

"Batty as a mortal bat in a bag." Gerth shook out his long hair as he wiped at the blood on his cheek. "A couple of years before the Crossing, Erikir's father and some of the other Chosen had a run-in with the Forsaken general. The general killed all of them except for Getyl."

"Tol's...uncle?" Addy asked, trying to put the pieces together.

Gerth nodded.

"And I look like the general?" Addy asked.

"Nah." Gerth waved a dismissive hand. "The Forsaken are all big, blonde-haired, and gray-eyed. She must have seen how tall you were compared to me," Gerth grinned up at Addy, "and just made the leap." He shrugged. "Although, technically, Getyl's the only Chosen still alive who has ever seen the Forsaken general. Every time we get a hint about where the general's hiding, she disappears into thin air."

"Oh," Addy managed, feeling somehow like she'd failed Tol by earning his grandmother's hatred before she had even opened her mouth.

She turned her anger on the Forsaken general. That woman was the reason why Addy's family was dead and Tol's beloved grandmother was going insane.

"Don't give it another thought," Gerth said, seeing Addy's distress. "Getyl is over seven-hundred years old, so she's ageing faster in the mortal world than the rest of us." Gerth paused, considering. "She hasn't been right since her husband didn't make the Crossing."

Addy remembered Tol saying that his grandmother talked to his dead grandfather.

"She thinks her husband is still alive," Addy said.

"Yeah." Gerth looped his finger by his ear, making the crazy gesture. "Anyone who believes there might have been survivors after what happened to the Old World is—"

"Batty as a mortal bat?" Addy supplied.

"Mad as a mortal hatter," Gerth confirmed.

They walked for a few minutes in silence. Addy used the picturesque landscape and peaceful stillness of the gardens they passed through to quiet her nerves. Gerth steered her around the outside of the manor and toward yet another shrub-lined path.

Tol, who was walking toward them, came to a stop.

"Gods, Addy."

His eyes roved over her. It should have made her feel exposed, but it didn't. She was drinking him in the same way.

He was wearing a tux like Gerth, and it looked incredible on him. His hair was pulled back in a bun, with a few of the shorter strands still framing his face. She could smell his spicy scent from here.

"If you two are finished swallowing each other with your eyes," Gerth began, but Addy didn't hear the rest of what he said.

She moved toward Tol.

"Whoa." Gerth got between them, holding his hands out to keep them apart. "We are in full view of no fewer than fifty curious eyes, wondering who the mortal in the purple dress is who has made the prince's tongue unravel on the ground. If they see you doing," Gerth flailed his hands, "whatever you're planning to do, their questions are bound to get harder to answer."

Tol shook his head like he was trying to clear it. "He's right," Tol said, sounding resigned. He gave Addy an apologetic look.

"I'm always right," Gerth said.

"You look," Tol began, and then shook his head. "I…."

Addy smiled at him. "You, too."

The way he was staring at her made Addy think of herself in a way she never had before. It felt exhilarating.

"Tolumus, quit stuttering," Gerth commanded. "Addy, stop drooling."

Gert put a hand on each of their backs and shoved them forward.

"You look like a goddess," Tol said as soon as they were across the lawn and Gerth had released them.

She was about to make some kind of joke, but when she turned to him and saw the look in his eyes, all words left her.

"Thank you," she managed, as Tol took her hand in his.

Gerth walked ahead of them on a path that was covered by flowered trellises.

"Oh, you're back," a musical, feminine voice called.

"Uh-oh," Gerth muttered.

Tol's hand tightened on Addy's.

The most beautiful person Addy had ever seen stepped onto the path. She wore a red dress that made Addy's look like a nun's habit in comparison. It was strapless and cut low between her breasts. Unlike Addy, hers weren't the illusion of cleavage…they were the real deal. A slit that went from the bottom of her dress almost to her hip showed off a flawlessly tanned and toned leg. The dress clung to her perfect hourglass figure.

She was tiny, making Addy feel more like the Hulk than the supermodel Gerth had called her earlier. Her glossy black hair hung all the way down to her waist and rippled with her every step.

She was a Barbie, Addy decided. A living, breathing Barbie.

"Hi, Nira," Gerth said in a sing-songy voice. "So lovely to see you."

She ignored Gerth, crunching up the path in stilettos that got her to about Addy's shoulder.

"Tol used to be Nira's plaything," Gerth whispered to Addy. "Or maybe, she was his. It was confusing." He raised his whisper so Tol could hear. "Fount stuff aside, I like you *much* better."

Nira reached them and, to Addy's shock and fury, put her tiny hands on Tol's chest. Her perfectly-manicured red nails traced a line down his front buttons before Tol reacted. Her hand went to his belt and rested on the buckle. It was suggestive and possessive. Addy wanted to rip her Barbie head from her neck.

"Ad-dy," Gerth hissed. "Your Haze."

Addy looked down to see the golden light that was seeping out of her. She forced her anger back down, and with it, the golden light receded.

Nira's eyes widened in surprise, which only made her prettier. "What in the two hells do we have here?" she asked.

Tol let go of Addy's hand to remove Nira's from his belt.

"Nira," Tol said, his voice tight. "I'd like to introduce you to Adelyne."

Nira jutted out her lower lip. "So, it's true? You've found the Fount."

Tol and Gerth exchanged a look. Gerth shrugged.

"We don't want anyone else to know yet," Tol said. "But yes, it's true."

Nira's beautiful, dark eyes scrutinized Addy from bottom to top, making her want to cover up. She felt her cheeks heat from embarrassment and anger. Her hand itched for the feeling of her garden shears, which she'd left in the cottage.

"Nira," Gerth said in a too-cheery voice, "let's go reserve seats near the good food." He took Nira's elbow and tried to drag her away. "You don't want to be stuck sitting next to Erikir, do you?"

She shooed him away like he was a pesky fly.

"Well, she could be uglier, I suppose." Nira gave Tol a pitying look. "If I had known last month would be our final time together, I would have made it really count."

She winked one of her beautiful eyes at Addy and turned before anyone could say anything. Nira strutted away, swaying her hips far more than the activity of walking required.

Gerth took one look at Tol, and then hurried after Nira.

"I should have told you about Nira," Tol said when they were gone.

"You think?" Addy didn't try to hide the sarcasm in her voice.

"I'm sorry." Tol took a step closer, but she twisted out of his grasp.

"She's the one, isn't she? She's the one you *made love* to." Addy hadn't forgotten their conversation in the hotel room or the way those two words had sounded in his black velvet voice. "And you were still together until now?"

"No, I mean yes, but it wasn't like that."

Addy knew that Tol had been with someone else, but she hadn't realized that whatever Tol and Nira shared, it wasn't as far in the past as she had assumed.

Addy's golden light was seeping back out again, but she didn't care who was around to see it. "Is the only reason you're with me because you have to be?"

"What? Gods, Addy. No."

"Then why was she acting like you two were still together?"

"Nira has always known what we had couldn't last," Tol said. "She'll forget about me soon enough."

Addy felt her anger growing by the second.

"I'm sorry this blood marriage thing is so strict," she said. "You must be heartbroken to be stuck with me when you could have had her instead."

A look of horror crossed Tol's face. "Addy, listen to me." Desperation tinged his voice. "I was angry and lonely, and I thought I was going to spend eternity with someone I didn't love, and who didn't love me. Nira was…a distraction. I care about her, but not like that. I didn't think I *could* care about someone like that."

Addy wasn't ready to let him off the hook yet, but she committed his words to memory so she could replay them later.

"It doesn't change that you're with me because you have to be, whether you want to or not," she said.

"Addy." Tol shook his head. "You are the only woman for me…in this world or any other. You are *my* chosen."

And just like that, Addy's anger evaporated. Her golden light withdrew, and the angry, twisted thing inside her went back to sleep.

She looked up at him, and a warm tingling spread through her as their eyes locked.

Tol took her face in both his hands. She felt warmth from his living flesh and coolness from the prosthesis.

"Addy, I—"

"Tolumus, there will be time for that after the blood marriage." Queen Starser, looking as regal and intimidating as ever in a fancier version of the suit she'd been wearing earlier, was frowning at them. She took Tol's elbow in one hand and Addy's in the other, and steered them forward. "Come along."

Tol's mother led them over a garden bridge where a weeping willow tree's branches kissed Addy's bare shoulders, and through a trellis that was dripping with purple and white flowers. When they stepped into the clearing, Addy gasped.

She had never seen anything so beautiful.

There were trees bordering the clearing, and blue hydrangea bushes just inside the trees. Beneath the canopy of the biggest tree Addy had ever seen was a long table set with crystal and china. Glass lanterns floated in the air over the table. The setting sun threw a golden tinge to everything, including the people milling around.

Tol, who had been watching her, smiled. He led her over to the head of the table where King Rolomens was already seated. A servant moved to pull out Addy's chair, but Tol got to it first. Before she sat, she ran her hand over the top of one of the glass lanterns hanging above the table, only to find it wasn't floating in the air, but hanging from the tree branches by nearly invisible wires.

Tol laughed. "I wish we had the levitating kind of magic."

Addy found herself sitting between Tol and Gerth, and across from Tol's cousin, Erikir. She was relieved that Getyl was too far down the table for her to have to make conversation with. After the old woman's outburst earlier, Addy wasn't sorry to have some distance between them, just in case Tol's grandmother went crazy again.

Addy had expected the dinner to be stiff and awkward, but it wasn't. Conversation flowed as freely as the wine, which tasted like honey and exotic spices. There was plenty of laughter, and a festive mood hung around the entire group.

The dinner was both like and unlike the food she was familiar with. It certainly wasn't farm fare, but the artfully plated delicacies were ones she knew existed in any fine restaurant in the States. Even though she'd never had quail eggs or white truffles, she got the sense that the ones served in even the best restaurants didn't taste as good as these. A servant stood behind Addy and Tol, refilling their wine glasses and switching out their silverware with every course.

Tol and Addy held hands under the table, even though Tol earned more than a few disapproving looks from his mom as he wielded his fork in his prosthetic hand with only mild success.

Everyone was more than kind to Addy, and she felt herself falling in love with Tol's family. The only exception might have been Tol's cousin. Erikir hated her from the moment they were introduced. He would have been handsome, if he wasn't always scowling. He had dark, almond-shaped eyes like Tol, but unlike the warmth that radiated from Tol's, Erikir's eyes were cold.

"Were your parents pro basketball players?" he asked, turning up his lip like the idea was so far beneath him he could barely stand to speak the words.

Before Addy could respond, Gerth loudly proclaimed, "Don't be jealous, just because you can't get a supermodel girlfriend like Tol."

After that, Addy earned only sneers from Tol's cousin.

The queen turned and said something to the servant standing behind her. The man snapped his fingers, and then all of the servants bowed and walked back down the path. More than half the people sitting at the table also got up, clearly having understood something Addy had missed. Only a small group remained seated at the long table. Addy was more than a little irritated to see Nira was still with them.

"We may now speak freely," the king announced. "But I would like to impress on all of you the importance of discretion, especially regarding the Fount. These are turbulent times, after all."

There were murmurs and stares in Addy's direction.

"To the Fount!" someone down the table shouted.

Everyone raised their glasses as Addy's cheeks turned to flame. Tol smiled at her over the rim of his glass.

"Did you know that, technically, I should be next in line to the throne?" Erikir asked no one in particular when the conversation had died down around them.

Tol just shook his head, like he was used to these kinds of comments from his cousin, and they had long-since ceased to bother him.

"The Forsaken general murdered my older brother before the Crossing," the king explained to Addy. "However," his eyes slid to Erikir, who wilted under his gaze, "now that I am king, my son is next in line to the throne."

Erikir lowered his head, his cheeks dark with humiliation.

"He's bitter Tol is more powerful than he is," Gerth said loudly into the awkward silence that followed.

Erikir scowled, but he didn't try to deny it.

"Tolumus is the most powerful of us all," the queen said, looking at her son with pride. "He will use his extraordinary gifts to lead our people to new heights we've never even dreamed of."

Addy looked at Tol, who had become very interested in the edge of the tablecloth.

"How about you, Addy?" Gerth asked. "Is your Influence as strong as Tol's?"

Addy looked at Tol.

"Her Haze is brighter than yours," Tol told Gerth in a mocking tone, "but we don't think she'll be able to Influence until after the blood marriage."

Gerth's brow creased. "But she tolerates the Source?"

"She doesn't need it. Her Haze only comes when she needs to draw on the Celestial's power. You should see her fight the Forsaken." Tol's voice was full of pride. "She's unstoppable."

Addy felt herself blush, not so much at the compliment itself, but at the fact that it had come from Tol.

"Well, that makes sense," Erikir said in a way that made Addy stiffen in preparation for the coming insult. Tol was braced for it, too.

"Careful, Cousin," Tol said in a tone that made Addy very glad it hadn't been directed at her.

"Brute force is much easier than Influence." Erikir gave Addy a knowing look. "It's why the Forsaken are weaker."

Addy decided Erikir must not have fought very many Forsaken if he thought they were weak, but she kept her mouth shut.

"Funny," Tol said, his eyes narrowing on Erikir. "You might—"

The king interrupted before Tol could finish. "Very little is actually known about how the Celestial's powers would interact with a mortal. I'm sure the full extent of Adelyne's abilities will present themselves in due course." He gave Addy a warm smile.

The king got to his feet and cleared his throat. The rest of the table went quiet.

"Our people have had eighteen long years to reflect on what happened to our world. The queen and I regret what was done more than words can express, although we have no regrets about our desire to improve the lives of our people."

They all waited while the king took a sip of his water.

"The gods gave us our gifts, not so that we could hide them away like squirrels hoarding acorns, but so that we could use them. Our race was blessed with superior power, and thus, it was our gift and burden to try to make our world a little better."

Addy felt Tol stiffen beside her. She remembered his fear that he wouldn't be able to temper his people's ambition. Addy could see now what Tol had meant. The king said he regretted what happened, but Addy wasn't sure she believed him.

"Our people have been punished long enough," King Rolomens continued. "When we return to Vitaquias, we will not be timid, as that would be akin to spitting in the gods' faces. Instead, we will use what we have learned during our exile."

Addy was beginning to doubt he had learned anything. It sounded to her like the king was justifying ruining their world in his quest for more power, and the others were agreeing with him. Addy exchanged a look with Tol, and she saw the same misgivings on his face.

"Our biggest regret, though, is the pressure that has been placed on our son's shoulders as a result of our miscalculation."

How could destroying an entire world be classified as a miscalculation?

"Our son has carried the weight of our race's survival for the last eighteen years. Now, he has achieved what we have all been praying for."

The king extended his hand toward Addy. She ducked her head as applause went down the table. Tol squeezed her hand.

The king raised his glass to Tol and Addy. "May your union bring life and liberty to our people. With your blood marriage, we will return to Vitaquias stronger than ever before."

Everyone except for Tol, Addy, and Erikir cheered.

"The Forsaken will fear us once again, and we will all live to experience the golden age of Tolumus Magnantius' rule."

There were cries of joy and well wishes shouted down the table, before another voice broke through the toasts.

"My son is a bit long-winded," Getyl began, earning a few appreciative chuckles from the others at the table, "so I'll keep my words brief." She got to her feet with the help of the people sitting on either side of her. "My praise is for Adelyne Deerborn, our true savior."

Addy froze as all eyes turned on her.

Tol, who seemed relieved that someone else was the center of attention, took his hand out of Addy's and draped it over the back of her chair. His finger traced light circles on the back of her neck while she died of embarrassment.

"To Adelyne, our savior."

Glasses were raised and drained.

"Adelyne Magnantius has a nice ring to it." Gerth elbowed Addy in the side.

"My last name is Deerborn," Addy said. "It will always be Deerborn."

All she had left of her family were her memories and her name. She would die before giving up either.

"That's not how things are traditionally done here, especially in the royal family," Erikir said, smirking at her ignorance.

"I'd like to know what about our relationship is traditional," Tol shot back. "A mortal has never become one of us, which means we get to make up our own rules."

Addy gave Tol a grateful look.

"Well, your family must be very proud of you at any rate," Tol's grandmother said in an attempt to clear away the tension. "I imagine your parents—"

Tol stood up so fast his chair overturned.

"I'm taking Addy on a walk before it gets dark," he announced.

"The guards will be posted outside the cottage tonight," the king said. "Be sure she's back at a reasonable hour." To Addy, he explained, "We can't take any chances with your safety while you're still vulnerable."

"And be sure you remember the rules of the ritual," Getyl said with a wink.

"Gran!" Tol's face had gone dark with embarrassment, while everyone else at the table laughed, clearly in on a joke Addy had missed.

"It's been a big night for my mother-in-law," the queen said in apology. Like Addy had a clue about what was going on.

"We'll see you in the morning," Tol told his parents. He put a hand on Addy's back and steered her away from the table.

CHAPTER 33

TOL

A re you okay?" Tol asked as soon as they were alone.

"Fine." Addy gave him a small smile.

"I'm sorry about that," Tol said. "I told Gran about your family, but her memory isn't what it used to be."

She nodded, but she didn't say anything more.

Tol hadn't been paying attention to where they were walking; he had just wanted to get Addy away from everyone's scrutiny. He realized he had led them up to the cliffs out of habit.

It was a rare clear night, and the moon shone over the water.

"Oh," Addy said, taking it all in.

"We can go somewhere where you can't see the water," Tol said quickly.

"No, that's okay. I'm not afraid." She smiled at him in a way that made him think the reason she wasn't scared might be because of him.

The wind picked up, and Addy shivered.

Tol took off his jacket and put it over her shoulders.

"Thanks," she said, pulling it closer around herself. He thought he saw her put her nose in the fabric and inhale.

Tol leaned over the stone wall and looked down at the water. "I used to come up here between trips searching for you," he said.

He had spent so much time worrying he wouldn't find her, and resenting the Celestial for what would happen if he did. It amused Tol in a dark kind of way that all the worries he'd had back then disappeared when the Fount turned out to be Addy. His worries now were of a much different kind.

Addy came to stand at the wall beside him and leaned her head against his shoulder.

Tol didn't take his eyes off the sea. "My parents want the blood marriage to happen as soon as we get Olivia back."

He felt Addy's intake of breath. He turned so he could see her face.

"Why do you look so unhappy about it?" Addy asked. "Is it because of Nira?"

"Gods, no." Tol recoiled. "I'm unhappy because I hate making you do something you don't want to do."

Addy's features relaxed, and she put her head back on his shoulder.

"You're risking more than just your life to help me get Livy back," she said. "I'll never forget that you did that for me."

Tol winced. He'd used her sister's disappearance as leverage to get what he needed, but he didn't want Addy to feel like she owed him anymore.

"I wish there was some other way for this to end," Tol said. He brushed back a lock of her hair that had come loose in the wind.

"Fred kind of asked me to marry him before I met you," Addy said.

These were not the words Tol had been expecting.

"That filthy, presumptuous farmer," he growled.

Addy laughed. "It threw me off guard because I'd never thought of him that way."

Knowing that Addy didn't love the bloke didn't make Tol any more tolerant of Farmer Fred.

"But then," Addy continued, "when he laid it all out for me, it made me feel like I was suffocating. Livy had described almost the same future, and I just felt so stuck."

"And now I'm doing the same thing to you," Tol filled in, making the connection.

"That's just it, though." Addy was playing with the joints of his prosthetic fingers. He wished she would do that to the hand he could feel. "I should have gotten that suffocating feeling when you told me about the blood marriage. I mean, the only thing worse than a future I don't want is a future I don't want that lasts forever."

Tol turned away from her. The guilt and grief and regret were too much for him.

"I didn't get that feeling, though," Addy said. "Don't get me wrong, I was pissed at you for not telling me sooner, even though I guess I can understand why you didn't."

Those words broke through the endless loop of *should have's* going through Tol's mind. He turned back to face her.

"If it was up to me, I wouldn't be getting married any time soon," Addy continued, "but I realized the thought of being stuck with you forever didn't scare me the way it should have."

"How…sweet?" Tol let the mockery in his words hide everything else that lay just beneath the surface.

"Let me finish," Addy said in that imperious way she had.

Tol waited, bracing himself for her to deal the blow to his heart.

"I've spent my life running away from a future that didn't hold any mystery. But I don't want to run away from this future. In fact," Addy paused, and Tol felt all the weight of that silence press against his ribcage, "I want to run toward it, because I'm running toward you."

Tol couldn't breathe.

"I love you." Addy put her hand on his cheek. The moon illuminated the flecks of gold in her hair and green eyes. "I love you so much, Tol. I *want* to spend forever with you."

He was speechless. There was nothing he could say to make her understand what her words meant to him. So, he didn't try.

He took Addy in his arms, holding her in a way he hadn't let himself touch her since their night in the cave.

"I am yours, Adelyne Deerborn," he said against her lips. "Now and forever."

And then, he kissed her.

✳ ✳ ✳

When they came up for air some time later, the sky was filled with stars. Tol was drunk on a happiness that was more powerful than all the Source on Vitaquias. He didn't know his heart could feel so full. One look at Addy, and he knew she was feeling the same way.

"Our life will never be boring, will it?" Addy asked.

"Never," Tol promised. "I want to explore every corner of Vitaquias with you, and once we get tired of it, I'll bring you back here so we can travel the mortal world."

"And we'll find a way to bring Livy with us?"

Tol nodded. "I don't know how it all works, but I do know there hasn't been a problem you and I couldn't solve yet."

Addy smiled. "Livy always wanted to see Stonehenge."

Tol laughed. "I think we can make that happen." He leaned in for another kiss.

"Ah, excuse me," a voice Tol knew only too well drawled. "I thought I'd be alone up here."

He turned to see Erikir sauntering up the path toward them. Tol stiffened, but he kept his face impassive.

"What are you doing here?" he asked.

This place had been Tol's refuge since they were kids. If Erikir was here, it was because his cousin had wanted to find him.

"Just out for a stroll," Erikir said with a shrug.

"A stroll," Tol deadpanned.

He straightened from where he'd been holding Addy against the stone wall and faced his cousin.

"Must be nice to have everything work out for you again, as usual," Erikir said.

Tol shrugged. "Things couldn't be anything but perfect with Addy by my side."

Erikir's shrewd eyes swiveled away from him and onto Addy.

"Consider your next words carefully," Tol warned his cousin. "And remember you are speaking to your future queen."

"I had no plans to offend her," Erikir said.

Tol didn't trust his cousin on the best of days, and he trusted him even less with that malicious smile.

"I wanted to apologize to Adelyne on behalf of the royal family," Erikir said.

Tol raised an eyebrow. "Apologize for what?"

Erikir made a show of cutting Tol out of the conversation and kept his eyes trained on Addy. "You deserve better."

"Better than the prince of a magical race?" Addy retorted.

"Well," Erikir said, his sly look turning on Tol. "At least a man who can hold you with two real arms." He gave a pointed look to Tol's prosthetic arm, which was resting on the stone wall beside Addy.

Tol flinched before he could stop himself. Erikir managed a short laugh before it was cut off.

Addy moved so fast she was a blur. Tol blinked, and the next thing he knew, Addy was dangling Erikir over the cliffs below by his tie. Erikir was wriggling like a fish on a line, but Addy's grip didn't falter.

"Apologize to your prince," she commanded.

"Let go of me," Erikir snarled.

"If you say so." Addy shrugged, and then she let go of him with her right hand. All that kept him from falling was Addy's one-handed grip on his tie. Erikir let out a strangled scream.

Addy heaved a dramatic sigh. "My arm is getting *so* tired. I don't think I'll be able to—"

"I'm sorry!" Erikir's face had taken on a blue tinge, and Tol was wondering at what point he should step in and end this.

"I'm sorry, *Your Majesty*," Addy said.

"I'm sorry, Your Majesty," Erikir gasped.

With that, Addy lifted him back over the wall and watched him slump to the ground. Erikir looked up at them with murder in his eyes. Then, he limped away like a dog with its tail between its legs. Addy and Tol watched him go.

"That was one of the hottest things I've ever seen," Tol said.

Addy raised an eyebrow. "*One* of the hottest things?"

Tol nodded. "The other is you in that dress."

He reached for her again. His only thought as their lips met was that eternity wouldn't be long enough for him to get used to kissing Addy.

CHAPTER 34

ADDY

It was late when Tol left Addy with her retinue of bodyguards. She hadn't wanted him to go, but when Marise and Viola had poked their heads out of the cottage and dragged her inside, she'd barely had time to say goodnight before the door was shutting with Tol on the wrong side.

The two women took off her beautiful dress and undid her hair. They helped her into a nightgown that was a far cry from the extra large T-shirts she usually slept in. It was pale green, which Marise and Viola assured her complimented her eyes. It had a similar cut to the dress she had worn earlier in the night, except it only reached down to her mid-thigh. She thought the outfit was wasted when Tol wasn't even going to see her in it.

After putting hot water bottles under her blanket and brushing her hair into silken waves, the women bid her goodnight. Addy heard their soft voices as they exchanged pleasantries with the guards outside the cottage, and then everything was quiet.

Addy got into bed for lack of anything better to do. She wasn't tired, but she knew she'd need her rest if she was going to be ready to take on an army of the Forsaken. As comfortable as the bed was, though, it felt too big and too empty. She realized she hadn't spent a night without Tol near her since they'd left the farmhouse. She had gotten so used to his warmth and comforting presence that she didn't think she could relax without him.

Her mind wandered back to the clifftop, where Tol had held her and kissed her breathless. Her back had been against the stone wall, and she had known the sea was behind her. Some part of her had known she could fall over the wall and go crashing into the black abyss below. It was the same part of her brain that felt the water sucking at her ankles and turned her anxiety to panic. But she hadn't panicked. The other part of her brain, the stronger part, had felt Tol's arms around her, all warm muscle in his right arm and cool sturdiness in his left. She had felt both safe and exhilarated all at once.

A scratching on the roof tore her away from her thoughts. The sound came again, but this time, it was closer to the high windows on the other side of the cottage.

Enough moonlight had filtered into the room that she could see every piece of furniture and every shadow. If the intruder managed to get inside before her guards discovered him, her red hair would immediately give her away.

She could scream, and the guards would come running. But what if it wasn't an intruder, and just a tree branch scraping against the side of the cottage? Maybe it was her paranoia about the Forsaken that was making her hear things that weren't there.

The window latch rattled. Heart hammering, Addy got out of bed as quietly as she could. She grabbed a brass candlestick on her bedside table and melted into the shadows beside her bed.

She was across the room from where she'd heard the scraping sound. If she moved quickly, she could be on the intruder and pin him down before he even caught his balance.

She forced herself to stay still and not give herself away too quickly. She waited for the quiet confidence that came on her when her golden Haze flared. Her pulse fluttered like a caged butterfly, and her hands shook.

Keep it together, she commanded herself.

The window, which was now creaking open, was high up. Her intruder must have climbed a tree to get onto the roof so her guards wouldn't spot him.

Clever.

Addy sunk deeper into the shadows as the intruder wriggled through the window. She let him land on the floor, and then, before he could regain his balance, Addy raised the candlestick and jumped out of the shadows.

"Tol!" Relief and adrenaline coursed through her. She didn't know whether she wanted to laugh or cry, run to him or hurl something at him for scaring her.

The candlestick fell out of her hand and thudded onto the floor. She threw herself into his arms.

Tol caught her, and the small package he'd been carrying fell to the ground, forgotten. Addy wrapped her legs around him as their mouths found each other.

Tol kissed her like a man who had been dying, and her lips were the sustenance that would bring him back to life. She kissed him with the same ferocious need. She couldn't get enough of his taste, his smell, the feel of him.

Addy hadn't even realized they were moving until her back hit the soft mattress. Tol followed her, his body settling on top of hers. His tongue slid across hers, awakening her senses and making her aware of her own body in ways she never had been before.

Tol's lips moved to her throat. She tipped her head back to give his mouth free rein over her. He kissed a line of fire down her neck and across her collar bone. He moved lower, kissing the place where the satin of her nightgown met the curve of her breast.

Never before had she thought drowning could be a good thing. But she was drowning now, and she'd never felt more alive in her life.

Tol's soft hair brushed against her bare skin, leaving another trail of sensation to follow the movement of his lips. She curved her body up to meet his. It was then that she noticed Tol was using his prosthetic arm to keep his weight off her.

He was being *careful* with her.

Addy wasn't interested in careful. Suddenly, it wasn't enough. She needed more of him.

She pulled his shirt out from his pants. She didn't bother with buttons and just slid it up and over his head. She got it almost all the way off when the material caught on the place where his prosthesis met his shoulder. Addy froze.

She knew how sensitive Tol was about his arm, and after Erikir's taunts.... She still had the shirt bunched in her hand as she tried to figure out what to do.

"Rip it off," Tol growled.

She did. The material tore, and she tossed the shreds off him.

Addy let her hands roam over his torso and back, feeling his muscles and bones ripple beneath his skin. A soft rumbling came from deep in his chest as her hands explored his bare skin.

Tol stopped kissing her long enough to meet her gaze. He kept his eyes on hers as he hooked a finger around the strap of her nightgown.

"Yes," she managed, answering his silent question.

He slipped the strap down her arm. His hand skimmed over her breast, and she gasped as pleasure rolled over her in waves.

Addy lifted her hips to meet his. She wrapped her legs around him and pulled their bodies closer together.

Tol groaned, but it sounded more like frustration, even torture, than pleasure. All of his muscles tensed beneath her hands. He cursed, and then rolled off her.

He lay on his back beside her, his chest heaving.

Addy went very still. She'd been so lost in the moment, so lost in *him*, that she hadn't even been thinking about what she was doing. Her body had taken over and done what it wanted. She realized now, too late, it must have betrayed her in some unforgivable way that would cause her endless humiliation as soon as she understood what it was.

"You'll be the death of me, Addy," Tol said, his voice raspy.

She turned to face him, her face hot with shame, an apology on the tip of her tongue.

His eyes were squeezed shut, and he was still breathing fast. His hair clung to his damp forehead. Had she somehow re-opened the wound on his chest without realizing it?

"I'm sorry," she began, confused and humiliated. "I didn't mean...."

Tol let out a short laugh. "You have nothing to apologize for, except maybe for being irresistible."

He still seemed to be struggling to get his breathing under control.

Addy was more confused than ever. "I thought you wanted me," she said, feeling her face get somehow hotter than it already was.

"Gods, I've never wanted anything more in my life." Tol opened his eyes. "I'm the one who should be sorry. I've never lost control of myself like that."

Addy scoffed. "That was you losing control?"

"Yes." He huffed out a breath. "I almost didn't stop. I almost...."

"I didn't want you to stop." Her voice was barely more than a whisper.

Tol's gaze softened. "Neither did I."

"Then why did you?" Her embarrassment was turning to irritation. Her body felt cold and abandoned without his warm weight on top of her. She quivered with unfulfilled desire.

"Remember when I said the blood marriage will bind us in body and spirit?" he asked.

Addy nodded.

"Well, for it to work properly, the union of the mind must come first. The Source impacts the strength of our minds, and so the telepathy part needs to happen first. If our bodies are joined before then," he cleared his throat, "then the union won't be as powerful."

He reached over and tucked her hair behind her ear. "Given our role in all of this and the uncertainty of a blood marriage between a mortal and immortal, we can't take any chances of weakening the connection."

"The rules of the ritual," Addy said, remembering what Getyl had said at dinner, and how it had rattled Tol. "Is that what she was talking about?"

Tol cringed at the memory of his grandmother's comment, and nodded.

"So, that means no sex before the blood marriage?"

"No sex before the blood marriage." Tol heaved a dramatic sigh that made Addy laugh.

"Fine, then," she said. "Let's do it right now." And then she clarified, "The blood marriage, I mean."

Now it was Tol's turn to laugh.

"First of all, it's quite a big deal. We need witnesses and Chosen wielding Source, and a sunset…I'm not sure why. Second, and more importantly," he locked eyes with Addy, "I made you a promise. Nothing else happens until we have your sister back."

Addy startled, and then she felt shame settle on her as she realized she hadn't even been thinking of Livy. All she'd been thinking about was Tol's perfect body, and the unacceptable distance between him and her.

If their positions had been reversed, Livy wouldn't have rested for even a second until she found Addy.

"You're right," she muttered.

As Tol pulled the strap of her nightgown back up, the tragic expression on his face replaced some of her anguish with humor.

"So, what now?" Addy asked.

"Oh! I almost forgot." Tol got out of bed and went over to the center of the room where he'd tumbled out of the window. "Sorry for startling you, by the way," he said as he stooped to pick up whatever had been in his hand when Addy assaulted him. "My parents are rather traditional, and the guards were given explicit instructions not to let me inside."

"Just be glad I recognized you before I bashed you over the head with a candlestick," Addy replied, watching Tol wind his hands around what looked to be a drawstring bag.

"What's that?" she asked as he came around to her side of the bed.

There was a serious look on Tol's face that hadn't been there a few moments ago.

"The blood marriage is a ritual that is purely from my world," he said, his voice low and quiet. "But since you're from this world, I wanted to do something symbolic that is more in line with your traditions."

Addy watched as Tol opened the bag and pulled out a small velvet box. She sucked in a breath as Tol went down on one knee.

"Adelyne Deerborn," he said, a shy smile curving his lips. "Will you do me the honor of being my wife," his smile broadened, "for eternity?"

Tears pricked at Addy's eyes. "Yes," she managed, reaching for him. "Yes, yes, yes!"

"Eternity means forever, you know," Tol murmured against her lips.

Addy laughed. "For a life with you, it won't be nearly long enough."

Tol looked at her with such wonder and adoration it turned her into putty in his arms.

When they separated, Tol opened the box. In the moonlight, she saw a ring with three large stones. It was difficult to tell their color in this light, but they looked black. Tol took her left hand and, kissing it, slipped the ring onto her finger.

"Tol," she breathed. "It's beautiful."

Tol turned on the bedside lamp, bathing the whole room in a warm glow.

"It was my gran's most prized possession," he said. "The Celestial gave it to my grandfather almost a thousand years ago. Gemstones from Vitaquias are incredibly rare, and these ones have a part of the Celestial inside them."

They both looked at the ring. Addy realized the stones weren't black like she'd first thought, but a blue so deep they almost appeared black. She'd never seen anything like them before.

Tol brushed his fingers across the ring. He said, "As far as I know, these are the only stones the Celestial ever infused with her magic."

Before Addy could even begin to process that, Tol continued, "The gems have a mind of their own and display different abilities depending on the wearer. For Gran, they would light up whenever she was in the dark and needed light. It'll be different for you, although the stones won't reveal their powers until a time of their choosing, probably at a time of great need."

"That's incredible," Addy whispered. She wiggled her finger, watching the play of light across the facets of the stones. Addy didn't know if she was just imagining it, but she thought she could feel some hidden strength moving within the ring, like electricity in a circuit.

"Do you like it?" Tol asked, his eyes searching hers.

"It's the most beautiful thing I've ever seen," Addy said. "But why would your grandmother give it up if it was so precious to her?"

Tol smiled. "She gave it to me after I told her about you."

Addy felt overwhelmed by the gesture.

"I'll never take it off," she said, admiring it in the light.

Tol kissed her forehead. "Should we try and get some sleep?"

Addy nodded, although she had no idea how she'd manage it with everything that had happened tonight. Tol lay down on his back and rubbed at his left shoulder. Addy looked at the straps across his torso and saw the way they dug into his skin. She frowned.

"Addy," Tol warned, half-joking and half-serious as she straddled him. "My self-control...."

"Don't worry," Addy said. "Your virtue is safe from me...for now."

Tol snorted. When she moved her hands to the buckle across his chest and he realized what she was doing, Tol went still.

Carefully, so she wouldn't pinch his skin, she undid the buckle across his sternum. Then, she peeled away the straps one by one until the arm was no longer attached. She laid the arm down on the floor next to the bed, and then kissed Tol's left shoulder.

She knew he was watching her for the disgust that, even after everything that existed between them, some part of him still expected. He'd never find it.

She kissed his shoulder again and then lay down in the crook of his right arm. She wound her legs through his and used his chest as a pillow.

For a few minutes, they just listened to each other breathing.

"I'm the luckiest man in two worlds," Tol said.

Addy smiled. "And I'm the luckiest woman."

They fell asleep like that, tangled in each other, with the unfamiliar and comforting weight of the ring on Addy's finger.

CHAPTER 35

TOL

"Tol, Addy," a voice hissed. "Get up."

Tol opened his eyes as a glaring light filled the room.

"Gerth, what the hells?" he grumbled, shielding his eyes.

Gerth tossed a bundle of clothes on top of the covers. "Get dressed. Now."

"How did he know you'd be here?" Addy asked, her voice soft with sleep.

"Because he knows me," Tol replied.

"Both of you, get moving," Gerth said, with none of his usual self-congratulating that he was right once again. "They know the Fount is here."

That woke him up. "Who knows?" Tol demanded, gently extricating himself from Addy, who somehow looked even more stunning this morning than she had last night.

"Everyone." Gerth threw another set of clothes on top of them.

Tol swore. "How did they find out?"

The only ones who'd been at dinner were his family's most trusted subjects....

"How do you think? Nira told them you had the Fount and weren't going to do the blood marriage. People are getting ready to storm the cottage. We have to get you out of here."

Tol sprung out of bed, putting on his arm. "Get a car. We have to get Addy—"

"Already done, mate." Gerth put out a calming hand. "Just get dressed. The limos are getting everyone in the manor, and then they'll come around here."

Gerth generously turned his back so Addy could get dressed. It was a true mark of their situation that Tol didn't have time to admire her.

Gods, what a mess.

Nira had wanted to hurt him, and she'd done it by hurting his parents. She must have gone straight to the small but growing contingency of Chosen who wanted to overthrow his parents for what had happened on Vitaquias. The king and queen had kept the peace through their constant assurances the Fount would be found and their world would be restored. But now, if the rest of their people knew the Fount was here, but that the blood marriage wasn't happening, it would mean more than just a nebulous challenge to his family's reign. It would mean chaos for them all.

Tol should have guessed something like this might happen. The only family members Nira had left were ageing too quickly in the mortal world. Along with so many others, their lives depended on the blood marriage, which he was staving off to go on a possibly suicidal mission to recover a mortal who objectively was of no relevance to his people's survival.

He understood Nira's desperation, which only made all of this worse.

"What's going to be in place while we're gone to maintain our authority?" Tol asked, turning to concrete matters that were easier to solve.

Gerth shrugged. "Anything we do to strengthen our position here will weaken us against the Forsaken. It's your call."

Tol looked at Addy. Her face was pale, and he saw that she understood the position they were in.

Damnit, Nira.

"We leave the guards here," Tol said. "All of them."

"But your parents said—"

"My parents won't have a throne when we return unless there's someone to protect it in our absence. We won't be able to defeat the Forsaken without my parents, but we'll have to do without the guards."

Gerth let out a long breath. Tol could almost see the cogs turning in Gerth's brain as he considered every possible outcome. Finally, he nodded. "It's a calculated risk."

Tol and Gerth moved Addy out of the cottage between them, shielding her in case anyone planned to do something foolish. Four stretch limos were pulling up to the cottage.

The sound of crashing glass and screams came from the manor. Tol went still, his heart in his throat.

"Tolumus!" his mother yelled from the first limo.

His feet carried him away from the cars, toward the mob that was hurling torches through the manor windows like barbarians. Like Forsaken.

"Addy, get back to the car," Gerth barked.

That got Tol's attention. He turned back to see Addy following him.

"You have to choose," Gerth told him.

Gerth didn't need to elaborate. It would take more than words to calm down this mob. And it would take time. Tol and his parents could subdue them, but it would be a state of temporary calm. His people's desperation would only be quelled by the completion of the blood marriage. If he stayed behind to deal with his subjects, Tol wouldn't be able to keep his promise to Addy.

He looked at her. With the light of the fires reflecting in her red hair, it made it look like she was on fire, too.

In that instant, his decision was made. Tol pushed Addy into the limo with his parent before ushering Gerth in. He had time for only a brief argument with his parents, which he won, before the three other limos were circling back around to the manor. Tol's parents barked instructions at the guards through a cell phone.

Part of the mob broke off, with Nira at its head. They were making their way to the cottage.

Their limo peeled away with a squeal of tires.

Tol sat back against the leather seat, his heart hammering, as guilt swept over him. This was his fault.

"Nothing like a woman scorned," Gerth muttered quietly enough that only Tol could hear.

Yet another thing Gerth had tried to warn Tol about, and Tol hadn't listened.

Tol wanted to slam his fist against the side of the limo. He wanted to rage at Nira. But he knew he had no one to blame but himself. He had done this. He had let Nira fall for him, even when they both knew there would never be a future between them, because he was trying to stave off the inevitable end of his freedom.

Stupid. Stupid. Stupid.

"Nice work, Adelyne," Erikir sneered. "Causing a coup on your first day."

"Leave her alone." Tol's voice was dangerous.

Tol turned to Gerth, who was toying with the vial around his neck. Gerth had that look on his face, the one he got when he understood he'd been right about something he didn't want to be right about.

Tol remembered Gerth telling him the rebellion was coming. He also remembered assuring his best mate it would all be fine once he returned with the Fount.

How had he managed to make such a mess of everything? He wasn't even king yet, and already, he had sabotaged his reign and put his entire family in danger.

Erikir rounded on Tol. "How can you call yourself a leader when you put the needs of one girl ahead of the rest of your people?"

"Your words are bordering on treason," Tol said. "You speak of your future queen, whose needs will always be more important than anything else."

Addy pressed her hand to her mouth as though to hold back a sob. Or a scream.

"She's not my queen yet," Erikir said, but the bluster had gone out of him.

Tol wished he could have left Erikir behind. As much as he hated to admit it, though, Erikir was powerful and good in a fight. Still, gods help him if he offended Addy.

"This is my choice," Tol said. His voice was savage...a challenge to the unspoken thoughts he felt hanging in a dense cloud over the others.

Tol's mother, the stoic, unflappable Chosen queen, turned her head into his father's chest. He saw her shaking with silent sobs. He saw his father's stricken look as he patted her back. Nausea roiled in Tol's stomach.

What had he done?

"I'm sorry," Addy whispered, her eyes wide.

Tol took her hand in his and rubbed his thumb over her knuckles. "You're saving our entire race. The least we can do is get your sister back first."

"There will always be loud voices who capture the attention of lesser minds," Tol's father said. "This sort of thing was inevitable. We've just sped it along, is all."

Tol was grateful to his father for not blaming Addy. It hadn't escaped any of their notices how Tol's mother didn't say anything. Her mouth was set in a tight line. Tol knew that look.

"We'll be back in a few days," he told his mother. "As soon as the blood marriage is done, this little rebellion will be forgotten."

Gran gave him an encouraging smile. To Tol's father, she said, "What's done is done. All we can do now is move on. Although I fear this is not the last bit of trouble Adelyne will cause us."

"Gran," Tol choked. His grandmother was the last person he expected to look at Addy with accusation in her rheumy eyes, and yet, that was exactly what she was doing.

Tol pulled Addy against him, as though to shield her from his gran's judgement.

"Maybe we should," Addy began, but then stopped, like she couldn't bring herself to say the words she knew she should.

"No," Tol said.

Olivia was the last member of Addy's family. He'd keep his promise to get her back or die trying.

CHAPTER 36

TOL

When they all piled out of the limo, Tol got to see how small and inconsequential their party really was. It was his gran, leaning on her cane and looking about as lethal as a wingless pigeon, his parents, Erikir, Gerth, Addy, and him. It would be the seven of them against the Forsaken general and all her best warriors. *What could go wrong?*

Security escorted them into Heathrow Airport and through the crowds of people.

"Addy!"

It took Tol a second to figure out why that voice, saying that word, filled him with rage.

"Fred?" Addy gasped as the pudgy farmer came running toward them.

"Should we fry his brain?" Gerth asked, his vial already unstopped.

Absolutely.

Tol shook his head and gestured for the others to wait.

"Did you know he was going to be here?" Tol asked Addy. He had to try very hard to make it a question rather than an accusation.

"No." She shook her head, looking as puzzled as the rest of their party.

When Fred reached them, his face red and sweat dripping down his bulbous nose, he actually put his hands around Addy. It took every ounce of willpower Tol possessed to keep from ripping the bloke to pieces with his bare hands, Source be damned. Addy was hugging him back, though, which filled him with a different kind of emotion.

"What are you doing here?" Addy asked, her voice muffled because the buffoon was suffocating her.

"How did you find us?" Tol demanded.

"Who are you?" Gran asked him.

Fred tore his eyes off Addy long enough to notice the rest of them.

"You," he said, his hands balling into fists as he stepped toward Tol.

Bring it, Farmer Fred.

"You did somethin' to me at the farmhouse, didn't you?" Fred demanded, spit coming out of his mouth. Without waiting for Tol's response, he continued, "If you try—whatever you did—ever again, I swear I'll kill you."

Tol laughed, the sound harsh. "Your mind is more moldable than clay. In fact," he reached for his vial.

"Please, don't."

Addy's hand on his arm stopped him. Her ring flashed with the movement, and Tol had a gratifying moment to see Fred's eyes pop out of his skull. Fred looked at Addy, and then at Tol, the question in his eyes.

You?

Tol lifted his eyebrows at Fred. *Me.*

Fred was beside himself, stuttering and making incoherent threats that would have amused Tol under different circumstances.

"How did you know we were here?" Addy asked.

Farmer Fred's hand went into his pocket, and Tol remembered him making the same gesture the last time he'd tracked them to an airport.

"I don't know, I just had…this feelin' you'd be here," he said, his eyes still on the ring.

Before Tol could speak the words on the tip of his tongue, Gerth reached into Farmer Fred's pocket and pulled out a cheap-looking bracelet.

"Hey, that's mine," the farmer snarled.

Gerth turned so Farmer Fred couldn't snatch it back as he studied the bracelet. "Adelyne," he said, reading the inscription Tol could now see engraved on the metal.

Tol turned to Addy.

"Fred gave me the bracelet the night my family—" she broke off, looking confused and sad all at the same time.

"What does this bracelet have to do with you showing up here?" Gerth asked.

"Who the hell are you?" Fred shot back.

"Answer him," Tol commanded, stepping forward until he was standing directly in front of the farmer.

"Fred?" Addy asked. Hers was the only voice free of menace.

"Okay, this is gonna sound really weird," Fred said, speaking only to Addy, "but I think this bracelet led me to you."

Tol and Gerth exchanged a look.

Gerth peered at something on the bracelet and then held it in front of Fred's face. "Is this blood on here? Is it Addy's?"

Addy was the one who answered. "There was a cut on my arm, and my blood got on the bracelet. But what does that have to do with—"

"If we keep standing here we're going to draw attention," Tol's father broke in. "Either bring the bloke with us, or Influence him and have done with it."

"No!" Addy said, giving Tol a desperate look.

"Addy, we can't bring him with us," Tol said, making a heroic effort to keep his voice reasonable.

"Fred," Addy began, her expression torn.

"Take me with you, Ads," he said.

Tol hated the nickname *Ads*, like Fred knew her so well that *Addy* wasn't familiar enough. He'd never experienced jealousy like this and knew it wasn't a good look on him. More to the point, he knew Addy wouldn't appreciate it. So Tol clenched his jaw until it ached and forced an impassive expression on his face.

"I'm so sorry," Addy began, but Fred interrupted her.

"You won't believe what your Aunt Meredith told me. You won't believe what your parents knew about *their people*. I can tell you everythin' and help get Livy—"

"Not a chance," Tol said. "Go back to your cows."

At the look that Addy gave him, most of Tol's pettiness and ire receded.

"I'm sorry," he told Addy. "But he'll just be a liability."

"You know that ain't true," Fred snarled. "I can help." He turned to Addy. "You're not the only one who cares about Livy."

Addy looked conflicted.

Tol's mother tapped her foot in impatience.

"By all means, come along," Gran said good-naturedly. "The more the merrier."

Traitorous old bird.

Please? Addy's eyes asked Tol. And that was the end of that.

"It's your funeral," Tol said to Fred as the mortal fell into step with them.

Fred's only comment as he boarded Tol's family plane was a muttered, "You gotta be kiddin' me" under his breath. Tol had to bite his tongue to keep from saying something he'd later regret.

They all sunk into their seats as the captain and stewardesses welcomed them on board.

There was so much they needed to plan and discuss, but Tol couldn't stop thinking about what was happening back at the manor. From his parents' quiet whispering and the worry on their faces, he knew they were sharing his thoughts.

Their plane took off, bound for Anchorage, Alaska, drawing them away from one set of problems and toward another.

"It must have something to do with the Celestial's powers in her blood," Gerth said, still examining the rust-colored speck on the bracelet.

Tol shrugged. "It doesn't really matter now." Farmer Fred had found them, and now he was sitting next to Addy on the couch. Tol curled his right hand into a fist as the farmer moved so close to her their knees touched.

Tol felt strangely removed as Addy and Fred cried together over her lost family and talked about the people he knew about, but had never known. Logic and observation told him Addy didn't feel anything for Fred akin to what she felt for Tol, but it was still like a kick in the gut when she leaned her head on his shoulder and cried for the ones she loved who she'd never see again.

"Tolumus, come here," Gran commanded.

With another look at Addy, Tol went to the back of the plane where Gran was sitting with her cane resting between her legs.

"Stop your pouting," she said as he sat down in the seat beside her.

"I'm not—"

"You're jealous because that boy has Adelyne's attention," she said. "And it doesn't suit you."

Tol felt his face heat. "I'm not jealous, I just don't like him," he muttered.

"That mortal boy is the only one she has left from her old life," Gran told him. "He's as much her family as Gerth is yours."

When she put it like that, Tol's baiting of Fred seemed so juvenile. Why did Gran have to be so gods-damn wise?

"Anyone with half a brain can see Adelyne is in love with you. But that doesn't mean she can't have affections of a different kind, just as you can. Don't make her resent you because you're trying to possess her every attention."

Tol sighed. "You're right," he admitted.

Gran patted his leg. "Put aside your differences. Do it for her."

He nodded, knowing she was right.

Gran inclined her head in Addy's direction. "I hope she's as worthy of such a ring as you believe."

Tol looked at Gran. "She is."

Gran smiled, but she was looking past Tol.

"Our grandson is growing up before our eyes, Walidir." She chuckled. "He's in love, and he's going to make a fine king."

"Thanks, Gran," Tol said.

"Alright everyone, gather round," Gerth called. He was sitting at one of the tables and had a mess of books and papers spread out in front of him. There was that twinkle in his eye that Tol knew only too well. "It's strategy time."

The problem was clear. It was seven of them—eight if you counted Fred—against what Gerth had estimated to be a hundred Forsaken.

"The objective is simple," Gerth said. "We get Olivia out of there without the Forsaken knowing about it. No fuss, no muss."

"The Forsaken might be expecting an attack," Tol's father pointed out.

"True," Gerth said. "But they won't be expecting the royal family and their chief strategist," he puffed out his chest, "to be the ones to do it. As far as they know, the only person who cares about Olivia is Addy. They're expecting her and Tol to come, not the rest of us. We'll use that to our advantage."

"If you're thinking of using Addy as bait," Tol began, seeing the direction his friend's mind was taking, "then you can forget it."

"It's the plan with the greatest likelihood of success," Gerth said with a shrug. "But I have a few additions to the usual procedure that will keep her as safe as possible and throw the Forsakens' brains into a tizzy." He grinned his evil scheming grin.

"It's fine with me," Addy said before Tol could argue. "I'll do whatever you need me to."

"We are *not* putting the Fount in harm's way," Tol's mother said. "She and Tol are our people's only hope for salvation. We cannot risk them."

"We won't be able to manage any of it without them," Gerth said. "And the odds of them coming out alive are at least 60-40 in favor."

"Doesn't inspire much confidence," Tol's father said.

"I can help," Fred began, but the others continued to talk over him. Tol saw Addy give him an apologetic shrug.

"Fine," Tol said. "But Addy and I stay together."

"Tolumus," his mother began.

"Addy and I stay together." He used what Gerth called *the king voice*.

Tol saw his mother about to protest, and then his father put a hand on her arm and shake his head. She went silent, but not before shooting an accusing look at Addy.

"Now," Gerth was saying, "here's the layout of the Air Force Base. We need to get here," he tapped a point on the diagram. "But my guess is there will be guards here, here, and here." Gerth frowned. "Well, everywhere, really."

"They'll see Tol's Haze a mile away," the king said.

"Our only chance against those barbarians is with Influence," Erikir argued. "Without it, we'll be dead before we set foot on the Base."

"If we could get on Base without having to fight through every mortal and Forsaken guard around the perimeter, we'd be in better shape," Gerth lamented. "But the first Forsaken who sees us will know who we are."

"They don't know who I am," Fred said.

"Unless you have magic running through your blood that you haven't mentioned, then that doesn't do us any good," Tol snapped, before remembering his promise to himself to be the better man for Addy's sake.

"That could actually work," Gerth said.

Tol narrowed his eyes at his best mate. *Traitor.*

"Think about it," Gerth insisted. "He's the only one the Forsaken won't recognize. He can get close without raising alarms."

"And what happens when he gets close?" Addy asked, echoing the question in Tol's mind.

Gerth grinned. "That's what I'm going to figure out."

✳ ✳ ✳

After they had done as much planning as they could, Tol's parents insisted they all try to get a few hours of rest before they landed. Tol sat on one of the couches, and Addy lay down next to him. She fell asleep with her head in his lap, her face pressed against his stomach like she wanted to breathe him in.

It put his animosity toward Fred at an all-time low, so he decided it would be a good time to try and smooth things over between them.

Fred, who was sitting in the seats facing them, wore a glower that pinched his pudgy face.

"Her parents would have hated you, you know," Fred told him.

Not an auspicious beginning. Tol bit his tongue.

"I'm sorry I'll never have the chance to know them," Tol said in what he hoped was a conciliatory tone. He'd never mastered the art of diplomacy the way his parents had.

Fred didn't say anything else. He was glaring at the ring on Addy's finger.

"I know we got off to a…rough beginning," Tol began.

"Oh, you mean when you kidnapped Addy?" Fred interrupted.

"And I'd like to start over," Tol finished, like Fred hadn't said anything.

"She would have been better off with me," Fred said. "I coulda kept her safe."

Tol bit down on his cheek until he tasted blood. He wasn't sure he could argue with that first part, and it ate at him more than anything else this insolent farmer had said.

"I don't think Addy would appreciate you talking about her like she's some helpless person who needs protection," Tol replied.

"Don't preten' like you know her," Fred spat. "You think there's anythin' you can tell me about my best friend I don't already know?"

As a matter of fact, Tol thought there were at least a few things he knew about Addy that Fred never would, but he felt Gran's eyes boring into him and stayed silent.

"She's my best friend." Fred's voice cracked. "If you hurt her, I swear I'll kill you."

If Fred was expecting Tol to lay bare his heart so the farmer could pick apart his motivations and desires, he'd be disappointed. Tol wasn't going to tell Fred how the woman in his arms had come to mean everything to him.

"I think Addy is the one point we can agree on," Tol said. "And for her sake, I'd like to set aside our differences." He gently moved his hand out from under Addy's neck and extended it to Fred.

After a brief hesitation, Fred took it. His grip was strong, which didn't surprise Tol—he supposed working on a dairy farm would lead to strong hands. It did surprise Tol when, instead of letting go after the appropriate two pumps, Fred gripped him harder.

"If you ever hurt her," Fred hissed, leaning in, "I swear it'll be the last thing you ever do."

Tol bristled. He didn't take kindly to threats, especially when they came from a mortal whose mind was so weak he could hold it in his sleep.

A pointed "ahem" came from the direction of his gran.

Do this for Addy, he reminded himself.

Tol looked Fred straight in the eye, and nodded. "Understood."

CHAPTER 37

ADDY

Addy's mind was filled with everything Fred had told her. After Addy had called Aunt Meredith from the farmhouse, her aunt had gone straight to New York. She'd found Fred, finishing up his gruesome task of cleaning away all evidence of her family's murder, and had broken down on their bleached kitchen floor. Afterward, she'd told Fred everything she knew…everything she knew because Addy's parents had told her.

Addy knew she and Livy had been born in Texas, and that for the first few weeks of their lives, they'd lived on the farm Aunt Meredith now called home. Neither Addy nor her twin had ever questioned why, weeks after their birth, their parents had moved away. They hadn't questioned why Aunt Meredith always came to visit them, but they never went to visit her. They hadn't questioned why they never went anywhere. And now, Addy knew. Or at least, she knew a little.

Fred's memory was hazy, and Addy was pretty sure it had something to do with the Influence Tol had used on him before they left.

What Fred had been able to piece together from his remembered conversation with Aunt Meredith was that something had happened soon after Addy and Livy were born. All Fred could recall was that Addy's mom had called Aunt Meredith to tell her something about "blue fire and aliens." It was after that when the Deerborns entrusted their farm to Aunt Meredith and moved to upstate New York. *Fled* to upstate New York…to hide.

Fred's story unearthed more questions than answers, and Addy was desperate for more. Her parents had known who...what...she was. She was certain of it. Why hadn't they ever told her? Why had they tried to make her normal, like them, when they knew she never could be?

The questions were a swarm of angry bees in her head.

Once she had Livy back, they'd figure it all out together. Her sister would find reason and understanding where Addy saw only secrets and betrayal. She needed Livy to help her comprehend why her parents would have kept her ignorant about her own identity.

Addy was restless. She slept for no more than an hour, comforted by the warmth of Tol's body and the familiar spicy cologne that made her think of moonlight reflecting off bronze skin.

Gerth had papers and maps spread out on the table across from her and was muttering to himself. He was scribbling down ideas like the master strategist he was. Addy felt an overwhelming gratitude to these people who had come with her to free her sister. She knew they weren't really doing it for her, but for Tol and the all-important bond she would soon share with him, but she was grateful nonetheless.

She also felt a crushing guilt. Before, Tol's people had been an abstraction in Addy's mind. Tol had said his people were dying, but it wasn't until she met Marise and Viola and saw their nearly-empty vials that Addy understood it was up to her to save them.

And now, instead of doing just that, she had abandoned them. She'd brought away their royal family and put them all in more danger than she had any right to. If they died on this mission, it wouldn't just be their lives that would be forfeit. Tol's entire race would perish, without any hope of ever getting back to their world.

Addy couldn't shake the memory of fire spilling out of the beautiful bay windows of the manor, or the look on Tol's face as they'd driven away.

She should have argued harder with Tol to do the blood marriage first.

But even as the thought crossed her mind, a terrible fear made the thought ring hollow. Livy had been these monsters' prisoner for almost a month. How could she let them keep her sister for even a second longer?

There was another possibility, but it was too horrible to even consider.

Livy was alive. She had to be.

"Work it out, work it out, work it out," Gerth was saying as he thumped his fist against his head.

"It's his process," Tol said, inclining his head toward his friend. "Nothing to do but wait until he's finished."

Gerth was drawing what looked to Addy like squiggles on a sheet of paper. "Once we're in, I've got it figured out," he said. "But getting in without them killing us or taking us prisoner ourselves is the issue."

"How 'bout a distraction?" Fred suggested. His face went red as everyone turned their attention on him. "You know," he coughed, "keep their attention on somethin' else while you all do your thing. If we do it right, there'll be too much else goin' on for 'em to even notice you."

Gerth drummed his fingers on the table. "What kind of distraction do you have in mind?"

Fred looked at Addy. In that one glance, she knew exactly what he was thinking. A slow grin spread over her face.

When they were twelve, Fred had rigged the Benz, the Deerborns' tractor, to run without a driver. He had installed complicated pulleys and sensors, weights and counterweights, that Addy couldn't begin to understand. When Fred was finished, they'd gone out with Mr. Brown's camcorder to film the Benz's first solo foray.

It hadn't been a failure, exactly. The Benz *had* driven itself. It had just driven itself right through the side of the Deerborns' garage. It took out the pickup truck and tore through bags of corn seeds her dad had been storing for the next planting season. It had been the only time Addy could remember hearing her father yell.

"I'll need a tractor," Fred said, returning Addy's smile.

Gerth looked at the king, who nodded. "I think we can manage that."

✳ ✳ ✳

Everything happened very quickly after the plane landed in Anchorage. There was a private airstrip for the Base, but they couldn't draw the

Forsakens' attention by landing there, so they'd landed at the International airport. They would drive from there to the Base.

During the flight, the king had been busy on the airplane phone. Addy had heard him talking quietly to whoever was on the other end, but when Addy saw the Hummer and tractor parked on the side of the runway, her jaw fell open.

"Will this do?" the king asked Fred.

Fred, who looked as impressed as she felt, just nodded. There were tools and materials neatly stacked next to the tractor, and were those…fireworks?

Addy hadn't really thought whoever was on the other end of the airplane's phone would be able to get the thousand-or-so things Fred had written down in his chicken scratch and given to the king. But there it was, waiting on the side of the runway.

As Fred got to work and the others piled into the Hummer, Addy lingered with Fred. As she handed him tools before he even needed to ask for them, it felt like they were back on Mr. Brown's farm under the "We Fix Everything" banner strung over Fred's garage. It was like every afternoon she'd spent for as long as she could remember. Except they weren't fixing the beat-up old tractors of the elderly farmers in town. And she wouldn't be going back home to her family.

"Addy, come on," Tol said.

"Go," Fred told her, when she hesitated.

"Fred, I—"

"Livy's my family, too," he said, already anticipating what she was going to say. "Whatever happens, I got no regrets." He gave her a rueful smile. "Well, at least, not about this."

Guilt coiled in her stomach. She'd hurt Fred, and she would need to fix it.

"Ad-dy!" Gerth shouted out the passenger window of the Hummer. "Make like a gazelle and get the bloody hells in the car."

Addy threw her arms around Fred and squeezed. After a short pause, Fred's tools thunked to the ground, and he hugged her back.

"Don't blow yourself up," she ordered him. And then she went over to the Hummer.

Tol stuck his head out of the window. "I told them about what you can do behind the wheel, so you're driving," he told her.

Addy gave him a quick grin before going around to the driver's side and climbing in. She hadn't been behind the wheel of a car since D.C., and she was itching to have a steering wheel in her hands and a gas pedal beneath her foot.

Addy had always thought if she was going to be a criminal, she'd be the getaway driver. She'd never in a million years had any idea how close she would actually come to this very role. If the stakes were different, she'd be thrilled out of her mind.

The Hummer raced along the spruce tree-lined roadway until they reached the closed access roads near the Base. At the intersection where Gerth had directed her to drive, they found a nondescript blue car idling.

"That's him," the king said, nodding for them to get out.

Addy had come to understand that Tol's father was personally responsible for ensuring that Chosen men and women occupied important political roles all over the world. Those politicians had power, and since Tol's father was their king, that meant their power was his.

The man who had been waiting inside the car got out. He unloaded duffel bags from the backseat of his car and handed one to each of them. Then, with a bow to Tol's parents, he got back in his car and drove away.

They unpacked the army fatigues and put them on over their clothes.

"Hide your hair," the queen barked at Addy. "You're conspicuous enough." Those were the only words she'd spoken to Addy since they'd left the manor burning behind them.

Tol gave Addy an apologetic look, but she shook her head. If she were Queen Starser, she'd hate herself, too.

Once they were ready, they climbed back into the Hummer and waited. Hours passed with nothing to do except look out the window at the trees and mountains in the distance. Once, Addy thought she saw a moose ambling through the trees, but she was too distracted to be sure. The wait was agonizing.

Fred hadn't been entirely clear on what they should be waiting for. All he'd said was that they'd know when it happened. He was right.

There was an explosion that made the ground beneath them tremble. Addy heard shouting from inside the Base, and then she saw people dressed in army fatigues like her own running in the opposite direction.

Addy's stomach clenched with anxiety for Fred. She knew her best friend was somewhere on the other side of the Base, trying to stay hidden while he remotely controlled the tractor. Fred had been confident it would all work out, but he didn't know the Forsaken like she did.

Popping sounds filled the air, and then color exploded overhead.

"That's our signal," Gerth said, getting out of the car. Of all of them, Gerth was the only one who seemed to be enjoying himself.

Tol and his parents were tense and focused. Getyl, who was managing to keep up even without her cane, had shed the look of Tol's grandmother. She wore an expression on her wrinkled face that made Addy feel sorry for anyone who got in her way. The old woman's arm was looped through Erikir's, and the two of them were walking with a single-minded intensity. They were here to help Tol and Addy, but they were also here on business of their own. The Forsaken general had murdered Getyl's son and Erikir's father, and they weren't leaving until justice had been served.

For her part, Addy felt like a barrel of snakes had gotten loose in her stomach and were slithering around.

Tol took his vial from around his neck and measured out a drop on his finger. The others did the same. They swallowed the Source, and their Hazes flared around them. Not to be outdone, the golden light inside Addy decided it was time to appear. She saw the shimmering gold surround her, and felt the sense of purpose that came with it.

Addy didn't know if it was the seriousness of their mission or seeing his Haze compared to the others', but Tol was almost blinding. It was like trying to stare at the sun. When she looked away, bright spots danced in her vision. He was beautiful and terrifying.

Their tiny army marched onto Base. Mortal guards still posted at the entrance opened their mouths. With no more than a flick of his eyes, Tol cut off their voices and stilled their limbs mid-step.

Gerth let out a low whistle, clearly impressed by the strength of Tol's Influence.

"Told you, mate," Tol said, sparing Gerth a grin.

"This way," Gerth said, motioning to the king and queen.

"Son," the king began, but then stopped. He must have known his arguments would fall on deaf ears now, just as they had on the plane.

"We'll see you all in a few hours," Tol said.

"Indeed." His mother sniffed and straightened her spine.

With one more look at Addy that was as sharp as daggers, the queen put her hand on the king's arm and let him lead her away.

Erikir and Getyl went with them, their Hazes nearly as bright as the king and queen's.

Tol took Addy's hand. "Ready?" he asked.

She pulled her garden shears from her back pocket.

"Ready."

CHAPTER 38

TOL

Tol and Addy ran in the direction of all the mayhem, away from the barracks where Gerth and Tol's parents were now headed to retrieve Olivia. Erikir and Gran would handle the Forsaken general. It was up to Fred, Tol, and Addy to make sure the rest of the Forsaken on Base would be chasing them and not the ones rescuing Olivia.

Smoke was rising from where the fireworks had started a small blaze. In the distance, Tol could hear the rumble of Fred's tractor. They ran toward it.

Shouts rose, and Tol knew his Haze had been spotted. Forsaken charged them from every direction.

Look at me, he silently commanded their enemy.

The Forsaken were well-trained and prepared. They all kept their eyes averted until they were in striking range, and then they lashed out with their weapons.

Addy wielded her shears with abandon.

"You wanted the Fount?" she screamed. "Well, come and get me!"

They were moving too much for Tol to get a hold of their minds. Addy whipped her garden shears through the air so fast they blurred. Blood sprayed across her fatigues and splattered on the pavement. She didn't slow her pace. Still, the Forsaken didn't let up. In seconds, Tol and Addy were surrounded.

One of the more eager Forsaken with a weaker Haze got too close, taunting them. Tol grabbed the man's sleeve, and before he could strike out with his sword, Tol pressed his fingers to the bare skin at the man's throat. The man went still.

"Look at me," Tol commanded.

He directed the Forsaken to turn his weapon on his comrades. While they were occupied, Tol took five more minds under his Influence. He made them fight alongside him and Addy, allowing them to move deeper into enemy territory.

Addy was fighting like a tigress, but she was one person, and she was up against the best fighters in a race of warriors. She was fading. Tol could see the strain in her movements and on her face.

The dozens of mortals trying to lend support to their Forsaken superiors weren't a real threat, but it took time and energy for Tol to take control of their minds, and he didn't have enough of either to spare.

The Forsaken had known to expect him, and they were going to great lengths to avoid looking into his eyes. Tol took too many risks diving within range of their weapons to make physical contact.

Move, he ordered himself as the strain of having so many minds under his control turned his legs to lead weights. Addy needed him, and every person he Influenced was one more enemy he could turn into an unwilling ally.

Even though he'd wasted precious seconds to take more Source, he knew their strength wouldn't hold out forever.

For every Forsaken Addy put down, three more took his place. They were relentless. It was taking Addy longer and longer to dispatch each opponent. Tol did what he could to control the minds of those clamoring for their chance to kill her. He must have been Influencing close to twenty Forsaken and almost as many mortals, and his hold over them was as frail as spider silk. If this lasted much longer, his tenuous hold on them would snap.

Tol heard the rumble of the tractor before he saw it. The machine steamrolled down the road and onto the grass, driverless. The seat was occupied by wooden cogs and strings attached to the steering wheel.

More of the fireworks went off, and one of the flares shot right past them. Tol pushed Addy to the ground and used his body to shield her as the explosion went off in a shower of purple sparks.

The Forsaken closed back in on them, undeterred by the explosion. Tol and Addy scrambled to their feet.

Addy had lost her cap, and her loose hair was whipping across her face. He saw the moment recognition fell across the Forsakens' faces who weren't under his Influence.

Just as he had feared, these barbarians knew exactly who Addy was. It was plain in their eyes.

Tol expected them to converge and swarm over him and Addy like an army of ants swallowing a wingless fly. Tol braced himself, even though he knew it was pointless now. They were outmatched and utterly spent.

And yet, the Forsaken hesitated. For some reason Tol couldn't fathom, they seemed not to know what to do.

Addy didn't hesitate. Her shears flashed as she moved from one to the next. Her enemy's gray eyes widened, but they didn't raise their weapons as she sliced their throats. Some of them were trying to speak to her, but she didn't give them a chance.

It was a bloodbath. All Tol could do was watch as Addy took out every remaining Forsaken who had surrounded them.

"Come on," Tol gasped, still Influencing the minds of their living shield of Forsaken.

"There are more of them," Addy said, waving her bloody shears.

"We've taken too long." Tol grabbed her hand. "We have to go."

Addy resisted. There was a gleam in her eyes Tol hadn't seen before. She looked a little mad.

"Come on." He winced as his hold on the Forsakens' minds slipped. "Let's go see your sister."

They made it to the edge of the Base. Tol gave the mortals and Forsaken still trailing them directions with the last of his strength, and then he released their minds.

He took two steps on jellied legs, and then the strain of the enormous control he'd just exerted over the warriors overtook him. He stumbled.

Addy, her eyes fierce, put an arm around his waist. Together, they stumbled into the woods beyond the Base.

Had Gerth and his parents gotten Olivia out of the barracks? Would they be at the meet-up, waiting for him and Addy, or had the Forsaken gotten them? Did Gran and Erikir kill the Forsaken general?

The questions swam through his foggy brain.

It was a two-mile hike to the meet-up Gerth had outlined on the map and made them all memorize. Tol wouldn't have managed it without Addy. His vision kept wavering in and out of focus. His feet felt like they had cement blocks glued to them. He stumbled over tree roots, rocks, and even pine cones scattered across the unworn trail. Still, Addy's hand in his made him keep going long after his energy was drained.

Addy's innate sense of direction got them to the meet-up, while Tol tried to will his overstrained mind back to full consciousness. When they were in sight of the clearing, Addy dropped his hand, and ran.

The sight that met Tol when he stepped into the small, round patch of dirt surrounded by pine trees infused him with joy and relief. His parents and Gerth were there, uninjured. And Addy was wrapped in her sister's arms. They were crying and laughing, and holding each other like they'd never let go.

Even as exhausted as he was, Tol's heart lifted at the sight. *They'd done it.*

They'd saved Olivia just like he'd promised. Now, they could go back and fix the mess he'd created at the manor. He and Addy would be a force to be reckoned with. Nothing could get in their way.

Tol felt his own smile spread across his face as Addy hugged her sister with so much ferocity the other girl was lifted off the ground.

Olivia looked nothing like Addy. She was petite, looking downright diminutive next to Addy. She had dark hair and eyes, and Tol found himself wondering what their parents must have looked like to have two such different-looking daughters. There was so much about Addy's family that he didn't know, and he wanted to know everything about her.

Fred stumbled out of the trees, looking soot-stained but otherwise intact. He took one look at the scene before him and raced for the sisters.

They made room for him, and the three of them somehow managed a three-way hug while jumping up and down at the same time.

Tol's parents and Gerth stood off to the side. Gerth and Tol's father were smiling at the reunion. His mother's mouth was pressed into a tight line as she watched the sisters' brazen display of emotion.

Gran and Erikir weren't here yet, but they were expected to return last. Gerth had done it. He met his best mate's eye across the clearing, and everything that needed to be said passed between them in a single glance.

Tol wanted to laugh. He wanted to pump his fist in the air and shout. He wanted to kiss Addy.

Once Gran and his cousin returned with the car, they'd all get back to the airstrip where their plane would be waiting. They'd go back to the manor. He and Addy would complete the blood marriage and save them all, and the rebellion would die. Tol's parents would pass on the monarchy to him and his wife, and they'd return to Vitaquias.

His wife.

As he watched Addy reunite with her sister, he felt a lightness in his heart that was so unfamiliar he didn't know it at first for what it was. Another beat passed before he understood. The worries that had plagued him incessantly for eighteen years were over. It felt bloody amazing.

At that moment, Addy looked up and caught Tol's eye. She dropped her arms from her sister and Fred, and ran to him. She threw herself into his arms, wrapping her legs around his waist as she crushed her mouth to his.

Tol heard his mother and Fred's twin sounds of protest. Tol wrapped his arms around Addy and kissed her back.

"Thank you, thank you, thank you," she said, her lips vibrating against his skin.

"Thank you for loving me," Tol replied.

CHAPTER 39

ADDY

Addy's heart was so full of happiness she thought it might explode. Livy was with her, safe and in one piece. They were together. And Tol was with her. After all the horror and grief and loss, she had the two people who meant everything to her.

When Addy and Livy got their breath back from so much crying and laughing, and she had seen for herself that her twin was truly intact, she forced herself to settle enough to have a conversation with Livy. While they waited for the roar of the Hummer on the road beyond the clearing, she talked to her sister for the first time since she'd come into the farmhouse and found the rest of her family lying dead on the kitchen floor.

"I knew you'd find me," Livy said, gazing up at her with the warm brown eyes Addy had feared she'd never see again.

"I'm sorry I couldn't come sooner," Addy replied, squeezing her sister's hands in hers. "You must have been so scared."

"I was," Livy admitted. "But the whole time, I thought about what you would do if you were in my position." She smiled, and it warmed Addy to her core. "I wanted so badly to be brave like you that I managed not to have a single seizure the entire time they had me locked up."

"I should have been there for you from the beginning," Addy said, all of her regret rising and making it difficult to speak. "I should have been there for all of you…."

"Don't." Livy closed her hands around Addy's, her eyes wide and pooling with tears. "You can't blame yourself. You weren't even home. I was." She swallowed. "The men came into the house, and they were the biggest people I'd ever seen. They all had weapons, and—" Livy choked on a sob, "—and they killed everyone." Livy could barely manage to whisper the words.

Addy's chest constricted with grief as fresh and sudden as if she were back in the kitchen kneeling in her family's blood.

"They took me," Livy said. "I tried to fight them, I really did."

"I know." Addy wrapped her arms around her sister, and they held each other.

"Addy," Livy said after a long pause. "Who are those people? What do they want from me?"

Guilt tore at Addy anew. "They were using you to try and get me."

It was then that Addy realized that Livy didn't know any of what Addy had learned in the last month. She didn't know about the Chosen or Forsaken, or that Addy was some kind of Fount who was destined to be queen of a magical race. All she knew was the inside of a dirty cell and the threats of cruel men and women.

Addy huffed out a humorless laugh. "Did those barbarians tell you anything?"

"They said Mom and Dad were thieves and had stolen from them." Livy frowned. "And they asked me a lot of questions about you."

"Did they hurt you?" Addy heard the danger in her own voice. She would kill this warrior general if Getyl and Erikir hadn't gotten to her first, but if the Forsaken had done anything more than lock Livy in a cell....

"No," Livy said, her voice soothing, while Addy's was tight with emotion. "It was cold and dirty, but they mostly ignored me when they weren't asking about you. No one treated me badly." A tear tracked down her cheek. "I almost wish they had."

Addy started. "What—"

"I saw them, Addy," Livy's voice broke. "Mom, Dad, Stacy, Rosie, Lucy...they killed them all. It should have been me on the kitchen floor and one of them you rescued."

"Livy—"

Addy didn't have the words to make her sister understand that none of this was her fault. She was only beginning to see how Livy, the one who had cared for their little sisters as tenderly as their own mother, was suffering.

"This isn't your fault," Addy said. "If it's anyone's, it's mine. The reason for all of this was because of me."

"Why are those people after you?" Livy asked. "They aren't normal. I saw them do things, or at least I thought I did, that shouldn't have even been possible."

Addy shook her head, overwhelmed by how much had happened since she last saw her sister, and having no idea where to begin.

"I have a lot to tell you," she said.

"Good." Livy laughed a little as she wiped at her eyes. "Because I have a lot of questions."

Livy's eyes immediately slid to Tol, who was leaning against a tree with his eyes closed.

"Let's start with him," Livy said, a twinkle creeping into her gaze.

Addy looked at Tol. As though he felt her gaze, Tol opened his eyes and smiled at her.

Livy coughed then. It was a rattling, dry cough that was no doubt the result of being left in a freezing cold cell for a month.

Addy pulled off the army jacket she was wearing and draped it around her sister's shoulders. Livy looked at the blood still drying on the fabric but didn't say anything.

Livy coughed again.

"We passed a stream nearby," Addy said, worry gnawing at her insides. "Can I bring you some water while we wait for the car?"

Livy nodded, her cheeks red from coughing. Tol, his brow creased with concern, walked over to them.

"Livy, meet Tol. Tol, meet Livy," Addy said, already running back to the trail. "I'll be right back."

✳ ✳ ✳

TOL

Tol and Olivia stared at each other awkwardly. After the way Addy had kissed him, and the way he'd kissed her, he figured Olivia knew more or less *what* Tol was to Addy. As for *who* he was, that was a different story. What did Olivia know? Anything?

"It's a pleasure to meet you," Tol said, his voice coming out formal and strange. "I'm Tol."

He was talking to his fiancé's sister for the first time, and he was nervous.

"Nice to meet you, Tol." Olivia's face stretched into a smile that immediately put him at ease.

She held out her hand to him, and he took it. The moment their fingers touched, Tol saw a flash of blinding white. And then he collapsed.

OLIVIA

Olivia always knew the millisecond before a seizure started. One second she was there, present, and the next moment the blackness was being pulled over her eyes like a veil. She always woke up seconds or minutes later, with no memory of what had happened in the between time.

This time was different.

The moment she touched Tol's hand, she felt her legs give way. Olivia felt herself hit the ground. But instead of the black veil, she saw a white light. Her mouth was moving, but the voice that was speaking was not her own. The words that came out of her were coherent, they just made no sense.

"The Fount and the prince are the salvation of Vitaquias and the gods' Chosen race. The answers will be revealed when the blood marriage is completed and the new king is throned. Be united by the Fount's nineteenth year, or relinquish the key to Vitaquias for eternity."

Olivia gasped. She put a hand to her throat, like she couldn't believe those words had come from inside her.

She sometimes spoke gibberish during her seizures. She never remembered anything she said, but her family told her afterward. This time, she remembered.

She tried to stand, but her legs felt too rubbery to manage even that simple act. A strange tingle ran through her veins. She felt like she'd just downed an energy drink. Or ten.

Olivia had just had a seizure, and she remembered every moment of it.

Olivia turned to the boy on his knees beside her, who looked as dazed as she felt. She realized their hands were still clasped in a handshake that had never ended. She let go, and instantly, the strange feeling in her veins drained away. Tol sucked in a breath, like he hadn't been able to get any air while they were touching.

What in the world had just happened?

Fred, who had raced to her side when she collapsed, looked as confused as she felt. But the other people in the clearing, the ones who had rescued her, looked stricken. Like something horrible had just happened, and they understood every bit of it.

Before she could make sense of feeling…something…when she touched her sister's boyfriend, Tol grabbed her shoulders. He had a metal hand, and it dug into her skin.

"What was that? What did you do?"

"I—I'm sorry," she managed, not sure what she was sorry for. "I have seizures sometimes. It's nothing—"

Tol gave her a shake that made her head snap back.

"Did that happen to you the night the thief broke into your house?"

"You're hurtin' her," Fred growled, grabbing his arm and yanking it away from her. "What the hell is wrong with you?"

"Did it?" Tol repeated, his fearsome gaze locked on her.

"I—" Olivia thought back to that night. She remembered her mother and Addy crouched by her side, and her father offering her a cool washcloth. "Yes," she said.

Olivia saw the color drain from Tol's face. His metal hand, the one that was still gripping her, slipped away.

"Oh gods," the other boy who looked to be about Tol's age said.

These people all seemed to understand something she didn't. Olivia looked at Fred, who shrugged, as puzzled as she was. One thing was clear. Something terrible had happened.

"It can't be." Tol's voice sounded broken. He was looking at the two older people in the clearing, who Olivia thought must be his parents.

"You didn't make sure Addy was the one?" the other boy asked, not unkindly, but in a direct, no-nonsense kind of way.

"Of course, I made sure," Tol ground out. "She saw my Haze…she had her own…." his eyes turned from molten fury to desperation.

Olivia didn't understand it, but her heart hurt for whatever pain he was feeling.

"Addy is eighteen. She's the right age—" he turned to Olivia. "You're her younger sister, right?"

Tol's eyes were pleading with her to say yes.

"We're twins," she said as gently as she could.

The look that came into his eyes scared her. She shrunk away from him.

"I just assumed from the way she talked about you," Tol said. He grabbed his head, like he was trying to press whatever realization he'd had back out. "She never mentioned…I never asked…."

Where was Addy?

Olivia needed her sister to come back. Somehow, that would make everything better. There had been some misunderstanding, but she wasn't clear on what it was, so she couldn't say the words that would wipe away that look in Tol's eyes.

"Tolumus," the older man said. His face and tone were serious, but there was a sadness in his dark eyes that seemed to match the woman's and the other boy's.

"No," Tol rasped. "Addy fought the Forsaken. She could sense where they were. She knew things she couldn't have known if she was just a mortal."

He spoke to the people standing over them like he was begging for something.

"There must be some other explanation for that," the other boy said. "But there's no question who she is." He jabbed his thumb in Olivia's direction.

"No," Tol said again. "It isn't possible."

"You said you didn't see her, but you saw through her," the other boy said. "She and Addy were in the same house. Think about it, Tol. It makes sense. You show up and there's only one person with magic. You assume she's the Fount. Any one of us would have made the same mistake."

"And now we know the truth." The woman who looked like Tol's mother turned to regard Olivia. "I like this girl better already. Now I won't have to worry about having grandchildren with ghastly red hair."

Tol's face turned an alarming shade of green.

Olivia looked at the woman, who was smiling at her. Her cheeks turned to flame as she understood the implications of what this woman was saying.

Tol looked like someone was holding a gun to his head and was about to pull the trigger. "I can't." He met Olivia's eyes. "I won't."

CHAPTER 40

ADDY

Addy returned to the clearing, the pitiful amount of water she'd collected and managed to keep from slipping away cupped in her hands. It hadn't occurred her until she'd reached the stream that she had no vessel to bring the water back.

The sight that met her as she stepped into the clearing was nothing like the one she'd left. Tol was on his knees and Livy was crouched beside him, with Fred just behind her. Gerth and Tol's parents were standing over them. Some part of her brain registered the identical looks on each of their faces, but her only thought was of Tol.

"What happened?" She rushed forward, only to stop a short way from them. There was a look on Tol's face she'd never seen before, and it turned her blood to ice.

He looked…gutted. So much so that her eyes went over him twice, certain there must be some mortal wound. But there wasn't a drop of blood.

Tol looked at her.

"Addy," he said, and his voice broke.

At that moment, they heard the sound of tires screeching on pavement. The Hummer's horn blared. No one in the clearing moved.

"What's going on?" Addy demanded.

"I had a seizure," Livy said.

Addy felt the tension drain out of her. She even laughed a little. "That's what you're all so upset about? It's fine. Livy's had seizures since she was a baby."

"No, Addy," Livy said, shaking her head. "It was different this time. I talked in a different voice, and I remembered what I said."

Okay, her seizure was a little different than it had been before. So what?

"What the two hells are you still doing here?" Erikir barked, his voice startling the others, who seemed to be in a trance.

Getyl hobbled into the clearing behind Tol's cousin.

"We need to go. *Now.*" Erikir made a wild gesture. "The general's still alive, and she's on her way with an army of Forsaken."

Still, no one moved.

"Rolomens? Starser?" Getyl asked, looking at the king and queen. "What happened?"

"Why are you all just standing here?" Erikir demanded, his rage barely contained. "We lost them only a little way back. They're going to find us."

No one paid any attention to him.

"The Fount isn't…who we thought it was," the king said heavily.

"Tol," Addy began.

There had obviously been some mistake…some misunderstanding. Whatever it was, they'd figure it out in the car. When Tol wouldn't look at her, she turned to Gerth. There was an apology in his eyes that she didn't want to understand.

Addy looked to her sister.

"I spoke some kind of prophecy," Livy told her, looking confused and apologetic. "I saw a vision of a woman, and it was her voice talking through me."

Addy opened her mouth and then shut it with a click. "No," she managed, even as those words started to form into meaning. "It has to be me."

"Son, it's time to face facts," the king said.

Tol was shaking his head.

"Tolumus—"

"She's her gods-damned sister," Tol said, his voice wrecked.

An invisible, icy hand reached inside Addy and ripped all the air from her lungs.

No.

"Livy's had seizures her whole life. They mean nothing," Addy said again, unsure who she was trying to convince. Then, she remembered something. "Tol felt me," she said, the eagerness plain in her voice. "He found me because he could sense me. How do you explain that, if Livy is the one with all the power?"

Addy expected Tol's eyes to light up, but his face only paled further.

"I didn't see you, I saw through you," Tol said, his voice faraway and inflectionless now. "At least, I thought it was you...."

"But you said yourself no mortal could fight the Forsaken the way I do," Addy persisted. "Remember how I could track them? Remember how I could swim even though I'd never learned? How do you explain any of that if I'm not the Fount?"

She knew how desperate she sounded. She didn't care.

"There are other possible explanations for that," Gerth said. "There is no other explanation for the connection between Tol and Olivia."

"I know you wish things were different," Tol's mother began, and then stopped, like even she didn't have the words.

No. No. No.

Everything Tol had told her about the blood marriage rushed back to her now. Bound in mind and body for eternity. Tol...her Tol...doing *that* with her sister.... She covered her mouth with her hand to keep from throwing up.

"Tol." Addy said his name like a prayer. She felt the hot tears sliding down her cheeks.

I love you. I don't want to live without you.

The tears came harder now, and there was nothing she could do to stop them.

"I won't do it," Tol said. "I won't do the blood marriage with anyone except Addy."

"You have a duty to your people," his father said, his voice turning dangerous. "Do not forget where your priorities lie."

"I'll abdicate," Tol said.

Everyone in the clearing sucked in a collective breath. Erikir took a step toward them, his eyes wide with shock. No one else moved.

"You can't," Addy managed. "You want to be king more than anything." He'd told her that.

"That was before you." The veil of grief over Tol's eyes seemed to clear a little. He nodded, as though he'd reached a decision. "Erikir can have the throne. He can marry Olivia."

Addy gasped. Livy's eyes went round as saucers. Addy saw the same horror she felt reflected on her twin's face.

Addy would rather slit her own throat than force Sweet Livy to bond with that evil boy whose only pleasure in life was torturing Tol.

The queen was the first person to break the silence.

"You couldn't abdicate, even if you wanted to," she said to Tol. "You are the most powerful of our people. You're also the true prince of the Chosen."

Tol looked up at Addy then, and the look in his eyes stole the life from her.

"Please." He said the word while looking at her, like she wasn't as helpless as he was…like her heart wasn't breaking right alongside his.

"Perhaps it's for the best," Getyl began, putting a hand on Tol's shoulder.

Tol wrenched away from her. "No," he said. "I love her." Tol's gaze cut straight into Addy's soul. "I love you."

"I love you, too," she managed, her chest heaving from the sobs she couldn't contain.

"If you truly can't live without her," Getyl began.

Tol, who was still on his knees, got to his feet. "What?" he demanded.

The king shook his head at Getyl. "This is how it must be."

"My grandson is in love," Getyl argued. "He's in pain."

"He'll get over it," the queen said.

"I won't," Tol snarled at his mother, before turning all his attention on his grandmother. "What were you going to say?"

"If you can't live without her," Getyl said again, "there might be another way."

CHAPTER 41

TOL

Anything," Tol said. "I'll do anything."

Addy nodded her agreement.

"Perhaps you could convince the Celestial to pull her magic from Olivia and give it to Adelyne," Gran said. "After all, it's the power within Olivia you need, not Olivia herself." She gave Addy's sister a kind smile. "No offense, dear."

Tol's heart sank. "The Celestial is—"

"Alive," Gran said.

"What?"

"Well, I assume she is," Gran modified. "If your Grandfather Walidir could survive, then I imagine she could, too."

"Getyl," Tol's mother said in a stern voice. "Don't put foolish hopes in his head. There is no other way."

"But it might be possible," Tol said. He knew he sounded as mad as his gran, but if there was any chance, in any world, he'd take it.

"Olivia's blood opens the portal," Gerth said. "We could just check it out."

"There's no *just checking out* a ruined world!" the king thundered. "Tolumus, I order you to blood marry the Fount—the *real* Fount—and dispense with all this nonsense."

"Rolomens, you may be our king," Gran said, "but I am still your mother. And I say that true love isn't nonsense."

Tol wanted to kiss his gran.

Gran continued, "If he loves Adelyne as much as he says he does, and you force him to go through the blood marriage with this girl while he still desires another, you know what will happen."

Tol's misery would become Olivia's misery a thousand-fold. It would turn them both mad and, eventually, kill them both. Not only would he be bound to the sister of the woman he loved, he'd be responsible for the death of the only family Addy had left.

"This is madness, Tolumus," his father said. "Your grandmother is not well. Ever since my father died—"

"Oh poo," Gran said. "Your father *is* alive, and his spirit has travelled from Vitaquias to speak to me. He thinks you should give the young ones a chance."

"We all saw what happened," Tol's mother said. "We barely made it out ourselves. There's no chance any who were left behind survived."

"I know what I know." Gran shrugged. "And I know my husband still lives."

Tol knew how she sounded. He also knew he was desperate enough to try anything. If there was any way in the two worlds he could fix this disaster, he'd do it.

"We have to try," Tol begged his parents. "Just give us until Olivia's nineteenth birthday. It's in—" he looked at Addy.

"Ten months," she said.

His father's face was purpling and sounds that weren't words were coming out of his mouth.

"You're going to go into a desert wasteland of a world," Erikir said, his telltale sneer in place, "to look for someone any of the scholars will tell you had no chance of surviving, for a girl you've known for a month?"

"I wouldn't expect you to understand," Tol shot back.

"Do you have any idea how many of our people will die while you go on this little quest?" Erikir demanded.

"Erikir is right," Tol's mother said.

Tol yanked the vial from around his neck and held it out to his parents like an offering. "Take it all and distribute it to the ones who need it. Use

what's left of the reserves. We don't need to save any of it to find the Fount anymore." Tol was breathless from talking, but he forged on before either of his parents could interject. "That'll be enough for six months, at least. That's all I'm asking for. No one will die."

"Don't be absurd," his father said, but there was less certainty in his voice than there had been a minute ago.

"The rebellion needs to be put down and the curse needs to end," Tol's mother said. "We simply don't have six months to wait for you to go on this fool's errand."

"If you distribute all of the reserves, it will be enough to pacify the people until Tol returns from Vitaquias," Gran said.

"Please," Tol begged, his voice cracking on the word. "Please, just let us try."

"And if you're killed?" his father demanded.

"We all die," Erikir supplied. "Some great leader you're turning out to be."

"Try not to be a prick," Gerth told him.

"We won't get killed," Tol said.

"I'll make sure of it," Gerth added, coming to stand next to him. "I haven't had a real challenge in years."

Tol's chest constricted at his best mate's show of solidarity.

"So will I," Addy said.

"Me, too," Fred said, coming to stand next to Addy.

Tol saw his mother's eyes softened a fraction. "And if you cannot find the Celestial in six months, or if she's already dead, then you'll come back and marry Olivia that very day. Agreed?"

Tol looked at Addy, who looked at her sister. Olivia wore a look of pure disbelief.

"Agreed," Addy said.

"Fine." The king turned away from Tol in disgust. "But you're bringing Erikir with you, and if your lives are endangered or six months have passed, he has my permission to drag you back here by any means necessary."

"Fine," Tol said.

The decision didn't ease Tol's heart. He knew what his parents would have to face when they returned to the manor. Even with the extra Source they'd be distributing, he knew the uphill battle they would have to fight while he was a world away. He knew an absence of six months would drain the rest of their Source completely. There would be no room for error. If he failed, it would be his people who paid the price.

He looked at Gran.

"We'll all survive until you get back," she said, as though reading his mind.

Tol knew he was insane for going on this quest in search of someone who everyone but his gran was certain was long-dead. He knew his duty mandated that he blood marry Olivia and save his race from annihilation. He knew that every day the Forsaken and Chosen remained at war in this world, the greater the risk would be to the mortals who lived here. And yet, he couldn't see any other path except for the one that left him with some hope, no matter how impossibly little of it, that he could wake up every morning with Addy in his arms.

"Back to the Hummer," Gran said, already making her way to the road.

Fred helped Olivia to her feet and followed the others. Addy leaned against Tol. They didn't speak. There was nothing to say. Tol could sense her every thought and emotion, like they were mirrors of his own...like they were already bound.

Tol heard his mother's scream first. Then, the woods were filled with shouting.

CHAPTER 42

ADDY

Addy burst through the trees with Tol on her heels. Forsaken surrounded the Hummer. Livy and Getyl were pinned against the hood, their hands held behind their backs by two of the giant warriors. The others were surrounded.

"Where is she?" one of the barbarians screamed in Livy's face.

Pure rage came over Addy. She heard Tol's voice, but not his words. She ran for her sister and the Forsaken woman standing over her. Addy shoved past the warriors who tried to stop her.

The Forsaken leaning over Livy turned around to face Addy just as she raised her shears. Addy stopped, her arm still raised, and gasped.

It was like looking into a mirror, if the mirror reflected her appearance in twenty or thirty years. The woman had the same green eyes, the same pale skin. Her hair tucked into her army cap was as red as Addy's, although some of the strands were streaked with gray. They were the same height, the same build, the same everything....

"I don't understand," Addy choked.

Her brain was trying to tell her something, but she couldn't—wouldn't—understand it. This woman....

"Daughter," the woman said, and she was looking at Addy when she said it. She reached up and put a hand on Addy's cheek, like she might be a phantom.

Addy flinched away.

"Who are you?" Addy demanded. Even though her eyes made an irrefutable argument, everything inside her rebelled at the idea.

The woman didn't say anything as her eyes raked over Addy.

Addy stood motionless. She could do nothing but stare at this woman.

Maybe her eyes were playing tricks on her. Maybe there was some kind of illusion magic at work here that Tol had forgotten to tell her about. Maybe—

"General?" one of the Forsaken addressed the woman. "What are your orders?"

General? This *was the Forsaken general?!*

"Lezha Bloodsong," Getyl howled. "You will pay for your crimes!" Tol's grandmother struggled against her captor. It was useless. The warrior behind her pinned her head against the hood of the car with one hand.

Lezha Bloodsong. That name was familiar. And then Addy remembered. It was the name Getyl had called Addy when she met her for the first time. Tol's grandmother had thought she was the Forsaken general...that she was the one responsible for killing Getyl's son.

Addy had written it off at the time. Tol's grandmother talked to her dead husband like he was standing right next to her. She was crazy....

But now, Addy understood. Getyl was the only one of her people who had ever seen the Forsaken general, so she was the only one who could have known about the...resemblance between Addy and the general.

Addy wanted to throw up. It made sense why Tol's grandmother had tried to attack her, and why, even after she realized her mistake, she hadn't seemed to like Addy very much. Addy wanted to press pause on this whole mess and explain everything to Getyl.

We just look alike, she'd say. *We aren't related. I could never be related to a monster like her.*

"Take them into custody," the general said without taking her eyes off Addy. "Chain and blindfold the royal family so they can't use their Influence, but do not remove their necklaces. We may have use for them yet."

Those words snapped Addy out of her stupor. Lightning quick, she had her shears pressed to the general's—for that was the only title she could imagine belonging to this woman—throat.

"Lay so much as a finger on any of them," Addy snarled, "and your general will be dead."

The woman didn't flinch. She didn't so much as blink, even as Addy pushed the blades against her skin hard enough to draw blood.

No one moved. No one spoke.

"Addy." Tol's choked voice came from somewhere behind her.

Addy turned, keeping the shears pressed against the general's neck. Tol was standing, his golden light blazing around him. There were Forsaken on every side of him, but their eyes were clear. Tol wasn't touching or looking at them. His hands were hanging by his sides. He wasn't even trying to fight. Tol was looking from her to the general, his jaw slack, his eyes wide in disbelief.

"Tol, it's not…she isn't…." Addy stuttered over an explanation she didn't have. There was no explanation for why she was the spitting image of the Forsaken general except for the one she wouldn't even consider.

Two of the Forsaken surrounding Tol wrenched his arms behind his back, while another yanked a blindfold over his eyes.

Tol didn't struggle. He was too stunned to try and fight them. Addy felt her own paralysis in the face of so much impossibility. First, she had found out Livy, and not she, was the Fount. And now….

It was too much.

"Lock them in the barracks," the general said, her voice smooth even as her throat grated against the blade of Addy's shears. "My daughter's actions will determine their fate."

My daughter…their fate….

Addy's brain was moving too slowly.

Livy cried out as she was shoved into the backseat of one of the army jeeps parked behind the Hummer. Fred struck out at the Forsaken holding him. The warrior cracked Fred over the head with his fist, and her best friend sagged against his captor.

"No!" Addy screamed, letting go of the general and racing after them.

Addy saw two of the Forsaken pick Tol up like he weighed nothing and toss him into the truck. He was blindfolded and his arms were handcuffed behind his back. He was yelling her name.

Tol. Her mouth formed the word, but no sound came out.

She was too slow. Everyone she loved was piled into the army jeep. It sped away before she could reach it.

Addy ran after the truck, fury warring with her growing helplessness. She kept running until she collapsed on the pavement. Then, helplessness took over. Her head drooped as her body folded in on itself.

Too late. Too late. Too late.

The hopeless refrain beat in time with her heart.

A rumbling came from somewhere behind her. She heard a car's engine idling, and then a door open and close. Addy saw the general's boots cross the pavement and come to stand, toes perfectly aligned, in front of her.

"I think it's time we get acquainted," the general said. She offered Addy her hand. It was a pale hand with long, slender fingers that looked identical to Addy's own.

It wasn't possible. It *couldn't* be possible.

Addy looked up at the woman. She was startled once again to see her own eyes staring back at her from another person's face.

It couldn't be. It just couldn't. If she was this woman's daughter, it would mean her parents weren't here parents. It would mean she wasn't Livy's twin. It would make her Tol's enemy.

Addy knew she was shaking her head back and forth, like she was saying a silent *no*, even though no question had been asked.

The general smiled at Addy, but it was the tight-lipped smile of someone whose face wasn't accustomed to the motion. It looked more like a grimace.

"I have been searching for you for eighteen years," the general said. She offered Addy her hand again. "But I never gave up hope that my daughter was alive. I always knew I'd find you."

CHAPTER 43

TOL

Tol's mind was in a fog. Addy wasn't the Fount. Addy was the Forsaken general's daughter.

So much that hadn't made sense before now clicked into place. Why she could fight but not Influence…why she knew how to track and swim and do all the other things any Forsaken child would know…why, if she wasn't the Fount, she had magic in her blood. Even her comment about getting angry, which was a decidedly Forsaken trait….

The facts all aligned, and yet his heart rebelled.

Addy's parents were two mortal farmers whose dead bodies were buried in a cornfield in upstate New York. Her mother wasn't—couldn't be—the leader of Tol's enemy. Her mother couldn't be the one who had murdered Tol's uncle and countless more of his people.

But no matter how much he tried to convince himself otherwise, his rational brain wouldn't allow any other explanation. Addy was the Forsaken general's daughter.

And yet, there was still something that made no sense. Addy's Haze appeared without her ever taking Source…something that shouldn't be possible for either Chosen or Forsaken.

"What's going on?" came Olivia's tremulous voice from somewhere nearby. "What did you do with my sister?"

Tol's heart gave a painful lurch. *What had the barbarian general done with Addy?*

Tol was shoved into a cell. His right shoulder slammed into hard stone. He heard a key turn in the lock. The moment the footsteps retreated, he scraped his cheek along the rough stones until the blindfold came loose. The cell was large, and they'd been locked in together—his parents, Gerth, Gran, Erikir, Livy, and Fred. Erikir and Fred had gotten their blindfolds off too, and between the three of them, they were able to help the others get theirs off. Not that it did any good. The Forsaken guards were standing too far for any of their Influence to stretch.

The prisoners could see, at least, but there was nothing to be done about the shackles on their wrists and ankles.

"Who are these people?" Olivia asked. Her face turned scarlet, like she was embarrassed to even be asking the question.

Tol opened his mouth to reply, but no words came.

"How about," Gerth said, "we figure out our escape first, and then we deal with the rest later?"

"Sounds like a good idea," Fred agreed.

"We're not leaving without Addy," Tol said, daring the others with his eyes to argue.

"One thing at a time." Gerth moved to the door and peered out through the bars.

"The general is only keeping us alive for leverage," Gran said, her voice full of unspent fury. She had come here to kill the woman who murdered her son. And now that woman was....

Gerth turned back to them. "The only issue is how to get out of this cell."

"Not the twenty armed Forsaken we'll meet on the other side?" Erikir jangled his chains to emphasize his point.

Fred moved to the front of their cage and leaned against the bars. He looked up at the ceiling, and then down at the floor. "I could get us out," he said, and then frowned, "if I had a wrench."

"All you need is a wrench?" Gerth asked.

Fred nodded. "Can't do anything about the chains, though."

"We may not need to." Gerth paced the length of the cell. When he made his way back around to the front of them, he was grinning.

"I have a theory I'd like to test." He looked at Tol, and Tol knew with a sinking feeling he wasn't going to like whatever came out of his best friend's mouth next.

"Tol, Olivia, hold hands," Gerth said.

Without thinking, Tol stepped away from Olivia. Seeing what must look like his disgust toward her, Olivia flinched. He felt an immediate flare of guilt. None of this was even close to her fault. Still, though, he kept his bound hands facing the wall.

When he touched Olivia before, he'd had no idea what would happen. When they clasped hands, there was such a rush of feeling and power, such a sense of inevitability, that it had felt like betraying Addy.

"I'm not asking you to sleep with her," Gerth huffed. To Olivia, he said, "Please excuse my mate's *terrible* manners. He's not usually such an idiot."

"Beg to differ," Erikir grumbled.

"Hold hands," Gerth commanded. "If what I'm thinking works, then I have a plan for getting us out of here."

Tol forced himself to turn around so his hands were facing Olivia. He felt ridiculous as he shuffled around and lowered himself so Olivia's bound hands could reach his. After a short pause, Olivia did the same.

This time, Tol was ready for the assault of power that hit him when their hands touched. Even so, he barely managed to stay on his feet. He was aware of his Haze flaring a blinding white, and Olivia's intake of breath as an onslaught of feeling tethered them. Raw power coursed between their clasped hands.

Everything around Tol faded. It was like the mortal world was an illusion, and reality existed in the space their touch had opened up. He saw mountains and trees, and a castle overlooking a sparkling, still lake.

Someone was calling his name. He had to squint through the brightness to see his friend.

Gerth was standing in front of Tol and saying something. Tol concentrated until the lake and castle faded, and Gerth came into focus.

"I thought that might work," his mate was saying. "I'd guessed that—"

Gerth's voice began to fade again as the blinding white light pulsed all around them.

"Hey." Gerth rattled his chains to get Tol's attention.

"See if you can get a guard over here," Gerth told him.

Tol and Olivia shuffled to the front of their cell, their hands still linked. The nearest guard was at the end of the hallway. No amount of Influence could reach even a tenth of the distance separating them. Tol could barely see the man at all, let alone make eye contact with him. It would be impossible to Influence him from here.

Even as the thought occurred to him, Tol felt something in the corner of his mind. He was acutely aware of Olivia, but he could also sense the minds of every person in the cell with them. He felt, more than saw, the Forsaken standing at the end of the hallway. The Forsaken's mind was right there, hovering overhead. All Tol had to do was reach out and grasp it.

Look at me, Tol silently commanded.

The guard turned toward the blinding light radiating from Tol.

"Come here," Tol said.

And, like a puppet on strings, the guard came.

CHAPTER 44

ADDY

Addy had been too overcome with everything she'd just learned to do anything as the jeep drove back to Base. She didn't struggle when *the general* and ten Forsaken escorted her into the main building. Every Forsaken they passed saluted first the general, and then her.

It was too much. The frantic desperation she should be feeling about Livy and Tol and the others was dulled by the way her mind cycled through one impossible truth after another.

Addy stood in the general's office. Two guards were posted outside the door, and there were more down the hall. But when the general shut the door behind her, they were the only ones in the room.

Addy glanced around. Everything in the office had a place and purpose, and had been organized with ruthless precision. Addy remembered the comfortable chaos of the farmhouse, and it sparked her hatred for this woman.

The general watched her, her hands clasped behind her back and feet spread in a military pose.

"You're not my mother," Addy said, seeing no reason to beat around the bush. "You will never be my mother."

This woman didn't seem like she could be anyone's mother.

"I'm sure you have a lot of questions," the general said, "and I'll answer them as best I can. But first, I want to explain something to you."

The general's tone was clinical, but her gaze was scrutinizing, like she was looking inside Addy and assessing her inner workings. It was almost like Gerth when he was solving a problem, except there was less swearing and joking, and all the joy had been stripped away.

This was the woman who, at least on some level, was responsible for the death of her family...her *real* family. Addy had no intention of letting this woman see another sunrise. But she also needed answers.

Addy forced herself to stand there, unmoving, as the older version of her stared back. It was unnerving and infuriating at the same time.

"You were hours old when Vitaquias started to burn," the general said. "I hadn't even had time to name you."

Anger flashed across the general's face.

"There was so much chaos at the Crossing. A group of Chosen tried to kill me." Her expression tightened in fury. Addy recognized it—it was the way she knew her own face looked when she was angry. It made Addy feel sick.

"There was blood and Source, and everything was wet. You slipped out of my arms in the portal. I couldn't find you."

For some reason she couldn't name, Addy felt her heart pounding.

"When we got to the mortal world," the general continued, "I searched everywhere for you. We all did. I've spent the last eighteen years looking for you. I knew you were alive in spite of all evidence pointing to the contrary.

"About a month back, when your Haze flared for the first time, I knew I'd found you."

Addy's throat felt like it had been coated with sandpaper. Even if she'd had any words, she didn't think she would be able to get them out.

That night, when she'd fought the thief like a seasoned warrior instead of a corn farmer, she'd felt something she had never experienced before. It was that anger and power coiled inside her finally being released. It was what she and Tol had both assumed was the Celestial's power inside her.

Now, she knew better. It had been Livy's seizure that brought Tol, and her Haze that brought the Forsaken.

The Forsaken had been able to track her the same way she'd tracked them...because they were one and the same. She hadn't been channeling the Celestial's powers like Tol had guessed. She'd merely been sensing some innate connection to her own people.

Addy didn't know if she wanted to rip this woman's face apart with her bare hands or crawl into the corner and sob her guts out.

If only the general didn't look so much like her, she'd be able to think. She'd be able to figure all of this out. But watching a monster with her face continue to stare at her and say words like *daughter* and *knew I'd found you* were enough to unravel whatever was left of Addy's composure.

"You aren't my people," Addy said. She was breathing as hard as if she'd just run a marathon.

Tol and Livy and Fred were her people.

If they'd still have her. The thought was like a knife to her heart.

She was only beginning to grasp what it meant to be the Forsaken general's daughter. *No longer Livy's twin...not really her parents' daughter...Tol's enemy.*

Addy sunk into one of the chairs beside the desk. The general appraised Addy in that too-keen-for-comfort way that, in the short time since she'd met this woman, Addy had come to loath.

"I sensed the power of the Bloodsong line in you that day," the general said, sitting in the chair across from Addy in a fluid motion. "I know I don't need to convince you. The proof is before your eyes."

It was true. There was no argument Addy could make that would explain why she looked so much like this woman. And still, Addy's heart refused to accept the truth.

"If you're my mother," Addy said, feeling dirty just from stringing those words together, "then who's my father?"

The general's eyes iced over. "He's not in the picture," she replied. "But I assure you, you are Forsaken, through and through."

"I'm not one of you," Addy said, her words coming out choked. She searched the room for something that might give her a way out of this new identity she wanted—needed—to reject. Her eyes landed on the small vial around the general's neck.

"There!" Addy said, almost manic. "I don't need Source to access my strength. That means I'm not like the rest of you."

A complicated array of emotions passed across the general's face. She seemed to be deciding how to phrase her next words.

"Life was…difficult for us on Vitaquias," she began. "The gods abandoned us, and they didn't hold the Chosen accountable for their greed and theft of the Source that was meant for all of us. When the world started to fall apart, many of our people died."

Addy waited. She could tell the general was working up to some critical explanation.

"The Forsaken were vulnerable. We were at the mercy of gods who had abandoned us. We did our best to hone our own strengths, but we were still dependent on the Source to survive. When it was clear Vitaquias wasn't a viable home for us any longer, I knew it would be even more difficult to protect you in the mortal world. You needed Source—more of it than would fit into a vial. I didn't know when, or if, we'd be able to return to our world, and I wasn't going to let you succumb to old age in the mortal world like the rest of us."

"How could that be possible?" Addy asked. The back of her neck prickled in warning.

"I brought you to the Source itself," the general said. "I…held you under the surface until you were forced to drink."

Addy was starting to hyperventilate. She gripped the arms of her chair until her knuckles turned white.

"I held you under until your lungs, your veins, your entire body was saturated with Source. I—"

"You drowned me!"

Addy's dream…the lake surrounded by trees…the oily water sucking her under. It wasn't a dream. That wheezing sound her lungs sometimes made…like she *actually* had water inside her that her body was trying to expel….

She'd always thought it was the first step in her descent into madness.

"You drowned me!" Addy was on her feet, shouting now.

"I didn't drown you," the general replied, her voice unreasonably calm given the news she was sharing. "I saved you. If I hadn't done what I did, you would have been vulnerable to an attack from the Chosen. Mortal disease could have killed you. You would have been defenseless."

"You sick bitch," Addy gasped.

The general's eyes flashed. "You've been with the Chosen. I can only guess at the lies they've Influenced you to believe." The general stood and leaned over until they were face to face. "*They* are the monsters. They stole all the Source, even though there should have been more than enough for all of us. They didn't care how many of us died. And when their greed was so consuming even the gods tired of them, they were the first to escape. They are murderers. We are the survivors."

An insane cackle came from Addy's lips. "You're not murderers? Then how do you explain the deaths of my parents? My sisters?"

"I am your mother," the general hissed. "Those mortals stole you. They hid you. For eighteen years, they lied to you. They kept you from your real family and the truth of who you are."

With a scream, Addy launched herself at the general. She clawed at the woman's face, her rage taking over as she kicked and tore and even snapped her teeth like a rabid beast. The general held her off, forcing Addy's hands to her sides and kicking out her legs until Addy was nothing more than a shaking, fuming pile of limbs on the carpet.

The door opened, and two Forsaken strode into the office. The general gave them a shake of her head, and they left again, closing the door behind them.

The general stood over Addy.

Addy's fury had retreated back inside her, and she was left with a yawning emptiness as she stared up at the general.

There was a quiet sort of conviction on the general's face. It made Addy less certain of who she should blame for the position she now found herself in. The resentment she had felt at the Deerborns, who had known more about her than they ever let on, had been licking at the edges of her consciousness for weeks. She'd managed to keep it at bay, but the more the general spoke, the more she felt it.

She remembered what Tol had said about the chaos of the Crossing. She could imagine how it had happened...two mortals in the right place at the right time. *Or maybe the wrong place at the wrong time.* A child they thought had been abandoned....

Her parents had always called her and Livy "their little miracles." They hadn't been secretive about the fact that their mother had struggled to get pregnant after multiple miscarriages. They had both wanted a big family. When they found an infant abandoned on their land, they must have seen it as some kind of gift.

Addy couldn't see right or wrong, who was to blame and who was innocent. It was all muddled together.

"No." Addy said it out loud, even as she argued within her own mind. "You murdered my baby sisters."

"Your parents refused to tell my people what they needed to know. They refused to give you up. I had ordered my soldiers to do whatever was needed to get those mortals to talk."

Addy moved so fast the general didn't have a chance to react. Her hands went around her mother's throat and squeezed.

Stacy, Rosie, and Lucy's broken bodies hovered before her...tiny phantoms whose lives had been stolen brutally...senselessly....

The door to the office flew open, and a dozen Forsaken stormed in. They ripped Addy away from the general, who was coughing but seemed otherwise unphased by what had almost happened. What *would* happen...the second the other Forsaken let her go.

Addy snarled and twisted as she screamed for the general's blood.

"Stop fighting," the general told Addy. Her voice was raspy. "I have no wish to hurt you."

"Imprisoning your own daughter doesn't make for a great first impression," Addy spat.

The general's lip quirked. "The girl you call your sister said your nickname was Firecracker Addy. Now, I can see why."

Addy screamed as she tried to wrench free from the Forsakens' grip.

"You are my daughter, and that is how I knew you would come here to rescue the remaining relative of the family who stole you."

Addy's hands had turned into claws. She raked at the men's faces, but they held her fast.

Kill them. Kill her. Addy's whole body pulsed with rage.

The general continued, indifferent to Addy's struggling and the blood that ran freely from her soldiers' faces.

"Taking that girl prisoner served a secondary purpose aside from bringing you to me. She has told me much about you in your early years. I look forward to getting to know the woman you will become. Someday, we will return to our home on Vitaquias together."

"I had a home," Addy replied, her voice trembling with unspent emotion. "You took it from me. But I still have a family, and it isn't you."

She went slack in the Forsakens' grip. Caught off guard, they relaxed their hold on her. Addy sprang.

Before anyone could react, Addy blasted her way through the Forsaken. She fisted her hand and thrust it into her mother's jaw. There was a crack as her knuckles connected with bone. The general stumbled back. Before she could recover or any of the guards could move, Addy pulled her garden shears out of her pocket and ran out of the office.

CHAPTER 45

TOL

Tol and Olivia raced toward the main building. His parents had given him ten minutes, the amount of time it would take Fred to hotwire one of the jeeps and drive to them. Tol had agreed, even though the only way he was leaving this place without Addy was in a body bag.

The doors burst open, and Addy came sprinting out. At least twenty guards were in her wake.

Tol gave himself only a millisecond to assure himself Addy was unharmed. Then, he looked past her to the guards. His hand, still coursing with the strength he borrowed from Olivia, vibrated with power. He willed the guards' minds under his Influence. Without eye contact or touch, they gave him their minds. The guards stopped mid-stride.

"Are you okay?" Addy gasped when she reached them.

"Fine," Tol said, trying to clear his vision from the brightness of his Haze, which made it almost impossible to see what was right in front of him. "You?"

Tol felt, rather than saw, Addy's eyes go to the place where his hand was still joined with Olivia's.

No, it's not like that, he wanted to explain. *I needed her power. I needed it to save you.*

He didn't say any of that, though. He dropped his hand from Olivia's like he'd been holding a scalding iron. At that moment, his hold over the guards fell away. They picked up right where they'd left off, like they weren't aware any time had passed.

A jeep screeched to a halt beside them, and the door opened.

"Get in!" Gerth shouted. Tol pushed Olivia into the car. He and Addy scrambled in next. Fred stepped on the gas and the jeep sped away.

Tol was practically on Erikir's lap, and the others in the backseat were similarly crushed together. Tol counted the people in the jeep. Miraculously, they'd all made it. No one had so much as a scratch on them. But no one was celebrating.

No one spoke except when Gerth was giving Fred directions. They bounced over grass as they neared the airport, cutting off some of the roadway to save time. The jeep came to a screeching halt on the airstrip.

"Hurry up," Gerth commanded, as they all spilled out of the car.

The airplane's propellers were already whirring.

Erikir and Tol pulled Gran along between them as the others ran to the plane. Police cars and more army jeeps were speeding down the road toward them.

"Let's get this plane off the ground!" Gerth shouted at the pilot.

Tol was the last one on the plane. He looked out just as a jeep skidded to a halt beside their abandoned one. The general got out, her eyes—Addy's eyes—on fire. It constricted his lungs to see Addy's face, her expression, on his enemy…on the one who had murdered his uncle and so many others.

Tol and his father yanked up the stairs, just as the general raised something metal that glinted in the sunlight. It thunked into the side of the plane.

The plane rolled forward.

"Can't this thing go any faster?" Fred demanded. He was looking out the window. Tol stared over his shoulder at the cop cars that were amassing at the other end of the runway. The plane picked up speed.

Olivia put a hand over her mouth. Addy wrapped her arms around her sister, like she could protect her if they crashed.

"Seatbelts," Tol's mother barked.

The plane ate up the runway, coming closer and closer to the pile of cars and Forsaken on the road. Tol felt the front wheels leave the ground.

"We're not going to make it!" someone yelled.

There was a scraping as the plane's belly grazed the top of one of the jeeps. And then they were leaving the swirling red and blue lights of the cop cars below. They were in the air.

Everyone on the plane seemed to release their pent-up breaths at the same moment. Gerth laughed and punched Tol's shoulder.

"Cut that one a bit close, don't you think?" Tol grumbled.

"What's the fun if we don't break a little sweat?" Gerth replied.

Gran was fanning herself with a handful of cocktail napkins. "I'm getting too old for this," she said, leaning back in her seat.

Tol breathed a sigh of relief. They were all here, and they were safe. His eyes went straight to Addy. They both rose from their seats on opposite ends of the plane and moved toward each other. Tol wanted to grab her, but there was something in her gaze that gave him pause. She looked uncertain. Her fists curled and uncurled at her sides.

"I," she began. "The general—"

And then, Tol understood. He pulled Addy against him, wrapping his arms all the way around her. "I don't give a damn who your mum is," he said in her ear.

She pulled back so she could look at him. He let her see the truth in his eyes.

"Nothing has changed for me," he told her. Tol swallowed. "Has…has anything changed for you?"

Addy shook her head. "I just thought you might have changed your mind."

The look on her face melted his insides.

"Never." He leaned in to brush his lips against hers.

Someone cleared his throat, reminding Tol that he and Addy weren't the only ones on this plane. Reluctantly, Tol stepped back. It was then that he saw his parents' faces. They were livid, their lips white with barely-contained fury. Gran and Erikir were wearing similar expressions. And they were all staring at Addy.

"Awkward," Gerth muttered, putting up his hands as though he were surrendering.

Tol looked at his family, and then at Addy. She seemed to shrink in on herself, like she was trying to become small enough to hide.

"Let's get something straight now," Tol said, his voice deadly calm. "Addy might be related to the Forsaken general by blood, but she had nothing to do with the deaths of our people."

"You can't seriously still be thinking about going to Vitaquias with her," his mother gasped.

"Of course, I am," Tol replied, puzzled. "Why wouldn't I?"

"You have a duty to your people," the king sputtered.

"And I will fulfill it," Tol shot back. "But I'm going to do it with Addy."

"The general's our enemy," his father said. "That makes her daughter your enemy."

"No, it doesn't." Tol's pulse sped in his growing anger. "The Forsaken are our enemy. Addy isn't one of them."

"Our people will never accept a Forsaken queen!" his mother said in a raised voice, which for her was the same as shouting.

"She will be a Chosen queen," Tol corrected. He took Addy's hand and pulled her forward so they faced his parents together.

His parents looked first to their joined hands, and then to the ring glittering on Addy's finger. Tol saw their faces go from disbelief, to dismay, to rage.

"You can't be serious," his mother said.

"You're an ignorant boy," his father said, his face red. "You used to have your priorities straight. You used to know your place. And now, and now—"

His mother didn't say a word. She was glaring at Addy with a look that could kill.

Tol felt a confusing array of emotions, ranging from guilty and ashamed for the reaction he'd provoked in his parents, who had never shown him anything but love and kindness, to righteous anger. He understood what he was asking of his parents...of his people.

Tol knew what his parents saw when they looked at him and Addy. They saw two starry-eyed almost-adults who couldn't see beyond their infatuation. They saw a passing fancy.

His parents couldn't understand. His mother and father loved each other, but it wasn't the desperate, burning need he and Addy felt. His parents hadn't needed that kind of love. His mother had come from the right sort of family, and everyone had blessed their union because it made sense. It was easy.

Tol wished everything with Addy could be easy. He wished Addy was the Fount who was destined to blood marry him, and they could be together because they were fated to be. But she wasn't the Fount, and it was clear fate had conspired to keep them apart.

He wouldn't let it.

Tol's father rounded on Gerth, who, unlike Fred and Olivia, was watching the argument with unabashed interest. "Talk some sense into him," his father commanded Gerth.

Any other Chosen would have bowed and done his father's bidding. Gerth did neither. He shrugged, and said, "I like Addy. And I like Addy with Tol. I think she'll make him a better king."

There weren't words to describe the gratitude Tol felt toward his best mate.

His father's face went from red to purple. "And you're willing to give your life for this...romance?"

"Some of the greatest mortal wars were fought for love," Gerth replied. The teasing veneer he always wore slid away. "I believe in Tol and the king he'll be, and I'd gladly give my life for him."

Tol bowed his head. There was a strange burning in his throat. Gerth's words humbled him.

"Gerth," he began, his voice hoarse.

His mate waved a hand, his easy grin back in place. "Besides, with me as your master strategist, no one's going to die."

"You have no idea what you're up against." Tol's father glared at each of them.

"We are going to Vitaquias," Tol said when he'd found his voice. "We're going to find a way to give Olivia's powers to Addy. Then, we'll complete the blood marriage and save our race." He looked at his parents. "I want to do this with your blessing, but I'm going to do it either way."

He should tell his parents how much he loved them, how much their words burrowed into his soul and made his chest ache. He'd given them no choice in any of this, and he hated the impossible position he'd put them in.

But Tol knew his own heart, and it screamed for Addy. He knew he could never live with himself if there had been even a glimmer of a chance they could be together, and he hadn't done everything in his power to make it so. If he didn't exhaust every possibility, every last hope, he knew he wouldn't be good for anything. He wouldn't be fit as a son or a king. If the Celestial was dead, then they'd cross that bridge when they came to it.

Tol would do whatever it took to fix this.

His father wasn't ready to give up. "You knew from the beginning the prince doesn't get to choose. The blood marriage was never going to be about love for you."

Tol looked at Addy. "It is now."

CHAPTER 46

ADDY

All of the boys had fallen asleep in the overstuffed chairs on either side of the table. Gerth and Tol were folded over the table, their long hair spilling over the edge. Fred's mouth was open as he snored. Erikir's head had tipped so that it looked like he was resting it on Fred's shoulder. Under different circumstances, the sight would have had Addy shaking with laughter.

But her mind was too full of horrible truths for her to think about much else.

She went over to the long couch and sat beside Livy. She looked at her twin, who wasn't her twin, and her heart gave a painful squeeze.

"I guess now it makes sense why we look nothing alike." Addy tried for lightness, but her voice broke. She knew she hadn't fooled anyone.

Livy laced her fingers through Addy's and squeezed. "You are my sister in every way that matters," she said, her voice unwavering. Her grip on Addy's hand was steady. "We've spent our entire lives together. No one can take that away from us."

Addy's heart swelled to the point she was afraid it might burst.

"I'm still going to kill that woman for everything she's done," Addy promised. "You, Mom and Dad, Stacy, Rosie, and Lucy are my family. That's never going to change."

Livy leaned against Addy.

"I love you," Livy said.

Addy wrapped her arms around her sister. "Love you more," she replied.

After Livy had curled up on the couch and fallen asleep, Addy worked up the nerve for a conversation she'd been dreading. She got up, stumbling as the plane hit some light turbulence. She managed to make it to the back of the plane without falling.

"Um," she said, feeling herself wilt under the unblinking stares of the king and queen. "Do you mind if I sit?"

The queen didn't say anything. After a short pause, the king gave her a nod. She sat.

"I don't blame you for hating me," Addy said. "If I were you," a small smile flitted across her face, "I'd probably kill me."

"We're not barbarians," the queen replied acidly.

Addy cringed, realizing her mistake too late. "I just meant," she began, but the queen cut her off.

"If you had any regard for our son over your own selfish desires, you'd disappear and leave him be."

Addy's breath caught in her throat.

"I…I can't," she managed.

"Our people are already turning on the Magnantius reign," the queen continued. "If the unlikely best-case scenario occurs and you return from Vitaquias with the powers of the Fount, Tolumus won't have a moment of peace if he marries you. If the more likely scenario occurs, you'll get our son killed." Her chin wobbled on the last word. "If you love him, you'll let him go."

Addy sat, frozen, unable to utter a word. She had expected Tol's parents to yell at her. But this was so much worse, because there was truth to the queen's words.

"If I did that," Addy said when she finally found her voice, "he'd be devastated."

"He'd get over it," the queen snapped.

Would he?

Addy imagined if Tol disappeared from her life. She'd never get over it.

"I've never lied to Tol about anything," Addy said. "I won't just disappear from his life without an explanation. But if the time comes when he has to choose, I promise I'll help him make the right decision."

The words felt honorable and true in her head, but when she spoke them out loud, they sounded like a cop-out.

The queen turned away from her, dismissing her. The king stared at her for a long moment. "Selfish girl," he said, his disgust hitting her with as much force as a blow to the chest.

"That's enough, Rolomens." Getyl, who Addy had thought was asleep, was glaring at the king from across the aisle. "That's the Prince's Chosen and my future granddaughter you're berating."

She patted the seat next to her. "Come sit with me, Adelyne."

"I'm sorry to have caused so much trouble," Addy said as the old woman studied her.

Getyl waved a hand at the flight attendant, who nodded like a bobble head and disappeared into the galley. The attendant returned a few seconds later with a silver tea tray. Her wide smile was all wrong and made Addy feel like she was being mocked.

"Have some tea," Getyl told Addy. "You won't find any on Vitaquias."

Getyl sipped from her own cup and placed it back on the saucer.

"Do you love my grandson?"

Okay, so no working up to the big question here....

"With all my heart," Addy said.

Saying those words out loud felt like walking into a crowded room, only to realize she wasn't wearing any clothes. But Tol's gran had asked the question, and the least Addy could do was tell her the truth.

"I believe you," Getyl said, her eyes alarming in the way they seemed to peer straight into Addy's soul. "And not even a blind fool could miss how much he loves you."

Getyl continued to stare at her with a clarity that erased Addy's earlier assessment. Tol's grandmother didn't seem crazy to Addy anymore.

"We are not our parents," Getyl said. Her glance slid over to the king and queen, who were talking quietly to each other. "If we were, there would be little hope for the future of our race."

"I'm nothing like the general," Addy said, but even as she spoke the words, she heard how empty they sounded.

She knew next to nothing about the general, except for the way she looked and that intelligent, calculating gleam in her eyes.

"You can be like her without being her," Getyl said, reading Addy's thoughts. "It's a distinction many fail to make, but it's an important one."

Addy didn't know how to respond to that, so she just nodded.

Tol's grandmother settled back into her chair.

"True love is the greatest blessing in the worlds, but it is not without its challenges," Getyl continued. "If normal lovers face bumps in the road, you and my grandson are headed for a maelstrom." She pierced Addy with her stare again. "Before you risk my grandson's life, and your own, I want you to think very carefully about how much you're willing to sacrifice for the sake of your love."

The answer was easy, but it was also an abstraction. Addy would do anything for Tol...to be with Tol. But she took Getyl's point. She had no idea what they'd face when they got to Vitaquias. She had only the vaguest sense of the impossible choices they'd have to make along the way. They'd already put Tol's family at risk by abandoning them when their people expected—demanded—the blood marriage.

What if Getyl was wrong, and the Celestial was dead, or there was no way to transfer Livy's powers to Addy? What if Vitaquias was too damaged for them to even get there?

Addy had promised the king and queen she'd help Tol make the right decision.

She thought she'd do anything to be with Tol, but did she really mean *anything*? Should she?

Addy had a sudden, desperate desire to talk to her mom...her real mom...the one who had bandaged her scraped knees and held her after she'd waken up from the dream....

The dream, which, as it turned out wasn't a dream, but a memory.

Addy didn't have the energy to even try to come to terms with that truth right now.

"One step at a time," Getyl said at whatever look was on Addy's face. She reached over and patted Addy's knee. "One step at a time."

CHAPTER 47

TOL

Tol jolted awake as the plane touched down in London. He looked out the window and saw the black car waiting to escort his parents back to the manor…or whatever was left of it.

He rubbed his hand over his face. He was sending his parents into the lions' den without him. They'd have to answer for the choices he had made.

His whole life, duty had come first. Tol had hated the notion of duty, but he'd never questioned it. He'd known his place and would do what was required of him. Everything was different now, though.

Tol knew his duty was to get into that car with his parents. He knew it, just like he knew he wouldn't give up on searching for a way to make Addy his, no matter the cost.

As soon as the stairs lowered, his parents walked off the plane. They hadn't spoken to Tol since he'd told them he was still going to Vitaquias. Tol went after them, wanting for the last words between them to be ones that weren't filled with anger and betrayal.

Henroix, his parents' chief of staff, was waiting for them. Tol took one look at the man and felt his heart drop.

Henroix's pristine suit was smudged with soot. His black hair, which was always in a tight braid, was loose and wild.

"Your Majesties." He bowed, moving to open the car door.

"Talk," his father ordered as he got into the car.

"The manor is destroyed," Henroix said. "The Jesul family has taken up residence in the cottage and has claimed leadership privileges. Rumors are spreading like wildfire, and people have taken sides."

Grief dragged at Tol.

"How many dead?" the king asked.

"None yet," Henroix replied. "They are expecting the blood marriage." His eyes slid to Tol. "If it happens today, I am confident we can avoid bloodshed."

"Well, that isn't going to happen." Tol's mother yanked open the other car door and got in before Henroix could rush around to help her.

"Mum," Tol said, holding onto the door before she could slam it. "Don't go back there. Go somewhere safe. Let the rebels have the manor...we'll deal with it all when I return."

Tol's father scowled, and then turned his attention to a file of reports Henroix had given him.

"We don't shirk our duties, Tolumus," his mother said.

Tol couldn't speak. When she grabbed the handle of the door and pulled it closed, he didn't try to stop her.

Gran waved away Henroix's offered arm.

"Gran, I'm so sorry," Tol said when he found his voice.

"Are you?" Gran asked, peering up at him.

"Yes," Tol said, taken aback. How could she think he was happy about letting his family go back and pick up the pieces of a kingdom he was responsible for destroying?

"Sorry enough to change your mind about where you're headed next?"

"I can't." Tol shook his head. "I'm sorry, but I just...can't."

"Then, don't be sorry," Gran replied. "Just stay safe and come back as soon as you're able."

Tol nodded. "I will," he whispered.

Gran reached up to him. Tol bent so she could kiss his cheek. "Your parents love you," she said. "And so do I."

"Thank you." Tol's voice sounded sand-papery and unused.

Gran gave his cheek one final pat and hobbled around to the front seat. She looked so delicate...so old....

"Gran." Tol hurried to her. "Please don't let them go back to the manor. Go somewhere safe. This is my mess, and I'll clean it up myself when I get back."

"Your stubbornness didn't come from your mother's side," Gran said with a knowing smile. "You have your place, and we have ours."

"Please," Tol said.

"Give your parents and I some credit, Tolumus." She got into the car. "This old voice still carries more power than you might guess."

She shut the door, and the engine started.

Gran rolled down the window and beckoned him forward. "And Tolumus," she said, "bring your grandfather back to me."

She rolled up the window before he could reply.

Tol stood on the runway as the car drove off. He watched until it was nothing more than a black speck in the distance.

"Mate," Gerth called from the plane. "Let's get this show on the road."

His steps heavy, Tol climbed the stairs and joined the others. Addy searched his face, her expression clouding with worry at whatever she saw. He tried to give her a reassuring smile. It felt more like a grimace. Addy took his hand, offering him more in that touch than she could have with words. She rested her head against his shoulder.

"I love you," she told him. "I will love you for the rest of eternity."

Tol turned his face into her, his nose grazing the smooth skin of her neck. "Eternity is a long time," he murmured.

She nudged him with her hip.

"Not long enough for a life with you."

OLIVIA

Olivia saw the haunted look on Tol's face when he got back onto the plane. She watched her sister wrap her arms around him. All the tension seemed to drain from his limbs as he settled against her. It was such a small gesture, but it was beautiful. Everything about Tol and Addy was beautiful.

And because of her, the love they so clearly shared was in jeopardy.

Olivia knew, logically, it wasn't her fault. She had managed to put together the pieces from the little Addy and Fred had told her, and she understood the gist of what they were trying to change. Olivia, the daughter of humble farmers, was some kind of Fount who held all the secrets of restoring a ruined world. It was completely insane, and yet, she had seen the impossible become possible with her own eyes. The seizures she'd had all her life weren't seizures at all, but prophecies she could only begin to make sense of when she was touching her sister's fiancé.

There was nothing Olivia hated more than being the center of attention or causing trouble for others, and now her very existence was doing both.

Her whole life, Olivia had believed there was order and meaning in the way the world worked. Now, she wasn't so sure. It seemed like fate had played a cruel joke on all of them. Addy—the one who had always hungered for more—should be the Fount. She should be the special one.

Olivia had spent her life content in knowing who she was. Now, she no idea how to be the person they all expected her to be.

Gerth poked his head into the cockpit. "All set," he called.

"Where are we going?" she asked him.

Gerth, Tol, and the boy with the angry eyes whose name Olivia hadn't caught, shared a knowing glance.

"Texas," they replied at the same time.

It was Olivia, Addy, and Fred's turn to exchange a look.

"We're going to the site of the Crossing," Gerth explained. "Where our people came into the mortal world eighteen years ago."

"Aunt Meredith's farm," Addy said. "Where the portal opened the last time."

The plane gathered speed as it hurtled down the runway.

As the plane climbed into the sky, Tol slid his arm around Addy's shoulders and said something in her ear. Olivia saw the way her sister's entire face lit up. Addy said something back, her words too quiet for anyone but Tol to hear. Tol raised Addy's left hand and kissed the finger where her ring sparkled. A strange flutter went through Olivia's stomach, and she turned away before she invaded their privacy any more.

"Now," Gerth said, motioning everyone over to one of the tables. "Let's talk strategy."

Olivia watched the others crowd around him, even the angry boy and Fred, both of whom hadn't been quiet about their disapproval of just about everything so far. They all watched as Gerth drew six columns on a notepad and wrote their names at the top of each column.

"Here's what I'm thinking."

As Gerth's plan started to take shape, the others jumped in with ideas and modifications of their own. Addy had found more pens, which she handed around, and they all leaned over the table as they made additions to each of the columns.

Olivia hung back, her unused pen in her hand. She didn't yet know what or how she could contribute to this group, or how she fit into it. But she knew she loved her sister more than anything. Olivia would do whatever it took to make sure Addy got the happiness she deserved.

In what felt like no time at all, the plane was descending.

"Howdy, ya'll," the pilot called from the front. "And welcome to Texas."

THE END

* * *

Because reviews are so important for a book to be successful, please consider leaving a brief review on your favorite retailer if you enjoyed *The Prince's Chosen*. Many thanks!

* * *

Sign up for Stephanie Fazio's e-Newsletter to learn about upcoming books at:
https://StephanieFazio.com/subscribe/

Acknowledgements

This project was so much fun, and I'm so appreciative of all the people who helped me bring it to life.

To my editor, Ellen Schaeffer. Your advice is always invaluable. Thank you!

To Keith Tarrier, for making such gorgeous covers that continue to exceed all expectations. Thank you also to Bob Brodsky, Rhoda Schneider, and the rest of my ARC team. Your advice, support, and encouragement are invaluable.

To Mom, Dad, and Rach. Thanks for always being there for me.

To my fantastic readers who have supported and encouraged me. Thanks for taking the plunge with a new series!

And to Andrew. For everything.

About the Author:

Stephanie Fazio is a fantasy author. She grew up in Syracuse, New York, and prior to writing full time, she worked in the fields of journalism, secondary education, and higher education. She has an undergraduate degree in English from Colgate University and a Master's degree in Reading, Writing, and Literacy from the University of Pennsylvania. Stephanie lives in Austin with her husband and crazy rescue dog. When she isn't writing, she's getting lost in parks, hosting taco nights, or ironically and miserably losing at word games, but having fun while she does it.

Connect with Stephanie Fazio:

Visit her Website: https://www.StephanieFazio.com
Sign up for her newsletter: https://StephanieFazio.com/subscribe/

Continue The Fount Series

Book 2, *The Forsaken's Choice.*
AVAILABLE APRIL 2020!

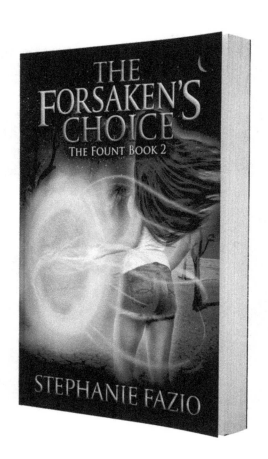

StephanieFazio.com

Discover other books by Stephanie Fazio

Bisecter Series

StephanieFazio.com

CPSIA information can be obtained
at www.ICGtesting.com
Printed in the USA
LVHW031208090320
649409LV00002B/342